# MCKINLEY RANCH DUET

KYLIE KENT

*kylie kent*

**Kylie Kent**

**Social Media:**
**Website & Newsletter: www.kyliekent.com**
**Facebook: @kyliekent2020**
**Instagram Follow: @author_kylie_kent_**

**This book contains scenes and discussions of non-consensual sexual acts, domestic violence, profanity, sexual content and violence. If any of these are triggers for you, you should consider skipping this read.**

ISBN 13:

Cover illustration by
Stacy Garcia - https://www.facebook.com/graphicsbystacy

Editing services provided by
Kat Pagan - https://www.facebook.com/PaganProofreading

*This book is dedicated to all the survivors. All who live with the internal and external scars left behind. Never stop fighting for you, never give up on finding your happily ever after.*

Book 1

# Prologue

## Emily

## 2010

Ten. That's how many times I have done this in the past three years. Ten new schools. Ten new groups of friends I had to fit in with. This one is in a league of its own though. I haven't had to try to fit in to this sort of crowd before. The elite offspring of the rich and famous.

I'm sure I stand out like a sore thumb. The scholarship kid, only here because her daddy died a military hero. I hate that everyone in this cafeteria knows who I am, knows that I'm the daughter of that soldier who died.

My face was plastered all over the news six months ago, when word broke out that my father died while saving the lives of five other men in his platoon. I should be sad. I should be missing my dad.

The thing is, I'm angry at him. Angry that he chose to save the lives of others instead of his own. Angry that he's not coming home this time. He promised me that this was going to be his last tour. I guess, in a twisted way, he didn't actually break that promise. I don't miss him though. I've grown up with him hardly ever around, so it's not a huge difference now that he's gone.

After the funeral, my mum packed up and moved us back to the Hunter Valley, a rural area just outside of Sydney. She applied for this scholarship—said it's the last time I'll have to change schools, so I might as well get into the best one there is. I'm fifteen; I have three more years of schooling left. Three years of being stuck in this gilded prison.

These rich kids know I'm not one of them. All morning I've had nothing but sneers and disgusted looks sent my way. No matter how much I paste on a smile (however fake it may be), one day, it will be real. I just have to keep pretending until it is.

I count to ten with the biggest, friendliest smile I can muster. My head high, I walk through the cafeteria looking for an empty table. Or a group willing to invite me to theirs. I don't find either.

What I do find is a table at the very back, one lone boy sitting in the middle of it. My breath halts, and my heart starts beating rapidly. This has to be the most beautiful boy I've ever seen. Golden blonde locks fall down past his eyes, complementing his tanned skin, the uniform doing nothing to hide his developing muscles.

Looking around, it's clear there is nowhere else to sit. With my head still high, and a smile so wide my face hurts, I go and sit across from the boy. The moment my tray hits the table, all sound in the cafeteria halts. I can feel eyes burning into my back, but I don't dare turn around.

Instead, I look at the boy across from me, who in turn, gives me his best scowl. A scowl I'm sure would scare off every other student here. Not me though. I am my father's daughter after all. I will not show fear.

"Hi, I'm Emily. The new girl, obviously." My voice does not give any indication of the anxiety I'm feeling from having his gaze sear through me.

"This is the part where you say hi back and tell me your name. Then, you know, we're BFFs and the rest is history. You'll be the cookie; I'll be the cream. You'll be the Tim to my Tam. You'll be the Vegemite to my toast. I think you get the drift." I stop rambling and look him directly in the eye.

There's a flicker of amusement, but just as quickly as it comes, it's gone. He tilts his head and stares at me for what seems like hours. Then, out of nowhere, he stands, picks up his milkshake and slowly, very slowly pours it over my head.

The gasp that leaves my mouth is the only indication of shock or annoyance that I'm willing to give him. My smile is plastered back on my face as I stare up at him. *I will not show him fear,* I remind myself again.

He leans down and whispers in my ear. "You'd do best to stay far away from boys like me. I'd destroy you, little girl. You're new here, so this is the one pass you get."

His cruel words and harsh tone confuse me. I know I should be scared. I should be pissed off—he just tipped milk all over me. I'm not though. I don't know what I am, but I don't want the interaction between us to stop. It's like I'm under some kind of spell.

Turning around, I straighten my back, pick up the sandwich on my plate and start eating it. I hear his heavy footsteps walk away. As much as I want to turn back and look at him, I don't.

Ten minutes later, a group of girls comes over, sits at the table with me and starts chatting away like we've always been friends. No one ever mentions the milkshake incident. I want to ask about the boy, the beautiful, heavily disturbed boy. But for a second time today, I don't.

# Josh

## 2014

It's the end of Senior year. Thank fucking God I'm finally getting out of this fucking soul-destroying hell they disguise as a school. The place is filled with pretentiousness on top of pretentiousness. The kids of celebrities and old money, spoilt fucking little brats. They wouldn't know a day of hard work if it hit them over the fucking head.

The one exception is *her*.

Three years and she's been the one thing I can't seem to break. It's only a matter of time though. Everyone is breakable. I take great pleasure in watching these fuckers succumb to their breaking points. I revel in their fucking tears, their pleas for mercy.

Not her, not fucking Emmy. She's a thorn in my side. No matter how much I want to break her, there's something niggling deep down that stops me from ever going too far with her. Something that makes me want to keep her in one piece. I try to ignore it, but I know it's a losing battle.

Emily. She's like an angel among the demons of hell. Her bright, sunny, happy disposition stands out like a nun in a whorehouse. It's sickening. I've tried everything to get her halo to shatter. None of my taunts or pranks have broken her.

But the thing I hate about her most is that I actually fucking like her. I've never liked anyone. Not even my own mother. I couldn't care less what happens to that woman. But Emmy, I've gone out of my way to make sure no boys here get close to her. They've tried, and they've all ended up with broken fingers or jaws.

After the first year, they got the message she was off limits. Off limits to them, and most fucking definitely off limits to me. The only thing I'd ever do is ruin her. As much as I want to do just that, I can't fucking make myself do it.

Standing in the shadows, I inhale the nicotine from between my fingers, attempting to calm the beast who wants to come out and play. I'm watching Emmy, *my* fucking Emmy, dance with some jock. A soon-to-be dead fucking jock. I heard he has scouts in a bidding war over him—he won't be any good to any footy teams with busted kneecaps.

I smile as the image plays over in my head, but it vanishes when I see the cocksucker lean in to kiss her. Fuck no, not fucking happening.

I storm up and rip him away from her. Throwing a right hook, I get him straight on his jaw; his head snaps back. He's a big fucker. I don't give him time to recover before I'm knocking his ass on the ground. I jump on top of him and land hit after hit to his head.

All I see is a red haze as the image of his lips on hers runs through my mind. I just keep striking over and over. Then I feel it, her hand on my arm, pulling me back. Her voice breaks through the fog.

"Josh, stop it. You're going to kill him," she whispers.

Blinking away the remaining haze, I stand up, grab her hand and lead her out of the ballroom. I have no idea what I'm doing. I've never dragged her off before, yet she's willingly following me.

Once I get to my Range Rover, I open the passenger door, pick her up and place her inside the car. Shutting the door gently, I run around to the other side and start driving.

Neither of us say anything. The drive is silent. I can feel her questioning gaze on me. However, she doesn't speak, not until I steer us through the ranch gates and start taking the back tracks past the bush. The ones I know lead to a little cabin in the middle of nowhere.

"You know, I should warn you. If you brought me out here to kill me, or I don't know, chop me up and feed me to pigs or something, I would have liked some warning, so I could have worn something more appropriate for the occasion."

"Pigs? Why would I feed you to pigs?" I ask her.

"Because they eat ninety-nine percent of the human body, practically don't leave a trace." She shrugs like that's a fact everyone should know.

"I'll keep that in mind."

I stop outside the cabin and turn the car off. "Relax, Emmy. If I wanted you dead, you would have been in the ground three years ago."

"Well, that's comforting," she replies as I'm jumping out of the car.

By the time I reach her door, she's already outside it. I don't understand this girl. Why the fuck would she follow me out to a deserted cabin? Why the fuck isn't she scared?

"Emmy, why the fuck do you trust me enough to let me bring you out to a deserted cabin in the fucking woods?" I question. I'm pissed off. Would she follow just anyone out here?

"I know you won't hurt me, Josh. You're an asshole, a little unhinged at times. But I trust that you won't hurt me." She looks me straight in the eye, momentarily sucking me into a trance.

"Come on. I want to show you something." I take her hand and lead her into the cabin. I came by earlier and hung fucking fairy lights everywhere. I had every intention of bringing her back here tonight.

"Oh my God, Josh, this is beautiful." Emmy turns in a circle, taking in the small room.

"Not nearly as beautiful as you are," I confess.

"Wait, what? You… Josh, you don't mean that." She stumbles over her words.

"I mean every word of it. Emmy, you are the most beautiful creature I've ever seen. I can't give you promises of tomorrow. What I *can* give you is tonight. Let me give you tonight." I'm practically begging her for one night. I hold my breath, waiting for her reply.

As soon as she gives a slight nod, I slam my lips onto hers and I've finally found my home. Finally found the place where I belong. The cookie to my cream, the Tim to my Tam.

# Chapter 1

## Emily

## Present

The tomato and herb aroma fills the tiny kitchen. I smile, inhaling the delicious smells. Trent is going to be pleased. Spaghetti bolognaise is his favourite; he's always happy when I cook this. I need to take one more walk through the apartment to make sure everything is orderly before he gets home.

He likes things a certain way. It's my job to make sure our home is up to scratch. I walk through the bedroom: the bed is made, the dark duvet wrinkle free, and the pillows are arranged with precision.

Next is the bathroom. I straighten the towels, taking extra care to make sure they are folded over the rail properly and are evenly spaced. Hearing the keys in the front door, I hurry back to the kitchen.

As soon as I get there, my stomach drops. The smell of burnt sauce assaults my nostrils. No, no, no! This cannot be happening. Rushing over to the stove top, I scrape at the pan, trying to salvage what I already know I can't. I don't have time to try to cover up my error. Trent's footsteps are heavy as he makes his way down the hall.

I reach over to the knife block and pick up a small filleting blade, holding it tightly in my hand. My heart beats rapidly as I await what's coming. There's a little glimmer of hope that things will be different this time. *Hope's a fucking bitch.* The words I was told seven years ago repeat in my mind every time I start to hope for something good.

"Trent, I'm sorry. I-I… just stepped away for a moment. I can fix this," I plead.

"You just stepped away for a moment. You stupid fucking bitch! How dumb are you? How many times have I told you not to leave things cooking on the stove top!" Trent yells as he makes his way into the kitchen.

"Are you trying to burn the place down? The home I work so fucking hard for! The home I provide you!" The frying pan goes flying across the room, hitting the wall before landing on the beige carpet. I have no idea how I'm going to get the sauce stains out of the carpet.

Instinctively, I take a step, backing up to the corner of the kitchen. I realise my mistake when it's too late. I'm trapped. I can't escape from here.

"You're so ungrateful. Is it too much to ask that dinner be properly cooked and not fucking charcoal when I get home? Huh, Emily. Why is the simplest of fucking tasks too damn hard for you?" Trent ends his sentence with a backhand across my face.

I don't dare move or make a noise. I know if I do, it will be worse. Sometimes he stops at one. Other times he doesn't. How did my life turn out like this? My dad would be rolling over in his damn grave if he knew what I was putting up with. What other options do I have though?

Trent smiles as he opens the second drawer and pulls out a wooden spoon. So, this is going to be one of the other times then. My hand grips the little knife tighter. I'm not even sure why I grabbed it. I learnt early on that it was pointless trying to stand up to Trent. He will always beat me. I've tried leaving; he's always able to find me.

I brace for the impact as I see the wooden spoon flying through the air at my face. Motherfucker, that hurts. I can't help but crunch into myself. The cry escapes my mouth as the left side of my face radiates with pain.

Trent drops the spoon, picks me up by my hair and begins to drag me out of the kitchen. I don't know what comes over me, but I start to resist. I try to escape his hold. This only makes him angrier though.

He brings his knee up into my stomach, literally knocking the wind right out of me. I fall to the ground. "Please, stop. Trent, stop," I beg.

"If I stop now, you're never going to fucking learn your place, you stupid dumb bitch." Slap, again his hand strikes my already burning cheek.

"If you can't please me with dinner, you can please me with the only thing you're good at." Trent starts to undo his belt. He's going to rape me, again. At least it won't hurt as bad as being beat.

He lifts my dress up. I'm not allowed to wear panties. I don't even own any. Trent pushes his cock deep inside me. I scream as he enters me dry. I feel like my insides are being ripped open.

Something digs into my hand. I remember I'm still clutching the little knife I picked up earlier. Trent hasn't noticed it. I look up at him; his eyes are closed as he pumps in and out of me. Without a second thought, I bring the blade up and jam it into the side of his neck. Pulling it out again, I repeat the action before he has a chance to stop me.

Trent's eyes go wide as blood spurts out of his neck. I watch as the colour drains from his face. It feels like time stops. Maybe I did it wrong. He hasn't moved, hasn't said anything. Then his body collapses on top of mine. This is probably the moment he ends me. He's not going to take kindly to me slicing him with a knife.

After lying with his dead weight on me for a few minutes, I take the chance and try to shove him off. I roll him onto his back before getting up on my knees. His eyes are open, his skin a pale grey colour. I'm going to be sick.

Running into the bathroom, I empty the contents of my stomach. Shit, fuck! What the fuck have I done? It's okay… it's going to be okay. He's going to wake up. I half expect him to be sitting upright when I walk back into the kitchen. He's not. He hasn't moved. There's a pool of blood around his head.

I have to get out of here. I have to leave. I wash the blood from my hands and throw on a black hoodie, a pair of jeans and my Converse. I pack the very little that's actually mine into a backpack. Heading into the bathroom, I lift the lid to the toilet cistern and retrieve the plastic bag that holds the phone and letter Josh left me to wake up to seven years ago. I've had it hiding in there all this time, only pulling the contents out to charge the battery once every couple of days, and to check if it's still connected.

So many times, I've been tempted to call the one number that is saved into the phone. I know it belongs to Josh; that is, if he hasn't changed his number since then. Seven years is a bloody long time. I don't even know why I've held onto the items for this long. I just can't seem to throw them out.

What I do know is that I need to get out of here, out of Adelaide, fast. I take the small amount of cash Trent had stashed in his bedside table. He always left it there to test me. I'd watch him count it every night. I wasn't stupid enough to ever take any of it.

I don't look at the kitchen on my way out of the apartment that has been my home, prison and hell for the last three years. Gently closing the door behind me, I pull my cap down low, my long hair hanging like a curtain on the left side of my face. I don't need to check a mirror to know what people will see when they look at me.

---

IT'S TAKEN me five days. I have ten dollars left to my name. But I'm here. I'm still unsure why I'm here, of all places. Why I would seek refuge in this dirty old cabin. The dirty old cabin that holds both my favourite and worst memories.

I hitchhiked with truckers from Adelaide, in South Australia, to the Hunter Valley in New South Wales. That's one thousand and six-hundred kilometres. Five days of not wanting to fall asleep, of always being on guard. I've listened intently to the radio, waiting to hear of the search that should be happening for me.

There was nothing. No mention of the murder scene I left

behind, no mention of a fugitive on the run. Nothing. Trent was a cop. I know you can't just kill a cop and get away with it. I'm not that stupid. Not to mention, his brother's also a fucking cop. One that will be after me, even if it's not being publicised on the news.

Shaking the dark thoughts off, I look around the small clearing in front of the cabin. No one is here. I don't know what I expected. I knew he wouldn't be here. That's why I came; no one will be looking for me in a cabin in the woods on the McKinley Ranch. I can spend a couple of days here to regroup and come up with a game plan as to how I'm going to get myself out of this mess.

With each step I take towards the cabin, the memory of the last time I was here hits me hard. There hasn't been a day I haven't thought of that night, a day where his face hasn't made an appearance in my mind.

*"What I can give you is tonight. Let me give you tonight," Josh pleads with me. I shouldn't be here. I shouldn't be anywhere alone with Josh, the boy who has tormented me, yet also protected me for the last three years.*

*I know he's the reason why boys stopped paying attention to me. I also know he's the reason why nobody ever gave me any kind of grief for being the poor girl at school. He has barely said two words to me since that first day in the cafeteria.*

*The only thing I ever get from him is a scowl and dirty looks. I've attempted to talk to him. Each time, he walks away from me like I'm a ghost, like he can't hear or see that I'm right in front of him.*

*The little notes that were left in my locker every day, I've always suspected they were from him. He just confirmed my suspicions when he called me Emmy; no one ever calls me Emmy. Those notes, they were all addressed to Emmy.*

*To have him standing in front of me now, confessing that he wants to give me tonight… My mind is telling me to run, run far and fast. This boy is psychotic. This is probably one of his sick and twisted games. I've seen the kind of stuff he's done to other students. Never me though. It was like I didn't exist—besides the occasional prank I've long suspected he's behind.*

*Yet, I can't help but nod, can't help but let him give me this one night. Within seconds, Josh's mouth is on mine, his smooth, full, soft lips pressing down hard onto my own. The spark I feel, the one that happens whenever I make physical contact with him, it's alight like fireworks and wreaking havoc through my body. I'm burning up.*

*Josh's tongue swipes against the seam of my lips; my mouth willingly opens for him. Our tongues fight against each other. Little moans sound through the room. I don't know if they're coming from me or him. I don't even care anymore. I need more. I want more.*

MY FINGERS TRACE along my lips as the memory of the best kiss I've ever had taunts me. I've never felt as safe as when I was in this cabin with Josh that night. Never felt more cherished, more treasured than when Josh took his time worshipping my body.

It was heaven. That night was the best night of my life. Then the morning came, and I woke up cold and alone. There was a note and a phone next to me. The same note and phone I've carried with me for seven years. I could recite the written words from memory. I knew then I would never see Josh again. I also knew then that I hated him, hated him with everything in me. I pull the scrunched-up paper from my pocket and read it again. I need the reminder of why I can't call him. Why I can't let him find me here.

. . .

EMMY,

*I'm sorry it has to be this way. You need to leave town. You need to leave and never look back. This is not the place for a girl like you.*

*You are the first person to ever make me feel anything. But you also make me hope, and hope is a damn bitch for someone with a soul as black as mine. That's why I can't keep you.*

*I know I'd only ruin you, tarnish your halo until it cracked and fell down. If I ever see you again, run. Run from me. Because I promise I won't be able to give you up a second time. I won't be able to let you go.*

YOURS ALWAYS,

*Josh*

P.S. KEEP *this phone with you always. I'm one phone call away if you need anything at all. Just know, if you do call, if you use the phone to contact me, it's the beginning of the end for us both.*

I READ it every time I think of caving and calling Josh for help. Deep down, I know he'd help me. I also know I'd never let him. Now is no exception. I will figure this out. I will get myself out of the mess I've created.

Just as I'm making my way to the door, I hear a woman shouting from inside the cabin. Peering through the dirty window, I see a dark-haired woman sitting against the back wall with her hands tied.

Please tell me this is not where Josh is bringing all of his women. Oh God, what if he's in there with her? She yells out "stop" and starts talking to someone about how Dean and Josh will find them. I duck down out of view and keep listening.

This girl needs help. She's obviously a friend or something of Josh's. As quietly as I can, I make my way back into the bushes and sit against a gum tree. What do I do? I can't call him. I can't let him find me. I also can't just leave that girl in there.

Pulling the phone out, I press the number I've wanted to press for so many years. The phone rings for so long I don't think he is going to answer. Then I hear his voice on the other end.

"Emmy, what's wrong?" Josh asks after a moment.

"Josh, I… I'm down at the cabin. Um… our cabin. There's a girl in there. She's in trouble, Josh. I saw through the window. I went to help her, but then she started yelling at someone named Sarah. And she… she said your name. I don't know what to do… What do I do?" I ask.

"Where are you now?" Josh's voice cracks. I can hear him start to run. Huh, maybe this girl is his girlfriend or wife, and he's really worried about her. I don't have time to analyse the way that thought makes me feel right now.

"I'm behind the cabin, in the bushes. I should go and help her, Josh. I can help her," I tell him.

"Stay hidden, Em. Do not come out of that spot until you hear me or Dean calling for you, okay?" Josh yells over the sound of an engine revving.

"Okay," I agree, although I have no plans of letting him find me. I'm just going to stay here long enough to know that he found the girl and that he can help her. Then I'm out of here. I need to look for a new place to hide out.

# Chapter 2

## Josh

As soon as I saw Emily's name flash across my phone, my heart stopped momentarily. I've waited seven fucking years to see that name on my screen. I've never allowed myself to hope that it would happen, because hope is a fucking bitch who only ever disappoints.

Letting her go was the one selfless act I've ever done. I've never cared about anyone before her, and I haven't cared about anyone the same way since. She took my breath away every time I saw her, made me murderous every time I watched another guy flirt with her. I wanted to destroy her and protect her all at the same time. It fucked with my already fucked-up mind.

Memories of Emily hit me like flashbacks as I speed through the bush on my dirt bike, towards the cabin. *Our cabin*, she called it our cabin. Like it was some secret hideaway of ours. When in all reality, it's the place I took her one time, where I worshiped her before warning her to get the fuck out of this town, my town.

She took my warning. I haven't seen or heard from her since. Until now. Of all the times she had to call, now was that time. Stopping five minutes down from where I know the cabin is, I cut the motor and signal for the rest of the guys to do the same.

"We need to walk from here. About five minutes away, down that direction…" I don't even finish my sentence before Bray starts running towards where I pointed.

Fuck! If his impulsiveness gets Ella hurt, or worse, Emmy, I will fucking kill him. The urge to maim and murder is strong right now. My skin feels like a hundred ants are crawling all over me. I need the blood. I need the destruction. There's one person who's first on my list.

Sarah, never met the fucking woman, but she's abducted Ella, my brother's new wife. That shit will not fly with me. The fact that she's a woman means nothing when she's threatening my family.

I may be a cold-hearted bastard with a black soul, but I have developed a soft spot for Ella. I don't know how, but as soon as she kneed me in the balls a week ago at Dean's house, I took to her. She makes me feel shit I'm not used to fucking feeling. It's different from the feelings Emily evokes though.

With Emily, it's like I'm only ever alive when in her presence. She's literally the other half of my soul, the light side, the good side. I remember when we first met, she said we would be best friends, some shit about being the Vegemite to her toast. She wasn't wrong about us being each other's match.

But she was wrong about us being best friends. I didn't have friends, and I sure as shit didn't have girlfriends. What I did have were the twisted mind games I liked to play on all the other spoilt little brats that went to our school.

I try to catch up with Bray, but that fucker is fast. I watch as he barges through the cabin door, before I hear the unmistakable sound of a gunshot. Fuck. As much as I want to look around the bush behind the cabin and find Emily, I need to make sure Ella is okay.

She has to be okay.

I wouldn't say I care deeply for my brother, but I don't hate him—which is a far cry from how I feel about every other fucker around here. I don't want him to lose Ella after just getting his shit together enough to claim her.

As I enter the cabin, I see Ella against the wall. Dean's already crouched down in front of her, untying her hands. I inspect her body from head to toe. She has dried blood on the side of her head—other than that, she looks okay.

Thank fuck. My eyes scan the room, landing on the woman currently on the floor; she's trying to crawl towards the gun only a few feet away from her.

A calmness comes over me as a smile graces my lips. *This*, I'm going to fucking enjoy. Effortlessly picking her up by her hair, I pull her so her back is against my chest. She lets out a little cry—music to my ears.

If she's seeking empathy from me, she won't find any. I'm not capable of it. My mother had me tested, and according to the experts she hired, I'm a lost cause. A textbook psychopath, no empathy, no conscience. I agreed with their findings until Emily came along and made me second guess my own level of fucked-up-ness.

I may not have empathy for anyone else, but for her, I think I do. I made sure no one ever bullied or outcast her at school. I made sure she was surrounded by friends and was accepted. Without my interference, she would have been a loner, ostracized for being the poor scholarship kid.

I force my thoughts back to the whining bitch currently in my hands. I lean in and whisper in her ear so that only she can hear me.

"I would really fucking love to take my time with you, love. But you see, I have a girl outside waiting for me. So, as much as I want to slice your skin from your body, inch by inch, and listen to your screams and pleas, I can't. I'd really fucking love to tarnish this perfect skin of yours with my knife. Unfortunately, we're both going to have to settle for me twisting your scrawny little neck though. Because, like I said, places to be, people to see. You know how it is, right?"

She doesn't get time to answer before my hands take hold of her head and I twist. I feel the moment her neck snaps as I let her body drop at my feet. Damn that felt good.

"I'll be back to clean this mess up later. Don't fucking touch it," I tell Zac—Ella's older brother and my own brother's best friend.

Just as I'm about to walk out the door, I stop and turn around to see Ella's wide eyes. Fuck, I should have taken into account who was here. Well, she's bound to eventually find out how fucked up her new brother-in-law is anyway.

Crouching down beside her, I reach out and tuck her hair behind her ear. I expect her to pull away from my touch, to be afraid of me. She'd be wise to be afraid of me. I don't know why Dean hasn't warned her away from me yet.

"I'm really fucking glad you're okay, sweetheart," I tell her, kissing her forehead.

"Thank you. I'm really glad you're okay too," Ella replies.

I get up and walk out of the cabin, stepping over Bray,

Ella's other fucking brother, who's currently on the ground with what looks like a bullet wound in his ass.

I make my way behind the cabin and call out to her. I know she's still here. I can feel her.

"Emmy, where are you?" I wait, expecting to hear her reply, or see her blonde head pop up from somewhere. All I get is the sounds of birds and the rustling of animals scurrying away from me in the bush. Even those fuckers know to steer clear of me.

"Emmy, I know you're here. I can feel you. You're better off coming out of your little hiding hole," I yell.

Still no answer. Huh, guess she really doesn't want to be found. Too bad, now that I can finally feel her presence again after seven years, I'm not about to let her go.

"I will find you, Emmy," I call out, still getting no response. I stop mid step and continue to listen.

I listen to the sounds of the foliage, the animals, the wind. I block it all out and listen closer. That's when I hear it. The tiny little sob. The sound that fucking guts me.

Why the fuck is she crying? She should never be fucking crying. I don't like this. I don't know how to deal with these fucking feelings. This is why I made her leave all those years ago. Fuck it.

I head towards where I heard the tiny sob. There, propped against a gum tree, is my Emmy. I approach slowly, sitting down in front of her. She doesn't look up.

Five minutes pass, and I'm still sitting here on the fucking ground, waiting for her to look up at me. I want to see those blue eyes of hers so fucking bad. I want to see her beautiful face. Right now, I can't see shit. She's wearing a black cap, her long blonde hair hanging like curtains around her face.

I can feel it in my gut; something is wrong. I know it's been seven years, but this is not my Emmy. This is not the bright, bubbly girl I spent years watching over.

I reach my hand out towards her face. My stomach drops as her whole body flinches away from me. She curls her arms around her legs. I drop my hand, my fist opening and closing. I'm out of my fucking element here.

This is the girl that never shied away from me. She never let me see fear, while all those other fuckers would beg, cry and plead for mercy. Not Emmy—she was capable of going toe to toe with the devil.

Now she's shrinking away from him. From me. I don't fucking like it.

"Emmy, look at me, please." My voice is hoarse. I'm practically begging her to look up at me. The moment she does though, I wish she hadn't.

"What the fuck? Who the fuck did this, Emily? I need a name right the fuck now!" I stand up and start pacing, my hands balling into fists. I can feel the blood rushing through my veins; never has the need to kill been this strong.

I stop and stare down at her. Half of her face is green and yellow. Some fucker has used her as a damn punching bag. Seeing her like this, curled into herself, bruised and broken… I can't process it.

Taking a breath, I sit back down in front of her and grasp onto her hands. She tries to pull away. I don't let her. I will not have her fucking scared of me. She's not fucking allowed to be scared of me.

"Emmy, you know I would never do anything to hurt you." I wait for her to acknowledge me.

A slight nod of her head is all I get. That's all I need.

"I have to know if you're hurt anywhere else." I don't want

to hurt her any more than she already is. I have to know what I'm dealing with here.

"I'm okay, Josh. I'm not hurt. I've had much worse. I'm sorry… I shouldn't have come here. I'm just going to go. I won't bother you again. I promise." Her voice is whisper quiet.

I tilt my head to the side and inspect her. I can't see much. She's hiding under a baggy hoodie and a pair of jeans.

"Babe, if you think I'm letting you walk away, you're crazier than I fucking am. Come on, let's go." I pull on her hands until she's standing.

Her back straightens, she picks her head up slightly, and I see a tiny glimmer of the Emmy I knew.

"I'm not going anywhere with you. I'm going…" Her sentence is cut off when I bend at the waist and throw her over my shoulder.

I'm an asshole. I should be more careful with her body in case she is hurt anywhere else. But I need to get her out of the fucking woods.

Emily starts pounding her tiny fists on my back. "Put me down, you asshole! I can bloody well walk, you know!" She gets more infuriated when I don't acknowledge her screams.

Good, show me your fight, baby. You are not some weak little girl. You're the strongest girl I fucking know. I will make sure that girl comes back, no matter who I have to fucking squash to make it happen.

Placing her on my dirt bike, I jump on behind her and kickstart the engine. We are off and speeding through the woods before she knows what's happening.

---

STOPPING right at the back door, I jump off the bike, picking Emily up with me. She doesn't fight me; she's oddly quiet as I carry her up the stairs to my room and straight through to the bathroom. I step into the shower and press the button on the wall that makes water fall directly on top of us from the overhead rainwater showerheads.

"Ahh, what the hell, Josh?" Emily shrieks as I put her down. I hold her arms until she is steady on her feet.

"Sorry, give it a minute. It'll warm up." Reaching behind my back, I pull my shirt over my head and dump it on the floor.

I then take the cap off Emily's head, before grasping for the bottom of her hoodie. Her hands are quick to come out and halt my movements.

"Stop. What do you think you're doing?" she hisses as she steps away, coming to a standstill when her back hits the wall.

"Either you remove the jumper, or I will. It's soaked, babe. You can't stay in wet clothes."

"They wouldn't be wet if you didn't turn on the shower. And I'm not getting naked in front of you." Her arms fold over her chest.

"You're forgetting you don't have anything I haven't already seen. Now, you can either let me help you, or you can remove that hoodie yourself. Either way, the clothes are coming off."

Emmy shakes her head no. She's forgetting who she's dealing with. People don't say no to me. But I can't be my usual asshole self with her. She's like a fragile little trapped bird at the moment, just looking for that open window to fly out.

"Emmy, I'm not going to fucking hurt you. I'm not going to touch you—well, not in any way you don't want me to. I just need to see how badly you're hurt, that's all." I don't make a move to close the gap she's put between us, even though my hands are screaming to rip her clothes to shreds already.

"I… I can't. Please, Josh, don't make me do this." Tears fall down her cheeks as she pleads with me.

I don't like her submissive pleas. It's not her. The sight of tears running down her cheeks does not sit well with me. I can usually take pleasure in others' pain and sorrow. Hers, it's different. And I don't fucking know how to deal with it.

I'm running out of patience and ideas. I have to get out of here before I do hurt her. Before I become the monster I am.

"I'll leave some clothes for you on the bed. Make no mistake, Emmy, this conversation is not over." Stepping out of the shower, I remove my wet boots and jeans before wrapping a towel around my waist. I can feel her eyes on my back the whole time.

I really need to fucking get away from this girl. I don't like people not doing what I tell them to, but I can't seem to bring myself to force her to comply either. I need to regroup. I will find out what the fuck happened to her, and when I do, someone's blood will stain my hands.

For now, I'm going to have to settle with feeding my pigs.

---

"BREAK STUFF" by Limp Bizkit screams out of the speakers. This shed is soundproof; there's no way to hear what goes on inside. To anyone looking, it's just an indoor pigpen. I've just thrown the last limb of that crazy bitch into the middle, watching as the pigs go nuts eating the human remains.

They love human meat. And *I* love that I can dispose of a body so easily and effortlessly. I remember thinking Emily was nuts when she thought I had a heap of pigs somewhere that I'd feed her to. It's because of her that I bought these guys as tiny piglets. I hand-raised them like they were my own children.

Leaning against the wall, I inhale the nicotine of my cigarette, watching as the smoke fills the air. I should go back into the house and check on Emily. I'm sure she's going to be pissed about the fact that I locked her in my room.

Flicking the butt of my smoke on the floor and squashing it with my boot, I turn to leave just as the door opens. Dean and Zac walk in; both men look towards the pigs and then back at me.

"You know I've done some messed up shit in my life, but this here is second-level fucking crazy, Josh," Zac says, shaking his head.

"You're welcome to leave, or better yet, be dessert," I inform him, to which, he just smirks at me. Cocky bastard.

"We're heading back into the city in the morning." Dean breaks the stare-off between me and Zac.

"Okay, tell Ella I'll meet her for breakfast at 7:30 a.m. If she's not there, I will be breaking your fucking door down."

"Sure, I'll let her know." Dean shrugs his shoulders before asking, "Are you sure you won't have your hands full? If you say you're meeting Ella, you have to be there. I won't have her disappointed if you don't show. For some strange ass reason, she likes you."

"Why wouldn't I show?" I ask.

"I don't know, Josh. How about that little blonde you have locked up in your room?" Dean knows way too much about my past with Emily. He's way too fucking intuitive when it comes to me.

"She won't be a problem. She also has a fucking name

asshole—*use it.* Now, if you'll both excuse me, I have things to do." Just as I think I'm getting out of this conversation, Dean stops me with a hand on my chest. I look down at his open palm, then back up at him. But he doesn't remove it. Anyone else, I would have chopped that hand off their arm already.

"Not so fast. What are you planning on doing with Emily?" he asks.

"That's really not any of your fucking business," I growl at him.

"I know how badly she messes with your head. It's not her I'm worried about. It's you. So again, what are your plans with Emily."

"It's simple really. I'm keeping her." I shoulder barge past him on my way out the door.

# Chapter 3

## Emily

The warm sun shines on my face. I pull the blankets up over my head to block out the light. Mmm, these blankets are soft, silky soft. Stretching out my limbs, I do a quick assessment of my body, cataloguing the various aches and pains.

The bruises on my face have become a dull ache. My ribs, a slight, sharp pain. It didn't help that Josh threw my body over his shoulder yesterday. Fuck, Josh!

I bolt upright at the memory. Looking around the luxurious room, I know it wasn't a dream. I really am in Josh's room right now. No, not just in his room… I'm in his bed.

Holding the blanket tight to my chest, I'm half expecting him to jump out of the shadows somewhere. He's not here though. I've always been able to somehow feel him whenever he's been close.

The room smells like him; he *was* here recently. Judging by the messed-up sheets on the other side of the bed, I'm guessing he slept there. He slept right next to me—probably explains why I don't remember waking up from the usual nightmares.

I need to get out of here before he comes back, before he can stop me from leaving. The asshole locked me in here after he left me in his shower. I walked out, saw the sweatpants and shirt he placed on the bed for me, and quickly changed. It only took ten minutes of trying the door handle for me to give up on it and climb into the bed. I told myself I would just lie down for five minutes, regroup and come up with a new plan.

That's exactly what I needed now, a new plan. A plan to escape this room. A plan to fix the shitstorm that is now my life. Reluctantly, I get out of what has to be the softest bed I've ever slept in.

I can take in more of the room with the sunlight shining through the large bay windows.

The dark timber, four-poster bed sits in the middle. It's masculine (and it's very Josh), covered with dark navy bedding and black satin sheets. There's a large chest of drawers with a few little knickknacks sitting on top of it. Other than that, the room is empty. There's so much blank space it's a little eerie. Why doesn't he have more furniture in here?

There are two doors; one I know leads to the bathroom. I head for that door and freshen up as quickly as I can. I run my hands through my hair, rub some toothpaste on my finger and pathetically try to brush my teeth.

It will have to do. I don't plan on seeing anyone anyway. I plan on sneaking out without being noticed. The only problem is I know how big this house is. I came to a house party here once. Josh's older brother, Dean, threw one when he was a senior at school. My friend Bella and I snuck in.

I had hoped to run into Josh, only he was nowhere to be found. That was basically my last years of high school—me, trying to get glimpses of Josh, while also hoping he would notice me. That he would see me.

I finally got that wish granted on graduation day. He noticed me. He cherished me, only to then abandon me and tell me to leave town. The memory both saddens and angers me. How dare he give me one night of pure bliss, of happiness like I've never known, only to shatter my world the next morning.

With renewed determination and a little anger, I storm to the door and yank on the handle. I'm expecting it to be locked again, so when it actually opens, I fall back with the force of my pull. Huh, what game is this psycho playing? I remember just how much he tormented the other kids at school. He loved playing mind games with everyone.

The hallway is clear; no one is around. The house is so silent I could mistakenly think I'm the only one here. I make my way down the winding marble staircase as quietly as I can. Once I get to the bottom, there are three different hallways, all leading in different directions. It's like a game of eeny meeny miny moe, and I have no idea which way to go.

One of these has to lead to an exit somewhere. Choosing the one to the left of the staircase, I follow the long walkway, tiptoeing past numerous closed doors. Why the hell are there so many doors in this place? How many rooms does one house need to have?

I get lost in my thoughts. By the time I realise it, I'm already in the kitchen with a pair of icy blue eyes staring back at me. My steps stop, my heart rate picks up, and an unfamiliar feeling rushes over me—a reaction to what I've walked in on.

Josh is sitting at the bench with the girl who was in the cabin. He has one arm around her, hugging her as she rests her head on his shoulder. My eyes flutter between Josh and the arm he has around another woman.

It's irrational of me to have any feelings of jealousy, yet I recognise that these feelings are just that—the kind of irrational, stupid jealousy that I have no right to feel. I don't even know Josh anymore. Then again, can I really say I ever knew him?

One night together does not count for anything. He clearly has not been hung up on me all these years. I can't help the violent thoughts running through my head, or the fact that I want to go and rip his damn arm off.

I can't remember a time I've ever been jealous before. Actually, that's not true. I used to get crazy jealous whenever the girls at school would talk about how hot Josh was, or how much they wanted just one night with him. Thankfully, I don't think any of them ever got that one night.

However, *I did*, and even though I hate him for how it ended, it was still one of the best times of my life. I can still feel the ghost of Josh's hands all over my body. What I wouldn't do to feel that again…

"You need a cool drink or something, Emmy?" Josh's voice breaks me out of my trance.

My face heats with embarrassment at the realisation he could possibly know what I was thinking. The girl beside him sits up straighter and looks in my direction. She only just noticed I was in the room.

"No thank you. And it's Emily, not Emmy." I cross my arms over my chest, trying to cover up the fact that I'm not wearing a bra. I can feel my hardened nipples rubbing against the fabric of his shirt.

My feet are frozen to the spot, my body betraying me. Josh stands up and walks around the bench. My mind is telling me to run, run in the other direction and never look back. But my feet don't move. They don't move when Josh approaches me as he undoes the buttons on his flannel shirt and takes it off.

They don't move as he wraps that shirt around my shoulders, unfolding my arms to guide each one through the long sleeves. My feet still stay rooted to the spot when Josh leans in and whispers in my ear.

"I know what you're thinking, Emmy. I also know your nipples are not rock-hard right now because you're cold. Unless you want me to throw you down on that bench and wrap my mouth around those delicious fucking nipples of yours right now, keep this shirt on." He straightens and takes my hand in his, leading me to the bench before sitting me on a stool.

"Emmy, this is Ella, my sister." He puts extra emphasis on the word *sister*.

I tilt my head and squint my eyes at him. Does he think I'm stupid? He doesn't have a sister. "Sister? Really? Since when did you get a sister?" I ask.

Josh smirks as one eyebrow raises. "Since a week ago, when Ella here was stupid enough to marry my brother."

"Don't be an ass, Josh. No matter what you think, it doesn't suit you," Ella directs to Josh before facing me. "I want to thank you for helping me yesterday. I'm really fucking glad you showed up when you did."

Before I know it, Ella is standing up and has her arms wrapped around me. She squeezes me in a tight hug. I wince at the sharp pain that radiates through my ribs. My body stiff,

I know I should hug her back, but I'm not used to this kind of thing. I haven't had anyone hug me for so long.

Ella pulls away suddenly. "Shit, I'm so sorry. Are you okay?" she asks with what seems to be genuine concern.

"Uh, yeah, I'm good. Just slept wrong. It was really nice meeting you, Ella. Congratulations on your marriage. Uh, I should probably be going."

Just as I stand up, Josh places a cup of coffee in front of me. "Sit down. We're having breakfast." His voice is rough, commanding.

I sit back down quietly. I'm so used to taking orders I don't even argue. Anxiety rains terror through my body as I wait for the yelling to start. Surely, it won't be long. It's probably better to just get it over with.

Only, when I look up, both Ella and Josh are staring at me and no one is yelling. I can see concern on Ella's features. It makes me uncomfortable and I can't seem to meet her eyes. Josh looks angry though; that's a look I can cope with. I know what to expect from anger.

Needing to get the attention away from me (and to calm Josh's rage), I pick up the cup and take a sip. My hands shake. I don't know why he's angry. I don't know what I'm supposed to do to make him happy. At least with Trent, I knew what made him angry. I could avoid upsetting him.

The image of Trent's lifeless stare, blood pooling around his head as he lies on the kitchen floor, haunts me. I can see it even with my eyes wide open. My hands are so shaky as I try to put the cup back down on the bench, that the coffee spills over and onto the pristine white marble benchtop.

Oh no! This can't be happening. I jump up. "I'm so sorry. I'm really sorry. I-I'll clean it up. I promise. I'll get it clean. You won't even know there was a spill," I stutter out, my eyes scanning around the kitchen for where I can find cleaning supplies.

I spy the sink and head for it. "It's my fault. I should have been more careful. I'll be more careful. I promise."

Just as I make it back over to the bench, arms wrap around me from behind. I automatically bring my hands up to cover my face. My body draws in on itself. Josh spins me around, caging me in.

I can't bring myself to look up at him. My hands are still raised defensively.

"I'm going to go pack. I'll come find you before we leave." With those parting words, Ella walks out. Josh doesn't answer her. I can feel his gaze locked on me.

He grabs onto my hands and pulls them away from my face, slowly, gently, tilting my head up with his finger. My eyes connect with his. I can't read what I see staring back at me. Gone is the icy glare, and in its place, something I've only seen reflected back at me once before.

"I'll never hurt you, Emmy. I promise." Josh's voice is a whisper.

I nod my head in acknowledgement. I don't know how to answer him. Deep down in my soul, I believe he wouldn't hurt me. But my body has been accustomed to protecting itself. It's all I've known for the past three years.

"I need a name, Emmy, now." Gone is the whisper, gone is the look of devotion I saw momentarily. Back is the icy glare, thc harsh tone.

I shake my head. I can't possibly tell him. He can never know what I've done. Plausible deniability. If the cops do catch up with me here, at least he has plausible deniability. He wasn't knowingly harbouring a fugitive.

"You know I'm going to find out anyway. It will save us both a lot of time if you just tell me."

"I can't, Josh. Just let me go. I'll leave and you can pretend you never saw me. Please."

Josh shakes his head. "There's only one problem with your plan, Emmy."

I'm afraid to ask, afraid to know the answer, but I question him anyway. "What?"

"I can't just forget I saw you. I haven't been able to forget about you in the past seven years. I can still taste you on my tongue. I can still feel the smoothness of you under my fingers." Josh traces his fingertips up and down my arm, leaving behind a trail of goosebumps.

I shouldn't be feeling turned on right now. I haven't been remotely interested in sex for a long time. My thighs tighten together; my body shivers. All I want to do right now is climb this man like a damn spider monkey. The thought of how quickly my body betrays my mind with just a single touch is terrifying.

"J-Josh, I..." I let my sentence drag off. I'm not sure if I'm begging him to give me the release that I so desperately want, or asking him to stop.

Josh pushes his whole body against mine. My back digs into the benchtop behind me. I can feel the hardness of his cock pressing into my stomach. I need to put a stop to this. I need to get some distance between us.

"Stop." My voice is nothing but a whisper as I push against his chest. The bastard doesn't even budge.

"Your voice is telling me to stop, but you don't really want me to stop, Emmy. Do you?" His tongue trails up the side of my neck. My head tilts, granting him better access.

Traitorous fucking body. Damn it feels good, so good. It

doesn't matter how good it feels, I know it won't end with *good feelings*. It never does.

"I need you to stop, please." As soon as the words leave my mouth, my eyes widen. Panic overtakes me and I wait for the slap that's bound to come. I wait and wait. Josh stares down at me without saying anything, his jaw clenched.

He pulls my stiff body into his and wraps his arms around me, burying his face into the crook of my neck. He whispers, "I've never felt the need to maim and torture as much as I do right now. When I find out who did this to you, Emmy, there won't be a stone they can hide under. I'm going to take great pleasure in staining my hands with their blood."

Little does he know... he's never going to get that opportunity.

# Chapter 4

## Josh

Holding Emily's stiff body tight against mine, I do my best to rein in the overwhelming anger threatening to take over. Anger is an old friend. I'm familiar with the sensation, but the level of anger I'm feeling now, it's at an all-time high.

I need to find out who did this to her. I need their blood, like I need air. I'm fucking angry that she didn't come to me sooner. How long has she been being abused? How long has some fucker been using her for a fucking punching bag?

I'm fucking furious at myself. If I hadn't been such a weak fucking coward all those years ago, this wouldn't have happened. I would have kept her. I would have protected her.

Picking her up, I carry her back to my bedroom—*exactly where she should be*. The sight of the perfectly made-up bed stops me. I know the maids don't come in here until at least 11:00 a.m.

"Did you make the bed, Emmy?" I ask.

"Yes. Is it not how you want it? I can fix it," she says, as she tries to shimmy herself down from my body.

"It's fine. But you don't need to do that. We have maids who will come in and tidy up every day."

"I don't mind doing it. I messed it up. I should clean it," she mumbles out.

Walking through to the bathroom, I sit her on the vanity while I turn the taps on to run a bath. I'm sure I've got some bubbles or shit somewhere in here. Digging through the cabinets, I find a bottle of jasmine bubble bath. I pour a good amount in, testing the water as I strip my shirt over my head.

I can hear Emmy counting quietly behind me. When I turn around, I find her counting the finger spaces between the hanging towels. I'm at a loss for words as I watch her rearrange the towels until they are evenly spaced apart.

Emmy is so transfixed by what she's doing, she doesn't notice me come up behind her until I have my arms wrapped around her, my hand covering hers on the towel rail.

Her porcelain white skin is the polar opposite of my tanned and tarnished hand. "The towels are fine, babe. You don't need to fix anything. You could throw them all down on the floor and I wouldn't care."

I lift her hand off the towel rail and drop her arm by her side before trailing my fingertips along her waist, slowly lifting the bottom of her shirt. My shirt. Burying my head into the crook of her neck, I gently kiss up and down.

"Wh-what are you doing?" Emmy asks softly.

"We're having a bath. And as good as you look in my

clothes, you're not wearing them in the tub." I lift the shirt over her head. Before she can protest, I drag the track pants down her legs, lifting each foot out one at a time.

"Come on." Taking her hand, I lead her over to the bath. She steps in and sits down, pulling her knees up to her chest while trying her best to cover herself up.

Smirking down at her, I undo my jeans and kick them off. Stepping into the bath, I sit on the opposite side of her. The water is waist-deep, and although the tub could allow for more of a capacity, I turn the faucet off. I don't want her whole body to be covered by water.

Grabbing her ankles, I pull until her legs straighten on either side of me. I'm aching to yank her towards me, to make her wrap those thighs around me. I'm aching to be buried into her heat.

"You don't ever need to hide from me, Emmy." I pick up a loofah and squirt bodywash onto it.

"I look horrible, Josh. I'm covered in bruises. Why would you want to look at me?" she questions, as she finally raises her head to peer up at me.

"You are the most beautiful person I've ever seen. These bruises don't hinder your beauty, babe." I gently run the loofah up and down each of her arms. She stares at me, silently.

"Can I ask you a question?" she prompts, her voice cautious.

"There isn't anything you can't ask me. I can't guarantee you'll like the answers, but I won't ever lie to you."

"Do you know someone else named Emmy?"

I'm not sure what I was expecting her to ask, but that was not it. I laugh. "No, I don't. Why?"

"Then why do you have my name tattooed across your

heart?" Her hand reaches out, her fingertips tracing over the lettering that runs across the middle of my chest.

"I had this done the day after… the day after our senior graduation. I have your name on my heart, because you are the only person I've ever loved. You are the only person I love."

Her hand stills and she removes it from me. I want her hands back on me. I want her touching me.

"If you loved me, then why did you make me leave?" There's a tiny flame of fire in her eyes, a tiny flame of the old Emmy.

"I was saving you *from me*. I'm not normal, Emmy. I didn't want you to be dragged down by me. You were like this piece of light in my dark world. I didn't want to be the one to dim your light."

"You're right. You're not normal. But I loved you anyway. I would have happily stayed in that cabin with you forever. I never cared what other kids said about you at school. I never listened to the rumours, even if I knew they were true. Because even back then, I knew. I've known since I first laid eyes on you…" she whispers.

"What did you know?"

"That you were the Tim to my Tam, the Vegemite to my toast."

"You forgot the cookie to your cream," I remind her, a vivid memory of the first time I saw her coming to me. "Did you forget the part where I tipped a milkshake over you? I'm not a nice person, Emmy."

"I haven't forgotten. I also haven't forgotten how no one ever picked on me at school. Or how every single boy who ever showed any interest in me would either leave school or come back banged up."

I shrug. "I did all those losers a favour. Also, they should have known better than to try to hook up with you."

I spend the next ten minutes rubbing the loofah all over her body, paying extra attention to her breasts and those pink nipples of hers that make my mouth water. Her breathing picks up; her cheeks are flushed. I can feel the twitch in her legs as she fights to close them. She's fighting the feelings. She doesn't want to be turned on.

Slowly lowering the loofah down her stomach until I reach her smooth, bare pussy, I press down harder and rub circles around her clit. Her head tips back and her lips part as her pelvis attempts to push into my hand.

Discarding the loofah, I replace it with my fingers, rolling them around her clit before dragging one down to her opening. My cock is hard as a fucking rock, aching to take the place of my finger as I slowly pump in and out of her.

Leaning over, my mouth closes around one of her hardened nipples, biting down gently as my tongue swirls around the tip. Fuck, I need to get my mind back on the game plan here. This isn't about my pleasure, or hers at the moment. As intoxicating as she is, as much as I want to watch her come apart from my touch, I want information more. I need the information only she knows.

Releasing her nipple, I kiss my way up her neck. *Slowly*. I want to stay right here, like this, forever. But forever doesn't exist. It's a concept only fools buy into.

"You want me to make you come, Emmy?" I ask as I slow my movements, her pussy trying to grind down harder onto my hand the more I pull away.

She nods her head, her long blonde locks falling back into the water.

"I need to hear the words. Do you want me to make you feel better than you ever have before?"

She picks her head up; her gaze locks with mine. "Yes." That one word, whispered out of her mouth… *That word*, I want to hear her screaming it over and over again.

"I want that too, Emmy. I want to make you come apart on my fingers, on my mouth, on my fucking cock." I groan as one of her hands tentatively wraps around my cock.

"Fuck." I have to remove her hand. I can't think straight when she touches me. Now is not the time to lose focus.

"I need something from you. If you want to come, I need you to give me a name." I'm hoping she's so far gone with need, she forgets that she's keeping this secret.

She's not though, and she hasn't forgotten. She shakes her head no. "Please, Josh, I-I can't." Her hips continue to grind into my hand.

I remove my fingers. I'm out of the bath and have a towel wrapped around me before she even opens her eyes.

"What are you doing?" she asks.

"If you can't, then neither can I. Finish yourself off, Emmy." With that, I storm out of the bathroom, slamming the door behind me.

*Fuck!* Losing control, I punch the closest wall I find. I keep punching over and over again until I feel the tear of skin. My knuckles drip with blood. I need to get out of here. I can't be around her when I'm feeling so out of control.

Why the fuck won't she tell me? Is she trying to protect the bastard who's been hurting her? Fuck that, if she won't tell me who the fuck it is, I have other ways of finding out.

Getting dressed, I decide on a new course of action and head down to my office.

I'VE BEEN SITTING in this office for an hour, making call after call, scanning emails and answering the ones that are worth my time. I've been debating over whether or not to investigate Emmy's life. I've never second guessed my choices before, never cared what anyone thought. But it's different with her. I fucking hate that she brings these feelings out of me.

Deciding it's always better to seek forgiveness rather than ask permission, I put the call through (the same call I've been holding off). Sam's the one guy I know I can trust to get me the information I need. There's a reason he's my second in command. He gets shit done, no matter what the task. There is no dirty laundry he can't uncover, no deal he can't make happen.

"Boss, what's up?" Sam asks.

"I need some information."

"Sure, what do you need?" I can hear him inhale, before blowing out a puff of air.

"I thought you quit?" I really couldn't care less, but this fucker has been kicking the habit for the last five years, obviously not successfully.

"I did. Then I remembered who the fuck I work for and figured there's no point in trying to prolong my miserable fucking existence anyway," he replies.

"You know, if you weren't so useful to me, your miserable existence would have ended years ago."

"So you remind me, at least once a month. What info do you need?"

"Emmy—Emily Livingston. I want to know everything about her over the past seven years. I want to know what she ate for fucking breakfast every day. Everything," I grunt out.

"Emmy, huh? Why now?" I knew he wouldn't miss the nickname I slipped out. He's been asking about Emmy for the past five years, ever since he saw the tattooed name on my chest.

"She's back." That's about all the information I want to give him.

"If she's back, why don't you just ask her?" He talks to me as though I haven't already thought of that.

"I have." I take a breath in. "She turned up here fucking black and blue. Some fucker has been using her as a fucking punching bag. I want to know who. Yesterday!" My voice raises to a yell. I pick the coffee cup off my desk and hurl it across the room.

"Oh, shit. Man, okay. I'll get every bit of information you need. I'll help you feed those fucking pigs of yours with what we find too." The sound of a keyboard being hammered on echoes in the background. He's already on the job.

"I'm not feeding my babies that kind of scum," I say. Even my pigs are too fucking good for that fucker.

"Josh?" Sam queries.

"Yeah?"

"Are you going to be all right? You know I can be there in a matter of hours if you need."

"I'm good," I lie. I'm not fucking all right. But then again, I've never been all right, have I? I hang up before he can question me further. If I was capable of having friends, Sam would come close to what I imagine a best friend would be.

Just as I hang up, Ella and Dean walk through the door.

"Hey, we're heading off. Unless you need me to stay… I can stay longer," Ella offers. I really don't understand the girl. Why would anyone offer to stay and hang out with me?

"It's okay. I'll be heading back into the city tomorrow

anyway." Walking around my desk, I wrap an arm around her shoulder, guiding her and my brother out of my office. "Let me walk you out."

"Are you sure you're okay? Wait, that's a stupid question. What are you planning on doing with your new houseguest?" She's cute when she's trying to get information out of me.

"Nothing that I can tell my little sister." I wink at her.

"Ew, gross! And we are the same age, idiot." She shrugs out of my hold.

I laugh at her reaction, which was obviously the wrong thing to do. Her arms fold over her chest. Her face hardens. She tilts her head and squints at me.

"Are you laughing at me right now, Joshua McKinley?" she seethes out.

Fuck, if I was anyone else, I'd probably be scared right now.

"So what if I am? What are you gonna do about it?" I taunt her.

"Oh man, trust me, you do not want to go there, Bro," Dean pipes in, stepping into Ella.

"Princess, he's not right in the head. You can't take him laughing at you seriously. He laughed at our grandfather's funeral when he was ten. Like full-on laughed his ass off when it was his turn to pay his respects to the man." Dean wraps an arm around Ella's waist, like he's trying to hold her back.

"It's okay. I won't do anything to him." Ella's voice drips with sweetness. She turns in Dean's arms. "I think I left something upstairs. I'll be right back." She starts running towards the stairs.

"Oh man, I'd be careful from here on out if I were you. She does not like being laughed at. This one time, she replaced

Bray's shampoo with hair remover. The guy was bald, even his eyebrows were gone." Dean laughs.

"I'm not scared of your wife, Dean. She can bring her best." I shrug.

After a minute of waiting for Ella to return, curiosity gets the better of me and I ask, "What do you think she's doing?"

Dean shrugs. Before he can answer, the front door opens and our mother struts in, staff carting her suitcases behind her. She stops as she sees both Dean and I standing in the middle of the foyer.

"Boys, you're both here. Good." She comes up and wraps her arms around Dean, kissing him on the cheek. "I've missed you. You should come home more often, darling."

She then moves onto me, hugging me even tighter than she had Dean. "Looking handsome as ever, Joshua." She steps back and smiles at us.

Dean and I share a look. Who is this woman and what the fuck has she done with our mother?

Laughter from behind me causes me to turn around. "Fuck no!" I say as I pull my shirt over my head, stomping towards Ella and Emily, who are currently walking towards us in bikinis. Where did those strips of fabric even come from?

Ella stands in front of Emily with her hands on her hips. "Stop right there! I'm going to show Emily here where the pool is." She looks over at Dean.

"Babe, you don't mind if we stay for an extra hour, do you?" she asks him.

"Ah, sure, whatever you want, Ella." The pussy-whipped fucker gives in to her every time.

"Dean, tell your wife if she wants to keep all of that pretty hair on her head, then she had better move out of my way." I hear my mother's gasp from behind me. I forgot she was even there for a moment.

"Wife?" Her head moves between Dean and Ella. I'm expecting Oscar-level dramatics any minute now, except, that's not what happens.

Mum walks over to Ella and pulls her into her arms. "Dean, I can't believe you got married and didn't tell me." She steps back and cups Ella's face. "Welcome to the family, sweetheart."

"Thank you, Mrs. McKinley. But it's not completely Dean's fault. It was quick. We didn't have a wedding, just signed the papers," Ella rambles.

"Ella, you can call me Julie. Don't you worry. I'll make sure you get a wedding fit for a princess."

She turns to me. "Joshua, put your shirt back on. You're distracting the staff." She makes a point to nod her head at the two young maids who are standing at the other end of the foyer with their mouths gaping.

Emily looks their way and glares. Huh? Well, that's interesting.

"Wait, why are these girls allowed to strut around without clothes on, but I can't?" I ask like a sulking child.

"They're not naked. They're going swimming," my mother, or the woman who has taken over my mother's body, answers.

"Ella, hunny, go ahead and take Emmy to the pool. I'll have some drinks and snacks brought out to the two of you."

Once Ella and Emmy are out of the room, my mother spins on my brother and me. Pointing a finger at Dean, she says, "I'll deal with you later."

"Now you," she directs at me. "For the love of God, please tell me that girl is here of her own free will, Joshua."

I raise my eyebrows at her question. "Of course she is." It's not a complete lie; she did come here of her own free will. However, am I prepared to let her leave? Fuck no.

"What happened to her?"

"I don't know. I'm trying to find out. She turned up here like that, Mum. I didn't fucking do that." I'm not sure why I feel the need to defend myself.

"I know you wouldn't hurt her, Josh. She's probably the only person on this godforsaken Earth who you wouldn't hurt." She pauses before asking, "Are you okay?"

Why the fuck is everyone asking me that? Like I'm going to fall apart or something.

"I'm fine. But are *you* okay? Are you dying?" It's the only conclusion for her sudden motherly attitude I can come up with.

"Never been better. I'm not dying. Is it so wrong for a mother to be concerned for her sons' wellbeing?"

"For mothers, no. For you, yes," I reply.

"Well, things are changing. I have daughters. I'm sure grandbabies aren't too far off."

"Ah, you have one daughter-*in-law*. Not plural. And let's hope those grandbabies look like fucking Ella and not this ugly ass." I look at Dean.

"Don't hold your breath for grandbabies anytime soon, Mum. I just got Ella to myself. I'm not ready to share her with anyone else yet." Dean's staring in the direction of where Ella just left, like he can see through the fucking walls to her.

"Okay, well, I have a wedding to plan. I'll catch up with you boys later." Our mother walks out of the room, already clicking away on her phone.

I look at Dean. "What the fuck was that?" I ask him. I

know I'm not the best at social situations, or emotions, but that shit was fucking weird as hell.

"No idea, man. But I'm going to go drag Ella out of here before we get stuck planning the wedding of the fucking century." He storms off towards the pool.

# Chapter 5

## Emily

Floating around in the pool, I feel free. Weightless. At peace. It's quiet in here. Dean came and dragged Ella out, saying something about escaping his mother's wedding planning before it was too late.

I like Ella. In another life, another time, I think I could have been good friends with someone like her. My life isn't destined for that. I'm not destined for the happily ever after. The sombre reality crashes over me, reminding me not to get too comfortable here. I need to plan my escape. I need to get out of here before I get Josh and his family in any trouble.

How my face isn't spread all over the news and on every paper out there, I don't know. I killed someone. Granted he deserved it, but he was still a living, breathing person and I killed him. The thing that's messing with my mind is the fact that I don't regret it. That realisation scares me. I should feel bad.

The nightmares come—maybe that's my subconscious telling me I did something I should feel bad about. In my nightmares though, I don't kill him. In my nightmares, he's still alive and he's coming for me.

What if I didn't kill him? No, I saw all the blood, the lifeless eyes. He was definitely dead. He has to be. I can handle going to jail for the rest of my life if it means never having to face him again.

A huge splash draws me out of my internal battle. I right my body, looking around for what could have made the splash. I can see the ripples in the water, but that's it. Nothing else. Surely if there was someone else in here, they would have to come up for air by now. Right?

The water stills and nothing and no one has popped up. I'm starting to get freaked out, standing here like a sitting duck. I head for the steps to get out of the pool when something grabs around my ankle and pulls me down, my scream silenced by the water. I kick out at the person holding me under. It's no use. Whoever it is wraps their arms around me and shoots both of our bodies up.

My lungs heave as I wipe the water from my face and swipe my hair off my forehead. Opening my eyes, I'm met with a sight that momentarily stops my heart.

Josh is smiling, a big beaming smile; even his damn eyes are twinkling. For a moment, a small moment, I forget that I'm mad at him, that I hate him. I get lost in those blue eyes of his. Then I remember I hate him.

Punching him on his chest while trying to wiggle myself out of his vice-like hold, I yell at him, "What the hell are you smiling about, asshole?"

"What's not to smile about? I've got the most beautiful woman in the fucking world in my arms—and she's all *wet.*" His voice is deep and husky.

"Does that line work on all the girls, Josh? Because if it does, you need to up your standards," I bite back at him.

"There are no other girls, babe. There is only you. There will only ever be you." He's so convincing with his words, I almost believe him. I almost want to believe him.

"Sure, whatever you say. Now, remove your hands from me before I scream bloody murder," I threaten.

Josh immediately removes his hands but doesn't move away from me. I take a step backwards myself, only to have him follow.

"You know, it wasn't that long ago you were begging for my hands to be on you, *in* you." He smirks.

"I had a momentary lapse in judgement. Don't flatter yourself. I ended up doing a better job myself."

I'm not sure where the courage to talk back to him like this is coming from. Why am I pushing him? Trying to get him to break? Get him to show me his true colours sooner rather than later? I'm waiting for him to snap and lash out at me. It's bound to happen, eventually. The longer I stay here, the more chance I have of being *that* girl again.

The one who lets a guy dictate her every move, the one who lets the guy use and abuse her to relieve his own frustration. I've decided I don't want to be that girl again. I never wanted to be her in the first place.

"You can push me as much as you like. Talk back to me with as much fight as you've got to give. There is nothing, and I mean *nothing*, you can do that will ever make me hurt you, Emmy. I may be a monster, but I'm not that kind of fucking monster," Josh says fiercely.

"You don't get it, Josh! All these bruises, all these scars. Yeah, they hurt. Yes, I've been beaten over and over again. But no amount of physical pain has ever amounted to the ache you caused when I woke up in that damn cabin alone!" I scream, and tears start running down my face. I didn't mean to tell him… I didn't want him to know how much he has the power to hurt me. *Had*. He had the power to hurt me. I won't let any man hurt me again.

Josh reaches his hand up to my face. I automatically flinch, turning my head. I feel my body go stiff, waiting for the sting. I don't feel it though; what I do feel is Josh's thumb wiping away the tears from my cheek.

"I wish you would give me a name, Emmy," Josh whispers.

I shake my head no. I can't let him know what I've done. I just need to get out of here.

"It's okay. You don't have to tell me. I'll find out anyway."

"You need to stop looking, Josh. You need to let me leave. I can't be here. I shouldn't be here."

"*Here* is exactly where you're meant to be. Here is where you belong. You can't leave, Emmy. You can't leave. You can't. Please just let me keep you for a little longer." Josh sounds almost desperate. His arms wrap back around my body as I let myself embrace his touch. I rest my head on his chest, right over where my name is printed on him.

I know I shouldn't give him reassurance, make promises I can't keep, but I do anyway. "Okay." The one word leaves my mouth, sealing my fate, his fate, our fate.

What will he do when he finds me gone? Because as soon as I get the chance, I will be leaving. No matter how much I want to stay right here in his arms, I know I can't.

---

I SPENT the rest of the day with my hand firmly gripped in Josh's as he gave me a tour of the farm. He introduced me to some of the staff, informing them I'd be staying for a while. I plastered on a fake smile and let myself believe the lie, the dream, for a little while.

This has been one of the best days I've ever had. I can almost picture a life here with Josh. Every time I let myself see a glimpse of what that might look like, a vision of dead eyes and a pool of blood overtakes my mind. I'm never going to have the fairy tale Josh is selling me.

I'm now wandering around Josh's room. He said he had some things to take care of, that he'd be in his office if I needed him. There's not much in here to look at. His closet is neat, too neat. All his clothes are perfectly hung and ordered by colour, his shoes lined up and again ordered by colour. I wonder if he does this himself, or if his maids do it for him.

Irrational jealousy overcomes me at the thought of other females doing anything for him. It should be me. I should be doing it all. No… no, I should not. What I should be doing is figuring out how to get out of this damn palace, because let's call it for what it is. This place is not a home; it's a damn museum.

I'm bored. I could wander out of the room. I know he didn't lock the door this time. But I'm so exhausted from all the walking around we did today. I decide to lie down. I figure a little nap won't hurt. Maybe Josh will come back in soon and I can talk him into taking me into the city.

---

*"DID you really think you could get away from me? You fucking whore!" he yells.*

*I shake my head no. "It was an accident. I-I didn't mean to. I'm sorry," I cry as I step backwards until I hit the wall. How did he find me? He's supposed to be dead; he can't be here. This can't be real.*

*But as his hand wraps around my throat, it's real. I feel it. I feel the burn in my lungs as they fight for air. He lets go, only to slap me across the face. I fall to the ground and curl up in a fetal position.*

*"No!" I scream out. "Stop, please. I didn't mean to!" I'm sobbing. I look up to him standing over me, his big, heavy, black boot lifted above my head and ready to come straight down. I scream as the boot starts making its descent towards my face.*

Jolting upright, I look ahead, dazed. Where am I? It was just another dream. It's okay. I'm okay.

"Emmy!" Josh yells as he crashes through the door, holding a handgun out in front of him. His gaze searches every corner of the room before landing back on me. He lowers the gun and walks over to the bed.

"Are you okay?" he asks.

"I'm… I'm sorry." My voice is hoarse. I must have been screaming from my nightmare.

"Are you hurt?"

I shake my head no. I can't even tell him what happened. How can I tell him I had a nightmare about the guy I killed coming back for me? Josh places the gun on the nightstand beside the bed.

I could end everything with that gun. I could stop it all. The nightmares, these confusing feelings I'm having for Josh, all of it could be gone in just one press of that trigger.

Josh's hand grips my chin, turning my face towards him. "Get those disturbing thoughts out of your fucking head right the fuck now, Emmy!"

My eyes open wide. How the hell does he know what I'm

thinking? There's no way he can know what just went through my mind.

"I won't let anyone fucking hurt you ever again. Even yourself," he vows.

"I-I…" My mouth shuts. What can I tell him?

"What did you dream about?" he questions.

"I don't remember." The lie slips out way too easy.

"You're lying. But that's okay, because whatever monster you see in your dreams, Emily, I can promise you… that monster has nothing on the darkness of my soul, of the monster within me, or the kinds of things I plan to do with *him* as soon as I find out who he is."

"Your soul isn't dark, Josh. I've seen it." I have no idea why he thinks he's such a monster. Sure, he's a little unhinged at times. But the way he is with me, the way he's always been, I know he loves me in his own messed up way.

If only love were enough to change things… If only love could fix this mess I've put myself in…

"You're probably the only person other than my mother that sees any good in me, Emmy." Josh stands up, tipping his boots off before pulling his shirt over his head. I get so lost in all that is Josh. Big, tanned, broad shoulders. Wide chest, abs that lead into a V right down his waistline. My eyes travel back up his body. His blonde hair falls onto his forehead, covering those blue eyes a little.

"Move over, Em," he orders as he pulls the blankets back.

"What are you doing?" I ask stupidly. I can clearly see he's getting into bed.

"I'm getting into bed," he says.

"But why here? Surely there are a million other beds in this palace?" I ask him.

He tilts his head and stares at me. "Emmy, this is my bed. I'm not sleeping anywhere else."

Shit, I didn't think of that. I go to get up. "I'm sorry. I can go into another room. Or leave, or, or… I don't know," I offer.

"Emmy, move over. We've already discussed this. You are not leaving. If you try to move to a different bed, I'll just follow you anyway. Save us both the loss of sleep and just shove over a little already."

I scoot to the other side. "Just so you know, this does not mean I like you. In fact, we should draw a line down the middle of the bed if we have to share."

Josh laughs, the sound unfamiliar. I'm not sure how often he ever laughs, but I know it's not often enough. "Babe, I had my fingers buried inside your pussy this morning. Not to mention, I've had my cock buried inside that pussy of yours. Even if it has been way too fucking long since, he's been there and plans on being there again."

"Thanks for reminding me just why I hate you! And that cock of yours won't be getting anywhere near me again." I huff as I start lining pillows down the middle of the bed.

"You don't hate me, Emmy. You only wish you could. You can't hate someone you love. Trust me, I've tried to hate you for years, thinking it would make things easier. I've hated you for the way you make me feel. I've hated you for making me want a different future. I've hated you for making me want a future at all. But even with all that, the love I feel for you outweighs all the hate even I could muster up," he says this as he throws the pillows I just laid out onto the floor.

"Yeah, well, I've hated you just as much. So, you hold on to that hate; it will save both of us in the end."

"Don't you know, Emmy?" he asks.

"Know what?"

"There is no end to us. There will *never be* an end to us," he says as he lies down, pulling me into his arms.

I hate that he makes this feel good. And I hate myself more for wanting this to last longer.

# Chapter 6

## Josh

The phone on my bedside table is blaring. Reaching a hand out, I pick it up before bringing the receiver to my ear.

"What?" I ask.

"Joshua, that's no way to answer the phone," my mother's voice chastises through the line.

"It's also not polite to call people at ungodly hours, Mother. Is there a reason you're calling me so early?" I ask.

"Well, I was just having breakfast with Emily and I thought you might like to join us," she sings.

At the mention of Emily, I bolt up straight and look to the empty spot on the bed, the spot where Emily should be.

"I'll be right down." I hang up. Throwing on a pair of grey sweats, I forgo the shirt. The first thought in my head is that she's trying to leave. Even though she told me she wouldn't, I didn't believe her for a fucking second.

I can read it all over her face. She's running from something, someone. I can't let her leave. I'm afraid if I do, I'm never going to see her again. Over the last two days, I've come to terms with the fact that I don't want to live without her anymore. I never should have pushed her away in the first place. It's true what they say: *hindsight's a fucking bitch.*

On my way downstairs, I check my messages—nothing from Sam. What the fuck is taking him so long? He usually gets me the intel I need within hours. Shoving my phone back into my pocket, I reach the kitchen to find my mother at the counter. The sight is odd. She never sits at the breakfast bench, always having her meals served in the dining room.

Looking around, I note that Emmy is nowhere in sight. "Where's Emily?" I ask, heading for the coffee pot.

Pouring a glass of black coffee, I gulp a mouthful down before turning and raising an eyebrow at my mother, who still hasn't answered my damn question.

"She went out to see the stables. She wanted to see the horses."

Fuck! She's gone outside. She's probably halfway to Timbuctoo by now. I slam my cup down. "How long ago did she go out there?" I growl at my mother.

"Joshua, calm the fuck down. You are not going out there to go all caveman on that poor girl. Don't you think she's been through enough? She doesn't need another man trapping her." My mother's words halt me. One, because I've never heard her cuss before, ever! And two, because she's right. I can't be another man caging Emily in. But I'll be damned if I'm ever going to let her go either.

"What do you know about what she's been through?" I ask. Maybe Emmy confided in her about what happened.

"She hasn't told me anything, Josh. And if she did, I certainly wouldn't be breaking her confidence and telling you."

"You are dying, aren't you? What is this? Some new kind of sick and twisted game? Playing the nice mother who actually gives a fuck?" My words are harsh, however true they are.

"I know I haven't been the best mother. But I'm going to be now. I'm sober, have been for six months. And the reason I know what Emmy's been through is because I've lived it. My whole marriage was one of control and abuse. I protected you boys from ever seeing it. I didn't want you to know. Your father was a smart, smart man; he never left marks where others would see them. Never lost his temper in front of anyone."

She looks down at the ground. I want to scream at her that she did a shitty fucking job of protecting us. Because my father was a cruel son of a bitch to both Dean and me. He was worse to me—the man wanted to break me more than I was already broken.

He should have read the books my mother used to read, the ones on raising a child with psychopathic tendencies. I can't tell her any of that though—it won't do us any good.

I wrap my arms around my mum, the feeling foreign. But I don't know what else to do to help her. There's a tiny bit of me that doesn't like seeing her sad, a very tiny bit.

"I'm sorry he didn't die sooner," I say.

"So am I," she confirms as she pulls away. "Now, how are we going to get Emily around to the idea of being the next Mrs. McKinley, because I'm not getting any younger and I want grandchildren."

"Ah, I'm not… I don't… She's not leaving. I don't care what I have to do. I can't lose her again," I admit.

"I know. Go out there and take her riding. You know she was on the equestrian team in school, right?" The fact that my mother knows this surprises me.

"Of course, I know. She was on every bloody team," I say as I make my way out of the house.

---

STANDING in the shadows of the stables, I remain quiet as I observe Emily interact with Jasper. A white Quarter horse with a soul as pure as hers. She looks at peace, talking to Jasper and brushing him down.

I smile at the sight of her in a pair of my track pants and my shirt. I really do need to get her some of her own clothes, but the possessive ass that I am just wants to see her in mine.

I want to mark her, to make sure every fucker knows she's mine and only mine. I get so lost in taking her in, I don't notice the stable hand enter the building until he's approaching her.

I watch as he looks her up and down, licking his lips like he's about to eat a delicious meal. He's about to *be* the fucking meal if he doesn't avert his eyes elsewhere.

The fucker has a death wish. And I'm the goddamn genie who's going to grant it. I stay hidden in the shadows; neither of them knows that I'm here. As soon as Emmy notices she's not alone, she glances towards both exits. Smart girl. She's already looking for a way to escape a possible threat.

The fact that she even has to think like that is fucked up. She should feel safe in her own home. That's exactly the way I plan to make her feel.

"Hey there, darlin'. You need a hand?" the dead guy walking asks her.

"Ah, no. Thank you. I'm fine." Emmy's voice is quiet.

"Yes, you sure are," the cocksucker says as he rakes his eyes down her body again.

I watch as Emmy folds into her own body. Her head hangs low, her blonde hair falling (as it so often does) in curtains around her face.

"Ah, you should go. I'm meeting someone. He should be here any minute now." Emmy looks to the entrance, almost like she's praying someone else walks in.

Pulling my phone out, I type a quick text to Paul, my head of security.

**Me:** Clean up in the stables

His reply comes in quick, my phone vibrating in my hand.

**Paul:** Really, Josh? It's eight a.m. What the fuck could you have possibly gotten up to already?

**Me:** It's what I'm about to do that's going to need cleaning up.

Putting my phone back into my pocket, I make my way towards Jasper's stable, where that fucker is blocking the entrance and trapping my Emmy in.

"I don't see anyone else around, darlin'. It's just you and me out here. No one comes by these parts for at least another few hours." He takes a step towards her; she steps back.

Jasper starts to get agitated. Emily tries to soothe him, patting his neck. She whispers something to Jasper. And I swear I see the horse nod in agreement with her. Fuck, I must be getting crazier by the fucking day.

Emily notices me standing behind the fucker, and her eyes widen. I bring my finger to my lips, telling her to keep quiet. Pulling the knife from the ankle of my left leg, I snap my hand around him, placing the blade firmly at the base of his throat.

"I'm pretty sure the lady asked you to leave her alone," I say.

"What? No, we were just talking, that's all. I was just on my way out," he tries.

"Really? Is that true, Emmy? You wanted to talk to this guy?" I look at her, but she's transfixed on the knife I'm holding at the guy's throat. She slightly shakes her head no.

"That's what I thought. You see, this here is my girlfriend, and I don't take kindly to anyone that tries to fuck with her," I growl. As much as I want to slit his throat here and now, I don't want Emmy to see me like that. I don't want her to see how truly dark I am inside.

"I never have been one to play well with others. But Emmy here, she's a fucking saint. Always thinking of others before herself. Even though she knows you had all horrible intentions, she still doesn't want me to hurt you."

Emmy's eyes widen, before she looks down.

"The thing is, I'm going to enjoy hurting you. And I've got some hungry fucking pigs to feed."

Paul comes running into the stables, three men behind him, all four with their guns drawn. Emily gasps as she takes in the four hulking men pointing their weapons in our direction.

"Put the fucking guns away," I growl at them, not once taking my eyes off Emily. She's backed herself right up against the far wall.

Paul comes up behind me, tapping me on the shoulder. "Boss, I'll take it from here."

Like fuck he will. This fucker had every intention of messing with Emily. I'm going to make sure my face is the last thing he sees. Then he'll know to run when I meet him in hell.

"Josh, let me take him to the shed. You need to get your girl inside." Paul steps in front of me, holding his hand out.

"Fine, but nobody touches him until I get there," I demand.

"Sure, boss."

Removing the knife, I'm pleased to see the tiny speckles of blood on it, before I hand it over to Paul. One of the other guys comes up behind the fucker and cuffs his hands along his back.

Stepping aside, I wait until they're all out of the building before I make my way across to Emily, who is still up against the back wall. Jasper keeps one eye on me. I wouldn't put it past him to kick me in the back.

Emily doesn't move. Her body is still—apart from the slight tremble I can see. As soon as I get close enough to her, my hand wraps around her throat and my mouth slams down on hers.

Her lips part a little and I take the opportunity to slide my tongue inside, swiping and swirling it all around her mouth. She's rigid for a minute. I don't give up on my assault of her mouth. She tastes fucking delicious, and it just now occurs to me that this is the first time I've actually kissed her since she's returned.

Why the fuck haven't we been joined at the lips for the past two days? Because I'm a fucking idiot. This right here, this is my heaven. Pressing into her more, while my hand tightens a little around her throat, I groan as I devour her. She's giving back too. Her hands no longer attempt to push me away—no, those tiny hands are pulling me closer.

I trail my fingertips down her body. Picking her up, I wait as she wraps her legs around my waist. I need to get out of here before Jasper decides he wants to keep her.

Spinning on my heel, I'm met with Jasper's glare. The

horse obviously doesn't like me as much as he likes her. Then again, who would?

Walking down the stalls, I find an empty one that looks like it hasn't been occupied for a while. I slam her against the wall, probably a little too roughly. But fuck, I'm losing my goddamn mind here.

Her little moans tell me she doesn't mind, her centre grinding up and down on my rock-hard cock. Clothes, why are we still wearing clothes? Unwrapping her legs from my waist, I hold her until her feet are steady. As I break away from her mouth, her eyes open, her gaze searing right through my soul.

"Do you trust me, Emmy?" I ask. I need her to say yes. I need her to trust me for what I'm about to do to her.

"Yes," she whispers out softly.

That one yes is everything to me. "Good, because you're going to really need to hold on to that trust right now."

# Chapter 7

## Emily

Did I really just say that I trusted him? I didn't even think about it before the word "yes" slipped out. It's not true, is it? I don't trust anyone. Yet, here I am, pushed up against the wall of a damn horse stable, letting Josh tie my hands above my head.

Shit. Wait! I pull on my wrists, but they're bound tight with rope. How did he manage to do that without me noticing? I was so lost in the pleasure-induced fog he keeps putting me under, I wasn't paying attention to what he was doing.

"Ah, Josh?" I question.

"Trust, Emmy," is the only thing he says before his lips fuse with mine. His taste is intoxicating. I can't get enough of it. As his tongue slips into my mouth, I suck and nibble on it. I want more. I want everything.

No, I don't want this. How could I possibly want this?

What does that make me? I'm so confused. Even as I drown in all that is Josh, my mind questions my every move. I want to let go. I want to let go and escape just for a little bit. I want my mind to just stop.

"Make it stop, please," I beg quietly. I don't intend for Josh to hear my pleas. When he pulls away from me, holding my chin in his hand, he keeps our eyes locked on each other.

"Make what stop, Emmy?" his husky voice asks.

I close my eyes as I answer. I can't bring myself to look at him—he's already making me more vulnerable than I'm used to. "My mind, I want it to stop. I want to escape."

When I open my eyes, I'm greeted with Josh's smirk, his own eyes sparkling. "That I can do. Hold on," he says as he drops to his knees in front of me.

Hold on? I'm literally tied to the damn wall. What am I meant to hold on to? Josh pulls my sweatpants down, discarding them out of the way. Kneeling, he reaches up to the collar of my shirt before tearing it in half.

He sits back on his heels and stares up at me. "This is the best fucking view I've ever seen."

Picking up my left leg, he trails his lips over my calf, biting down on the tender skin behind my knee before continuing to drag his tongue along my thigh. It's a slow torture. By the time he reaches my aching centre, I'm dripping—literally dripping—juices down my inner thighs.

Josh's tongue licks all around the lips of my pussy, without touching the spot I want him most. My hands pull on the rope, while the skin on my wrists burn with each tug.

"Please," I beg. Before I even finish the word, Josh's mouth covers my mound, his tongue licking from bottom to top. Holy fucking hell. This, yes, this is what I need.

Josh picks up both of my legs, positioning them on his

shoulders. His hands are over my waist, pinning my back to the wall. The grunts and groans coming out of him are on a whole other level. He's like a starving man, someone who just found a waterhole after being lost in the desert.

His tongue swirls around my clit before trailing down and pushing into my slick entrance, pumping in and out a couple of times. He continues this pattern, travelling up to my clit before sinking back inside of me.

I'm losing my damn mind. My body is tight; my muscles become rigid. I can feel a sheen of sweat covering me, the cold breeze creating goosebumps all over my skin.

If my hands were not tied, they'd be buried in those blonde locks, holding his head to me. My hips grind into his face mercilessly. I'm chasing a release I haven't felt in years. I don't think anyone other than Josh has ever been able to make me feel this good.

My head tips back, his name leaving my lips as my thighs tighten around his head. The orgasm washes over me, and I feel it. I embrace it. The sense of pure bliss, nothing but pleasure.

Josh abruptly removes my legs, placing my feet back on the ground as he stands up. Tugging his sweats down a little, he pulls out his rock-hard cock. I don't get time to admire the view. His mouth is back on mine, the taste of my release on his tongue. It makes me hungry for him all over again.

I can still feel my core convulsing with aftershocks. Josh picks me up, my legs automatically wrapping around his waist. I moan at the feel of his smooth cock as he rubs the tip over my clit before lining himself up with my entrance.

He just holds it there, pulling his face away from mine. I open my eyes to see him staring down at me. What the fuck is he waiting for? Oh God, I swear if he leaves me hanging again, I'll… Okay, I don't know what I'll do, but it will be messy—*that* I can guarantee.

"Josh?" I ask

"I want to see your eyes, Emmy. I want your eyes open when I finally get to slide my cock into you again."

That's it? He wants my eyes open? Well, my eyes are open. I decide to take over. I'm not waiting any longer. I arch my back off the wall, tighten my legs around his waist and sink myself onto his cock.

"Fuck!" Josh grunts out.

He's so big, stretching my walls out. The slight sting I feel stops me once his cock is fully inside me. Josh's forehead falls onto mine as he slowly pulls out before sliding back in.

"You feel so fucking good, Emmy! I thought I had made it up," he says.

"Made what up?"

"How fucking perfect you are! How this pussy of yours was made for me. You are mine!" He grunts as he starts to pick up his pace.

"Say it!" he growls.

"Say what?" I ask.

"That you're mine, that you're not leaving again. Say it!" he demands.

I can't say that. Instead, I tell him the one thing I can say, the one thing I want more than anything right now.

"Fuck me, Josh. I want you to fuck me harder." I bury my head in his neck and bite down.

Josh really picks up his pace then. He drives into me, his fingers pinching into the skin on my hips so tight… it's almost like he's afraid I'm going to disappear into thin air if he doesn't hold on. I'm going to have bruises from his fingertips after this.

Those marks, I will wear gladly. Neither of us are quiet as pleasure overtakes us. I wouldn't be surprised if the whole farm could hear me screaming right now. I can't seem to care though; all I care about right now is how Josh is making me feel. How close I am to tipping over the edge again.

"I need… Oh God, that, yes, keep doing that!" I cry out as Josh somehow manages to angle my hips, his pelvis grinding against my clit.

Within seconds of this new position, I'm coming undone. My pussy clenches his cock, not letting him pull back out. My whole body quakes. Josh grunts as he comes, the warm liquid coating my walls.

We stand there, our chests heaving. After a moment, reality comes crashing into me. I just gave myself to the devil, the same one I swore I'd never play with again. The same one I dreamt about playing with, over and over again for the past seven years.

Fuck! I wiggle around as Josh's hold tightens under my ass. I need to get out of here, before I get myself in any more trouble than I'm already in. Getting caught in Josh's world is most certainly a recipe for disaster for me.

Josh finally slips his cock out of me and lets me stand. I don't know how I thought I was going to get away, considering my hands are still bound by rope above my head.

"Josh, you need to untie me now!" My panicked voice raises.

"No," he says as he takes a step back.

"What? What do you mean *no*? Untie me the fuck now, Joshua. This isn't funny!" I scream at him. Internally, I'm chastising myself. I know better than to scream and make demands—that only ends up with me covered in cuts and bruises.

"No, it's not funny. But do you know what *is* fucking funny, Emmy?"

"What?" I'm so angry right now. I'm literally tied up to a wall, with nothing but tattered material that used to be a shirt.

"It's fucking funny that you think you *can't* yell at me. Yell at me all you want, sweetheart. I can take your anger. In fact, your fire only turns me on. I don't remember you having that at school. You were always the people pleaser, always had a smile plastered on your face no matter what anyone said." He steps forward again, bending so his face is level with mine.

"But it's fucking hilarious that you think you're going to run out of here. It's fucking funny that you think there is a single fibre of my being that will ever let you leave. You're not leaving, Emmy. I don't care if I have to keep you tied to my bed for the rest of our lives. You are not leaving!" By the end of his tirade, he's pacing up and down the small space of the stable, pulling at his hair.

I've seen this Josh many times. He doesn't know that I've seen him. I always stayed out of sight when he would lose his shit at school. I know all the other kids were afraid of him. Not me though. I was drawn to him. I wanted to help him, just like now.

Everything in me wants to reassure him that I'm not going anywhere. That I'll stay here. However, if I say any of that, I'm more afraid I'll start to believe it myself. Because more than anything, I want the future he thinks we're going to have.

He stops pacing and stares at me, a lost look in his eyes. "Josh, you can't keep me locked away. This should never have happened. I should never have come here." I turn my head, not able to maintain eye contact with him. That expression on his face breaks my damn heart.

"But you did. You did come here. Why? Why'd you come

back, Emmy?" His voice sounds pained. This is my fault. It's always my fault.

"I-I didn't know where else to go," I admit. When I left that apartment, the first place I thought of going was the cabin. It's all I thought about while hitchhiking with truckers across the country to get here.

"Why? What are you running from? What are you afraid of?" He's never going to stop asking, and I'm never going to be able to tell him.

I shake my head no. "I can't tell you. I can't. It's better for everyone if you don't know. It's better for everyone if you just let me go, Josh."

"You can tell me—all you have to do is open that damn pretty mouth of yours and talk. You won't tell me. There's a difference between *can't* and *won't*. But don't worry, I'll uncover all of your secrets, Emmy. And when I do, I have a feeling that hell is going to rain down on this town." He pivots on his heel and goes to walk out.

"Josh, wait!" I yell out. He turns his head and looks back at me, raising one eyebrow.

"You can't leave me here tied up like this, Joshua. Anyone could walk in and see me."

"Fuck!" He stomps over to me, his jaw clenched tight. He's angry. But I'm not afraid. Of all the people in the world I could choose not to be afraid of, it has to be him.

Once my arms are free, he rubs along my wrists, inspecting the red marks. "Wait here," he says as he runs out the gate. I pick up the discarded sweats and put them back on. I have to roll the waist over a few times so they don't fall down.

Grabbing the two sides of the ripped shirt, I tie them together in the middle, creating a little midriff top. Huh, it's actually not a bad look.

Josh comes back in, holding a riding jacket. He looks me up and down before saying, "Put this on."

It's pink, and clearly a female jacket. "No." I fold my arms over my chest. I am not putting on one of his floozies' jackets.

"What do you mean *no*? Put the fucking jacket on, Emmy. You are not walking out of this stable dressed like that. I can see… *everything*," he says.

"Really, well then, maybe you shouldn't have ripped my shirt. I am not wearing that. Deal with it." I stomp past him.

I don't get far before his arms come out, wrapping around my waist. He presses my back to his chest, bending his head to talk quietly into my ear.

"Emmy, there is a lot of staff on this property. Some I would hate to lose. But, so help me God, if anyone gets a glimpse of you like this, I will fucking cut their eyeballs out of their head before slitting their damn throats. You'd be surprised how hungry those pigs can get."

He lets go and smirks. Stepping in front of me, he holds out the jacket again.

"Your call, babe. What's it gonna be?" His eyebrows raise as he waits for an answer.

"You're not serious. You're not going to kill your staff just because they get a glimpse of my stomach." Even as I say the words, I know that his promises are not empty ones.

"Want to test the theory? I don't mind. Because at the end of the day, I'll still sleep at night—*with you right the fuck next to me*."

Fuck it, I'm not going to have anyone else's blood on my conscience, especially someone who's innocent. Taking the jacket, I put it on and zip it up.

"You're fucking crazy, you know that." I stomp past him for the second time in a matter of minutes.

"Yeah, I've been told once or twice. But who's the crazier one here? Me, for being clinically insane, or you, for loving me that way?"

My steps momentarily stop. It's on the tip of my tongue, to refute his claims. To correct him. *Loved.* I loved him once, but I don't anymore. At least, that's what I've tried to convince myself. I don't say anything. Instead, I huff and storm towards the house with Josh hot on my trail.

# Chapter 8

## Josh

I followed Emily all the way through the house and into my bedroom. I don't even think she realises she automatically heads to my room, which I should really start thinking of as *our room*, considering I'm not ever letting her leave it.

I follow her across the room to the en suite door. She turns as she steps into the bathroom, sending me an icy as hell glare as she rips the jacket off and throws it at me, before she slams the door right in my face. I laugh, making sure she can hear it through the closed door.

The fact that she is beginning to stand up to me, beginning to feel comfortable around me, enough to be herself and not the scared girl I picked up from the woods two days ago… That fact is everything. I honestly didn't know how long she would be cowering from me. How long she would be afraid of what she says, afraid of what my reaction would be to the things she says or does.

Whatever she's been living through, I'm going to make sure it doesn't keep a hold on her. I wanted to climb inside her head last night, just to kill the demons that haunt her dreams for her. I hate that I can't fix that. I hate that she's dreaming about another man, even if it is a nightmare. No motherfucking other man should be taking up space inside her mind.

Fuck, I need to get my hands on this fucker. Pulling out my phone, I dial Sam. He picks up on the second ring.

"Why the fuck haven't you called me yet?" I yell through the phone.

"Well, hello to you too, boss. Good to see you're having a great day." He laughs.

"Fuck off, Sam. Start talking. What have you found?"

"Not much, which is why I haven't called. It seems Emily Livingston passed away at age twenty-two. Three years ago," he says.

"Well, obviously that's not fucking true. She's currently in my fucking bathroom."

"About that, I think I'll make a trip up there. Check this Emily out for myself, make sure you're not just, I don't know, batshit crazy and talking to the dead."

"Don't bother. I'm heading to the city tonight. I'll be bringing her with me. What else did you find out? How did she supposedly die?"

"The coroner's report says suicide. Last known address was in Adelaide."

"Adelaide? What the fuck was she doing there?" Heading over to the little bar I keep in my bedroom, I pour a glass of whisky—it's five o'clock somewhere.

"There's something else," Sam says.

"Well, go on, mate. Don't hold back," I urge.

"There was a trust that one—Joshua McKinley—had set up in her name. She was due to get it when she turned twenty-two."

"Don't be a dick. I know about the fucking trust."

"Well, did you know it was emptied three years ago? One day before she apparently committed suicide?"

"I never bothered to check it," I admit.

"It was five million dollars, Josh. You never checked a bank account with five million dollars in it? Gee, guess that's how the other half rolls, hey?"

"Who made the withdrawal?" I ask.

"The name on the check is hers. Think she somehow managed to fake her own death? Maybe she ran out of money and that's why she's back?"

"No, she wouldn't do that. Send me a copy of the coroner's report." I hang up on him.

Within seconds, my phone buzzes in my hand with his email. Opening up the report, I have to remind myself it's fake. She's real. She's in my bathroom. Even I'm not so fucking crazy that I've conjured her up.

Emily comes out of the bathroom with a towel wrapped around her, steam billowing all around her. Her blonde hair hangs down her back. She's every man's fucking wet dream. Those long, toned legs and slim waist…

She walks over to the bed and sits on the edge. Going into my wardrobe, I walk back out with a shirt for her to put on.

"We need to go shopping and get you some clothes of your own. As much as I love seeing you in my things, they're not going to work for every occasion." Handing her the shirt, I watch as she stares at me.

"Thank you, but you don't need to take me shopping. I'm

fine." Her head lowers again as she wrings the fabric of the shirt between her fingers.

"Emmy?" I ask.

"Yeah?"

"Do you know anything about this?" Offering over my phone, I wait as she reads the report on the screen, her hands shaking.

"No, he wouldn't have… How could he? No." She shakes her head, tears forming in her eyes.

Kneeling down in front of her, I grab hold of her hands. They tremble under my touch.

"Emmy, it's okay. I can fix this. Whatever this is. I can fix it for you. You just have to tell me what you know."

"I… I don't know. I didn't know about this. I don't understand. I'm right here. Obviously, I'm not dead."

"Thank fuck for that." I swipe the lone tear that escapes down her cheek with my thumb. "Do you need money? Is that why you came here?" I prompt, feeling like a complete jerk for even asking her that.

"What? No. I don't need your money. I told you I can leave. I'll never bother you again. I don't need you to give me anything." She starts to stand up.

"I know. I just… You won't tell me a damn thing, Emmy, and I find out you were pronounced dead just a day after withdrawing five million dollars from your trust account? I don't know what to think here, Em."

"I don't know what this is," she says, waving my phone around. "But I didn't have a trust account. I was the scholarship kid, remember? Not a trust fund brat," she spits out at me.

"I set up a trust for you. You were able to access it the day you turned twenty-two. It appears you withdrew the whole amount in one go, then transferred it to an offshore account."

Emmy shakes her head. "No, I didn't. And why the hell would you set up a trust for me? Five million dollars? Really, Josh? What the hell would one person need that much money for?"

"I wanted to make sure you were taken care of. That you wouldn't ever need to worry about money again," I tell her.

She laughs, full-belly laughs. "That's funny. Because for the past three years, I haven't." Her mouth snaps shut.

"You haven't what?" I pry.

"Been alive apparently," she answers before mumbling under her breath, "Ironically… it's not far from the truth."

This conversation is not going to get either of us anywhere. She doesn't know about the trust or the death certificate—*that* I'm sure of.

"Get dressed, you can find some sweats in the closet. We're going to the city," I say as I walk out the door.

---

I'VE BEEN WAITING at the bottom of the stairs for thirty minutes. What the fuck could be taking her so long? I've had time to sort through some files, and pack my laptop and other essentials into a bag. All she had to do was throw on some sweatpants.

I'm about ready to go up and drag her out, when I hear her footsteps. Turning around, I see her coming down the steps. No. Fuck no!

She's put on a blue flannel shirt, and somehow tied a black belt around the middle of it. It looks like a dress. A short fucking dress that is showing off her every fucking curve. She's put her Converse back on her feet. Her hair, now dry, hangs in loose curls over one of her shoulders.

"That doesn't look like sweats," I grunt out.

Emily looks down at herself, running her hands over her body and smoothing out the flannel material.

"Mhm, I suppose it doesn't, considering, you know, it's not sweats." She shrugs.

It's a three-hour trip into the city. Deciding I don't really have time to win the argument about her putting more clothes on, I let it go. Or, more accurately, on the outside, I let it go. On the inside, I'm fucking seething at the thought of other people seeing that much of her skin.

"Emmy, whatever you do, don't let go of my hand," I tell her as I take hold of her open palm.

She looks up at me, confused, her eyebrows drawn down. "Why?"

"Because when you're touching me, I feel less murdery. Also, it's a little harder to slice someone's throat with just one hand, though not impossible. It just takes longer," I answer as I lead her outside to the waiting Range Rover.

She doesn't question me. What she does do is squeeze my hand tighter.

---

EMILY FELL ASLEEP an hour into the trip. Sitting in the back seat with her head resting on my shoulder, she never lets go of my hand. Even as she sleeps, she still has a tight grip on that hand.

She's been sleeping for the last hour and a half. Whatever's happening inside her head now is not peaceful. She's stirring, her body jerking around slightly. Her fingernails pierce into my skin to the point I can feel tiny drops of blood escape.

I should wake her up. That would be the right thing to do. The only reason I'm not waking her from this nightmare is she's mumbling out incoherent words. I'm waiting for something to slip out of her mouth that I can actually use. Something to tell me what the fuck she's running from.

I sit still as her nails dig in, her head shaking no. She looks tortured; she looks like she's in hell right now. Sweat coats her forehead while blonde hair sticks to her face. If I was a better man, I'd wake her up. I'd stop this torture.

I've never pretended to be good. I'm not ashamed of who I am. A soul-tearing scream leaves her mouth before she bolts upright. "No, Trent, stop!" she screams.

Her eyes are staring ahead, but she's not fully awake. Finally, I have a fucking name. Not much to go on, but it's more than I had before.

"Emmy, it's okay. It's just a dream. You're safe," I whisper, as I pull her into my arms and give her the comfort I've been holding back. "You're safe; no one is going to hurt you ever again." Moving the hair off her face, I gently kiss her forehead as I whisper promises I'll die in order to keep.

"Josh?" she asks.

"Yeah, it's me. You're okay."

"I'm sorry. Did I wake you?" Why the fuck is she apologising to me?

"Emmy, you have nothing to be sorry about, babe. You didn't wake me, and even if you did, I wouldn't care."

My phone vibrates in my pocket. I shuffle as I retrieve it. Emmy tries to move over. I have to grip her tighter as I bring the phone to my ear.

"Yeah."

"Boss, what did you want done with the occupant in the shed?" Paul asks.

"Fuck, I fucking forgot about that cocksucker." How the hell did I forget about the fucker that had Emmy held up in a stable this morning?

"Yeah, I figured you've got other things on your mind," Paul says.

"Keep him on ice. I'll only be gone a couple of days. I'll deal with him when I get back."

"Sure thing. Also, your mother just asked me about increasing security for the wedding. Congratulations," he says loudly through the phone. I know Emmy hears him when she tenses and looks away.

"It's not for me, asshole. It's for Dean's wedding."

I hang up. I don't need to be discussing details for a fucking wedding—not until it's my wedding we're planning.

"It seems my mother's planning a wedding for Dean and Ella. It's probably a good thing we got out of there. She would have ended up planning a double wedding. She's taken by the idea of you being her daughter-in-law." I smile at her. She does not smile back. Instead, she chooses to ignore me, changing the subject.

"Are we nearly there? Will we be seeing Dean and Ella when we're there?" she asks as she looks out the window.

"About fifteen minutes away. Do you want to see them?"

Emmy shrugs her shoulders. "I like Ella; she's nice."

"She is nice. Why the fuck she married Dean's ugly ass, I have no idea."

Emmy quickly turns her head in my direction as her eyes squint at me. "You and Ella seem close," she says.

"As close as two people can be who only just met weeks ago. I suppose."

"You don't like people, Josh. You've never been close to anyone. Well, at least you didn't used to. It's been a while so maybe you like people now. I don't know." Her rambling stops.

"Nope, still can't stand fucking people. They're a bunch of idiots. The only person I've ever liked is you, Emmy. You know that."

"And now Ella," she clarifies.

"And now Ella," I confirm, pausing a little. "Are you jealous that I'm friends with Ella?" I ask with the biggest smile on my face.

"What? No, I'm not bloody jealous. Curious is what I am, considering you never had any friends in school. Not that you ever wanted friends… though I can guarantee any one of the girls back then would have chopped off a limb to be *friends* with you." She frames the word "friends" with air quotes.

"Ella's my sister, Emily. There is absolutely no reason for you to be jealous of anyone. No one has ever been able to measure up to you."

"I'm not jealous. I can see why you'd be friends with Ella. I mean, it's been a long time since I've had any friends, but I can see she would be a good one to have."

"Why haven't you had any friends, Emmy. You were always surrounded by people at school. It seemed everyone wanted to be your best friend back then."

"They weren't really my friends, Josh. They were just too scared of what you would do to them if they weren't. People had this assumption that if they were friends with me, you'd leave them be. God only knows why they thought that—it's not like *I* was spared from your torture."

"Trust me, babe, I spared you in high school."

"You literally tipped a milkshake over my head the first time we met." She holds up one finger before she continues.

"Then there was that time you got me kicked off the cheer-leading team. I still don't know how you managed that, but I know it was you." Her second finger goes up.

I smile at the fond memory. "I bribed the coach. But, in my defence, that uniform showed off way too much skin," I argue.

"You weren't my boyfriend, Josh. You wouldn't even speak to me."

"I was trying to save you from me."

The third finger goes up. "The time you put red hair dye in my shampoo. My hair was bloody bright red. Do you have any idea how embarrassed I was to walk out of the girls' locker room that day? That shit stayed in my hair for months."

"I thought it would make you uglier, less appealing to others. That one backfired because you looked hot as fuck with that fiery red hair. Do you know how many guys I beat up in those few months? My knuckles were constantly fucking bruised."

Emmy's mouth hangs open as she shakes her head. "That, just—wow. You're just… Wow," she says, then holds up a fourth finger. "The time you slashed my tyres."

"That was your fault."

"How do you figure that?" she asks.

"You offered Jackson a ride home that day."

"So, I do a good deed for someone and you decide that I needed to be punished for that?" Her eyebrows go up to her hairline.

"Not punished. Just stopped from having another guy in your car. Besides, I made sure you had a ride home that day *and* I replaced your tyres."

"You had your limo driver take me home. Do you have any

idea how embarrassing that was? To turn up in my neighbourhood in a damn limo?"

"Emily, you lived in the suburbs, not the fucking Bronx."

"Doesn't matter. It was embarrassing." She holds up a fifth finger. I take hold of her hand, stopping her.

"As much as I'd love to continue this trip down memory lane, because really there are so many fond memories of us during those high school years, we're here. Come on."

"You do realise those fond memories are all one-sided in your own head, right? Those moments weren't *fond* for me at all," she says as she climbs out of the car. I have to step in front of her to prevent someone from getting a view of her ass.

If I thought I'd get any peace tonight, I was mistaken. As soon as we step through the lobby, we're greeted by Sam and Tony. Tony is Sam's assistant. I've never liked the prick, but I like him even less right now with the way he's looking at Emmy.

# Chapter 9

## Emily

Josh pulls me slightly behind him as we enter the lobby, or yet another museum-lookalike building. He stops in front of two hulking men in suits. My first thought is maybe they've found me—they're probably detectives. Then Josh shakes the hand of one.

"Sam, what the fuck are you doing here?" he asks.

The guy Sam looks directly at me behind Josh and smiles. "First, I wanted to make sure you weren't conjuring up the dead. Now that that's settled, I have some documents that need your signature." He waves a briefcase in the air.

The other guy stares at me, and not in a friendly way. It creeps me out. I step further behind Josh, trying to escape the man's gaze.

"It couldn't have waited until tomorrow?" Josh asks as he

starts heading towards the elevator, pulling me along with him. The two men follow close behind.

"No, it couldn't. It's the Casey merger. It needs to be finalised today," Sam says as we all enter the lift.

Josh steps behind me, wraps an arm around my waist and pulls my back against his chest. As the doors shut, he buries his head in the crook of my neck. I hear him inhale before he whispers in my ear, "Emmy, I really need you to hold my hand right now."

My eyes go wide. I look up, staring at our reflection on the metal doors. I place both of my hands in his. One hand curls over the fingers holding my hip, while the other grabs the hand hanging down at his side. I squeeze tight.

I can feel his hands trembling. What the fuck happened out there that's got him this messed up? It can't be the fact that he has to sign papers. Surely that's the kind of thing he does all the time.

I watch the numbers as the elevator travels up. I know we're heading to the penthouse by the PH button that Sam pressed. My thumbs rub tiny circles on Josh's hand. I'm not sure what to do to help him. I do know that I *want* to help him. I shouldn't want to, but I do.

I really need to find a way to get away from him. The longer I'm around, the further I slip into the Josh fog. That place where I can pretend that everything is normal, that we have a chance at a future together. I'm constantly reminding myself that we don't, that I can't have that.

It's better for everyone if I disappear… *sooner rather than later*. Even as I tell myself this, my heart is hurting. Josh was right. There was a reason that I came to him. That when I finally got free, the first place I thought to go was that damn cabin. The first person that I wanted to see was Josh. Not that I can ever admit any of this to him.

The elevator finally stops, and the doors open. I release the breath I didn't even know I was holding. Stepping out of the lift, I don't let go of Josh's hand. He leads me further into the room. It's elegance at its finest. It's McKinley-level elegance. The foyer where we are standing is white, white, and more white. White marble floors, pristine white walls. We're standing under a huge sparkling crystal chandelier; the thing looks bigger than me.

Past the foyer, the floor steps down into a living room. White leather couches face each other with a grey marble coffee table between them. Beyond the couches are floor-to-ceiling windows—the view currently being obstructed by sheer (yep, you guessed it) white curtains.

All the white and light is such a contrast to how I would have imagined Josh's place. I feel so out of sorts here, like I'm going to mess something up or break something I can't afford.

Yeah, like I've been able to afford *anything* for the past three years. I met Trent four years ago—the first year was perfect. He had me completely fooled. The last three years were utter hell. I wasn't allowed out of the apartment, unless I was with him. I wasn't allowed to have access to money. I didn't even own a purse. The thought of not being able to afford something is laughable. I can't even afford a damn happy meal at this point.

The little amount of money I took from our apartment didn't go far. I think I have around five dollars left and tucked into the lining of my backpack, which has been shoved into the corner of Josh's closet.

"Emmy, the kitchen is just through there. Go get yourself a

drink, or whatever you want." Josh lets go of me and points towards an entryway off to the left of the room.

I nod my head. I wouldn't mind a moment alone anyway —some time to get out of the Josh fog. As I'm about to walk in the direction that Josh pointed, Sam steps in front of me. I have to tilt my head up to meet his eyes.

"Since this asshole doesn't have any fucking manners, I'll introduce myself. I'm Sam, Josh's friend." He holds his hand out to me in greeting, a hand which I have no intention of shaking.

Instead, I put my hands in my pockets. Who the fuck does he think he is, calling Josh an asshole and talking about his lack of social skills? It makes me want to knee him in the nuts.

"I'm Emily. But you already know that, I'm sure. I would advise you though, if you ever want the chance to father children in the future, I'd refrain from calling Josh an asshole or making comments on his social skills. If he wanted me to meet you, he would have introduced us."

I'm not sure where my sudden courage to speak to anyone like this has come from. Maybe Josh is rubbing off on me more than I thought. Deep down, I do know I'm safe if Josh is around. Maybe that's why I feel like I can say what's on my mind.

As I go to walk around the jerk, I'm pulled back by Josh, who spins me around so fast I lose my footing. His arm goes around my waist, steadying me while also pulling me tight against his chest.

My first thought is that I've made a mistake. I've made him mad. I should have kept my mouth shut and been polite to his friend. All those thoughts get blown out of my head when his lips descend onto mine, his tongue hungrily diving into my mouth.

I don't know if it's relief I feel or just my pure wanton need for the man, which makes me pull him closer, desperately trying to climb into his skin as I return his kiss tenfold. A little groan leaves his mouth as he pulls away from me.

Josh smiles down at me. "Want me to turn him into pig feed?" he asks, as he nods his head to Sam.

I look over my shoulder at Sam and consider Josh's offer, or at least pretend to consider it. "Tough call, but you should probably keep him around. I'm going to see what I can find in the kitchen. I'm suddenly starved," I say, as I walk past Sam and the weird guy who's creeping me out by just standing in the background and staring. Even as I walk away, I can feel his beady eyes pinned to my back.

---

I'VE JUST OPENED the fridge when I hear Sam shout out, "Josh, stop. Don't do it!"

I shut the door and tiptoe back out to the living room, where I can see that Josh has the creepy guy by the throat and up against the pristine white wall. It's not the tattooed hand wrapped around his throat that has me frozen to my spot. It's the gun Josh is holding to the man's head.

"Give me one good reason why I shouldn't blow your fucking brains out right now?" Josh seethes.

"I-I'm sorry. I didn't mean any disrespect, sir," the guy stammers out.

"Disrespect? You've been nothing but disrespectful since the moment we stepped through the lobby downstairs. Do you think I haven't noticed the way you were looking at her? Do you take me for a fucking fool? Think I don't know the thoughts running through your head?" Josh screams in his face.

"No, I didn't. *I don't.*" He shakes his head.

Holy shit, this is about me. Josh is losing his shit over me. I should say something, put a stop to this. I knew something was eating at him in the elevator, but I didn't think it would be because someone was looking at me. Even though I know I should try to stop this, my feet are frozen in place, fear gripping me. What if he blames me? What if he thinks this is all my fault? I should have worn the sweats like he wanted me to.

"Josh, man, calm down. Put the gun away. You don't want to do this in front of your girl." Sam nods his head towards me.

Josh turns and looks at me. "Fuck!" he mumbles out, as he lets go of the guy before stepping back. He holds the gun down by the side of his leg, tapping it repeatedly against his thigh. I'm afraid he's going to accidentally shoot himself if he keeps doing that, yet I'm still frozen to my spot. I still can't seem to make my feet move. They should be running the hell out of here. Any reasonable, sane person would be running out of here.

"Fuck, man, you're batshit crazy over a damn bitch. Talk about being fucking pussy-whipped. Must be a fucking gold-plated pussy," the creepy guy, who has just been renamed in my head as *dumbass*, spits out.

Josh raises the gun up and shoots, hitting the man's left kneecap. He doesn't even blink as the guy falls to the ground. "That was a warning shot, motherfucker. The next one will be in your fucking head."

The guy is rolling around on the ground, screaming incoherent nonsense—the once pristinely white floor and wall now covered in blood. Josh turns and looks me up and down.

"Clean this mess, and shut him the fuck up, before I do it permanently," he says to Sam as he walks slowly towards me. This is the moment I should run; in my head, I know that. But my heart, it wants something completely different. It wants the devil who's making his way to me, slowly, carefully, like I'm a wounded animal about to take flight. I fear it's too late to run—even if I could, I'm not sure I would.

"Emmy." Josh takes a breath in, releasing it slowly before continuing, "I'm sorry. You shouldn't have had to see that." He's standing in front of me, apologising.

I nod my head. I don't know what to say. His grey sweats and white shirt are now stained with blood and he's still clenching the gun in his hand. Yet, all I can think is how badly I want to climb him, claim him as mine.

My thighs tighten together as I feel myself getting wetter and wetter by the minute. I'm not wearing any underwear, and I'm at risk of having my desire run down my inner thighs right now. I can feel my hardened nipples rubbing against the flannelette fabric of the shirt.

"Josh, where's the bedroom?" I ask.

He nods his head behind me. "Down that way. Why?" he says with a smirk.

"I-I'm going to need you to take me there now," I whisper.

Josh wraps one arm around me and picks me up. My legs encircle his waist and cling on. My hands go to his hair as my mouth finds his. His groans of pleasure run through me as he walks us down a hall.

I'm so lost in all that is Josh that when I'm thrown down on a bed, confusion and dizziness take over as I open my eyes. Josh is standing at the end of the bed, pulling his shirt over his head.

I lick my lips as his perfectly-sculpted, tanned body comes

into view. I really need to book an appointment with him. Hours long, where I can run my tongue along all those grooves. Draw the outline of those tattoos that cover him with (yep, you guessed it) my tongue.

Even as I lie here, conjuring up all of the things I want to do to his body, I know it's wrong. I know that it's only going to hurt more when everything I've done comes crashing down on me, on him, and ends up ruining us.

"I fear the longer I keep you, the more I'm going to ruin you," Josh confesses as if reading my inner thoughts.

"And just how do you suppose you're going to ruin me exactly?" I ask.

"My darkness is going to overtake your light; my darkness is going to ruin every good thing there is inside you. I can see it's already happening. Yet, I can't seem to let you go. I won't ever let you go again, Emmy."

"You can't ruin me, Josh. I'm already ruined."

"No, you're not, but you will be." He smirks as he strips off his sweats.

He doesn't know that he already ruined me in this way… years ago. I've never wanted anyone the way I want Josh. Even in the beginning with Trent, when it was good, it wasn't Josh-level good.

Josh climbs on the bed and undoes the belt, his belt, from around my waist. "As much as I want to tie you up and have you at my mercy, I want to feel your hands all over me. I want to feel those nails scratching my back when I make you come like you've never come before," he says as he throws the belt across the room.

He climbs up and straddles my thighs, slowly reaching for the top of the shirt. He undoes one button at a time. What happened to just ripping the damn thing open? I'm all for that right now. But no, he ever so slowly undoes one, then the next. When he gets to the last button and spreads the shirt apart, his eyes go wide.

"Fuck, Emmy, you've been naked ever since we left the house. How the fuck have you been naked this whole time and I didn't know?"

I'm not sure if he's asking me, or himself. I answer anyway. "I wasn't naked. I had a shirt on."

"You're not wearing panties, Emily. That's naked!" Josh emphasises the word *naked*. "If I had known I had unrestricted access to this sweet-ass pussy of yours the whole way here, it would have been a much more pleasurable car ride." His fingertips twist and pull on my nipples as he talks.

My back arches off the bed. "Oh yeah, with your driver watching through the rear-view mirror?" I ask.

"Sure, why not?"

"You'd seriously let someone watch you strip me naked and fuck me in the car?" I don't know why the idea is so damn appealing, but I'm locking that shit down tight, shoving the idea in the vault for another time.

"Yep, I'd cut their fucking eyes out afterwards, but I'd let them watch." He shrugs as he brings his mouth down onto my nipple.

They're so sensitive. I'm a squirming, begging mess within minutes of his mouth taking turns at torturing each nipple. As much as I try to move, I can't. He's still straddling me. My hands pull at his hair, alternating between trying to pry his mouth away from me and pulling him even closer.

I'm out of my mind with need. "Josh, please, I need…"

He lets go of my nipple, a plop sound echoing in the room. "What do you need, Emmy?" he asks.

He's going to make me say it. Asshole. He knows what I need. He always knows what I need.

"I need you. I need you inside me now, damn it," I scream.

"Babe, all you had to do is ask. I'm not a mind reader." The bastard smirks. Moments later, he jumps off and flips me over, positioning me on my knees with my ass up in the air.

Josh's hands spread my cheeks open. I feel his tongue lick from top to bottom, right along my slit. My fingers curl around the sheets. I'm trembling. I'm ready to burst. When I feel the tip of his cock at my entrance, I push back.

I can't wait any longer. As soon as his cock bottoms out inside me, the moment it rubs along my G-spot, I lose all control. I scream as my pussy convulses around him.

"Fuck, Em, I fucking love how hungry your pussy is for my cock. Hold on, babe, the show is only just beginning," he says, right before he starts to slam in and out of my still quivering core.

# Chapter 10

## Josh

I watch Emily sleep peacefully next to me. She passed out shortly after her sixth orgasm. She's so fucking beautiful it hurts. I can't believe I let her go all those years ago. I've wasted so much time. She's obviously endured a lot of crap that she shouldn't have. And she wouldn't have, had I manned up and kept her like I wanted to.

Tugging the sheets higher, I cover her up as I stand, gently kissing her forehead before I slip out of the room. As much as I want to stay curled up in this little world with her, and just her, I've got shit to sort out. Sam mentioned the Casey merger, which is code for *confidential*, and not necessarily something that's work-related.

Fuck, I hope he's got a better lead on who the fuck has been abusing Emily for God knows how long. I make my way out to the kitchen; I need a fucking drink. Of course, I find

Sam, cooking some shit that smells fucking delicious on the stove.

"Make yourself at home, mate," I say as I walk past him to the fridge. Grabbing the OJ, I drink from the bottle, not bothering with a glass.

"Don't worry, I will," Sam replies.

"What'd you do with Tony?" Not that I really care, but I'd like to know the fucker is not still in the apartment. Not still in the same space as me. Even with Emily draining me of every bit of fucking energy, I'm still buzzing to cause damage to that fucker—well, more damage than I did by blowing out his kneecap.

"Clean up crew. He'll be fine," Sam says. "I, however, am now in need of yet another new assistant. Thanks for that," he grunts.

"*Please*, I did you a favour. What else have you got for me?"

"Not much—found a death certificate for her mother, dated two years ago."

"Fuck, I was wondering why she didn't turn to her mum for help."

"That's not all. Mum didn't cark it; she's alive and breathing. Same address you gave me as Emily's last known."

"What the fuck does that mean? Who the fuck's out there writing up death certificates for people who are fucking alive and breathing?"

"No idea, man. That's all I got. Everything's been buried bloody good. It seems someone didn't want anyone finding these documents. She tell you anything yet?" he asks.

"No, I've stopped asking. She did let a name slip in her sleep though," I say, remembering the nightmare she had in the car.

"Care to share?" Sam prompts, as he serves up three plates of what looks like some kind of stir fry concoction.

"Trent." I raise my eyebrows at him. "You expecting company?" I nod at the three plates.

"Nope, but you gotta eat. And I'm not gonna lie. I think I like Emily more than I like you. And it seems I have some serious grovelling to do to win her over."

"She's asleep. You're out of luck." I smirk, recalling just what exhausted her to sleepiness.

He hands me a plate and fork, walking around my fucking kitchen like he owns the place. "Eat," he says, as he picks up another plate and fork before heading out of the kitchen.

"Where are you going?" I ask him.

"To wake her up. She needs to eat," he offers simply.

"Take another step towards that bedroom and I'll fucking shoot you," I warn him. Like fuck, I'm about to let him walk in there while she's fucking naked. Just the thought of a naked Emily makes my cock hard.

"Fine, but when she wakes up, make sure she knows I cooked this shit for her, not you." He places cling wrap over the plate before putting it in the fridge.

"Why do you care if she likes you anyway?" I ask.

"Because she scares the shit out of me," he admits.

I laugh. How the hell can a tiny little Emily scare the shit out of a six-foot something hulk of a man? "How so?"

He looks me in the eye, quiet for a moment, then with all seriousness, he says, "She'd only have to say the word and you'd slice my fucking throat for her, without a second thought."

I'd like to say he's wrong. But he's not. So, instead, I just dig into the food. He's one hell of a cook. I'll give him that.

"So, Trent…? Did you happen to get a last name, or are

we just going to run around the country burying every fucker named Trent?" Sam asks.

"No last name," I grunt. I'm fucking pissed that I don't know who the fuck I need to kill yet.

I hear the bell on the lift ping, and groan when I look at the screen on the wall showing me who just arrived. Fucking Whitney.

I listen for the sound of her heels clicking against the marble floors as she makes her way through the apartment to the kitchen.

She stops short when she sees me and Sam. "Josh, I heard you were back in town." She plasters on what is supposed to be a seductive smile. All it's doing is making my cock, which was hard minutes ago, fucking limp—and to think, I used to fuck this bitch.

"What the fuck are you doing here, Whitney?" I growl.

"I came to see you, silly. I thought we could have some fun." She places her hand on my chest. Sam chokes on his mouthful of food as he tries not to laugh.

"Yeah, well, you thought wrong. Leave," I tell her, removing her hand from my chest.

"Come on, Josh, you know I'll make you feel good." Her hand runs up my thigh and begins to rub my cock. I'm wondering what I ever fucking saw attractive about her when Sam coughs loudly, gaining my attention. I look at him and he nods behind me.

I don't even have to look to know who's there. *Emily*. And she's watching another woman rub her hands all over me right now. Fuck. I push Whitney off me as I jump up and turn to Emily, except she's already walking back down towards the bedroom.

Following, I get to the room just as she's turning to walk

back out, only now she's holding a gun in her hands. My gun. The sight of Emmy pointing a gun at me should not turn me the fuck on right now, but it fucking does.

I make no attempt to hide the fact that I have to readjust my cock, my boner standing tall and proud. The disgusted look that crosses over Emmy's face tells me she's less than impressed.

"Move out of my way, Josh," she says as she points the gun right at my chest. Her hands are frighteningly steady.

"You'll have to shoot me if you think I'm going to let you walk out of here." I fold my arms over my chest and stand in the doorway.

Emily tilts her head and stares at me. Fuck, I think she's actually contemplating fucking shooting me.

"Why? It's obvious you don't need me here. Not even an hour after you've used every inch of my body, you have one of your whores at your beck and call. The bed's not even fucking cold yet, Joshua!" she screams. I can't help but smile at her jealousy. Fucking finally, she's letting her feelings for me show.

"What the fuck are you smiling at?" she asks.

"You're jealous. But I've told you before. You don't need to be, Emmy. Nobody will ever measure up to you. I didn't invite her here. I told her to leave. You can ask Sam if you don't believe me," I offer.

"You asked her to leave, yet she was still standing there rubbing you up and down to the point that you're now in front of me with a fucking hard-on." She points the gun in the direction of my cock.

Okay, that's a little much. "Babe, if you're going to shoot me, then do it anywhere other than there. Please," I practically beg. "I told her to leave. *This.*" I point to my hard-on. "…is because of *you*. You standing here pointing a gun at me is hot as hell."

"You're demented," she huffs like it's not old news. "If you really did ask her to leave, then you won't mind if I go out there and shoot her, instead of you."

"Be my guest." I wave my arm and step out of the doorway. She smiles and walks past me. Well, fuck. That backfired. I didn't think she'd actually walk out there.

I follow close behind her. I'm a little intrigued at how this will play out. I'm not about to let her shoot someone though. I know she'll regret it later. She has way too much of a conscience for that shit.

Emily stands in front of Whitney. "I don't think Josh wants you here. You need to leave." She speaks clearly, calmly.

Whitney laughs. "Oh, hunny, I think you're the one that needs to leave. Josh, did you let Sam bring in the trash again?"

"Maybe all the Botox has fried your brain cells, so I'll tell you again. *You need to leave.*" Emily points the gun at her.

Whitney gasps as she eyes the other end of the barrel. "Josh, are you seriously going to let this bitch threaten me?"

Okay, I've heard enough. I was ready to see how far Emily would take this. But Whitney has said one too many things about my girl for my liking.

I'm quick to step in front of Emily as my hand wraps around Whitney's ponytail. "You see, I was prepared to let you walk out of here unscathed. *Mostly*. But then you had to go and open your mouth and talk shit about my girl."

Whitney's eyes go wide. "You can't seriously want *that*… over me." She's so fucking dumb. She doesn't know when the fuck to shut up. As much as I want to snap her neck, I'm trying to not let my darkness rub off on Emily more than it already has. Bloodshed and dead bodies should not be normal, everyday occurrences in her life.

"Sam, escort the trash out. Make sure she can't get back in." I watch as Whitney smiles, until Sam comes up and grabs her by the arm and starts leading her out.

Turning around, I see Emily now sitting on the couch, the gun in front of her on the coffee table. I go and sit down next to her, pulling her into my arms. She comes willingly, thank God.

Holding her head to my chest, I wait for her to say something. After a few minutes, she speaks, but doesn't move. "Josh, I'm scared," she says so quietly.

"What are you scared of, Emmy?" I ask, wanting to slay all of her fucking demons.

"I'm scared I'm not going to be able to let you go again when the time comes."

"That time's never going to come, Emmy. I'm not letting you go." I kiss the top of her head.

"You'll think differently soon. I'm not the same person I was in high school."

"I'll never think any differently of you than how I already do, than what I always have. You are perfection, Emily."

"I hope you're right," she whispers.

"I know I am. I am very rarely wrong, you know." I smile.

"In your head, maybe. But you were very wrong that time you thought I was dating Jimmy. You scared the poor kid out of school."

"I did, didn't I? And if you weren't dating him, then why the fuck did he think he could put his arm around you constantly?"

"He did that one time, Josh. And I was certainly not dating him. He was way more into you than me." She laughs.

"What?"

"He was gay. As in, had a bigger crush on you than I did back then."

"Wait, you had a crush on me? How did I not know that?" I ask sarcastically.

Sam walks back into the apartment and heads straight to the kitchen. As he passes us, he yells out to me, "If you don't bring her in here to eat, I'm going to bring the food to her."

Emily's head pops up; her eyebrows draw down. "Does he have a weird food fetish I should be aware of?"

I laugh. "No, he's just trying to win you over. He's afraid if he doesn't, I'm gonna end up shooting him or something."

"Oh, okay. Well, I'll be nicer to him, put his mind at ease," she says as she jumps off my lap.

"Where are you going?"

"To eat. I'm starving." She heads into the kitchen.

I enter right behind her. Sam places a plate of food down on the bench next to my half-eaten meal.

"Do you want a drink, Emily?" he asks her.

"Ah, sure, water's fine." Emily says, looking between the two of us. She smirks at me before walking up to Sam, who hands her a bottle of water.

She wraps her arms around him. "Thank you so much, Sam. I can't believe how good this food smells."

Sam eyes me. Holding his hands out to the side, he doesn't return the hug. But that doesn't deter Emily from attempting to push my buttons, even though I know what she's doing.

"I don't think anyone's ever cooked for me before," she says.

"I made you cookies that one time in year eleven," I remind her.

She spins around, folding her arms over her chest. "That

was you? *Of course,* it was you. Who else would give me Valentine's Day cookies that were full of laxatives!"

"I saved you from a disastrous date with Matthew. I heard he was trying to take you out to the old rock. You know, people only went there for one reason, Emmy," I tell her.

She shakes her head no. "What if I wanted to go to the old rock with Matty? What if I wanted him to do unspeakable things to me in the back of his BMW? He was on the football team after all."

I raise an eyebrow at her. "Did you? Did you want Matthew to do unspeakable things to you, Emmy?" I ask, ready to hunt the fucker down and do *unspeakable things* to him.

"Ah, no?" she questions.

"Right answer."

"You know you two are fucking twisted as shit, right?" Sam says as he sits on the bench and continues eating.

"Wait, *him*, I get. But what's wrong with me?" Emmy asks as she sits down. I sit next to her and drag her chair over so she's much closer to me.

Sam laughs at her question. "That's a loaded gun, babe. I'm not answering that."

My fork flies across the room, barely missing his head. "I won't miss next time, fucker. Her name is fucking Emily!" I grunt.

Emily grabs hold of my hand. "Joshua, stop tormenting the one person who is probably your only friend. I like him. I think we'll keep him around." She smiles at me.

"Yep, well, on that note, I'm out of here while I'm still fucking alive. Josh, I'll see you in the office tomorrow." *Yeah, I know.* I'll be there.

# Chapter 11

## Emily

I'm woken up by something tickling my face. Scratch that, something sloppily kissing my face. I swipe at the culprit, groaning as I roll over and try to escape. Then I realise my mistake and jump up. "I'm sorry. I'm sorry. I'm awake," I say, as I wipe at my eyes.

My vision starts to focus in on the room. I'm not at home. It's okay. I look up into a pair of blue eyes. Blue eyes that are staring at me with concern, while a storm is brewing within them in the background.

Did I make him mad? I don't know what to do. I don't know what I'm supposed to do, so I pull the sheet up to my chest and sit there. I should make breakfast. I can make myself useful if I make breakfast.

"Emmy, stop. Whatever thoughts are going through your

pretty little head right now, tell 'em they can fuck right off. You're here with me. You're okay."

"Do you want breakfast? I can cook," I offer, not willing to share what exactly those thoughts were.

"We'll get something on the road. I gotta go into the office for a few hours. Come on, I want you to come with me," he says.

Now that I'm fully awake, I notice that he's in a suit, a really nice freaking suit. A charcoal jacket and pants with a white business shirt and light grey tie. He's wearing a tie. Josh, my Josh, does not wear ties. What happened to the ripped jeans and sweats?

"Why do you look like that?" I ask.

Josh glances down at himself. "I have to go into the office. I'm the boss, Em. I have to wear a suit."

"Yeah, but do you have to wear it that well? I mean, surely we can find you like an oversized jacket or something. I hear plaid is back in style," I offer up suggestions.

Josh smirks at me and stands up, doing a complete three-sixty. I get the full, head to toe view. Okay, my eyes didn't make it to the toes; they got stuck on the ass. Damn, what an ass that is.

"My eyes are up here, Emmy." Josh laughs as he catches me staring.

"Uh?" I pretend to play dumb. I *am* blonde, so it should work.

He shakes his head. "Come on, get up. As much as I love you naked, you need clothes on. You're coming with me," he says.

"Wait, what? I can't go to work with you. I'll just be in the way." Think, Emily, you have to get out of this. You cannot go into an office building and risk being seen.

"You're never in the way. I want you there," he argues.

"Josh, I'm tired. I'd rather stay here and wait for you to come back." I pray he will let me just stay locked up in this tower. It's much safer than being out and about in the city, in broad daylight.

"Besides, I have no clothes suitable to wear to an office." That's not a lie. I literally have no clothes on me. I don't know what he did with the jeans and sweatshirt I left in his bathroom that first day he found me.

Josh contemplates his options for a minute before pulling his phone out and calling someone.

"Ella, how's my favourite sister-in-law?" he asks.

I can't hear what she says back to him, as I'm only getting the one-sided conversation.

"Still counts. I need you to come over to my apartment and show Emily around some shops. She hasn't been out in the city and I don't want her getting lost."

My eyes go wide, and I shake my head. I am not going shopping. No way, no how.

"Now would be good. Tell him he'll manage." Josh hangs up the phone.

"I'm only going to be gone for a few hours. Ella's going to take you shopping. I'll wait for her to get here before I leave." He comes and sits on the bed. I start to shake my head no and protest.

"You need clothes, Emmy," he says as he pulls out a shiny black card from his wallet. "Take this—there's no limit on it." He grabs my hand and wraps it around the card.

"I-I'm not sure I can go shopping, Josh. I haven't been out to the shops for a really long time. What if I can't do it? What if something happens? I'd rather just stay here." My breathing picks up at the thought of being out in public, of being caught.

"Okay, how about I set the computer up, and you and Ella can do some online shopping? Have it delivered to the farm. We'll be back there tomorrow."

I nod my head. I have no intention of spending his money, but if it means I can escape the conversation, I'll agree to it.

"Do, um, do you want me to cook you breakfast before you go?" I ask.

"Emmy, you don't have to do anything you don't want to do. I'm a grown-ass man, capable of getting my own food if I have to. If you want to cook, then by all means, go and cook. If not, then don't. I don't want you to do anything you don't want to be doing," he says as he brushes the hair away from my forehead.

"Okay," I whisper. I'm just more confused now. I don't know what the right thing to do is. Yesterday, I felt so confident. I felt almost like myself again. Then, today, I wake up as the girl who's afraid to make her shadow appear on the wall the wrong way. I can't keep up.

"Emmy?" Josh asks.

"Yeah?"

"Promise me you'll be here when I get back." His voice is husky and vulnerable.

"I promise that if I'm not here, it's not because I didn't want to stay. The only thing that could get me out of this apartment today is if I'm dragged out." I give him the best I can offer.

"No one's going to be dragging you out of here, Emmy. You can't get up here without passing security and having the passcode, which I've just changed by the way. You are safe here." As he talks, he pulls out his phone, firing off a few text messages.

I don't bother to correct him. I know it's only a matter of

time before everything catches up with me. I just hope that I don't end up destroying him in the process. I'm selfish to want to stay as long as I can. I know the longer I stick around, the harder it's going to be when we get torn apart.

Josh puts his phone away and walks into his closet, coming back out with a shirt and sweats.

"You should definitely change into that," I say, pointing at the clothes he's holding. "It's much more suitable attire."

He smirks at me. "These are for you. I'm sure you don't want to be naked when Ella arrives. Come on, I'll make you coffee."

I just stare at him. When was the last time someone made me coffee? I can't even recall. I had coffee yesterday with Josh's mum, but her chef made it. No wonder Josh doesn't want me to cook for him. He's grown up with five-star chefs cooking his every bloody meal. I'm such an idiot, thinking he'd want to eat anything I made.

"Sure," I say as I climb out of bed and take the clothes into the bathroom.

Closing the door behind me, I lean against it and stare at my reflection in the mirror. It's not until I'm alone, in this quiet space, that I let the tears fall. I've always been good at hiding my emotions and faking happiness. I've done it my whole life. But when I'm alone, I don't need to pretend to be happy, to be normal.

As I look in the mirror, I don't recognise the woman staring back at me. The bruising on my face has dimmed to a pale yellow. It won't be much longer until it's gone, although the scars will always be there, both physically and mentally.

I'm surprised Josh hasn't asked about them yet. I know he sees the scars from the numerous stitches I've had. He's licked and kissed over them, but hasn't asked.

Wiping the tears from my face, I freshen myself up and get dressed in Josh's clothes. I can smell him on the shirt. I bring it close to my nose and inhale, his scent having a somewhat calming effect on me. I brush my hair with the hairbrush that's been left on the counter. It's new, still in a packet. Did Josh leave this for me? Does he think I need to be better presented? That's probably why he wants me to go shopping with his money. He is a McKinley; they do have an image to uphold.

What kind of image does it give him to be seen with me? An unkempt, domestic violence victim—no, not a victim, *a survivor*. I am a survivor. Even if I did have to kill Trent to escape him, I managed to get myself free. I survived years of torture from that asshole. I need to get out of my own head and stop second guessing myself.

Opening the door, I find the bedroom empty. I make the bed and pick up yesterday's discarded clothes, placing them in the laundry hamper before I go off in search of Josh. I find him in the kitchen, cooking eggs. He looks… I'm not sure what the word is… But seeing him dressed in that damn suit and standing over the stove cooking eggs, I'm suddenly hungry for something that's not food.

He hears me enter and turns around. He gives me a once-over, from head to toe, and his jaw clenches. I can't bring myself to meet his eyes. I don't know what I've done wrong. I can never tell with Josh, and it makes me nervous as hell. Did I take too long in the bathroom?

He puts down the spatula and walks over to me. It takes everything in me not to back away. This is Josh. He's not Trent. He is not going to hurt me. In my heart, I know that he won't hurt me, but in my head, there's always that little fight or flight button telling me to fly.

Josh brings his hand up to my face, and although he does it

slowly, I still flinch away from him. I close my eyes and, like all those times before, wait for the slap… but it never comes. His fingers brush underneath my eyes. Blinking them open, I see a whole whirlwind of emotions staring back at me. He's fighting with his own feelings just as much as I'm fighting with mine.

"You've been crying. I don't like it," he says as he pecks the softest of kisses under my eyes, while his tender touch only makes them water more. I don't understand his feelings towards me, when he clearly can't stand anyone else.

"Why do you like me, Josh?" I blurt out.

He's taken aback by the question and stares at me for a moment before answering. "Why do I like you? That's like asking why is the sky blue, babe. It just is. I don't know how to answer that. But I do know from the first day you made the terrible mistake of sitting at my table, you sealed your fate. Something inside me clicked for the first time in my life. I didn't know or understand what was happening at the time. I even talked to my mum about it. She was drunk, so it's probably a conversation she doesn't remember happening. But she cried and told me that I loved you—that's why I felt this overwhelming urge to protect you and make sure nothing bad ever happened to you."

He takes a breath in before continuing, "I don't just like you, Emmy. I love you. I always have. We both know that. Nobody gets me like you do. When you're around, I feel almost normal. I don't feel like I have to pretend to fit in with you because we just fit together."

I think about all that he said. "She remembers, you know? Your mum… I did know you loved me. I also knew you didn't want to. So, why now?"

He shrugs. "I've been going through life for the past seven years in black and white. The moment I heard your voice over the phone, my world became colourful again. I'm not giving you up for a second time, Emmy."

"Sometimes we don't get to choose our fates, Josh."

He doesn't get a chance to answer as smoke starts filling the room. Josh rushes over and turns off the stove, placing the frying pan in the sink. I wait for the yelling to start, the blaming me. Even though I wasn't the one cooking, I had distracted him.

I have to fix it. I have to make it right. "I'll fix it. Go sit down. I'll make something new," I say as calmly as I can while I open the fridge, inspecting what ingredients I have to work with.

"Babe, you don't need to fix shit. It's only burnt eggs, not a big deal," Josh says as he runs water over the frying pan.

"I can fix it. It's okay. It'll be okay." I keep repeating the mantra in my head. If I say it enough times, it might be true.

Josh comes up and shuts the fridge. He pulls my body tight to his as his arms wrap around me. "Emmy, it's okay. It's just burnt eggs. It doesn't matter. You're okay. I'm okay. We are okay." He kisses the top of my head.

My fingers curl around the lapels of his jacket. I don't want him to let me go. I want everything he says to be real. I want us to be okay, even though I know we never will be. We have an expiration date. He just doesn't know it yet.

"You need to get out of your head, Em. I'm not him. I'm an asshole. I'm not going to pretend that I'm not. But I'm not the monster haunting your dreams. There is nothing you can do that will ever make me want to hurt you."

"I know that. Deep down, I do know that. I just can't help the constant feeling that I'm going to do something wrong. I'm not the same girl you knew in high school, remember, Josh?"

"Of course you're not the same. You're better. You're more

real now than you ever let yourself be back then. I don't need a fake, plastered smile on your lips constantly, Emmy. I'd love nothing more than to always see genuine happiness written all over your face. But I love you no matter what you're feeling. When you're scared, I still love you. I want to hold you and make you feel safe. I want to slay every motherfucking demon you have that makes you scared. If you're angry, I still love you. I may want to throw you down on the bed and fuck the shit out of you, because, damn, babe, you're fucking hot as hell when you get fired up. Don't even get me started on when you're jealous. If you're sad, I still love you. I want to be the one to wipe your tears away. I want to be the shoulder you cry on."

I don't know how to respond to any of that. This Josh… This fierce, overbearing, protective Josh… This is the one I fell in love with when I was just fifteen. It's twisted and fucked up, I know. After all the shit he did in high school, after taking my virginity and warning me to leave town the next day, I should hate him. I try to remind myself I hate him. But the truth is, as much as I want to, I can't.

No one has ever loved me the way he does, even if it is a little crazy. Okay, *a lot crazy*. But I've never felt safer than I do right now, in his arms.

"Some days I really hate you; I remember waking up alone in that cabin and I hate you. But most days, even on the worst days of my life, all I wanted was to be held by you."

"Why didn't you call me sooner, Emmy? I would have come for you."

"I know you would have—that's why I never called. I knew what you would do. I don't want you to get in trouble over me, Josh."

"There is no amount of trouble you're not worth," he says as a ping sounds through the room.

Then I hear the clicking of heels on the marble floor and I step back. My body tightens. Please don't let it be another one of Josh's *friends*. I don't think I can handle that.

"Josh, why do I have two men, who look like they just stepped out of the WWE, following me up here?" Ella's voice carries through the house.

I raise my eyebrows at Josh in question. He laughs as he grabs my hand, leading me out of the kitchen. I've never really felt too self-conscious when I'm around Josh. But right now, with how glamourous Ella is in her skin-tight, little black dress and red pumps—her hair falling down over her shoulders in thick dark waves and red lipstick painted on her lips—I can't help but think she looks like a goddess. And all I want to do is crawl under a rock and never come back out.

"What the fuck, Ella? Does Dean know you left the house looking like that?" Josh asks.

"Don't be stupid. Of course he doesn't know. He wasn't exactly invited to our little shopping trip, which, by the way, I'm going to need one of your fancy McKinley money credit cards." Ella holds her hand out.

"Hasn't anyone told you?" Josh asks as he digs out his wallet, removing yet another black card and handing it over to her without question.

"Told me what?"

"That you are a McKinley. I happen to know you have a card with the name Ella McKinley on it. I ordered it myself."

"Well, yeah, but it's more fun to spend *your* money."

"It all comes from the same place, Ella," Josh says. "Also, change of plans. Emily's not feeling up to going out in the city.

She's going to use the computer in the study and do some online shopping."

Ella looks directly at me and smiles. "Emily, blink once if you need help. Twice, if you want me to knock this one on his ass. I've done it before."

My eyes open in surprise—surely she can't actually put him on his ass. "Ah, I'm okay. I just don't feel like going out. I'm sorry for interrupting your day." My hands wring the fabric on the bottom of my shirt.

Josh takes hold of one of them. "Emily, this is Ben and Jacob. They'll be your security detail whenever I'm not here."

I glance over to the two hulking men in suits. They don't say anything. They just stand there, looking scary.

I hold Josh's hand tighter. He's not actually going to leave me here with the two of them, is he? Ella must notice my distress and she speaks up.

"Josh, they are not hanging out inside the apartment. I'm inviting my sisters over, and we're having a girls' day. Your wrestlers can serve and protect from downstairs."

"Okay, but Reilly is not helping Emily buy clothes." Josh agrees to have the men wait in the lobby.

He cups my face between his hands and slowly brings his lips down onto mine. The moment our mouths touch, I forget that we're not alone in the room. Everything else drains out, everything but the feel of his lips on me.

The kiss ends way too soon for my liking. I cling to the lapels of his jacket tighter. I'm not sure I want him to leave. Maybe I should go with him. No, my mind is such a mess right now. Some distance will be good.

"You okay?" Josh asks.

"Yeah, I'm fine," I answer. "You are coming back, right?" I

ask. What if this is one of his cruel, twisted games from the past and he's going to leave me here?

"Emmy, I promise there is nothing that will keep me from coming back to you." He kisses me again. Leaning down, he whispers in my ear, "There's a phone in the bedroom drawer for you—use it if you need me. My number's saved. There's also a gun placed in that drawer, one in the top left drawer in the kitchen, one in my study under my desk, one in the lounge room under the coffee table and another in the entry table, middle drawer. Shoot first, ask questions later if you have to." He winks at me as he backs away, my eyes wide. Why the hell does he have so many guns in the house?

# Chapter 12

## Josh

The whole way down the elevator, through the lobby and getting to the car, I fight everything in me not to turn around and go back to Emmy. As soon as I get in the car, I pull out my phone and press the number I've stored for Emmy. It rings out. Fuck, I told her there was a phone in the bedroom if *she* needed to call *me*, not the other way around.

I dial Ella's number instead. The call almost rings out before she answers. I was prepared to jump out of the car and run back upstairs.

"Did you forget something?" she answers in a singsong voicc.

"Put Emily on the phone," I grunt out.

"What if she doesn't want to speak to you right now? Let me check." Ella laughs.

"Emily, there is one overbearing asshole with separation

issues on the phone and wanting to speak with you," Ella says to Emmy.

"What?" Emily asks, and the moment I hear her voice, my muscles begin to relax.

"Josh is on the phone. You want me to hang up?" Ella asks her.

"Don't you dare fucking hang up on me, Ella," I yell loudly. I know she hears me when she laughs.

"It's okay," Emily says tentatively. Seconds later, she's speaking into the phone.

"Josh, are you okay?" she asks.

"I am now," I breathe out.

"Okay." She waits for me to say something else. I don't care how crazy I look or sound when I'm around Emily. She's seen me at my worst and loves me anyway. Even though she hasn't said those words back to me yet, I know her heart.

"Emmy, I need you to go into our bedroom for me," I instruct her.

"Sure, hold on," she says. "Okay, I'm in the room."

"Open the top bedside drawer and take out the phone that's in there." I wait for her to follow the instruction.

"Okay, got it."

"Now turn it on."

"It's turning on. Are you sure you're okay? You don't sound like you are."

"I didn't know it would be this hard," I admit.

"What would be?"

"Leaving you in the apartment, being away from you, not being right next to you."

"Yeah, I know…"

"I want you to keep that phone on you. Text me, call me,

send me pictures throughout the day. Please." I'm practically begging for any morsel of attention she'll throw my way.

"You want me to send you pictures… what of?" She laughs.

"Your face. I miss seeing it already."

"Okay, let me figure out how to work this fancy phone first. I haven't…" Her sentence cuts off.

"You haven't what, Emmy?" I urge her to continue.

"I, um… haven't had a phone for a while so I'm a little out of touch, that's all."

"How long is a while?" I ask. The more info I can get, the more I can use it to find out who (or what) she's running from.

"Three years," she answers.

"Fuck!" My fingers grip the phone so tight I'm surprised it's not crumbling in my hands. Three fucking years! She's been living under someone else's control for three fucking years. She's been beaten and abused and God only knows what for three fucking years.

"Josh?" Emmy's voice is strained. It took a lot for her to tell me that little bit of information, and I've just yelled my frustration through the phone.

"I had a dream last night, babe," I tell her. It's a lie, but I need to change the topic. I need to reassure her that she's okay. That she's safe.

"You had a dream? Okay, what about?" she asks.

"You were riding Jasper. You were wearing these little denim shorts and a white top. Tan boots. Your hair was blowing in the wind behind you. Fuck, now I'm hard again, picturing that image of you in my head."

"Me, on a horse, turns you on? That's… *strange*, Josh, even for you," she says.

"*You* turn me on, Emmy. But that dream, I want to see it. Make sure you buy those tiny shorts and boots today."

"Sure. How long do you have to be at the office?" she asks, her voice quiet.

"I'm going to be in and out. I'll be back before you know it. Unless you want me to turn the car around and come back now?" Part of me is begging for her to say yes. To give me any reason to go back to her.

"No, it's okay. I think it might be fun to hang out with Ella and her sisters."

"Emmy, remember, it's your home. You can kick them out whenever you've had enough of them. You don't owe anyone anything," I tell her.

"It's your house, Josh, and I'm not about to kick your family out of it."

"It's *ours*. And the only one who is family is Ella. The other two are her family, not ours. The redheaded one is batshit crazy. Don't let her choose clothes for you."

"Okay."

I know I need to hang up, but I don't want to. I don't think she wants to either.

"I gotta go. I love you, Emmy. Don't ever forget that." My voice chokes with emotions I'm not used to feeling.

"I know," she replies.

"I know too, babe," I tell her; she doesn't have to say it back. I know she will when she's ready.

---

I'M annoyed as fuck the moment I walk through the office. "Mr. McKinley, good to see you back, sir," Kathy, my sixty-year-old assistant, says from her desk outside my door.

"Kathy, what am I in for today?" I ask her. If anyone knows what's going on in this building, it's her.

"We have you until two. You have a meeting with the board at ten, a lunch meeting with Hunter Jackson from Jackson Imports, and then a meeting with the legal department at one thirty."

"What the fuck does the legal department want?" I ask. They're not the ones who usually call for meetings.

"Something about your brother getting married without a prenup. The board isn't too happy about that either." She smiles.

"Well, the board can kiss my ass. Ella is now a McKinley; she's entitled to the shares that are being transferred into her name. I want to make sure she's protected if anything were to happen to Dean," I tell her. "Besides, they should be more concerned over the fact that *I* fully intend on getting married without a fucking prenup."

The thought leaves my lips, then my words sink in. Did I just say I'm getting married? Kathy's eyes widen and a huge smile spreads across her face.

"Did you meet someone? Who is she?" she asks.

I don't answer her. Shaking my head, I storm into my office. My love life is not going to be the fucking talk around the water cooler. Sitting down at my desk, I send a text to Emily.

**Me:** Did you buy those shorts yet?

**Emmy:** Not yet. Ella says I need to buy out the whole store of some place called La Perla. Don't worry, I told her I'm doing no such thing.

*La Perla*, I know exactly what that is. And I fucking approve. Fuck, I'll buy the fucking franchise if it means I get to see Emily in all of that shit.

**Me:** Yes, you are! Get clicking, babe. One in every style, every colour. I want to see the fucking rainbow on you!

**Emmy:** I'll check it out.

**Me:** I gotta go, but if you don't shop up big there, I'll just go there myself and buy everything.

**Emmy:** Don't work too hard. XX

Checking the time, I have ten minutes until this fucking board meeting. I need to catch up with Sam before I go in there. Stopping in his office doorway, I see him hitting at the keyboard on his desk.

"What did that keyboard ever do to you?" I ask.

He doesn't stop, totally ignoring my comment instead. A minute later, he smiles. "Gotcha, motherfucker!" he shouts.

I raise my eyebrows in question. It's not unusual for Sam to get animated or excited when he finally manages to get into something he was being kept out of.

"I have the name of the fucker who registered both death certificates." He smiles at me.

"And that is?"

"Gregory Jones. Detective Gregory Jones," Sam says, picking up a pile of files and walking towards the door.

"Who the fuck is Gregory Jones, and what the fuck does he have to do with Emily?" I ask aloud.

"No idea. *Yet*," he replies. "Try not to kill off any of the board members," Sam adds as we walk into the boardroom.

The room falls into silence as I take a seat at the head of the table. I've always fucking hated these meetings. They're full of stuffy, old, overweight men. Men just like my fucking father.

It was supposed to be Dean in this seat, not me. He never worked a day in his life in this company—my father gave up trying to mould him. Instead, the son of a bitch focused all his energy on me, making me the next head of McKinley Industries.

Let's just say, he's not a man who's missed by anyone. The only reason I gave Emily up when we were kids was because I was so afraid I would turn out like my father. An abusive, entitled asshole. I didn't want to ever put that on Emily.

My hands clench on the desk as I think about the three years of abuse she's endured anyway. Three years I could have saved her from… I *should have* saved her from. Whoever made up that shit about if you love someone let them go is a goddamn fucking idiot. If you love someone, the only way to keep them safe is to fucking keep them in the first place.

"Mr. McKinley, we're ready whenever you are, sir," Sam says from next to me. The sooner we get this shitshow over with, the sooner I get back to Emily. I nod my head, indicating that I'm listening—even if I'm only half paying attention.

---

IT'S one in the afternoon by the time I get five minutes to myself. I send Emily a quick text to check in, something I've wanted to do for a while.

**Me:** How are you?

**Emmy:** Reallllly goooood. How you doinnn?????

Her reply comes in quick, almost like she was watching the phone for it to ring, although I'm not sure what to make of her message.

**Me:** I'd be better if I was home with you. What are you up to?

**Emmy:** I'd be better if you were in me too.

Great, now I have a fucking boner. I'm sitting in the car heading back to the office with a fucking boner.

**Emmy:** With. Not in. Although, now that I think about it…

I don't bother to text back. I dial her number. She picks up straight away.

"Hellooooo," she sings.

"Babe, what are you doing?"

"Um, well, Ella's sisters are here and they made these drinks. I didn't want to be rude so I drank some. And now I feel good. Like really good, Josh. But not as good as you make me feel," she slurs.

"Are you drunk?" I ask, already knowing the answer.

"Um, I don't know. Hold on," she says. I don't think she pulls the phone away from her ear as she speaks to Ella.

"Ella, Joshua is asking if I'm drunk. Am I drunk?" she asks. I hear a heap of laughter before some shuffling of the phone.

"Joshy, she's not drunk. *Much.* Where are you anyway? You're missing the fun," Ella says.

"Ella, what are you drinking? What is Emmy drinking? Has she eaten? Had any water?" I fire off. The only response I get is more laughter.

"Give the phone back to Emily," I growl out.

"Joshua, remember that time in high school when you took me home from that party?" Emmy asks.

I'm surprised she remembers that; she was out of it. She passed out in my car. I don't know how much or what she was drinking at the party, but when I turned up and saw how wasted she was, I dragged her ass out.

"You remember that?" I ask her

"Yep!" She pops out the P sound. "I wasn't drunk that night. I faked it because I knew you'd take me home. It was the first time you told me that you loved me."

"You were supposed to be asleep when I said that."

"I know. But I'm not faking drunk now. So, you know, if you want to tell me now, that's okay too," she says, not making any sense.

"I love you, Emmy. Have you eaten anything today?"

"Mmm," she hums.

"Emmy?"

"Oh, hang on." She returns her attention to the girls. "I lick, drink then suck, right?" she asks.

Fuck me, they're giving her tequila shots. I hear a bunch of females cheering before Emmy starts talking again.

"I don't get it… it tastes like shit, Josh. Why do people do this?"

"Emmy, drink some water, babe. I'm coming home," I tell her.

"Oh, can we do that thing again?" she asks.

"What thing?"

"You know that thing you do with your tongue. Down there," she attempts to whisper.

"Babe, I will be doing that thing with my tongue on a daily basis. Don't you worry about that."

I can hear giggles and wolf whistles in the background.

"Emmy, I'm hanging up now. I'm coming home."

"Josh, are you mad? I don't want you to be mad at me."

"I'm not mad. I just really miss you, that's all."

"Yeah, I miss you too. The girls want to go to some place called The Merge. But I don't want to go, Josh. What if they find me there?" she says.

I pause. "Emmy, who? What if who finds you?" I prompt, hoping like fuck that she's drunk enough to let something slip.

I hear a bang. "Emmy, Emmy?" I yell through the receiver.

"Oopsie-daisy. I dropped the phone, but don't worry, it's

not broken or anything," she says before she starts rambling on again, "Josh, my lips are numb, but I really want you to kiss them. I like your kisses. They're nice."

I laugh. I like drunk Emmy. I need to call my brother though, which means I need to hang up the phone.

"Emmy, babe, have those lips ready for me. I plan on kissing the hell out of them as soon as I get home."

"Well, hurry up then," she says before the phone cuts out.

I dial Dean straight away.

"Yeah?" he answers.

"Your wife is currently in my apartment giving Emily tequila shots," I grunt.

"Last I checked Emily was an adult?" he replies.

"I currently have four drunk women in my penthouse, Dean. Three too many. Come and fucking get them."

"What do you mean four? Who else is there?"

"Ella, Reilly and Alyssa."

"Fucking hell. I thought Ella was taking Emily shopping."

"Emily wanted to shop online. I don't know how the others got involved. But you need to come and get them."

"Okay, Zac and I are on our way."

I hang up as I pull up out front of the building.

# Chapter 13

## Emily

My head is spinning. This tequila is really good stuff. As soon as I hear the ping of the elevator, I get up and run to the foyer (at least I try to run). I stumble my way through the penthouse. The moment I see Josh, or two of him, I jump up, wrapping my legs around his waist.

My lips find his, my tongue pushing its way inside his mouth, not that he puts up any resistance. Before I know it, he's got me pinned up against the wall. He takes control over the kiss, tilting my head to give him better access. I can feel his hardness against my centre, every movement of his hips sending me further and further into a frenzy.

Josh slows down the kiss, before pulling away. "Miss me?" he asks.

"You were gone a really, really long time," I tell him with a pout.

"I know."

"Emily, it's your turn!" Ella shouts from the living room.

"Oh, it's my turn. Put me down. Put me down. It's my turn." I unwrap my legs from his waist, my feet landing on the floor. Josh doesn't let go. His arms hold me close as I struggle to keep myself upright.

Once I've got myself steady, I look up at him. "It's my turn. Let's go."

"It's your turn for what?" he asks as he holds me still.

"Our game. Come see." I unlatch his arms and drag him by the hand through to the living room, where the three girls are waiting for me.

"About time, I was about to take your turn," Ella says.

"Damn, Josh, who knew you'd clean up so well." Reilly whistles. I glare at her. It's just like high school, when all the hot girls would be pining for Josh to give them some attention.

Josh ignores her. Instead, he wraps his arm around my shoulder, pulling me into his chest. "Mmm, you smell good. Why do you smell good?" I ask him.

"Because I showered?" he questions back.

I shrug. I don't really care why he smells good, as long as I can stay tucked up in here and sniff him.

"Gross, Emily, it's your turn. Hurry up and get that little ass of yours down here," Ella squeals.

I take my seat next to her. "Okay, sorry, but I'm not really sorry. He has a really good tongue," I whisper back to her.

"So does his brother." Ella winks at me and I laugh.

I lick my hand and hold it out. Ella sprinkles the salt on it. "Oh, wait! I have a better idea. Josh, get over here, and lose the shirt."

Josh raises his eyebrows at me. "Lose the shirt? Why?" he asks as he strips his jacket off and loosens his tie.

"I want to lick you," I say simply. All the girls start laughing, and I join in with them. "If you knew how good he tasted, you'd want to lick him too." I point to each of them.

"Trust me, Emily, we do not want to know. Besides, nothing tastes as good as Zac," Alyssa says.

"My husband has a pierced cucumber. And when you lick it…" Reilly laughs.

"Argh, God. Josh, shoot me now," Ella grumbles.

Josh squats down behind me, picking me up before placing me in his lap. His arms close around my waist. "Sorry, El, I happen to like you, which is rare, so you're not getting shot." He lifts up my tequila and downs it in one go.

"Hey, not fair. That was mine," I complain.

"Okay, where're you licking, babe?" Josh asks as he undoes the first few buttons of his shirt.

"Really, I can lick you?" I'm so excited. I jump up and down. Josh's hands go to my waist, stilling my movements.

"Anytime, anywhere," he says.

I pull his shirt off his shoulder a little and lick a spot at his neck. "Salt," I say, holding my hand out. Ella places the salt in my open palm.

I pour it over Josh's neck. "Okay, where's my shot?" Josh hands me a glass. Then he places a slice of lemon between his teeth.

I don't waste time. I lick, drink and suck on that lemon. It tastes gross. My nose scrunches up. "Ugh, I don't know why people like this stuff."

"Have any of you had water since you turned my living room into a bar?" Josh asks. Why is he suddenly sounding like the responsible one?

I look around. "Water? Yep, it's clear, just like water." I

point to the three bottles of tequila that are on the table. They're all open and half empty.

Josh looks at the bottles. "Wait, is that my…? Fucking hell. Ella, did you raid my bar or did you bring these supplies with you?" he asks her, nodding to the table.

"*Yours*. You have the good stuff too, you know." Ella smiles.

"You do know that's a two-thousand-dollar bottle you're spilling all over my damn table? I'm sending your husband the bill," Josh says to Ella.

I, on the other hand, just about choke. I've been drinking a two-thousand-dollar bottle of tequila. Who the hell pays that much for one little bottle?

"Alyssa, you look the most responsible. Can you please go get some water bottles from the fridge?" Josh asks.

"Sure," she says, as she goes to stand up and starts tumbling.

"Fuck me, you're all as bad as each other. Alyssa, sit your ass down. I'll get you water."

"Oh, pizza, that's a great idea, Josh. I'll have a meat lovers," Reilly squeals.

"Yes. Pizza, pizza, pizza!" Ella starts cheering.

I can't remember the last time I ate pizza. Do I even still like it?

"Pizza actually is a fucking fantastic idea. Let me order some. What kind do you want, Emmy?" Josh asks me.

It seems like everyone's eyes go to me. "I don't mind. Whatever you all want is fine," I say.

"Chicken, no, cheese. Oh, pepperoni!" Ella says.

"Okay, I've got this. Emmy, help me in the kitchen." Josh stands, picking me up with him.

"Oh, *help*. Is that what the kids are calling it these days!" Ella winks. All three women burst into laughter.

"Where's Zac, because I could really use his *help* right now." Alyssa giggles.

"Gross, no. Josh, wait for me. I'm coming." Ella goes to stand up but wobbles so much she falls back down in a fit of laughter.

"Fuck my life. Change of plans." Josh pulls his phone out of his pocket and presses some buttons, before sitting back down.

"Where the fuck are you?" he yells through the receiver.

"Almost there. Why?" A rough voice comes over the speaker.

"Oh, Dean, hunny, are you coming to *help* me? 'Cause I really need *help*!" Ella yells. We all burst into laughter with her.

"How much has she had to drink?" Dean asks.

"I don't fucking know, but they're all fucking drunk as skunks. Hurry up and get your ass here. And bring pizza. They want pizza."

"Do I look like a delivery boy?" Dean says.

Josh holds the phone out in Ella's direction. "El, tell Dean to bring pizza."

"Oh, yes, pizza!" Everyone starts shouting.

Josh hangs up the phone and throws it on the table.

"Josh, your brother's a little scary," I tell him.

"You're scared of Dean? When you sleep next to *that one* at night?" Reilly asks me.

"That one? You mean Josh? He's not scary at all. Are you, Josh?" I turn into him.

"No, babe, not at all. Remember that." He kisses my forehead, and I melt into him.

---

ARGH, God, why is my head pounding? I feel a body move behind me and I tense up. What did I do last night? I don't remember what I did to make him mad. I try to catalogue my other injuries. But all I feel is nausea. I need to find the bathroom. I climb out of bed as quietly as I can. Nothing other than my head hurts, so maybe it's not that bad.

Although it must have been a pretty big hit, for me to feel this nauseous. This doesn't happen that often. But when it does, it can last for days.

I find the bathroom, my stomach emptying as soon as I'm near the loo. My head pounds as I lean back against the wall and close my eyes.

"Babe, here, drink some of this."

I must be dreaming because I just heard Josh's voice. It's times like these that I wish I could go to him. I wish I could take the phone out of the cistern and call him. Why can't I just call him?

"Emmy, open your eyes. You need to drink a little," he says.

"If I open my eyes, you'll be gone, and I'll be back in hell. Just let me dream a little longer," I whisper. I cannot let Trent know I'm awake. I don't have the energy to deal with him yet.

"Emmy, I'm right here. I'm not going anywhere. Open your eyes, babe." I feel his hands place a bottle in mine. That feels a little too real. I jolt back, my eyes springing open.

"Josh?" I ask. How did he find me? "How… how did you find me?" I say the question aloud this time.

"Emmy, you're okay. Look around. You're not there anymore." He scoops me up and carries me back to bed. The room I'm in… it's not where I thought I was. I'm in Josh's apartment. The last few days come back to me. Mostly.

"Why does my head hurt so much?" I ask him.

"Tequila. You and Ella both finished off the bottle." Josh hands me two pills. "Take these. This is just ibuprofen—it'll help with the headache. And this one's for the nausea."

"I think I'm dying," I complain. I don't handle being sick well at all. Now that my heart has calmed down a bit, blurry parts of last night are coming back to me.

"You're not dying. You're just hungover. Haven't you ever been hungover before?" he asks.

"No, I wasn't allowed." I shut my mouth, choosing to shove the pills into it instead. I'm obviously getting way too comfortable around Josh for me to keep slipping up like this. He doesn't need to know about the last few years of my life. The less he knows, the better.

"Argh, why didn't you stop me?" I groan as I lie back down and snuggle into the blanket.

"You were having fun. You're also a full-grown adult, Emmy. If you want to let loose and blow off steam, I'm not about to stop you."

I think about what he said. He's not about to stop me. I wonder if he'd stop me if I was to get up and walk out the door now? The only problem is, I'm too scared to test the theory. What if he didn't stop me? I don't know if I want to leave this dream yet.

I watch as he pulls on a pair of grey sweats. God, what is it with this man and grey sweatpants? How many pairs can one person have? He comes over to the bed, leans down and kisses my forehead while stroking his hand through my hair.

"I promised Ella I'd meet her for breakfast. Do you want to get up and come eat?"

I shake my head, which was a mistake. "Argh, no. I'm just going to stay right here."

"I doubt Ella is actually awake anyway. I'm going to bring you back some food." He gets up and walks to the door.

"Josh?"

He turns and looks at me, waiting for me to speak up. I get a little lost in all of the tanned muscles and ink currently on display on his bare chest.

"Need something, Emmy?" He smirks.

"No, but you need a damn shirt. And don't you have any other colour sweatpants than grey?" I ask.

"No, I like grey. But I will put a shirt on. For you." He walks into the closet and comes back out with a tight white V-neck on. Is he purposely messing with me?

"Better?" he asks.

"Not at all," I grumble and roll over. I hear him laugh as he walks out the door.

---

*"NO, stop. Trent, stop. Please, I didn't mean to. I'll fix it," I beg him. He doesn't listen.*

*"You fucking stupid whore. How fucking hard is it to place the damn towels on the towel rail. Look at them." He shoves my head into the rail.*

*I hear the crunch of bone, a searing pain tearing at my face. I scream. Blood pours out of my nose.*

*Trent lets go of the hold he has on my hair and I fall to the floor, landing on my hands and knees.*

*"Now you've gone and made a bigger fucking mess. The shit better be fucking cleaned up when I get back." I see his booted foot come for my head. I scream.*

I jolt up in the bed. Someone is screaming. Who's screaming? The door bursts open and Josh runs in, holding a gun directly at me. Dean comes in after him. Both men stop when they see me. Josh scans the room quickly then lowers the firearm, his jaw tense.

"Fuck!" Josh screams. He turns and punches the wall behind him, not just once but three times.

"Josh, calm the fuck down, *now*," Dean growls.

I just sit in the middle of the bed, watching. Waiting. I don't know exactly what I'm waiting for, but I'm waiting. Josh places the gun down on the dresser. His icy blue eyes stare, meeting mine.

I've made him angry again. All I ever seem to do is make people angry. I don't know what to say, what to do, so I just sit and wait.

"Emily, are you okay?" Dean asks me. I nod my head, but I don't take my eyes off Josh.

"Good. Joshua, a word." Dean walks out of the room. I think that Josh is going to follow his brother, but when he gets to the door, he slams it shut and locks it instead. He bangs his forehead on it a few times before turning back around and heading to the bed.

I should be looking for a way to get out of here. Any normal person would not want to be alone in a locked room with Josh right now. He's acting like a caged lion, ready to rip the head off anyone who's close. I'd be lying if I said I wasn't a little unsure. *Not scared.* I've never been truly scared of Josh, but *unsure*.

I'm unsure of what's going through his head. I'm unsure of what I should be doing to help him.

"Josh, I need you to tell me what to do. I don't know what I'm supposed to do." I'm trying to not let the tears fall—trying and failing miserably.

Josh comes and sits on the bed, pulling me into his lap. He brushes the sweaty hair out of my face. I still slightly flinch when his hand reaches up. He doesn't mention my reaction, just continues to brush the hair off my face.

"You don't have to do anything, Emmy. You aren't meant to do anything. I'm sorry if I scared you. I'm sorry. I'm so fucking sorry that I can't slay the demons that haunt you in your sleep."

"It's not your fault," I tell him.

"It is. If I didn't make you leave, if I had just kept you back then…" His words trail off but I know what he doesn't say.

How can he possibly think any of this is his fault? This is my fault. I should have been smarter, gotten out sooner.

"Josh, it's not your fault. Whatever choices were made, I made them, not you." I take hold of his hands. "Can we go back to the farm?" I ask, wanting to change the subject, and maybe distract him from his own thoughts.

"Yeah, let's shower then we'll head back." Right as we are about to get up, the door opens.

"What the fuck! Josh, out. Emily and I are having a girls' morning. We will accept a delivery of mimosas." Ella comes barrelling in with her hands full of bags.

"How the fuck did you even get in here?" Josh asks, making no move to get out.

"I picked the lock. Bray taught me how when we were kids. Never really thought I'd be thankful for those painful hours. But here we are." She drops the bags on the bed.

"Babe, want me to send her back to the loony bin she came from?" Josh asks me.

I shake my head no. "No, I want to keep her," I tell him.

He smiles. "Okay, I'll bring you back some food, and mimosas, *and water*."

---

AFTER WHAT FEELS like hours of being primped and prodded, Ella declares that we're ready.

"Are you sure about this, Ella? We're only going to be spending a few hours in a car heading back to the farm. This is too much."

I stare at my reflection in the mirror. Ella gave me a royal blue dress; it's made of a light, sheer material. The dress has thin spaghetti straps that crisscross at the back, with a deep V-cut along the neckline that shows off way too much cleavage. The fabric falls halfway down my thighs, so although it's not that short, it feels short. So much of my skin is showing.

Ella put soft curls in my hair, leaving them hanging down my back. It's my face that has me most confused. I don't recognise the woman staring back at me. All the fading yellow bruising has been covered over and hidden under the flawless makeup Ella applied. Shiny pink lips and dark eyeliner make my blue eyes appear bigger than I've ever seen them look.

"You're stunning, Emily. Josh is going to be tripping over his own tongue. I can't wait. Come on, let's go. Remember, confidence. You are a strong, confident woman, and no one, not even Josh, is going to be telling you what to wear." Ella's pep talk hits me harder than it should.

I can't bring myself to tell her how wrong she is. I'm not strong or confident. And honestly, if Josh hates the dress and wants me to change, I'm probably not going to argue with him about it. As much as I want to have Ella's confidence and self-esteem, I just don't. What I *can do* is fake it for a little while.

"Okay, let's go."

# Chapter 14

## Josh

Emmy's been holed up in the bedroom with Ella for two hours. What the fuck could they possibly be doing that takes two hours? I've attempted to go in a few times, only to be screamed at by Ella telling me to get out.

I've tried to distract myself, going through emails and boring-ass reports for work, but every few minutes, I'm pulled back to the image of Emmy sitting up in the bed, screaming at the top of her lungs with tears running down her face.

I'm such a fucking idiot for not controlling my reactions better. I should have been able to keep my cool. I'm surprised she's not running for the hills with how I acted, unless she's too scared to try. Fuck, is she only here because she's too scared of what I'll do if she tries to leave? I did tell her I'm not about to let her go.

And I'm fucking not, but I also would not hurt her either.

I'll do anything to keep her. I'll also do anything to make her nightmares disappear. Dragging my fingers through my hair, I can't help but think how much I'd fucking love a drink right now. But I'm refraining. I need to be as clear-minded as I can be. I need to figure the fuck out who did this to Emmy, who the fuck is continuing to haunt her.

"You look like shit," Dean says as he walks in with two large coffee cups.

"Thank you, I do try hard," I remark.

"Here, drink this. Are you sure you're going to be okay?" he pries.

"I'm fine. I just need to find the fucker who did this to her."

"I get that, I do. But I worry about you. With her, it's different. Your obsession with her has already been a little much. But now that she's back, it's off the fucking charts—hospital territory," Dean says.

"Yeah, how's that differ from your obsession with Ella?" I ask him.

"If Ella wanted to walk out that door without me, I'd probably let her. Can you say the same?"

"Fuck no. But I also don't care. I let her go once, and look what happened to her."

"Josh, whatever happened to her is not on you. It's on the fucker who did it. Not you."

"I always thought if I kept her around, I'd end up like him. Like dad. That's why I sent her away. Guess the joke's on me because the life I thought I was saving her from, she ended up having anyway."

"You are not like him. Never have been. Do you think I'd leave you alone with Ella, even for a minute, if you were? Fuck that. He does not define who you are."

Dean gets worked up whenever the topic of our asshole father comes up. I don't actually know why, but he hates him more than I do. And from what I remember, Dean hardly had anything to do with him at all in the later years. No, that shit was all left up to me.

"I know that now, but when I was eighteen, I obviously wasn't as smart." I sip at the coffee; it's burnt and fucking disgusting, but I drink it anyway. "How much longer do you think they're going to be?" I ask, looking at my watch.

"Your guess is as good as mine." Just as he sits across from me, I hear the sound of Ella and Emmy laughing as they come down the hall.

I'm too impatient to wait for her. I get up and meet her just as she's about to enter the living room. The moment my eyes land on her, I'm speechless. Fuck me, Emmy is always beautiful. But right now, fuck, she's fucking gorgeous.

My eyes travel up and down her body numerous times. I wouldn't be surprised if I was drooling right now. I have an instant fucking boner.

Emmy stands still, wringing her hands in front of her. "If you don't like it, I can change," she says.

If I don't like it? Is she blind? The only reason that dress is coming off her is because I'm ripping it off to worship the body underneath it.

"Emmy, do you like the dress?" I ask her.

"I like it." She smiles at me.

"So, keep it on then. You look fucking gorgeous, babe," I tell her as I pull her close to me. I don't think I can ever get enough of her being in my arms. "Are you ready to head back?"

"More than ready," she says.

"Oh, Dean, I'm heading up to the farm with Emily and Josh for a few days," Ella adds in. That's news to me.

"Why?" Dean and I both ask at the same time.

"Because your mum invited me. She said something about wedding planning."

"Okay, I'll come down tomorrow. I need to sort some things out here first." Dean picks Ella up off the ground, kissing her.

Yep, don't need to see that shit. I'm surprised he's not insisting on coming down today with her. I do suspect he'll be there before midnight. There's no way he's going all night without Ella attached to him.

"Okay, we'll be downstairs. Car's leaving in five minutes, El, with or without you," I tell her as I lead Emmy to the elevator.

---

NEVER AGAIN! Never fucking again will I take a fucking three-hour road trip with both Ella and Emily together. If I didn't already have shares in a paracetamol company, I'm about to fucking buy some.

Nonstop talking and laughing the whole trip. Add in the off-key singing and you have yourself a fucking migraine. The only reason I didn't tell them both to shut the fuck up was because of how happy Emily was. Hearing her laugh and be carefree is what I imagine angels sound like.

Not that I'm ever going to meet any angels, other than Emily. I'm sure if there is a maker up there somewhere, he'd be chewing someone's ass out for their mistake of making Emily and me soulmates. Her pureness should never have gotten mixed up with my level of evil.

Too late now, motherfuckers. She's mine and I don't give a fuck what anyone has to say about it. Pulling up in front of the house, I glare at the fucker who is about to open Emily's door for her. He quickly walks around the car, choosing to open Ella's instead. I know he's doing the job I fucking pay him to do, but I want to be the one opening doors for her, not any other fuckers.

"Thank you." Emily smiles at me as she climbs out of the car.

"Anytime." I smirk. Taking her hand, I lead her inside with Ella following behind.

"Shit, I probably should have thought about this whole night without Dean thing a little better," she says.

"You'll be fine. It's one night, El," I tell her.

"Sure, I'll be fine. It's only one night," she repeats.

Something is off with her now that we're here. I don't like it. I don't like the way she's withdrawing into herself. I've seen her do it a few times before. I've seen the way she rubs at her wrists, and I've seen the scars she tries to cover up.

"Babe, can you take this to my office for me? I'm just going to grab a drink, then I've got a few things I need to catch up on. I thought you and Ella could hang out a bit while I work." I hand over my laptop bag to Emily.

If only she knew how much trust I'm putting in her hands right now. I don't let anyone touch that laptop. There is access to literally billions of dollars on that one machine. Emily looks between Ella and me before nodding her head.

"Sure, how about I have a quick shower and meet you at the pool?" she asks Ella.

"Yeah, sounds good," Ella responds, a little vacant. Emily's eyebrows draw down, but she silently turns around and heads towards my office.

I wait for her to be out of earshot before I speak to Ella.

"What's wrong? And don't fucking try to lie to me. I already know your tells. You can't lie for shit."

"Nothing's wrong. I just don't know how I'm going to get through a whole night without Dean. I mean, if you were having sex with him, you'd understand what that man can do." She smirks.

"Try again," I say.

"I… okay, I don't know. What if I can't do it? What if I get that urge to…?" Her sentence trails off.

"Then you come to me, Ella."

"You don't know, Josh. You don't know what I do," she says quietly, averting her eyes as if she's ashamed.

"El, you don't have anything to be ashamed of. And you don't need to say it either. *I know.*" I hold her wrist, turning it over. "These scars do not define who you are. They are a part of you, not the whole you. Do you know who you are, Ella?"

"Who am I?" she asks.

"You're Ella fucking McKinley. The McKinley Princess is what they're calling you in the papers. Hold your head up high. You don't bow down to any motherfuckers. You make them bow down to you."

"Okay, thank you," she says as she's about to walk away.

"Ella, I may not be Dean or Bray. But I know better than anyone about battling internal demons. If you need to talk, you come to me."

"Thank you." She heads for the stairs.

When I walk into the office, Emily is sitting at my desk typing on my laptop. She's so focused on what she's looking at, or for, that she doesn't notice I'm there. I wait, giving her more time. More time to search for whatever it is she felt the need to hack into my computer for. Not that it would have been hard

—the password is *Emmy*. She would have guessed that right away.

I'm surprised I'm not more furious about the fact that she's on my computer. Anyone else would have a bullet between their eyes right now. But with Emily, I'm more intrigued to find out what she's looking for. She doesn't realise this, but that computer has software that tracks every single keystroke. Even if she tried to delete what she's searching for, she won't be able to.

Deciding to make myself known, I step out of the shadows I was hiding in. "If you're looking for porn, babe, we can always make our own." I smirk at her.

Emily jumps out of her skin. She presses a few buttons on the computer quickly and slams the lid closed. She looks guilty as shit, like she just got caught stealing cookies from the cookie jar. The guilt quickly morphs into worry and trepidation. *Fear.*

This look, I've seen it many times, across many faces. I usually relish this look. But I never want to see this look on her. Am I pissed as fuck that she's hiding shit from me? Fuck yes, I am. But am I about to take out my frustrations on her? Fuck no.

She needs to learn that there is nothing she has to fear from me. "So, is that a yes to the home porno? Because I can have a camera set up in a few seconds. Want to play the role of my naughty secretary?" I ask as I approach the desk. She doesn't move, doesn't even blink.

Walking around the desk, I move the laptop out of the way before picking her up and sitting her in its place. I take the seat in the chair she's just vacated. I run my fingertips along the inside of her thighs, pulling the fabric of her already short dress up higher.

"You know, I don't need the camera. There is no way I'll

ever forget the vision you're giving me right now, babe." I bend down and lick and nibble on her inner thigh. This started out as a way for me to ease her fear. But now, this is about me getting a taste of that delicious pussy currently staring me in the face and begging me to drink from it.

"I forgot to get my drink. I think I might just drink from here instead," I say as I move the lace panties aside, her wet, pink folds now unobstructed.

# Chapter 15

## Emily

Oh my God! Did he say he's going to drink from me? Is he playing games with me here? I can't tell. I hate that I can't tell. He just caught me red-handed on his laptop, which was password protected, not that the password was hard to figure out.

I tried to search my name, to see if there was any news about me or what I had done. I got nothing, not a goddamn thing. No one is looking for me. I searched Trent's name, and again, nothing. Does that mean nobody has found his body yet? Is he still lying in a pool of his own blood on the kitchen floor?

I don't know why Josh isn't mad that I was on his computer. Why is he acting like everything is fine?

"Emmy?" His husky voice breaks me out of my internal monologue.

"Uh-uh?"

"Mind if I quench my thirst?" He smirks at me.

"Is that even a real question? If you don't, I'm sure I can find someone else who will." As soon as the words are out of my mouth, I know I've made a mistake.

Josh growls and his fingers dig into my thighs, spreading them wider than they already are. "Emily, if you ever let another man near my pussy, you'll be signing their death certificates. Because I will fucking kill them." He looks me dead in the eyes. It's not his words that tell me just how serious he is, or the fact that he said Emily and not Emmy. It's his eyes. The soul-piercing icy stare, the same gaze I imagine the devil would have.

But isn't that exactly who I've been in love with all my life? The devil currently staring back at me? I smile at him.

"I'd help you bury the bodies. Because I promise, if another man got anywhere near me, it wouldn't be because I wanted him to. Now you, on the other hand… I very much want you near me, on me, in me."

"Fuck, Emmy!" Josh grunts out, as he buries his face in the apex of my legs again. He doesn't waste any time before his tongue is slicing between my folds. My head falls back against the desk.

"Oh God, don't stop," I moan. Josh's hands go under my ass as he lifts my hips off the table, his tongue alternating between pumping in and out of my centre and circling around my clit.

My hands fist his hair, pushing his face into me, while attempting to hold him still in just that one spot. That spot that's going to let me fly over the edge. He doesn't let me control the show. The more I pull and push on his head, the further away he moves from the spot I want him licking.

"Argh, I'm so close!" I groan. I feel him laugh, the vibrations going straight through me. He's torturing me on purpose, keeping me hanging off the edge with just enough promise of ecstasy but not delivering.

"Josh, please, I-I need." What is it that I need? I don't even know anymore.

"I'll give you everything you need and more, Emmy. All you have to do is ask," Josh says, peering up at me. I have a feeling he's talking about more than just making me come.

"I need to come, damn it," I growl. Why did he take his tongue off me?

"Your wish is my command." He smirks.

He inserts two fingers into me, while his tongue goes straight for the kill spot. I detonate. Stars, fog, the whole thing. My body quivers, and my pussy grips his fingers as my release gushes out of me.

Josh doesn't stop licking, drinking until I'm nothing but a puddle of electrified nerve endings, sprawled out on his desk. He kisses his way up my body, his lips claiming mine. Tasting myself on him turns me on way more than I ever thought it would.

Fuck, I want him. I want him so much it scares the shit out of me. This isn't healthy; I can see that. But right now, I don't care. All I can focus on is getting access to his cock. I push him back until he's sitting in his chair again.

Smiling, I slide off the desk, kneeling in front of him. It's my turn. Let's see how much he likes being kept within arm's reach of nirvana. My hands grasp for his belt. I keep eye contact with him as I undo the loops and then move onto getting his jeans undone.

Josh holds my hands still. "Emmy, you don't have to do

this." His voice is strained, like although he means every word he says, he doesn't actually want to say them.

"But I want to. Do you not want me to?" I ask.

He lets go of my hands. "I want it. More than you fucking know," he grunts.

I go back to my task of freeing him from his jeans. I smile as I achieve my goal, my mouth watering at the sight of his hard cock, precum dripping from the top. My tongue glides easily along the tip, licking up what he's offering.

His taste is a little salty, musky. My hand wraps around, firmly gripping his length as I glide my arm up and down. I take turns pumping him with my hand, and running my tongue along the underside of his cock, from his balls right up to the tip, twirling around the top.

"Fuck, Emmy!" Josh growls, but other than his hips slightly pumping upwards with each stroke I make, he doesn't move. His hands grip the armrests of his chair, his knuckles white with the force.

After five minutes of teasing, I can't take it any longer. I need him in my mouth. I slide my lips down over his length. My hand grips onto the base of him. I can't fit the whole of him in my mouth.

I close my eyes, savouring the feel of him, the taste of him. I groan around him, his thighs shaking underneath my arms. I want to make him feel good. I've had a few boyfriends, but I've never wanted to please someone as much as I want to please Josh right now. I need it. I need him to lose control because of me.

Is it a healthy feeling? Probably not. I know Josh thinks he's the one with issues here, but he doesn't know the depth of my instabilities yet. He doesn't know the things I've done over the last few years to survive.

I continue to suck and stroke his length. After a very short few minutes, Josh growls out, "Fuck, Emmy, I'm going to come." Is he really warning me? Like I'm going to suddenly pull away? I increase my efforts, sucking harder. My free hand cups his balls and rolls them around.

Josh grunts as he comes, the warm liquid filling my mouth. I swallow as quickly as I can, not wanting to waste anything he's willing to give me.

Once he's completely finished, and I've licked his length clean, Josh leans down and lifts me under my arms, bringing me up to straddle his lap. He holds me close, my head leaning on his chest as both of our hearts beat rapidly.

Josh runs his fingers through my hair, something I've noticed he does a lot. It's a nice feeling, comforting somehow. Maybe it's because I haven't felt cherished like this for a very long time.

"I know I don't deserve you. I haven't done anything good enough to have someone like you fall into my lap. But I'll be damned if I'm ever going to give you up again, Emmy."

"I don't want you to give me up, Josh. But some things are even out of your control," I tell him.

"There is nothing that is going to keep me away from you, Emmy. I don't care what I have to do. I know you don't want to tell me what you're running from. But know that I will find out, and whether you like it or not, I will fix this for you, for us." He kisses the top of my head.

I don't know what to say in response to that. I don't know how to get him to stop looking. He's going to think very differently about me if he discovers what I've done. The best thing for him would be to forget about me again. I need to figure a way out of this mess. I can't let Josh drag himself down with me.

---

"YOU KNOW WHAT WE NEED?" Ella asks. She's currently sitting on the daybed next to me, sipping at some concoction in a fancy glass with a little umbrella. They just keep bringing these drinks out to us.

We've been lazing by the pool all afternoon, drinking and eating ourselves into a food coma. Now Ella's all pepped up again.

"No, what do we need?" I laugh. It may be the drinks, but I like the free feeling I currently have. I'm not lost in my internal monologue, my own inner nightmare, for once. I just feel free.

"We need to go dancing. Yep, get up. We're going dancing." She jumps up and pulls at my arm.

"Dancing, I can't go dancing. Besides, look around, Ella. We're in the middle of bloody Timbuctoo. Where do you think there is to go dancing around here?" I wave my arms.

"Well, I just happen to know a little country pub about thirty minutes down the road." She smiles, proud of herself.

"I know the place you're thinking of. I went to school in this town, remember? That's not a pub we need to be at." How can I talk her out of wanting to go out? What if someone notices me? Although it appears nobody is even looking for me, which just freaks me out more. There is no way they haven't discovered what I've done.

"Come on, get up. It'll be fun. Besides, I need to go dancing. I need to let off some steam." She pouts at me.

"What about Josh?" I ask. There is no way we're both getting off this farm without him noticing. He thinks I haven't seen him lurking in the shadows every twenty minutes, watching us. But I've noticed. He stands there for at least five minutes before going back inside. Then twenty minutes later, he comes back out and watches again.

"Emily, I grew up with two very overbearing big brothers. I know a thing or two about sneaking out. *Trust me*. No one's going to notice we're gone until it's too late." She winks.

This could be my opportunity to get away from Josh, before I drag him down into my mess. My heart hurts at the thought of leaving him. Although I know it's for the best, it's the last thing I want to do.

"Okay, let's do it. But we need to change first. We cannot go into that pub looking like this." I point to both of our bikini-clad bodies.

"Woohoo, yes! You're already my favourite sister-in-law," Ella shrieks.

"I'm not your sister-in-law, Ella," I remind her for what seems to be the tenth time today.

"*Yet*, but you will be," she says as she takes hold of my hand and drags me through the house like she owns the place, which, I guess, she kind of does.

---

SITTING IN THE BOOTH, in this little old country pub, I can't help the feeling of being watched. I've been overtly looking around for the last half an hour, trying to figure out who it is that's watching me.

"Will you stop? You look like you just robbed a bank and are waiting for the cops to burst in here looking for you," Ella says from the other side of the booth.

She looks hot as hell and has not been short on drawing the attention of everyone in here. She's wearing a denim skirt and a black singlet, complemented by a pair of tan and black

Ariat cowgirl boots. Her dark hair falls in two perfectly sculpted braids.

I'm not sure where the hell she got these outfits from; it's almost like she was planning this trip for longer than she admits. She put me in a little pair of denim cutoffs and a white blouse that falls off one shoulder. I'm also wearing a pair of tan and aqua Ariat boots, my hair hanging in loose curls.

When I looked in the mirror before leaving the house, the first thought I had was that I looked like me. The old me, the naïve eighteen-year-old, who left this little country town without so much as a plan.

Unlike now. Now, I do have a plan. A plan, which involves sneaking out the back door of this pub and hitch-hiking out of this town. I don't care where I end up. I just know I need to get my mess away from Josh. I shouldn't have come back here. He shouldn't be dealing with my issues.

"Ella, can you promise me something?" I ask her.

"Depends on what it is," she answers while sipping at her beer. With each sip, she screws her face up. She hates it, but refused to order anything else in a pub.

"Promise me you'll look out for Josh when I'm not around anymore."

Ella puts her drink down before gripping my hand. "You're not going anywhere, Emily. I get that you think you probably need to, but please reconsider whatever it is you're planning. Josh needs you just as much as you need him. Don't do this to him, please."

"I'm not planning anything; some things are just out of our control," I lie. "I've gotta pee. Can you order me another beer please?" I ask her.

"Sure," Ella says with a sad smile. I think she knows something. But how could she possibly know what I'm planning to do?

I give her the bright, fake smile I mastered in high school and head towards the bathroom. Once I make it to the hallway, I chuck a left and head through the back kitchen area. No one even looks in my direction as I beeline for the back door. My heart hammers the whole way.

What am I actually doing? I don't want to leave. But I can't stay either. I'm doing the right thing by Josh. I have to leave so he doesn't get in trouble for me being around.

I push the heavy door open and step out into the alleyway. The door closes with a loud clanging sound of metal hitting metal. I get two steps down the alley before a hand wraps around my mouth and I'm pushed into the wall.

# Chapter 16

## Josh

I've been looking into finding out everything I possibly can about Trent Owens—the name Emily was looking up on my laptop. Her search didn't bring any results. So far, I've managed to discover he's a dirty fucking cop who lives in Adelaide. What the fuck is his connection to Emily?

She also searched her own name, which again, brought up no results. Just like Sam said, it's as if Emily never existed. I know that she's been abused. I can see the signs. I can still see the slight yellow bruises. If it was this Trent asshole who caused them, I at least now have a target to unleash my demons on.

Then I remember that there is someone else deserving of my wrath. Someone here on this farm who I've yet to deal with.

I make my way to the shed where that fucking stable hand is being kept on ice. The stale stench assaults me as soon as I walk through the doors. The smell of faeces and piss (as well as the stench of the fucker's fear) hangs in the air.

Pulling my shirt over my head, I hand it to one of the guys standing at the door. In return, he gives me a questioning look. "It's one of my favourites. I don't want to get blood on it." I shrug.

"What's your name?" I ask the fucker who's hanging limply from the chains.

One of his eyes is already swollen shut. He stares at me through the other, as he contemplates how to answer the simple question.

"It really doesn't matter either way, but I do prefer to know the names of stupid cunts. I'd hate to one day call my children the name of some dead fucker who should have known better."

I walk slowly over to the table, which is currently housing a lineup of knives. I pick up a big, heavy, serrated blade and weigh it around in my hands. Putting it down again, I choose a lighter one.

Just for dramatics, I pick up the whetstone and start polishing the blade, even though it's already razor sharp.

"You still haven't given me a name," I say as I stop in front of the fucker.

"Glen. The name's Glen." He shakes as he speaks.

"Glen, how long have you worked here?" I ask him.

"Three years, sir," he says proudly. I'm not sure what the fuck he's proud about.

"Three years. I'm sure within those years, you've heard of how I can sometimes be a little… *unstable*. So why the fuck would you think it's a good idea to corner my girlfriend in a fucking stable in her own home?" I scream.

The word girlfriend does not sit well with me. Emily is so much more than a girlfriend, although I'm not sure there is a word to describe what she is to me. I might settle for wife. I wonder if I can get away with a quick wedding like my brother somehow managed. He married Ella over a fucking dinner with her family. Papers signed, sealed and delivered within hours.

"I-I-I didn't know she was your girlfriend, sir."

"So that makes it all right? You didn't know she belonged to me, so you have the right to scare her and trap her in a stable?" I ask.

"No."

"That's right. Unfortunately for you, she does belong to me, which means I plan on making an example out of you. I can't exactly have people thinking they can mess with what's mine. Especially her."

I walk around him, debating what I'm going to do first. All of my pent-up anger, resentment and frustrations are about to be unleashed on this fucker.

---

THREE HOURS, that's how long I dragged out Glen's death, keeping him conscious enough to know what was happening and that the end was near, but not giving him the out he so desperately begged for. It was gruesome—probably some of my best work yet.

I had three men in that room run for a trash can to empty their stomachs. I'm debating whether or not I need fuckers that weak on my security detail. If they can't handle a little blood and guts, then what good are they?

Finally showered, in clean clothes and sitting back at my desk, I'm about to start digging into this Trent fucker when Paul enters the office.

"Ah, boss?" he asks pensively, stepping inside with a look I don't ever like to see on the face of my head of security.

"What happened?" I ask, getting up and walking around the desk.

"Nothing, *yet*. But Mrs. McKinley and Emily are about to head into town. They're planning on going to Hughes Pub," he says.

"Ella and Emily are going to Hughes? Follow them, but not close enough that they know. I want at least five men placed around the pub before they even enter." Picking up my wallet, phone and keys, I'm out the door.

Let's see what trouble these two find themselves in at Hughes. Why the fuck Emily would go there, I have no idea. Ella, I get; she doesn't know how rough that place can be. She also has a rebellious streak. But Emily doesn't have a rebellious bone in her body; she's the straight-A student. The kid who was literally friends with everyone and couldn't stand the thought of someone not liking her. That someone being me. She knows what Hughes Pub is like, the kind of people who choose to hang out there. Why the fuck would she want to go there?

Unless she's still got it in her head that she needs to leave… No, she can't. I won't let her destroy us before we've even had a chance to begin.

"Paul, I want your eyes on Emily the whole time. Do not let her out of your sight. Have someone at the front door. I'll be at the back door behind the pub," I demand. I'm struggling to contain my anger right now. The thought of losing her again does not sit well with me.

"Sure, boss," he says as he leaves, already talking into his earpiece.

Heading out to the garage, I jump on my black Ducati Superleggera V4, choosing speed over anything else right now. I want to be able to get to the pub before the girls arrive. I want to see them walk in. And if my suspicions are right, I want to be there at the back door when Emily walks out.

The whole way to the pub, I hope that I'm wrong. I know… hope is a bitch, but I really fucking want to be wrong about this. Can I really keep her here if she doesn't want to be here? No, I can't. I know she wants to be here; I know she thinks she's doing the right thing by wanting to leave.

If only she would tell me what the fuck has her running scared, I'd be able to fucking fix it. We'd be able to move forward. I want more than anything to help her, to give her the future she should have already had.

Pulling in behind the bar, I hide the bike next to a dumpster and wait. About fifteen minutes is all it takes for Ella and Emily to pull up in a fucking town car. How the fuck did Ella manage to get a town car all the way out here? Maybe she's a little more resourceful than I gave her credit for.

I am a little impressed, that is, until they come into full view and I see what they're both fucking wearing. Or, more accurately, what they're not wearing, which would be fucking clothes. My eyes are pinned on Emily; she's wearing little fucking denim shorts with a white shirt that doesn't even cover both shoulders. Those damn cowgirl boots she's wearing are going to look fucking good wrapped around my waist later tonight.

I have to adjust myself in my jeans; just the sight of her

has my cock hard as a fucking rock. The thought of every other fucking guy in that bar getting their eyes on her is not sitting well with me.

As much as I want to barge in there and drag her ass back home, I can't. I need to know if she's planning to run or not. I need to know if I'm all in, while she's got one foot out the door. It's driving me fucking insane, more than I usually fucking am.

After twenty minutes of waiting, that little fucking bitch, hope, makes an appearance again. I know better than to entertain her, but I do anyway, that is, until the back door slams open and shut and out walks a leggy blonde—one I know very well.

I can't believe she's doing this. She's in a fucking back alley. Anything could happen to her out here. Is she that hell-bent on leaving that she's willing to put herself in danger?

As soon as the door shuts, my hand wraps around her mouth and I'm pushing her up against the brick wall. I'm an asshole, I know, but we've also already established this. I let my emotions get the better of me, which is always the fucking case when it comes to Emily.

"Going somewhere, Emmy?" I ask into her ear.

I feel her whole body relax when she notices it's me who's got a hold of her. Where most other people would be shitting themselves, she's thanking the gods that it's me and not someone else.

She shakes her head no before biting down hard on my hand and stomping on my foot. The shock of her standing up for herself makes me loosen my grip. She doesn't miss the opportunity to slip out of my grip and turn around. When she does, I'm staring down the barrel of a Glock.

I can't help but be proud of her right now. She's taking a

stand; she's showing the fighting spirit that I always knew she had. And I fucking love it.

"What on earth are you smiling at, Josh?" she asks, not moving the gun at all.

"A couple of things really. One, I'm so fucking proud of you right now—you have no idea. Two, you look hot as fuck. And three, if it's at all possible, I think I might have fallen in love with you even more in the last minute."

"That's messed up. You realise I'm the one pointing a gun at you, right? You should be hating me right now. You should want nothing to do with me. You should be moving away, not closer!" she screams.

"Emmy, there is nothing you could possibly do that would make me hate you, *ever*! I want everything to do with you, and I'm never walking away. You step back, I'm following you."

"No, Josh, you need to let me go." Her voice is quiet, her hands shaking a little.

"You're going to have to shoot me then. Because I'm not letting you fucking leave me, Emmy. Why? Tell me why? Tell me what the hell has you so determined to leave me? I know I can be a little much at times. Okay, *all the fucking time*. But I love you, Emmy. I've loved you since I was fifteen. I'd do anything for you. I want to give you the fucking world at your fingertips. Why is it not good enough?"

"You are enough, Josh. You've always been enough. I'm the one who's not okay. I messed up. I did something bad. I can't fix what I did. I can make sure that my mess doesn't get you in trouble though… and that's what I'm doing. I need to leave to protect you. Because I love you." Emmy drops the gun to her side, tears streaming down her face.

I wrap my arms around her. I don't care if she shoots me or not. I'm not fucking letting go. "You know that's the first time you've ever said I love you to me," I say, my voice hoarse. I feel tears on my own cheeks.

Emmy reaches up and wipes my face with her hands. "You are enough, Josh. Any girl would be blessed as hell to be loved by you. I'm sorry... I'm so sorry I can't give you what you need."

"All I need is you, Emmy. I don't need anything else, just you." I lean down gently, kissing her lips.

"You have me, Josh. You've always had me," she says. I can tell she still thinks she needs to leave.

"Let's go home." I'm not taking any chances on her not coming home with me. If she thinks she is staying out here on these streets, I'll be staying right here with her.

"Okay, take me home, Josh."

After calling Paul and telling him to drag Ella's ass home, I tighten my helmet on Emily's head and sit her in front of me on the bike. I don't rush home. I want time to just be with Emily without words, just us. That's what we need, time to be *just us* without any other outside forces playing against us. I know just the place we can go to do that.

# Chapter 17

## Emily

"Emmy, babe, wake up." Josh is kissing me all over my face. I slap a hand out to stop him. When I try to roll over to avoid him, he jumps on top of me, straddling my thighs.

"Why? I just want to sleep," I complain, slowly opening my eyes.

"I have a surprise," he says excitedly.

"That's nice. I hope you enjoy it."

"The surprise is for you, Emmy. Wake up." His fingers find my waist and start circling underneath my shirt.

I'm instantly awake. My eyes spring open. My hands land on his forearms, attempting to stop his movements.

"Okay, okay, I'm awake. Stop, please. I'll wake up." I laugh as my body thrashes under his attack.

"You'll wake up?" he asks.

"Yes, I'm awake." My hands are still on his forearms. As they roam up and down, it occurs to me that they are the definition of arm porn. Strong, muscled, tattooed arms. Arms that I feel the safest in, the most cherished in.

"You have nice arms," I blurt out. Josh laughs.

"Yeah? You like my arms? What else do you like?" he asks, lifting his shirt a little and showing off his abs, his very well-defined abs.

My eyes travel from the top of his jeans up to his chest. He's fully dressed. Where is he going?

"Why do you look so nice? Are you going somewhere?"

"Thank you. And yes, I am going somewhere. With you. *We* are going somewhere. Just as soon as you get up."

"Okay, but where are we going?" I ask. "Also, you need to get off me if you want me to get up."

"I really fucking like being on top of you. But we do need to get going. I left a dress for you in the bathroom," Josh says as he stands.

My body freezes. He left a dress for me in the bathroom? This is how it starts; he's going to control me just like Trent did. Why did I think he would be any different? The only difference is it hurts so much more, because it's Josh. I've built him up so much, put him on a pedestal so high, I can't even reach it.

But when it comes down to it, they're all the same. Men just want to control me, hurt me. I'm looking at the door and calculating if I can make it there before he catches me. I can't, so my eyes search the room for anything that I can use to defend myself, or cushion the blow.

"Babe, did you hear what I said?" Josh's voice breaks through my internal hell.

I should have been listening. What's he going to do when

he finds out I wasn't paying attention? I don't know what to say, so I don't say anything at all.

"What's wrong?" he asks as he walks back towards me.

"Uh, nothing. I'll get dressed. Thank you." My voice is robotic, monotone, just how Trent used to prefer me to answer.

"Something's wrong. Whatever is going through that pretty little head, forget it. You are safe here, Emmy. If you have something to say, then say it. I want you to say what's on your mind. I want to be the one you tell your secrets to, the one you share your fears with, your happy thoughts with. I want them all. I'm selfish like that." He winks before pulling my stiff body into his arms.

"I… what if I don't like the dress? Will you be mad?" I whisper.

Josh pulls his head back and tilts my chin up. I flinch away from his touch. I see his jaw clench, his eyes narrow, and he takes a deep breath. I wait for it, for his anger over my question.

When his eyes open, all I see in them is love, patience and understanding. "Emmy, if you don't like the dress, throw it out. I don't care what you wear. You wear whatever you want. I didn't pick the dress to take away your choice. Ella left it at the door this morning and said to give it to you. I just moved it to the bathroom. That's all."

I feel so stupid. Why do I always think the worst? Why do my thoughts always put Josh in the same category as Trent? He has never done anything to deserve my doubt.

Well, maybe all the shit he did in high school… But we all do stupid shit when we're young.

"I'm sorry. I don't know… I'm sorry," I tell him. I don't even know how to explain what was going through my mind.

"You have nothing to be sorry about, Emmy. Now, how about we finish getting ready so I can show you the surprise?"

"Okay."

---

AN HOUR LATER, we are pulling up to a private airstrip. I wait for Josh to come around and open my door; he has a thing about wanting to open my door all the time. To be honest, I like it. Stepping out, I hold down the fabric of the dress I'm wearing to make sure it doesn't blow up in the wind.

The dress Ella left was beautiful. A bright yellow sundress. It has a corset waist with a light cotton fabric skirt that hangs loosely to the midpoint of my thighs. I put my hair up in a high ponytail, which I'm thankful for now. This wind would have played havoc on my curls.

"Why are we at an airport, Josh?" I ask him.

"I'm taking some time off. We're going to get away for a few days. Or weeks." He shrugs.

"I can't go anywhere. I don't even have a passport. Where are we going?"

"You don't need one for where we are going. And we are going to one of the family vacation homes. Don't worry, we're not leaving the country. Come on." He takes hold of my hand and starts leading me towards the runway, where there is a small jet with the McKinley Industries logo on the side of it.

"You have a jet?" I ask. Of course, the McKinleys have a jet. Is there anything they don't have?

"You know all of this is going to be yours when I can talk you into marrying me?" Josh laughs.

But I don't laugh. I try to smile at him, but it's strained.

I'm not sure that I can ever get married so I decide to change the subject. It's not a discussion I can have right now.

"So how long is the trip?" I ask.

"It's a few hours. But don't worry, I've got plenty of ideas on how we can use the time wisely." He smirks.

"Oh yeah, did you pack a deck of cards or something?"

"I was thinking more along the lines of the mile high club kind of activities. You ever joined the mile high club?" he asks.

I'm just about to tell him no, that I have not, when he interrupts me.

"Don't answer that. I was thinking today could be a day where I don't have to kill anyone."

"You wouldn't actually kill them. But, just in case you're still wondering, no, I have not ever joined the mile high club."

"Make no mistake, Emmy, I'm crazy enough to kill any fucker who has ever laid a hand on you. Whether you wanted them to or not. You and I both already know that."

What the hell do you say to that? I have nothing. Again, Josh leaves me speechless. Somehow, I do believe he is just that crazy. I remember the look he had when he was holding the knife to that guy's throat in the stable. He was more than ready to take his life. And he wouldn't lose any sleep over it.

Me? I took a life and I'm left with his ghost haunting my dreams every night… and this god-awful feeling of someone watching me constantly. I look back over my shoulder and I swear I see a figure in the distance next to a shed. My steps stop and I look again. Is this it? Has someone found me?

"Emmy, you good?" Josh asks.

"Ah, yeah, sorry. I thought I saw someone." I turn back around and continue walking. Josh glares over his shoulder in the direction I was looking, then he turns back and wraps his arm around me. He starts typing out a message as he guides me up the stairs of the plane.

I stop at the entrance of the cabin. This is not an ordinary plane. This is fancy with a capital F. I feel so out of place. When I see the two stewardesses glaring in my direction, I want nothing more than to run off the plane.

Their looks change when they see Josh step in behind me. "Mr. McKinley, welcome back. I've set up your usual spot with your drink ready for you. I'm sorry… I didn't realise you were bringing a guest. Can I get you anything else?" The blonde bombshell bats her lashes at him.

I don't like her. I'm ready to rip those eyelashes off her damn pretty face. Let's see how she bats them when she doesn't have any.

"Josh?" I turn my head to look at him. "I'm gonna need you to hold my hand right now," I tell him. I figure holding hands helps calm his fire down, so maybe it will help with mine.

Josh's eyes open in surprise. He looks from me to the stewardess. He takes hold of my hand, pulling me into him. His lips slam down on mine and he claims me in front of both stewardesses. I do nothing to stop him; instead, my tongue hungrily meets his.

When he finally pulls away, he smiles down at me before turning to the stewardess. "Crystal is it?" he asks the blonde one.

"Yes, sir." She beams at him.

"You're fired. Get the fuck off my plane," he growls as he walks past her, dragging me behind him.

"But-but… I've worked for your family for years. You can't just fire me," she stammers out.

Josh stops walking and steps in front of me. "You see that

name embroidered onto the seats? That's my name. I very much can fire you and I just did. Don't make me repeat myself."

"Are you crazy?" she yells at him. Something in me snaps. I've always hated when people call Josh crazy. He's not crazy, just different. Okay, maybe a little crazy, but he's my kind of crazy. No one else is going to get away with calling him names.

I step in front of Josh. He lets me move him aside, allowing me to get in front of him. There's a drink on one of the side tables. I don't know what's in it or whose it is, but right now I don't care. I pick it up and throw the liquid at the stupid bitch.

"He's not crazy. But if you call him any more names, you're about to see just how *crazy* I am," I threaten over her shrieks.

"You stupid bitch!" she screams and starts charging towards me. Before I can even blink, I'm pushed behind a big body. When I finally look around the wide shoulders obstructing my view, I see that Josh has the woman up against the wall of the plane. His hand is wrapped around her throat.

Shit, this escalated way too much. Josh's body is vibrating as he holds her in place but I am blocked by the figure in front of me. I can't get to him.

"Do you want to know what happened to the last person who threatened her?" He tilts his head behind him, in my direction. The woman doesn't answer, but he continues.

"I took my time. It wasn't quick. Three hours, he held out for three hours before I finally let him die. Do you know how it feels to have your skin removed from your body, bit by bit? To watch pigs eat the fingers and toes that have been cut off? All the while, knowing the rest of your body will end up in the pigpen too?"

The girl goes white. Surely, he didn't… did he? Even

though I know he's probably telling the truth, I can't bring myself to look at him any differently. I saw him shoot someone right in front of me, yet I never thought of it again. He does that to me, the Josh fog. Whenever I'm with him, it's like the rest of the world doesn't exist. It's just us.

Right now, I need that. I need it to be just me and him again. "Josh, I-I need…" I don't even know what I need. What do I say to get him to let her go? I try to step around the hulking man who's blocking my way, but he doesn't let me.

"If you don't move out of my way, I'm going to shove that gun—the one I can clearly see under your jacket—so far up your ass you'll be shitting bullets for weeks." I fold my arms over my chest and wait for the man to move.

The whole plane goes silent, all bar Josh, who is currently laughing under his breath. What the hell is so funny?

I look up at the guy in front of me; he doesn't look impressed. Oh shit, I then realise what I just said. Where the hell did that even come from? I take a step back, my throat dry.

I hear Josh yell, "Fuck!" but my eyes don't leave the hulking guy. Although he hasn't moved, my feet are still stepping away from him, that is, until my back hits a chair and I can't move any further.

# Chapter 18

## Josh

Seeing Emily stick up for me, wanting to defend me, is the biggest fucking turn on ever. My cock is painfully hard right now. Hearing her threaten Paul for not letting her past him, that made my day.

My girl is starting to come out of her shell, starting to say what's really on her mind. And I fucking love it. What I don't love is the look of terror that immediately came over her face after she told him she'd shove his gun so far up his ass he'd be shitting bullets.

Not even I could have come up with that line. It's not one I'll be forgetting in a hurry. Paul might not be impressed, but I'm proud as punch with her.

"Deal with *that*. Make sure she leaves quietly," I tell Paul, motioning to the stewardess who just escaped my wrath. I have more important things on my mind now; for one, my brain is counting the minutes until we are in the air and I can finally get to bury my cock into Emily.

I can't fucking stand the look of fear on her face, and the fact that I know where that fear has come from. At least I suspect where it's come from anyway. She's afraid of repercussions for speaking out, for threatening a guy on my payroll. I don't give a shit who she wants to threaten. I'll keep reassuring her that she's safe, for as long as it takes to sink in. She never has to sensor herself around me. If anyone else doesn't like what she has to say, they can find the fucking door, because she is the queen of this castle. She just doesn't know it yet.

Walking up to her and caging her against the seat she's backed herself into, I lean down and whisper in her ear, "Emmy, you are safe here. Don't ever be afraid of anyone when I'm around. I'll never let anyone hurt you. You know that, right?"

"I'm sorry. I shouldn't have said that," she apologises.

"Yes, you should have. You should always say what's on your mind. And never be sorry for it, babe. I fucking love your mouth, every word that comes out of it. Not to mention, how it feels wrapped around my cock. Fuck!" I have to adjust my cock in my jeans. Emily looks down at my hand then back at me with wide eyes.

"I'm always hard when I'm around you, but I almost came in my fucking jeans when you wanted to defend me. You don't need to by the way. I don't care what people say about me. But fuck, I love that you do." I kiss along the side of her neck and up to her ear, before sucking the lobe into my mouth.

Emily's arms go around my neck, and she pulls me in closer. "I don't like when people call you crazy. I never have. It makes me so angry I want to rip out their tongues and show them what crazy really looks like," she says.

I laugh. I could not imagine Emily actually doing any of that. She's always been sweet little Emmy, who is friends with everyone. The people pleaser, who always has a smile on her face, or at least she used to.

That smile was always fake—I could tell. Even when we were kids, I could see the pain and loneliness disguised behind her smiles. I love the real Emmy, the one she lets me see. I could live without watching her experience those fucking nightmares and the constant fear, but it's only been a few days and we are making progress. I don't care if it takes the rest of my life. I will get her to be the strong, confident woman I know she can be.

"Remember that time in year eleven when Jessica projectile vomited all over John in science?" she asks.

"Ah, yeah. Why?"

"Well, I overheard her in the bathroom that morning, telling Cassie how you had asked her out, but she turned you down because you were too psycho for her." Emily smiles at me, one of her bright, real smiles. "I might have put something in her iced coffee at recess."

"You made her sick? Because you thought I asked her out?" I ask, confused.

"No, well, maybe. Mostly because she was calling you names. And a little bit because I was jealous and angry that you'd ask her out and not me." She pouts.

"Babe, I never asked her out. There was only ever one girl I wanted in high school."

"Who?" Emily pulls away from me and folds her arms over her chest.

"You, of course. I never dated or hooked up with anyone before you, Emmy," I confess. That night was not just *her* first time.

"Really, I was your first too? You were so good at it I assumed you'd done it before."

"Well, it's not exactly a hardship to love you, Emmy. Come sit, we need to get ready for takeoff."

I lead her over to one of the four sets of chairs in this cabin. As soon as we are in the air, I plan on taking her into the bedroom and not coming out until landing time. Leaning across the seat, I buckle her seat belt for her.

"Thank you?" Emily questions.

"Trust me, it's my pleasure." I have to readjust my cock yet again; he's fucking raging to get out and into his home between Emily's thighs.

"You okay over there?" Emily raises her eyebrows at me.

"No, not at all," I grunt out.

"Sir, ma'am, can I get you all anything before we take off." The second stewardess, who has just been standing in the background the whole time, timidly approaches us.

"No, I'm good. Thank you. Emily, do you need anything?" I ask her. She's chewing on her bottom lip, contemplating if she can request something or not.

"Babe, whatever you want, I'll make sure you get it. What do you need?" I prompt.

"Uh, do you have a blanket at all?" Emily asks the stewardess.

"Yes, absolutely. I'll go get you one now." The stewardess, who's name I really should learn, walks away like her heels are on fire.

"You cold? Want me to get you a jacket?" I ask her. Why didn't I think to bring a jacket for her?

Emily shakes her head shyly. "I'm okay. A blanket is fine."

"Here you go, ma'am. Please let me know if you need

anything else. We're about to take off any minute." The stewardess walks away.

Emily kicks off her heels and folds her feet underneath her on the armchair. She places the blanket over her lap before stretching it out and spreading some of it over my thighs.

"Emmy, you don't need to share the blanket with me. I'm not cold. You keep it." I go to pull it off me, intending to wrap the whole thing around her legs, when she stops my movements.

"You need the blanket, Josh, trust me," she says sternly.

"Yes, ma'am." I laugh and keep the blanket on my lap. I'm not about to contradict her when she's being so forceful and insistent.

The plane starts its trip down the runway, with it, Emmy's hand lands on my knee, slowly creeping its way up my thigh. I don't stop her explorations. It's fucking hard (pun intended) not to grab her hand and place it directly over my cock.

Just as the plane takes off from the runway, Emily's fingers are undoing my belt, then my button, slowly unzipping my fly. The moment her tiny hand wraps around my cock, I let out the moan I've been fighting off.

"Argh, fuck!" My hips lift off the seat with her first stroke. Her thumb swirls around the tip, collecting the precum that's dripping freely. She lets go of my cock, and I'm just about to take her hand and force it back on there, when I watch her bring her thumb up to her mouth and suck it in.

Her eyes close with the gesture. "Jesus, are you purposely trying to kill me, woman? Because it's fucking working," I growl.

Her eyes now open, she releases her thumb with a plop sound. "No, I just wanted to get a taste of my new favourite flavour." She's quick to wrap her hand back around my cock. This time, she gets right to pumping me up and down.

Her grip firm, her strokes are a perfect mixture of fast and slow. I need to get inside her pussy now. If I can't get my cock in there, my fingers are going to have to be buried in her. The moment my hand slides under the blanket and up her thigh, she moves it away.

"Fuck, babe, I need to feel that sweet fucking pussy of yours," I grunt out.

"You want to feel how wet I am for you right now? Feel the juices dripping from me?" she asks.

Her words shock me, yet turn me on more *if that's possible.* "Fuck yes I do!" I pant as she increases the speed of her strokes.

"Mmm, you're going to have to wait. I'm busy right now, and I don't want to be distracted."

"Please, I need it," I beg. When she just shakes her head no, I have to ask, "At least tell me, are you dripping wet for me, Emmy. Is your pussy craving to be filled by my cock right now?"

"Yes." Her voice is husky, her cheeks flushed red as her body leans into me more. With that one word, I come hard all over her hand and my jeans.

"Fuck, Emmy, God!" I moan loudly, not giving a fuck who hears me. She might have wanted the blanket for privacy, but I don't give a shit who knows what we're up to back here.

"Shh, everyone is going to hear you," she whispers harshly.

"Let them. I want everyone to know that you're mine!" I tell her right as the seat belt sign goes off.

Thank God, finally. I rip both of our seat belts off, scoop Emily up and carry her into the bedroom.

"Wait, what? Oh my God, your plane has a bedroom?"

She squeals as I throw us both down on the bed. Me, on my back. Her, on top of me.

"We can discuss the floor plan of the plane later, Em. My cock needs to be buried inside you now," I growl as I unzip the zipper at the back of her dress.

"Oh, but you just, wow, okay," she says. I pull the dress over her head, her breasts bouncing free right in front of my face. She's left in only a pair of the littlest white lace panties.

"I hope you're not too attached to these," I say as my fingers trace the top of them.

"Why?" she asks.

Giving her my best smirk, I don't bother to answer her. Grabbing the material in both hands, I rip the lace in two. Then, lifting her hips, I position my cock at her entrance. Emmy's eyes go wide as I slowly sink her down onto me.

"Ah, fuck, this is fucking heaven," I moan, her tight, wet pussy gripping my cock like a damn glove. Once she's fully seated, she looks at me with shock. "This… is…" She cuts her sentence short. She seems unsure.

"This is…?" I push her to continue, pumping my hips up. She squeaks (yes, *squeaks*).

"Oh, God. That's good. It feels different," she says as she slowly wiggles around. I'm restraining myself from coming again already.

"Different? How? Good or bad?"

"Oh, it's good. I just don't know. I don't think I'm good at this. I've never…"

"You've never what?" I ask her confused. Then it hits me, she's never been on top before.

"You've never been on top before?" I smile as I repeat the sudden revelation.

"No, I wasn't allow…" Again, she stops mid-sentence. But

I got enough to know what she was going to say. I lay my hands under my head. As much as I want to take control and fuck her into the next galaxy, I want to give her something she desperately needs. I want to give her control, choice with her body and over what she's doing.

"This is your show, Emmy. You are in control. And trust me, there is no way you could do it wrong. Just having you sitting on my cock right now is everything right in the world. You do whatever you want to me. Nothing's off limits." I smirk and wait her out.

It takes only a minute before she smiles. "Anything I want?" she repeats.

"Anything," I confirm.

"Okay, but will you tell me if you don't like it?" she asks shyly.

"Sure," I lie. If she discovers something that she *does* like, I'll learn to love it if I have to. I'm not going to take this away from her. She's a goddamn fucking queen, and it's about time she realises it.

# Chapter 19

## Emily

Oh my God, I can't believe how good this feels. I've never been on top before. I didn't realise it would be so different. The kind of control I have right now is intoxicating. Josh is doing this for me. Handing the reins over, no matter how much I can see that he wants to take me. He's letting me explore, letting me feel like I have a say in how this goes.

My hands slide up under his shirt. Why the hell is he still dressed? This needs to change. Pulling at the fabric, I tell him, "Lose the shirt, *now*!" My hands tug it up. He obliges.

"If I must." Hc sits up slightly to pull the shirt over his head. His movements cause his cock to hit all different heights inside me. "Mmm, God." I grind my pelvis down on him harder, little sparks of pleasure going right through me.

My fingertips trail up his abs to his shoulder and I push

him back down. I can't believe I'm doing this. I've dreamt about having my way with this body, and now I actually get to.

I run my hands over his shoulders, down his arms and back up again. Leaning over, I lick around one of his nipples, lightly biting down on it.

"Fuck, Emmy, goddamn," he grunts out.

I pop my head up and smile. "You said anything!" I shrug my shoulders before ducking my head back down. I trail my tongue over the lines and swirls that mark his chest. When I reach the spot just over his heart—the spot with my name on it —I kiss it three times. One time for our past, one for the present, and one for the future I wish we could have.

Reaching his other nipple, I suck it into my mouth, biting down a little harder than the first time. I feel his cock twitch inside me so I do it again and again, as I start to move my hips up and down.

Sitting up straight, I pull his hands out from under his head. I need him touching me. I love seeing his tanned, tattooed skin against mine. I place his hands on my breasts. I don't have to guide him on what else to do. He rolls my nipples between his fingers, twisting slightly. My back arches as I continue to glide up and down on his cock.

I'm so close to coming, goosebumps erupting on my body as the cold air hits the tiny beads of sweat. I feel like a thousand bolts of electricity are circulating through me, and each time I bottom out on him, a flame is igniting higher and higher.

It's there. It's so close I can see it—*that release.* I just can't seem to reach it. I need something else, but I don't know what. "Josh, I need… something," I pant as I continue to chase my orgasm.

Josh sits up and repositions us with his back against the

bed. His hand comes up to my throat and he squeezes lightly. It's wrong, so wrong, to let him do that. It's even more wrong that I fucking enjoy it. The moment his hand wraps around my throat, my pussy gushes liquid. I can feel it all down my thighs.

The next thing I know, my body is tightening up and my muscles spasm as I come undone. I think I'm screaming. I'm not really sure if it's in my head, or if I'm actually making those noises. I don't really care either way.

My pussy convulses around his cock, like it can't get enough of him. I feel his cock get even bigger as it jerks inside me, painting my walls with his seed. As I come down from my high, I finally have enough brain cells working to notice that we have been having a lot of sex without protection. I'm trying to recall when I'm due for my birth control shot.

I collapse onto Josh's chest. His hands stroke my hair, my mind reeling at trying to remember that bloody date. I can't for the life of me remember. I should know this. The one time I stuffed up and forgot to get it, Trent made sure I learnt a lesson I'd never forget.

"I can hear you thinking. What's wrong? Did I hurt you?" Josh picks my head up, our eyes connecting. I shake my head no.

"No, I just… I can't remember," I tell him.

"Can't remember what?"

"When I last had my birth control shot," I say quietly. I wait for him to explode, for him to throw me off in disgust. He does none of that.

"That's all you're worried about?" He leans in and kisses me, ending the gesture way too soon. "Emmy, you know if you fall pregnant, we will be okay. You'd make a fucking great mother."

"You're not worried? Josh, we can't have a baby. *I* can't have a baby. I'm flat out looking after myself. How am I supposed to look after a baby?" I ask him.

"You have me. I love you. I'd never abandon you, Emmy. You wouldn't be alone."

"Do you even want kids, Josh?" There's something about the way he's phrasing his words that doesn't sit well. He's not talking about a child; he's talking about me. He'd look after *me*. He wouldn't leave *me*. But what about the hypothetical child who would be his as well?

"I want you, Emmy. It's not that I don't want kids. Because I want everything with you. But, let's be honest, I'm not normal. What if I don't love it, the baby? That's a very real possibility. There is one person I've met in my whole life, Emily, who I can honestly say I love, and I'm looking at her."

I think about what he's saying. He really has no idea just how great he would be as a father. If I ever do get to have a child (which, let's face it, *that* is not in my future), I wouldn't want it to be with anyone other than him.

"Josh, you are more capable of love than you give yourself credit for. You do love other people. There's your brother, your mum. Ella. It's not just me." I don't know how to get him to see how much he does love other people too.

"No, I might care about them a little. But it's not love, Emily. What I feel for you is different; it's more intense. I've never had that with anyone else."

"It's meant to be different. But that doesn't mean you don't love them. I loved my parents too, but not the same way I love you. With you, it's like you consume me, like every fibre of my being comes to life when I'm around you. I feel like I can do anything, be anything, with you. With my parents, I was heart-broken when each of them died. But the thought of something happening to you, I wouldn't survive that kind of loss. There wasn't a day that went by over the last four years that I didn't want to call you. That I wasn't thinking about you. Thoughts of you got me through some of my darkest moments."

I'm not sure I will ever be able to tell him all the details of what I've done, but he does deserve to know that he is loved, unconditionally, by me. That no one will ever measure up to him.

"Emmy, what happened to your mum?" he asks. Shit, how do I answer that? How do I tell him that I'm the reason my mum is dead?

"Emmy? You can tell me anything. There isn't a damn thing you can't tell me. What happened to her?" he presses on. I can't stop the tears from falling down my cheeks. Josh is patient. He swipes the wetness away and waits for me to speak.

"It-It was my fault. I should have known better. I shouldn't have…"

"Babe, it's okay, breathe. Try again. What was your fault?"

"My mum, he-he killed her because I tried to leave. I left… I did leave. But he found me, and the next day, he showed me… he showed me photos and a death certificate. It was my fault. If I didn't try to leave, my mum would still be here." I'm sobbing by the time I get it out. I've never said the words out loud. Oh God, I can't believe I just told Josh that. What is he going to think of me now? He's going to know that I'm the reason my mum is dead.

Josh squeezes my body tight against his; he holds my head on his chest. "I'm going to fucking rip him apart when I get my hands on that fucker," Josh growls.

He won't ever get the chance. I'm shaking. I try to snuggle in more, but I can't seem to get close enough. Maybe if I hold on tighter, he won't be able to walk away from me.

"Emmy, look at me," Josh says after a few minutes. I lift my head, expecting to see disgust on his face. Josh has a single tear trailing down his cheek. He's crying? Why?

"You didn't kill your mother, Emmy. What that bastard did to you was not your fault. And I want to know every little fucking thing he ever did. So that way, when I find the prick, he will know just what it feels like." Josh's voice is quiet, contradicting his harsh words.

I shake my head no. There is no way I can tell him everything. I can't…

"Emmy, your mum isn't dead. She's still in the same house you guys lived in when you left."

"What? No. I saw the pictures, Josh. I saw the death certificate. I went to her funeral!" I yell at him. Why is he being cruel? Is this it? Where it starts, the nastiness, the cruelty?

"Emily, stop. I'm telling you the truth. I've had someone do a little digging on you. That's how I found out there was a death certificate for you. I've seen your mother's too, but I've also seen photos of her around town. In her house. She isn't dead, Emily."

"No! You need to stop looking, Josh. You need to stop. You need to stop," I repeat the words over and over. I try to get off the bed. He doesn't let go of me.

"There will never be a day where I stop, Emily. You don't get it. I can't just let it go. I can't let that asshole breathe after what he's done to you. And I'm only guessing at what you've been through. When you're ready, you will tell me. Until then, I'm never going to stop loving you."

"Josh, she's really alive? Do you… do you have the photos?" I ask him. I need to see her, before I let myself hope.

# Chapter 20

## Josh

"Emmy, wake up. We're here." I kiss her forehead and run my fingers through her hair. I've just pulled up to one of the family farming properties in Western Australia. It took a five-hour plane trip and a three-hour drive to get out here. But this is the perfect spot to be alone with Emmy. No one comes to this cabin; the staff who work the farm live in housing on the other side of the property.

There is nothing to see but red dirt and dust. But I fucking love it out here. No fuckers to piss me off or get on my nerves. No need to attempt at being social, even though all I want to do is rip everyone's head off every other minute. This is the one place I've been able to just be me, without judgement.

I doubt anyone other than the staff here even knows this cabin exists. I built it three years ago, when I needed an escape from the world. I spent six weeks out here before I went back home and faced my father's rage. People think I'm psychotic and cruel, but I've got nothing on what that man could do. At a minimum, *I* have some limits. Or, at least, I like to think I do.

Emily's not budging. I get out of the car and jog around to her door. Reaching in, I get a whiff of that scent I want to surround every room of every house I own in. Emily, she's fucking mind-alteringly intoxicating, like I'm on a constant high when she's near me.

She stirs in my arms but doesn't wake up. She exhausted herself on the plane. Her breakdown tore me in half, just seeing her fall apart like that, hearing the small snippets she told me about what that fucker Trent did to her. I bury my head into her neck and breathe in. I need to calm the inferno that's blazing inside me.

Emily deserves this getaway; she deserves some happy memories—ones filled with being loved and worshiped like the fucking goddess she is. I don't care what it takes. I will give her as many of those moments as I can.

"Mmm, where are we?" she asks as I'm walking up the steps.

"This is one of the family farms; it's secluded. There's no one out here except you and me, Em. This is what I call fucking paradise."

"Okay, I'd like to be thoughtful and tell you that you can put me down. I won't though. I like being in your arms."

"Well, it's a good thing I like you being in my arms too."

Opening the door, I carry her through to the living room. Emily spots the windows at the back of the cabin.

"Oh my God! Josh, put me down. Put me down!" she shrieks.

"But you just said I could keep you here in my arms, Emmy."

"Yeah, but that was before I saw this. Put me down." She jumps out of my arms and practically runs over to the windows.

"Josh, it's so beautiful. I can't believe it. Look at them." She's pointing at the mob of brumbies in the fields. It's a sight, that's for sure.

"I knew your family had horses, but this is something else. Isn't it spectacular?"

"Yeah, it is. These aren't ours though, babe. These are brumbies; they're wild."

"I don't care. I love them. I could sit here for hours watching them."

"How about I cook us up something to eat. You can go sit out on the patio and watch them while you wait." I wrap my arms around her, trailing kisses up the side of her neck.

"Mmm, I can cook dinner. You've been driving for hours; you should sit down and relax."

"Emmy, go and sit outside. I'll bring you out a glass of wine. I want to cook for you. Let me cook for you."

"Okay, but I can help if you want."

"What I want is for you to go and sit down and watch the brumbies."

I wait until I see her settle into a lounge chair on the patio, before I head into the kitchen and find something to eat. I had some of the staff head up here today and stock up for us.

Deciding on omelettes, because I don't want to be away from Emmy for too long, I get all the ingredients out. I pour her a glass of red wine and put some grapes, cheese and crackers on a platter. Taking it out, I set the platter on the table next to her and hand her the wine.

"It's a little chilly out here. Do you want a blanket?" I ask her.

"Thank you. I'm not cold. I love it out here."

"Okay, I'm making omelettes. You do still eat eggs, right?"

"How did you know I ever ate eggs?" She smirks.

"I used to watch you eat in the school cafeteria. I'd watch as you'd suck on your spoon or fork and imagine that it was my cock you were wrapping your lips around." I shrug. I leave her with her mouth hanging open as I go back inside.

---

"I DON'T THINK I could eat another bite. Where on earth did you learn to cook like this?" Emmy says around the last forkful of food from her plate.

"I took classes. I find keeping busy helps."

"Helps with what?"

"The noise in my mind." I debate over how much to actually tell her. She knows I'm different, unhinged. But she doesn't know the extent of it. She doesn't really know how my mind works. I'm afraid if she did, she'd be running for the hills, not that I'd let her get far before I brought her back.

"Well, what else do you do to keep busy?"

I guess she's skipping the whole noise in my mind thing. She's the only person I've met that doesn't look at me like I'm crazy, or like they're scared I'm going to rip their hearts out.

"I ride?" I shrug.

"What, like horses? Bikes?"

"Horses, dirt bikes, road bikes, *you*." I smirk at her and watch the blush creep up her neck and face.

"We should go riding together someday. I haven't ridden for years."

"Well, you can ride me any day, babe. But I'm sure I can

rustle up a couple of Quarterbacks for us tomorrow if you want."

"Really? Yes!"

"I'd like to think your excitement is about the riding me option. But I'm pretty sure it's more for the horses."

Emily laughs, and I fucking love it. "Well, can I pick both options?"

"Emmy, you can have whatever you want. All you have to do is ask."

"Did you become a genie? What do I have to rub to get my three wishes?"

"I've got something you can rub." I raise my eyebrows at her. "You don't have to do anything, Em, and your wishes are boundless—*there is no limit to what I would do for you, give you.*"

"Mmm, okay. So how does this work? I just ask for something and you make it appear?" She laughs like it's a big joke.

"Sure, try it. What's something you've always wanted but never thought you could have?"

Emily thinks about it for a minute, then looks me in the eye as she says, "You."

"Well, that's an easy one, because you've always had me. You just didn't know it. What else?"

"Um, well, I've always wanted the *Beauty and the Beast* library. When I was a little girl, I used to pretend that I was Belle and I could go and save my daddy from the bad guys he was fighting. Then he died anyway. I very quickly learnt that fairy tales don't exist."

"I'm not too sure they don't exist, Emmy. Looks to me like you found your beast, because you sure as fuck are my beauty."

"Yeah, but you're not a beast. You're the nicest person I've ever met."

Okay, now it's my turn to laugh. Shit, how the fuck am I the nicest person she's met? "I'm pretty sure literally every other fucking person would lock you up in a nut house for that sentence."

"Okay, so you're an absolute asshole, a jerk, to everyone else. But to me, you're not—well, not anymore. And that's what matters to me."

"Wait, what do you mean *not anymore*? When have I been an asshole to you?"

"We don't have enough time to rehash high school. But for one, June, year ten, science class. You made sure we were lab partners for that assignment. But then you disappeared, and I had to do the whole thing on my own."

"Nope, I wasn't an asshole. I was protecting you from having to be partnered with all the other dumb fucks in that class. Besides, that class was seventy percent males; you would have ended up being partnered with someone else. You would have ended up studying with that person after school. They would have tried to hit on you. I saved you from that whole ordeal. Really, I'm like your regular knight in shining armour."

"I'm not sure what worries me more: the fact that you truly believe your own words, or the fact that I don't actually care about all the shit from high school."

"You didn't really have that bad of a time in school, did you? I really did try to make sure everyone was nice to you." I will go back and hunt the fucking idiots down if they didn't treat her well.

"Everyone was too scared not to be nice to me, Josh. I had lots of friends, but they were only my friends because they didn't want to be on your bad side. Not to mention, those girls who thought you would notice them more if they hung out with me."

"Like I would notice anyone other than you, Em. I'm sorry if I made your final years of school horrible. I really am. I was young and stupid."

"You didn't. You know, you're the first boy I ever crushed on. I tried so bloody hard to get your attention that first year. But nothing seemed to work. Then I gave up, thinking that you were just out to make my life hell. Until that party where you told me you loved me. That was one of the best nights of my life."

"You were supposed to be asleep. I can't believe you heard that whole conversation and didn't say anything. There was more said than just the fact that I love you."

"Oh, you mean like the part where you said you wanted to kidnap me and run away somewhere? Or that part where you said that I gave you hope, that you could see a better future when you looked at me?"

"Look around you, Emmy. I essentially have kidnapped you and ran away." I laugh, waving my arms around.

"Yeah, but I came willingly. You know, I would have followed you anywhere, even back then."

"I know, which is exactly why I stayed away from you. I would have only ruined you. I probably still will ruin you."

Emily looks at me, her eyes sad. "You can't ruin me, Josh. I'm already ruined and there's not enough duct tape in the world to fix me."

I get up and squat down in front of her chair. Taking her hands in both of mine, I look her directly in her eyes. "There is absolutely nothing wrong with you, Emily. You are perfect, beautiful inside and out. Anyone that tells you otherwise can go and fuck off."

"Can I use one of those magic wishes of yours?" she asks.

"Your wish is my command." I wink.

"I wish that you would pick me up right now, kiss me like it's the last time you're ever going to get to kiss me, and take me to bed."

That's a wish I can deliver on. Picking her up, I carry her into the bedroom. I lay her down, fall on top of her and do exactly what she just wished for. Then I kiss her like it's the last time we will ever kiss.

# Chapter 21

## Emily

*"Did you really think I'd let you get away that easily? Huh, that you could outsmart me?" he yells, picking up a vase and throwing it across the room.*

*"N-no, Trent, I'm sorry. I'm sorry. I wasn't thinking." I'm not sorry that I left; what I'm sorry for is that I didn't get far enough away before he found me.*

*"You weren't thinking. That's your damn problem, Emily. You're never fucking thinking. You keep making me punish you over and over again. Do you think I enjoy fucking punishing you?"*

*I know he does; the sick fuck gets off on it. "No, you don't need to punish me. I won't do it again. I promise."*

*"You're damn straight you won't fucking try it again. I'll make sure this is a lesson you'll never forget."*

*"Noooo!" I scream as I bring my hands up to cover my face. I know that was a mistake as soon as I hear the snap of my arm.*

"Emmy, wake up. Wake the fuck up!" Josh's voice is yelling at me.

My eyes snap open as I come face to face with Josh. He doesn't look so good. His jaw is clenched tight, and there's a dark storm brewing in his eyes. What happened? Why is he looking at me like that?

"Josh, what's wrong?" I ask.

"Nothing's wrong. Are you okay?"

He's lying. I can tell something is bothering him. I can tell he's on the verge of losing the plot. I'm not scared though. His hands are gripped firmly around my forearms. I wince at how tight his hold is, wriggling my arms a little. He immediately lets go and curses under his breath.

I nod my head. "I'm fine. What's wrong?" I ask again.

He doesn't say anything. Instead, he leans in and claims my mouth, his tongue circling around mine. I get lost in his kiss, in the passion, the love he puts into one simple gesture. My arms wrap around his neck, pulling him closer. No matter how close he is, it's never enough.

He pulls back, breaking my moment of bliss. "We have to leave this bubble and go home again."

"But I love our bubble. This has been the best week of my entire life. Why does it have to end?"

"I love our bubble too. Emmy, you are my bubble. It doesn't matter where we are, or who is around us—this bubble is ours to keep." Josh brings my hand up to his lips, kissing my palm before placing it over his heart. "I won't let anything destroy our bubble, Emmy."

"You can't stop the inevitable, Josh. Nothing this good lasts forever. Someone once told me that hope was a bitch best left alone."

"Well, that person was a fucking idiot, obviously." He rolls his eyes.

"Can we go riding before we leave?"

"Sure, babe. Hop up and get ready. I'll go out and saddle up the horses." He leans down and kisses my forehead before he leaves the room.

Stretching my aching muscles out before I even attempt to get out of bed, I welcome this kind of soreness. It's the result of the activities from the last week. It's been a week packed full of horse riding, hiking, and Josh. *So much Josh.* I shouldn't be enjoying intimacy after what Trent put me through for years, or at least I think I shouldn't… I've been so blissfully happy this last week here with Josh, I can almost trick my mind into believing the last few years were just a nightmare.

With Josh, everything is different. Every time we're intimate, it feels like the first time, new and exciting. He makes sure I'm always enjoying it. I've never had to fake an orgasm with him. Instead, I'm spent, fighting them off while trying not to combust every damn time he so much as touches me.

---

I MIGHT HAVE SPENT way too long in the shower under the hot water. When I walk out to the living room, the smell of bacon fills the air. Josh has insisted on cooking every meal since we arrived. He at least lets me help clean up afterwards. Who knew washing dishes could be so much fun?

I find Josh in the kitchen, just as he's placing a full plate on the bench. "Thought I'd have to come drag you out of the shower."

"Sorry, I lost track of time. This smells delicious." I sit

down at the bench in front of a plate full of bacon, sausages, scrambled eggs and hash browns. He must have had it cooked for a while; he's already cleaned up. The kitchen is pristine. I know Josh calls this a cabin, but it's no regular cabin.

This kitchen is something out of an interior decorating magazine. Pristine white marble benchtops, dark-stained wooden cabinets. The sink is a huge, square, farm-style basin. I love it. It's got such a homey feel to it. I could almost picture raising kids here, having a little soccer team full of tiny Joshes. If only that dream was a possibility…

"Don't be sorry. *I'm* sorry I wasn't smart enough to join you in there." Josh winks.

"It would have been a lot more pleasurable if you had, but then I wouldn't have all of this in front of me right now." I shove a forkful of the fluffiest eggs into my mouth. "Mmm, damn, these are good."

"Fuck, Em, my cock just went from half to a hundred, watching you eat eggs. It's like high school all over again."

"Except now you're not too chicken shit to talk to me." I smirk.

"Well, there's that." Josh laughs.

Over the past week, I've come out of my shell a lot. I still second guess myself (and the things I say) most times. But Josh has really put a magic spell over me, allowing me to be more myself than I've been in years. I can joke around with him and not get backhanded for talking back. I can ask him for something and he somehow makes it appear.

"Eat up. The horses are ready and there's a spot I want to show you." He points at my plate as he sits down next to me.

"You mean there's still places we haven't been to yet?" We've spent hours out on the horses every day we've been here. I love it. It's so freeing, being in the bush on horseback and riding through all the trails.

Josh laughs. "Babe, this property is over three hundred hectares. We've barely scratched the surface."

I shovel the food into my mouth, eager to get back out on the horses. It takes me no longer than ten minutes to finish the whole plate. "Okay, I'm ready."

"Well, don't let me keep you. Let's go," Josh says, grabbing my hand and leading me outside.

"Hi, Cherry girl," I coo at the horse I've come to think of as my new best friend. Josh approaches me with the helmet he insists I wear, even though he doesn't bother wearing one himself.

"Thank you." I'm not going to admit it any time soon, but I secretly love his protectiveness over me.

"Jump up." He waits for me to be settled on Cherry before getting on Herbert. Herbert's a big, brown, grumpy Quarterback who's perfectly matched to Josh.

"Lead the way." I smile as innocently as I can. I love riding behind him. I get to watch that perfect ass of his bounce around.

"Try not to get too distracted." Josh smirks as he leads us out into the fields.

It takes an hour for Josh to pull up to a stop. He jumps down from Herbert. I follow his lead and dismount from Cherry. However, I may have been a little too distracted by that ass of his in those tight denim jeans, because I somehow misstep and end up falling. I let out a little squeal as I land on my side, my left hip and arm hitting the ground.

Within seconds, Josh is by my side, panic clear all over his face.

"Fuck, Emmy, are you okay? No, of course you're not okay. Fuck. Stay still. Don't move. Where does it hurt?"

I can't help but laugh. I go to get up but he stops me. "Emily, do not move. What if somethings broken? You just fell off a fucking horse. Stay still." He pulls at his hair and looks around the bush we're currently isolated in, like somehow someone's going to pop out and help him.

"Joshua, stop it. I'm fine. I didn't fall off the horse. I just misstepped. That's all. It's just a scrape, see?" I hold my arm out for him to have a look—it really *is* just a scrape. I'm not sure if I should tell him my hip hurts like hell though. I can already feel the bruise forming.

"You're not fine. You're bleeding, Emmy. Shit, what do I do? Should I call the helipad? Fuck, there's a doctor on the farm. I'll get him to meet us at the cabin."

Josh goes over to his saddle bag and pulls out what looks like a mobile phone from the dinosaur era.

"Yeah, doc, I'm gonna need you to get to the cabin. My girlfriend fell from the horse." He's silent for a minute before he speaks again. "No, the horse wasn't moving. She fell when she was dismounting."

I'm officially mortified. I get up and dust myself off. "I'm really fine, Josh. I don't need a doctor."

"We'll be there in an hour. I expect you to be ready by the time we make it back." Josh hangs up the phone.

"We need to get you back to see the doctor and make sure you are fine." His eyes travel up and down my body, more than once.

"Josh, trust me, it's just a scrape. Besides, I've had much worse than this before. I'll be fine."

"How do you know nothing's broken, Emmy? Shit, what if there's internal bleeding, or worse?"

"I've had broken bones before, Josh. I'd know if something were broken."

Shit, that was not the right thing to say, judging by the look on his face. "What broken bones have you had, Emmy? And how did you break them?"

I shake my head no. "You don't really want to know that, Josh. Let's not ruin the end of this trip."

Josh comes up to me, walking me into the tree. My back pressed up against it, he cages me in, one hand above my head with the other running through my hair. "What broken bones have you had, Emmy?"

"Uh, my arm?" It comes out as more of a question.

"Which arm? What else?"

"This one," I say, holding up my right arm.

"What else?"

"What else *what*?" Maybe I can use the dumb blonde card.

"What other bones have you had broken, Emmy?"

I don't miss his wording: not what bones have *I broken*, but what bones have I *had* broken.

I close my eyes. I can't see the look of disgust that's bound to happen when I tell him. "Ribs, mostly my ribs. A few fingers and toes. My arm—twice." I wince.

"Emmy, open your eyes," Josh whispers. I can feel his breath against my lips.

"Never again," he says as his mouth meets mine.

His kiss is quick, too quick. I need more.

"You're riding with me. Come on."

Josh picks me up, sitting me on top of Herbert before climbing up behind me. My hip is hurting like hell. But I don't say anything. It's nothing I can't handle.

He rides slowly back to the cabin, while guiding Cherry along next to us. I'm not going to lie—it's nice riding with Josh like this. I can feel him all around me, the warmth of his body mixed with the scent of his woodsy cologne surrounding me. By the time we make it back to the cabin, all I want to do is rip his clothes off and attack him.

"The doctor should be here by now," Josh says as we stop in front of the stables.

"I really don't need a doctor, Josh. You're overreacting. It's just a scrape."

"Humour me then, will you?" Josh says as he leads me into the cabin. The doctor is waiting in the living room. He stands up when he sees us.

"Mr. McKinley. Nice to see you, sir."

"Doc," Josh replies as he shakes his hand. "This is my girlfriend, Em—"

"Ember. And I really am fine. Josh is overreacting." I cut Josh off just as he's about to say my name. I didn't think about this. Fuck. Josh doesn't say anything, but he is sending me a very inquisitive look right now.

"*Ember* here fell off Cherry as she was dismounting. She landed on her left side." Josh looks right at me as he annunciates my alias.

"Okay, how about you take your jeans and shirt off and we'll have a look," the doctor says.

"Like fuck you will!" Josh yells. I grab his arm as he starts heading for the doctor.

"Sir, I need to be able to examine her." The doctor stands firm without backing away.

"You can do that with her clothes on her fucking body," Josh growls.

I, however, let go of Josh's arm, stand in front of him and strip my shirt over my head. Let's see how much he thinks I need a doctor now.

"What the fuck? Emmy, put that back on."

"You're the one who wanted the good doctor here to check me out, even though I'm fine. Well, now you have to deal with it. He's right. How's he supposed to see if anything's broken if I'm all covered up." I smile.

"Fuck, if I see one second of anything that I deem inappropriate, I will put a fucking bullet in your head, doc."

"No worries. I assure you I'm old enough to be Ember's grandfather. I'm also a professional, which is why you hired me in the first place."

"Okay, let's get this over with so you can go home, doctor. I'm so sorry Josh is wasting your time."

"Your wellbeing is far more important than anyone's time, Em." Josh sits down on the couch. His eyes do not leave the doctor's.

I undo my jeans and start pulling them down. I can't help the wince I let out when the denim rubs over my hip.

"Fuck, I knew something was wrong!" Josh is up and beside me like The damn Flash.

"I'm fine. It's just a little bruise."

"Stop, let me help." Josh removes my hands from my jeans and starts tugging them down. When I wince again, he stops and pulls a knife (one I didn't even know he had) from his ankle. Holding the denim as far away from my skin as he can, he slices it in half all the way down my left leg.

"Fucking Jesus, hell. Fuck. Em, that is not a fucking little bruise. Goddamn it," Josh curses and yells. He throws the knife behind me. I hear it hit a wall with a thud. I flinch and step away from him. I can't help it—it's instinctual.

He notices right away. "Emmy, I'm sorry. Sorry…" he says quietly as he slowly steps into me.

"Come, sit down—no, you should be on a bed. She should probably be in bed, right, doc?"

"Ah, let me have a look." The doctor bends down and lightly presses around my hip. For a bit, he's just prodding and poking.

"It's just some bruising. Apply ice twenty minutes on, ten minutes off, and rest. Don't go doing anything strenuous," the doctor finally says.

He packs all his equipment away before asking, "Mr. McKinley, can you walk me out?"

"Ah, yeah, sure." Josh picks up a throw and wraps it around me before sitting me on the couch. "I'll be back with an icepack. Don't move."

"Okay."

I know I said I wouldn't move, but after they leave the room, I follow anyway. I need to know what the doctor has to say. What if he recognised me?

Leaning against the wall, I catch bits of their hushed voices.

"Multiple wounds, scars," the doctor says.

"I'm aware," Josh grits out.

"I should be reporting this. It's ethical to report it. She's clearly in some type of trouble, Josh." Huh, he's calling him by his first name. They must be closer than they made it out to be.

"I appreciate your discretion, doc. I'm looking into it. Believe me when I say she *will* get her justice," Josh says.

I limp to the couch. I just get settled in when Josh comes back over. "You know, all you have to do is ask," he says.

"Ask what?"

"What the doctor had to say. I'd never lie to you, Emmy."

"Sorry…"

"Don't be. Here, hold this on your hip. I'm going to pack the car. Do you need anything else?" He hands me an icepack and a bottle of water.

"And take these," he instructs, handing me pills.

"What… what are they?" I ask warily. I don't like just taking random pills. Trent used to force me to take pills that would make me sleep for days. I had no control *or memory* of what he did with my body during those days. I'd wake up every now and then, wishing I hadn't.

"It's just Panadol, babe. Here." He pulls out a sheet of sealed pills, showing me the Panadol label. Rather than take the sealed sheet, I take the pills he already has out. This is Josh. I trust Josh. I swallow the pills before I can change my mind.

---

THREE HOURS OF DRIVING, five hours of flying, and now we're almost at Josh's place. We're sitting in the back seat. Josh didn't want to drive so he had a car pick us up. I'm anxious as hell. I don't know what it is, but something is wrong. I can feel it in the pit of my stomach.

Josh is holding my hand, just like he always does in the car, his thumb absently twirling around my fingers.

"Josh, in case I didn't already tell you, I had a great time. I loved every minute with you. I love you, more than you'll ever know. Thank you for giving me this week," I tell him.

"Emmy, you don't need to thank me. There will be plenty more weeks like this in our future, babe." He smiles. I try to return the gesture, but it's fake. I know he can tell by the wrinkle in his eyes.

"What's wrong?" he asks as his phone rings. He takes it out

of his pocket and looks at me. "Sorry, I have to take this." Squeezing my hand, he picks up the phone.

"What is it?"

I don't hear the other side of the conversation. But when Josh's eyes turn to me, I know it's not good.

"What's the name of the detective?" Josh asks into the phone. I wait, holding my breath.

"Detective Jones," Josh says, looking right at me. My body goes cold. I'm shaking. I can't stop the shaking. He's found me. How has he found me?

"Tell Detective Jones that I haven't seen Emily Livingston since high school. Last I heard, she died a few years back." Josh hangs up the phone. He tilts his head.

"John, change of plans. Take us back to the airport," he orders the driver before pressing a button and winding up the partitioner.

"Emily, care to explain why there is currently a Detective Jones at the farm with a warrant for your arrest?" Josh asks quietly.

He's too quiet. I can't tell if he's angry or not. I can't tell what he's thinking.

"I'm sorry. I'm so sorry. Just let me out here, Josh. You don't need to worry. I won't have you get into trouble because of me."

"You're not getting out of this fucking car, Emmy. I'm not letting you go. You need to tell me why there is a cop looking for you though. I can't help you if you don't talk to me."

"You can't help me, Josh. No one can…" I whisper.

"Whatever it is, Em, it can't be that bad. Just tell me, please."

"I-I killed him," I stumble out.

Josh doesn't even flinch, doesn't blink. His facial expression is blank. I just admitted to killing someone, and it's like I told him I wanted an ice cream cone or something.

"Who, Emmy? Who did you kill?" he urges.

"My husband."

Book 2

# Chapter 1

## Josh

Married, she's fucking married. Or *was* married. How the fuck did I not know that? Why do I feel like my heart just fucking shattered into a million pieces? That should have been me, only me. She went and married someone who wasn't fucking me.

"Fuck!" I yell, pulling at my hair.

"Josh, just stop the car. Let me out," Emily whispers while moving as far away from me as she can get.

I look at her, really look at her. She's scared. I don't think I've really ever seen her this scared before. I need to calm down; my yelling is not helping her at all. But fuck, she fucking married someone else.

"I can't." My voice is hoarse, the words barely audible.

"*You* don't need to. Just tell him to stop the car and let me out."

"I can't let you go, Emmy. I'm never going to be able to let you go. You knew that before you came back. I warned you if you came back, I'd be keeping you."

"You have to let me go. You don't understand… They're going to find me, and I'd rather not drag you down with my mess."

"Your mess is my mess, Emmy. I'll fix this. I can fix this."

Emmy shakes her head no. She doesn't say anything, just looks down at her hands and continues to shake her head no repeatedly.

"Tell me why?" I ask. I need to know why she fucking married someone else.

"You want me to tell you why I killed him? I was cooking dinner; it was his favourite. I thought he'd be in a good mood because he liked when I cooked spaghetti. When I heard the door jingle, I ran into the bedroom to check the bed, then to the bathroom and redid the towels. By the time I got back out to the kitchen, the sauce was burning."

Emmy hesitates and stares at me, silently begging me to tell her to stop. I probably should. I know I'm not going to like whatever it is she has to fucking say. But fuck, I need to know. When I asked her to tell me why, I was referring to the whole marriage thing. I want to fucking know why the fuck she married him.

I wait her out, not breaking eye contact. I can do this. I can sit here and listen to whatever it is she has to say. I need to do this.

"He… I knew he was going to be mad. I don't know why I did it, but I picked up a small knife out of the block and hid it behind my back. He…" Emmy shakes her head no again.

"He what, Emmy?" I ask her, not moving a muscle. I'm so

afraid I'll scare her off and she'll stop talking. This is the most she's ever fucking talked to me about this prick.

"He got mad, threw the sauce. He hit me a few times. I don't know why I did it. I don't know why now. It wasn't different from any other time. But when he was..." She glances at me briefly then looks away. Again, I wait, with the patience of a damn saint.

"When he was raping me, I remembered I had the knife in my hand. I don't know what came over me. I just brought the knife up and jammed it into his neck. There was so much blood. It was everywhere."

"Stop the fucking car now!" I yell at the driver. He's quick to pull over to the side. As soon as I jump out of the vehicle, I'm bent over, throwing my fucking guts up. I watch the black SUV come to a stop behind me, and looking over my shoulder, I see another one just up the road in front a bit.

Paul springs from the SUV at the back with a bottle of water in hand. Fuck me, I've gutted and cut up human bodies like a bloody butcher and never once have I spilled my guts over that. But the image of Emily being beaten, being… *raped.* The thought of her having to endure that for years is too much. I want that fucker's blood. The inferno that's roaring inside me is the most intense I've ever felt.

I'm fucking losing it. Bending over, I'm clutching at my knees, trying to breathe through this. Attempting to calm the fucking beast within. I know I need to be the strong one here. I need to not let Emmy see me fall apart so easily. But fuck me, this is hard.

What's worse? It's all my fucking fault. If I hadn't made her leave town, this would never have happened to her. I'll never be able to forgive myself. How can I expect Emily to forgive me?

"Boss, you all right?" Paul asks, holding out the bottle of water towards me.

I take the bottle and swish some water around my mouth before spitting it out. "No, I'm obviously not fucking good," I grunt out.

"Well, you might want to get over whatever it is real quick. We got company and that girl of yours needs to be out of sight." He nods his head towards Emily, who is standing on the other side of the car, glaring straight at me with an expression I can't read.

"Fuck!" Passing the water bottle back to Paul, I make my way over to Emmy. "Babe, you need to get back in the car."

She just stares at me. I don't like the blank look on her face. Why the fuck can't I read what she's thinking? I've always been able to. It's like she's shut down, closed off all emotions.

"Emmy, get in the fucking car, now." I growl when she makes no effort to move. The moment the sound leaves the back of my throat, I know I fucked up again. I need to remember to be gentler with her. Right now, though, I need to get her back in the car and out of view. I see a black SUV coming up the road before slowing to a stop.

"Fuck, I'm sorry, Emmy. I'll make this up to you later," I whisper as I manhandle her, picking her up and sitting her in the back seat of the car. I make sure I flick the child lock on the door before shutting her in.

Turning around, I see some ass stagger out of the SUV that's just pulled up behind Paul's car. Four of Paul's guys jump out of the vehicle in front of mine, coming to a stand behind me. Paul goes to step forward and I pull him back.

I wait for the ass to speak as he stops directly in front of me, obviously knowing who the fuck I am.

"Mr. McKinley, you're a hard man to track down."

"Depends on who's looking," I reply.

"Detective Jones." He holds out a hand. I look down at his outstretched palm and dismiss it. Like fuck, am I shaking hands with this fucker.

"What can I do for you, detective?" I ask.

"I'm looking for a woman—Emily Livingston. Know anything about her whereabouts?"

"Emily Livingston. I haven't heard that name since high school." I shrug my shoulders. Everything in me wants to end this motherfucker right here. "I heard she left town right after graduation. Why are you looking for her? What'd she do?"

"That's classified, but if you do run into her, here's my card. I'd like to ask her a few questions." He holds out a card, which I take and pass off to Paul.

"Sure."

I watch as he turns and walks back to his car. "Detective," I yell out before he gets in. Turning back, he raises his eyebrows in question at me.

"I'm curious… how exactly do you plan to question a dead girl?" I smirk, knowing full well this is the asshole who signed both Emily and her mother's death certificates. The smile falls from his face momentarily, shock replacing his confidence.

"My sources tell me Miss Livingston is very much alive and breathing. For now," he says as he climbs into the car. Paul steps in front of me, stopping me in my tracks.

"Do not let him rile you up, Josh. You reacting right now is exactly what that prick wants."

I know he's right, but fuck, I want to gut the fucker. I want to hear his screams as I skin him alive. Nobody will ever threaten Emily and walk away unscathed. He may think he's walking away, but I now know who he is. Before the day is out,

I'll make sure I know everything there is to know about Detective Jones.

As soon as the detective drives off, I open the door of the car, instructing the security detail that they are not to leave any room between the convoy. I will not take chances with Emily's safety.

When I get in the car, Emily is sitting on the very far side, scowling in my direction. Fuck, how the fuck am I going to fix this? Reaching across, I pull the seat belt over her shoulder and plug the buckle in. Lingering a little in her space, I inhale her scent.

She always smells so fucking good, like wild berries. "I'm sorry, so fucking sorry, Emmy. I know it's not forgivable, what I've done, but I will try every day to earn your forgiveness."

I sit back on the other side of the car. "We're going to the penthouse," I instruct the driver before pressing the button and winding up the privacy screen. As soon as the divider's up, and it's just Emmy and me, I breathe a sigh of relief. I don't need to pretend with her. I don't need to be anyone other than me.

Leaning over, I grab at my hair as my head hangs down. I breathe in and count to ten, over and over again. I'm trying everything I can to stop myself from reaching for her. She needs to make the first move. The disdain on her face when I got in the car was clear as day.

She hates me. *Rightfully so, too*. I'm a fucking asshole. She's never going to be able to forgive me for what happened to her, the fact that none of that would have happened if I never chased her out of town.

"Josh?" her quiet, timid voice asks.

I look over to see her eyes red, silent tears staining her cheeks. Every time I see her cry, I feel her pain right down to my core. It shatters something in me. As broken as I am, it surprises me that there is anything left to break, but for Emily, there is always more.

I reach a hand up slowly to her face; she doesn't flinch at my touch. It's a small, hollow victory. "I'm sorry," I repeat as I wipe her tears away with my thumb.

"I understand. I won't be a problem for you anymore. Just stop the car and I'll get out," she whispers.

"You're not fucking going anywhere, Emmy. You don't understand. I refuse to lose you again. I won't lose you again. I can't."

"Josh, I'm only going to bring trouble to your life. Just hearing what I did, what I've done, made you sick. How can you even look at me? I can't even look at myself in the mirror without seeing it."

"The only thing I see when I look at you, Emmy, is a fucking angel, my fucking angel. A survivor. When I look at you, I see everything that's good in this world." Fuck me, she thinks I was sick because of what she did. "God, Emily, I wasn't sick because of what you did. What happened to you should never have fucking happened. It's my fault. I should never have made you leave town. If I didn't, then none of that would have happened. I would have been around to protect you."

"No, it's my fault. *I* left town, Josh. *I* made choices that led me to Trent. What he did is not on you. It's on me. I should have been smarter, gotten out of that situation earlier."

"This isn't something we are going to agree on, babe. But know that from here on out, it's me and you. Just the two of us against the world. Nothing will take you away from me, Emmy. I will fix this."

I lean in and claim her lips with mine. Her hands reach up and pull my head in closer to her. She unclasps her seat belt and straddles me, her pussy crashing down hard on my cock. "Fuck, babe, as much as I want you, this isn't safe. You should have a seat belt on."

"Shut up," Emmy growls as her hands rip at my own buckle. Okay, guess we're doing this. Her fingers are frantic as she tries to undo my jeans. I take over for her—thinking there'd be less chance of a zipper injury if I do it myself.

As soon as my zipper is lowered, her palm wraps around my shaft, pumping up and down a few times. My hands go to her ass as she hovers above me. Moving her panties aside, I line my cock up with her entrance, her pussy sliding down on me like a goddamn glove, pulsing and clenching at my cock.

She stills as she bottoms out. Her head leans back, her mouth open and her eyes closed. I wish I had a camera to capture this look right here. This has to be one of my favourite expressions of hers. Her body shivers as she tilts her head back upright, locking those blue eyes of hers onto mine.

# Chapter 2

## Emily

Locking eyes with Josh, I try to tell him everything I struggle to say in words. How much I really love him, need him, cherish him. I want to believe in the fantasy he's trying to sell me. That we will get our happily ever after, but no matter how much I try, I just can't see how reality is going to let that happen.

Right now, I can give in to this feeling, this need to have him as close as I can possibly get. I lift my hips and start rocking back and forward. Every time I come back down, my clit hits him right on his pubic bone. The sensations going through me are unbelievable. I was in such a frenzied rush to get him inside me, but now that he's there, I don't want it to end. I want to take my time and drag this out as long as I can.

My hands roam up and under his shirt, over the ridges and

grooves of his abs. All I can think of is how much I want to run my tongue along these grooves. I ride him as slowly as I can. Josh's hands squeeze the globes of my ass, his grunts and groans filling the car, but he does nothing to take control of the speed or tempo of my movements.

"Fuck, Em, you were fucking made for me. This pussy was made to ride my cock." Josh growls into my ear as he takes the lobe between his teeth and sucks.

"Mmm, I don't want this feeling to end, Josh."

"This is never going to end, babe," he promises as I pick up my pace again, chasing that bliss that I know will come crashing over me in waves of pleasure. I lean my head back as Josh moves his mouth to the crook of my neck. His teeth gently graze the delicate skin there before he bites down.

The pain of the bite sends jolts of electricity straight to my core, and I explode. My juices flood him as he holds my hips still, riding me through my orgasm and finding his own release.

"You. Are. Mine," he states as he empties himself inside me. I collapse into him, my head falling to his chest, my fingers wrapping around the fabric of his shirt. I'm not ready to let go of this feeling yet.

Josh runs his hands through my hair, laying tender kisses to my forehead. It confuses me how he can be so gentle and loving towards me, yet cold and closed off to everyone else. The way he makes me feel like I'm the most important thing in the world to him is dangerous. I want to keep him. Knowing that I can't is eating me up. I know I'm going to have to let him go eventually. Nothing good lasts forever and this right here, sitting on his lap, being wrapped up in his arms—this is a good feeling.

Shaking the thoughts away, I slip off his lap and slide back into my seat, pulling the seat belt back on. I can't even look at him right now. What the hell is wrong with me? I'm so afraid he's going to be able to see right through me. I can't let him in on the internal struggle I'm currently having about staying.

I know the best thing is for me to disappear. It will ruin him, but in the end, it will also save him. I can't let anyone else go down for the mess I've made. I just need to figure out how to get away from him.

Josh reaches across the car and picks up my hand, entwining his fingers with mine. I can feel his eyes on me as I stare out the window. He's silent. The stroking of his thumb on my wrist is comforting in the strangest way. Just his touch soothes all my aches and pains. Whenever his skin makes contact with mine, it feels like I can breathe again after being held under water.

If I were to ask a shrink, I'm sure I'd be told I was developing an unhealthy, co-dependent relationship with Josh. Even knowing this, I still want him.

"Emmy, whatever you're thinking, stop. I promise it's going to be okay. I will fix this."

"You can't possibly know what I'm thinking, Josh." Annoyed that he reads me so bloody well, I try to pull my hand out of his. He just holds onto it tighter, refusing to let me cut off our connection.

"I know that you've got one foot out the door, ready to run at any given chance."

"I can't let you deal with my mess. I'm a mess, Josh. I have so many issues up here right now. Why the hell would you want me around?" I ask, pointing to my head. He has to understand how damaged I am.

"*You* think you're a mess. I think you're fucking beautiful.

*Perfect.* Whatever we have to do to deal with this situation, we will do it together. I won't have it any other way."

"I'm far from perfect. I can't get these images out of my head. I can't close my eyes and not see it, not see what I did."

"*What you did?* Let me tell you what you did, Emily. What you did was survive. What you did was brave, courageous and fucking amazing. You didn't do anything wrong; you have nothing to feel guilty about. Do you hear me? *You have done nothing wrong,* Emmy. You survived a situation you should never have fucking been put in."

"But that's the thing, Josh. I don't feel guilty. I'm not sorry for what I did. When I close my eyes, I'm not consumed by guilt, but fear. I'm so tired of being scared all the damn time."

Josh unclips his seat belt and moves to the middle of the car, right next to me. He holds my face in his hands, resting his forehead on mine.

"Tell me what you're afraid of most in the world, Emmy. What's your biggest fear?" he asks.

I think about it for a while. I'm scared of the future, of what my future looks like. I'm scared that I didn't kill Trent and he's going to find me again. I'm scared that I'm going to spend the rest of my life behind bars for what I did. But my biggest fear, the thing that terrifies me the most, is Josh.

I close my eyes and confess this realization to him. "You. You're my biggest fear, Josh. I'm so afraid that you're going to wake up one day and decide that you're finished with me again. I'm afraid that you're going to send me away. I'm scared that you won't be able to look at me the same way… now that you know what I did. My biggest fear is losing you… again."

When I open my eyes, I'm met with Josh's blue orbs sucking me into his trance. I can see so many different emotions in his eyes. But the one that stands out the most is love. When he looks at me, I can always see love.

"Emily, I swear on everything that you will never lose me. You are the only person I've ever loved. You are the only person I *will* ever love. I'm sorry that I've made you feel like you didn't always have me, but I promise I've always been yours. Only yours."

"What kind of future do you really think we can have, Josh? I have the police looking for me. I killed someone…" I whisper.

"Babe, I've killed someone on every day that ends with a Y. It's not a big deal. And that cop will not get anywhere near you."

"Why do I feel like you're telling me the truth?"

"Because I always do and always will tell you the truth. Emmy, you watched me shoot someone in our apartment. You've never once questioned me about it or looked at me differently. Why do you think I would love you any less?"

"I know you, Josh, and that's crazy, considering our history. But I know your soul, and it's not bad. I can't answer why what you do to others doesn't bother me. It just doesn't." I shrug.

"Good, because I will stop at nothing to make sure you are safe."

---

I'M jolted awake as I feel my body being lifted. "Shh, it's okay. I've got you," Josh says. I let my head fall onto his chest momentarily before my brain makes the connection that he's carrying me.

"Wait. I'm awake. Put me down." I wiggle around, which only makes his arms hold me tighter.

"No."

"Josh, don't be ridiculous. Put me down. I can walk. You don't need to carry me."

"I know I don't need to. I want to, so I am."

"Look, I didn't want to say this, but you're making me. You should really take better care with your back; you're not getting any younger. You should probably leave the heavy lifting to the young folk."

"Are you calling me old, Emmy?" He laughs.

"If the shoe fits." I smile up at him.

"You do know we are the same age, right? Also, I'm more than happy to prove to you just how much vitality this body of mine still has."

"We *are* the same age, which is why I know how old you are. I'm pretty sure I saw a grey hair yesterday."

Josh stops abruptly. "Babe, that's not something to joke about. Where was it? It's probably just dust. I am not going grey. There's no fucking way." Shaking his head, he continues walking, pressing the button for the lift with his elbow.

"I meant on me. I saw a grey hair on me, not you. I didn't know you were so vain. Are you really worried about a grey hair?"

"On me, yes. On you, not at all. In fact, I can't wait to see you old and wrinkly with a full head of grey hair."

"That's weird. Do you have a granny fetish I should know about?" Josh laughs as the doors to the lift open and he steps in. Turning back around to face the door, he shifts all of my weight into one arm so he can use his thumbprint to send the lift to the penthouse.

Huh, I wonder if my thumb would do that?

"I don't have a granny fetish. I have an Emmy fetish. Everything Emmy turns me the fuck on. But mostly, I'm looking forward to seeing you old and grey because it will mean we'd have had a whole life together."

"Will we be sitting on rocking chairs next to each other on the porch of an old cabin?"

"We will be doing whatever it is you want to be doing, Em."

"Mmm, well, I think that when we are old, I want to be sitting on a porch in a rocking chair while we watch our grandchildren play in the yard." I don't tell him that I can't see how we can ever have that future—*the dream.* Instead, I do what I'm good at. I pretend. I pretend that Josh and I have a future together, that we will have a soccer team of kids and more grandchildren than we can count.

We'll spend holidays watching the brumbies run free and wild at the cabin we just spent a whole week in. If I had it my way, we'd be going back there. Out in the middle of nowhere, just the two of us. And all the horses of course.

Josh finally lets me down when he walks into the penthouse, holding me until he's sure I have my footing.

Josh looks around the room, his jaw tightening the more his head turns.

"Come on, I think you need to rest," he says, grabbing my hand and tugging me towards the bedroom. With his free arm, he pulls his phone out of his pocket and starts typing on it one-handed.

When we get into the bedroom, he escorts me straight into the walk-in closet, closing the door behind him. He places his finger up to his lips, indicating for me to keep quiet.

I don't know what's going on. Panic starts to kick in as I take note of Josh's posture, his taut jaw clenched. His eyes stormy blue, a cold, calculating look to them. Yet, I'm not scared of him. He looks like he's ready to pounce on anything that's willing to jump out at him.

I don't understand why he makes me feel so safe. I should be looking for a way out of this closet. Instead, I'm standing here, waiting for his next instruction. If I'm honest with myself though, I'd follow Josh into the pits of Hell if it meant I'd get to stay with him.

# Chapter 3

## Josh

I'm fucking fuming, trying my hardest not to let the anger inside me take over. Emily does not deserve to see the shit show that would happen if I let this rage seep out. It's burning me up. I can feel my veins heating up and pulsing as the fire tries to engulf me whole.

I need to calm down. She is safe; she is with me. If I let the rage win, if I let her see what happens when this overwhelming anger finds its way to the surface, I have no doubt that it will scare the shit out of her. And that's the last thing I want to do.

She's just starting to show moments of her spark, her humour and sass. I don't want to do anything that will take that away.

I knew the moment I walked into the penthouse that someone had been there. There were shoe prints on the white marble tiles. The maid service has never left so much as a speck of dust in this place.

The tiny cameras disguised as ornaments were the other tell. Most people probably wouldn't notice an odd ornament on a shelf they barely look at, but I'm not most people. A little OCD? Maybe, but when something's been moved, or in this case, added, I can always spot it. That, and the fact that they were subpar. I could see the tiny red light blinking from a distance.

I counted three, just in the living room. Taking Emmy into the bedroom, I saw another two sitting on the dresser. The fact that someone is watching us, watching her, pisses me the fuck off.

Looking around the closet I've locked us in together, I can't see any more surprises in here. But I'll be damned if I'm letting Emily out until those fucking cameras are gone.

I hold my finger up, indicating for Emily to be quiet. I don't know if those cameras in the bedroom have audio or not.

I've sent a message to Sam. If anyone can come and clean those cameras and find out what IP address they're feeding back to, it's him. He's thirty minutes away though, so I guess Emily and I are going to have to get comfortable in this closet, because I'll be fucked if I'm going to let whatever fucker put those cameras out there get another glimpse of her.

Pulling her to the very back of the closet, I sit on the bench seat that's positioned against the wall before tugging her down onto my lap. She doesn't hesitate, straddling me as she wraps her arms around my neck.

Leaning into her ear, I whisper, "Get comfy, babe. We're going to be staying in here for at least thirty minutes."

She looks at me, so many questions held in her gaze. "Why?" she mouths.

"I don't want you to worry. I promise I will never let anything happen to you. I just noticed some things in the apartment that shouldn't be here—that's all. Sam's on his way over to get rid of them."

"What kind of things, Josh?" Her voice is barely above a whisper.

"Cameras."

Emily's eyebrows draw down as confusion crosses her features. "Why would someone put cameras in your apartment?"

"No idea, but I'm sure as fuck going to find out." I trail kisses up the side of her neck. "In the meantime, how do you suppose we can kill thirty minutes?" I waggle my eyebrows up and down at her, attempting to put her at ease.

"Mmm, well, you could braid my hair?" She smiles.

"You want me to braid your hair?"

"Well, what are my other options here?"

"I could do that thing you like. You know, the one where I use my tongue to paint one of the classics on your pussy."

Emily's hips wiggle slightly, her pussy pressing onto my hardening cock. Just the thought of tasting her is giving me a raging hard-on.

"As much as I like that idea, and believe me I do, I'm not sure I'd be able to stay quiet. Considering we are whispering right now, how would I be able to whisper scream out your name when you make me come?"

She's got a good point. "Okay, hair braiding it is." Standing up, I sit her on the floor and walk over to the opposite side of the wardrobe—the one I've had fitted out for her.

The racks are lined with clothes, shoes and accessories; I had Ella help me out in getting this done while I took Emily to the property in Western Australia this past week.

There's a dressing table with stacks of bottles of girly shit. I find a brush and a pack of plastic hair bands. When I turn around, Emily is scowling at me. It's hard not to laugh; she looks so fucking cute.

"What's wrong?" I whisper once I'm seated behind her. Her shoulders are stiff. She shakes her head no.

"Emmy, what's wrong?" I ask again.

"I'm fine. It doesn't matter."

"It matters to me. What's wrong?" She's silent. She doesn't want to tell me. I decide to wait her silence out and start brushing her hair.

After three minutes of combing through her loose curls, her body is still stiff. I don't fucking like it.

"Okay, you need to tell me what the fuck is wrong, Emmy. I can't fix it if you don't tell me."

"You can't fix everything, Josh."

"When it comes to you, I *will* fix everything. At least let me try."

Emily turns around, crossing her arms over her chest, and my eyes are drawn to the cleavage she's practically shoving in my face.

"Argh, why the hell do you have a closet full of women's stuff?" she huffs out.

I laugh a little, trying to disguise it as a cough. "I have women's shit in here because a woman lives here—*with me.*" I stab at my chest to signify myself.

"Who is she?" Emily stands up, looking around the closet like someone is going to pop out.

"Only the most beautiful girl I've ever laid eyes on. The smartest, bravest and most loyal person I've ever had the pleasure of meeting. Not to mention, her pussy is…"

"Stop, do not say any more unless you want to find yourself missing a beloved body part," she seethes at me.

I get up and wrap my arms around her. She tries to fight me off so I tighten my grip.

"Emmy, that girl is you, babe. The woman who lives here with me is you. The one all these clothes are for… is you."

"Me?"

"Not sure why you're having a hard time comprehending that. Yes, you."

"Where did all this stuff come from?"

"I had Ella help me out, while we were at the cabin."

"You shouldn't have done that, Josh. This must have cost you a fortune."

"In case you haven't noticed, I'm not really short on cash."

"That's not the point. If I want clothes, I can buy them myself."

"Just a thank you would suffice, Emmy. I'm not having this argument with you. You needed shit. I got you shit. End of story."

"Really. Well, you can take it back. I don't need it."

"I'm not taking it back. It's yours. And we really need to be fucking quiet in here."

"Fine, I'll be as quiet as a damn mouse," she spits out as she sits back on the floor in front of the bench seat.

I guess we're back to braiding hair. Sitting behind her, I run the brush through her hair for a few minutes before it dawns on me that I have no fucking idea how to make a braid. I'm not going to admit that to her though. She wants her hair braided, so I'm going to figure out just how to do it. How hard can it be?

Putting the brush down, I pick up the strands of her hair and start twisting parts around each other. I'm sure I've seen girls do that. I get to the ends of her hair, and I don't know what the fuck I've done, but it doesn't look like a damn braid.

Letting the strands go, I run my fingers through her hair to separate the pieces. I slide my phone out of my pocket and pull up a YouTube tutorial on hair braiding. Emily is still quietly fuming as I watch the muted video. *Twice.*

Right, I've got this. Copying what the girl did in the video, I manage to get an end product that looks somewhat like a braid.

Emily reaches her hand around and runs her fingers down the braid. "Not bad. Not gonna lie, I didn't actually think you could braid hair. Thank you."

Well, thank fuck the silent treatment's over. "I didn't know until about five minutes ago when I watched a tutorial on YouTube."

She stands up and turns around. "You watched a tutorial, just now? To learn how to braid hair? Why?"

"Because I didn't know how to do it, and you wanted your hair braided. How else was I going to learn?"

"You really didn't need to do that. I could have done it myself."

"If you ask me to do something, Emmy, chances are I'm going to figure out how to do it."

I hear footsteps enter the bedroom. Reaching under the bench seat, I grab the Glock that I had stashed there. I shove Emily behind me and aim the gun at the door of the closet. I'm pretty sure it's going to be Sam out there, but I'm not willing to take any chances.

Seconds later, Sam opens the door. "Don't shoot." He raises his hands, laughing.

I lower the gun. "Took you bloody long enough, mate."

"I figured I'd disconnect the cameras around the place before I opened the door to the closet." Sam peers over my shoulder. "Figured you two kids would be playing seven minutes in heaven."

Emily steps out from behind me. "Oh, I played that game once in high school. It's not what it's cracked up to be."

"Back the fuck up! Who the hell played seven minutes in heaven with you?" It's not until I see the shock, the fear on her face, that I notice how loud I raised my voice.

Emily starts backing up until she hits the island in the middle of the closet. Fuck. I really need to learn to rein in my reactions. I fucking hate seeing her like this. Gone is the feisty girl who gave me hell for having women's clothes in here five minutes ago. In her place is a scared, shattered soul, afraid of what's coming next.

She shakes her head no. Her mouth opens, but no words come out. How the fuck do I fix this?

"Emmy, I'm sorry. I shouldn't have yelled." I raise my hands up, like I'm surrendering to her. Her eyes dart to the gun I'm still clutching in my right hand. Flipping it over, I hold the Glock out for her to take.

"Here, hold this for me." I'm hoping offering her a weapon will show her I'm not about to fucking hurt her.

"Why?" she asks.

"Because, right now, you're scared. I don't like it. Take the gun, Emmy. If anyone scares you, shoot them." I grab her hand and wrap her palm around the handle of the gun.

"No, I don't want it. I don't know what's wrong with me, Josh. I can't control this. I don't know how to stop these images from running through my mind. I want it to stop. I want to stop seeing it. Make it stop, please."

I hold her face in my hands, connecting my eyes with hers. Leaning in, I kiss her forehead before pulling back. "I want to make it all better for you, Em. More than anything else in this world, I want that. But I don't know how. Tell me what I need to do to help. I'll do anything."

"You can't fix this, Josh. No one can help me. I need to figure it out for myself."

"We will figure it out together. You're not alone, Emmy."

Emily shakes her head no. "I'm sorry." She puts the gun down on the island bench behind her.

"You don't need to be sorry, babe. *I'm* sorry. I shouldn't have yelled."

"I'm not scared of you, Josh. I just forget sometimes. Some things just take me back. I don't want to be that girl anymore. I'm tired of being scared of my own shadow." Tears fall down her cheek.

"As much as I don't like seeing you scared, it's okay to be scared, Emmy. Everyone is scared of something."

"You're not scared of anything. You never have been."

"That's not true. There's one thing I'm scared of," I admit.

"What?"

"You. I'm scared I'll wake up one day and you'll be gone. I'm scared that you're going to realise just how good you really are—too good for someone like me. I'm fucking terrified of what I'll become if I lose you again."

"You've been just fine without me for the last seven years. You will survive without me again." She says it like it's already a done deal, like she already knows she's not sticking around.

"I've been anything but fine, Emmy. If I lose you again, it will ruin me."

"I don't want to ruin you, Josh."

"Then don't."

"We don't always get to say how life ends up."

"I get to say how we end up, Emmy. And in my story, we will win out over any odds."

# Chapter 4

## Emily

"Ah, I'll leave you kids to it. I'll be in the kitchen if you need me, Emily," Sam shouts as he walks out, leaving Josh and me alone. The moment his footsteps can't be heard anymore, Josh picks me up and sits me on the island bench. Spreading my thighs apart, he places himself between them. His fingers trail their way up the outside of my legs, leaving goosebumps in their wake.

Using one hand, Josh pulls his phone out, presses a few buttons, then shows me the screen with the seven-minute timer.

"What arc you doing?"

"Giving you a *seven minutes in heaven* memory to replace the other one you shouldn't have had—which, by the way, I'm gonna need a name."

"I don't know. I'm pretty fond of the first memory," I tease.

"Emmy, you do not want to poke the beast right now. Do you really think I won't go on a rampage and murder every fucking boy you went to school with?"

"That would be a lot of boys, considering I went to ten different schools. And what makes you so sure it was even with a boy?"

"Emmy, did you kiss a girl?" Josh asks, then shakes his head. "You know what… it doesn't fucking matter if it was a girl, a boy, or a fucking unicorn. Whoever it was touched something that didn't belong to them. So, name, Emmy. Who was it?"

"That name will go with me to the grave, which is exactly where you're going to be real soon if you don't shut up and kiss me already."

Wrapping my legs around his waist, I lock my ankles, one over the other, to hold him in. My arms go around his neck and drag his head towards me. My lips hungrily find his, my tongue pushing its way into his mouth. Not that he puts up any fight, his tongue eagerly swirling around my own.

My emotions are so messed up at the moment. One minute, I'm scared. The next, I'm crying. And now, I'm bloody horny as hell. I wonder if my increased libido is just a coping mechanism for escaping my own mind. Am I using Josh as an emotional outlet?

My thoughts are quickly forgotten as Josh grabs hold of my braided hair, yanking my head back and tilting my face at an angle that allows him better access. He devours me.

"Mmm." Tightening my legs, I shamelessly dry-hump him, the outline of his hard cock beneath the denim of his jeans rubbing against my clit. I can't get enough. I need more. I want more. It's always *more* with Josh. I can never be close enough.

Josh's hands reach behind him and unwrap my legs from his waist. He pulls away from my mouth, taking a step back. My body unconsciously follows his, almost causing me to fall off the damn bench.

"Why'd you stop?"

Clutching the phone, which I now notice he's holding up as it's blaring some god-awful bell alarm, he says, "Time's up, babe."

"No, I need more time, Josh. Set it again. Practice makes perfect. We should practice this whole seven minutes in heaven game." My stomach chooses this moment to make itself known, the rumble so loud it echoes in the room.

Josh laughs as he reaches out and helps me down, waiting for me to be steady on my feet. "Sorry, I need to feed you before that monster gets out."

Pain radiates through me as I put all my weight on my left foot. I wince slightly—a wince that Josh does not miss. I've been doing so well with not letting on how much my hip hurts. I can deal with the pain, block it out to a point.

"What's wrong? What happened?"

"Nothing. I'm fine. What have you got to eat in this place anyway?" I try to change the subject.

"Nice try. You're in pain. Why didn't you say something sooner? Fuck, Em. Should I get the doctor over?"

"NO! Do not go calling any more doctors. I'm fine. Trust me, I've had worse."

His face goes blank. His body stiffens. I guess that was the wrong thing to say. "Josh, I'm fine. Really. I just need to eat."

He takes a deep breath in, closes his eyes, and is he…? I think he's counting to ten in his head. When he mouths ten, he opens his eyes again. Smiling at me, he scoops me up in his arms.

"Let's get you fed."

"Put me down. I can walk."

He doesn't respond, just looks at me with his eyebrows drawn down, and shakes his head, continuing his way out to the kitchen.

Josh sits me on a bar stool at the counter, kissing my forehead before he stalks into the walk-in pantry. I swoon, like full-blown swoon. Why does being kissed on the forehead feel so good? It's such a simple gesture, yet one I haven't had in a very long time.

"What happened to you?" Sam asks me. Where did he come from? I didn't know he was even still in the apartment?

"Nothing." I smile.

"Bullshit. What happened, Emily?" he asks again, crossing his arms over his chest.

"He's being overdramatic. I fell while dismounting Cherry this morning. That's all. It's just a little bruise." I shrug my shoulders.

"There's nothing little about that bruise, Emmy. Here, take these," Josh says, holding out two white pills.

I can feel the sweat rolling down my back. They're just pills. I have to calm down. I cannot freak out again. *They're just pills*, I repeat to myself. Swallowing, my throat dry, I ask, "What are they?" My voice quakes, even though I try not to let it.

Josh screws his eyes. I can see the intake of breath he draws before he marches over to the bin and dumps the pills. I watch as he silently walks back into the pantry, returning with a packet in his hands.

He holds the box out to me—a *sealed* box of paracetamol. "It's just paracetamol, Em. Take two."

I go to take the box, when he holds my hand still. "We will

be discussing this later," he says before letting go. Sam places a glass of water down on the bench in front of me.

"Here you go, love." He winks.

Josh slaps him across the back of the head. "Her name is Emily, asshole."

"Thank you." I take two pills out of the sealed packet and swallow them. I can't look in Josh's direction right now. I know I need to trust him. And I do. But these moments I have, where I second-guess his motives, they are driving me insane. I don't know how to stop it. The guilt is drowning me. Josh has never done anything to warrant my distrust. Well, nothing to make me think he's out to hurt me… physically anyway.

He loves me. I've always known that, even when he didn't want to admit it to himself. I wonder… when did he accept the fact that he loves me? He seems to have no problem telling me now. Yet, seven years ago, he wanted me out of town.

I get that we've both grown, changed, and had experiences that have turned us into different people. But whatever this connection is that I've always felt with Josh, it's never gone away. If anything, it's intensified now that I'm back here with him.

"So, I'm cooking. What'll it be, kids? Your options are steak, steaks, or steaaaaaaks?" Sam says, pulling a pack of steaks out of the fridge.

I laugh, appreciating that he's attempting to put a knife through the current tension both Josh and I are throwing out there. "Ahh, guess I want steak?" I question back to him.

"Right answer." He winks again.

"Emily, you can have whatever you want. Don't listen to this jerk. If you don't want steak, I'll order in. What do you want?" Josh is staring straight at me, through me, like he can see deep down to my soul. It's unnerving.

But what bothers me more than his soul-piercing gaze is the fact that he called me Emily and not Emmy. I'm not even sure why it bothers me. He's the only person who has ever called me Emmy. Everyone else will say Emily or Em. I feel like I'm going crazy. It's just a name. The fact that he called me by my name is fine. It doesn't mean anything, right?

"Don't overthink it. It's just food. There is no right or wrong answer, Emmy. What do you want to eat?" Josh pulls me out of my own head, again.

"Steak sounds good. Although, I don't see a barbecue in this fancy apartment of yours. Can you really call it steak if you don't barbecue it?" I ask.

"Don't you worry. I got you covered. See you at the top." Sam collects a tray and walks out of the kitchen, leaving Josh and me alone.

"At the top? Where is he going?" I ask Josh.

"To the rooftop. There's a barbecue up there."

"Oh, well, should we go up with him?" I ask, hopping off the stool.

"We will," Josh says as he steps in front of me, trapping me between the bench and the brick wall of muscle that is all Josh. Reaching up, he tucks a loose strand of hair behind my ear—the gesture, soft and comforting, a total contradiction to the storm I see brewing within those ocean blue eyes of his.

"Right after you tell me about the pills." His arms fall to each side of me, before he rests his hands on the benchtop behind me. He has me trapped. I can't escape.

Looking all around, I try to find a way to flee, a way out of this. Not so much to get away from Josh, but more to get out of this conversation I do not want to be having.

"You can't run away from this, Emmy. We need to face this

head-on. And I can't fucking help you if I don't know what I'm dealing with. So, let's start with the pills."

He's right. I know he's right, yet I still can't seem to bring myself to tell him.

"You really don't want to know, Josh. It's not something I want to think about, let alone talk about. Please, just drop it. I took the paracetamol. Can't that be enough?"

"The pills, Em, why didn't you want to take the ones I tried to give you first? I saw your reaction. Fuck, I fucking felt it. The fear, mistrust, confusion that you feel, I feel it too. That shit cuts right through me. So, I need to know why. Please, let me understand why. Let me be the one to help you."

Goddamn it. "How do you do that? You make me want to tell you everything. But I'm so afraid that when I do, I'm going to wake up and find you gone. Again."

"I promise you will never wake up and find me gone. The pills, Em, why?"

I can do this; he should probably know what he's dealing with when it comes to me. I can't stay anyway, right? So, what's it matter what he thinks of me. *It doesn't.* "Okay, sometimes he would give me pills, and when I woke up, days would have passed. I lost a lot of days being unconscious." I'm looking down, not able to meet his eyes. I don't want to see the disgust reflected in them.

Josh puts his hand under my chin. "Thank you for telling me." He leans in and kisses my forehead. "I have one more question that's been eating at me."

"What?"

"Why did you marry him? Did you love him? Do you love him?" he grits out through clenched teeth.

I shake my head no. I was never in love with Trent. Lust maybe, at the start, but it was never love. "No, I didn't have a choice. I would never have married anyone if it were up to me. It wouldn't be fair to enter a marriage when your heart and soul belong to another man."

"What do you mean you didn't have a choice?"

"Two days before my twenty-second birthday. That's the first time I saw who Trent really was. He told me if I didn't sign the paper, then he would have someone pull the trigger on my mum. He… he showed me video footage of my mum in the garden—someone was watching her."

"Motherfucker!" Josh screams, taking a few steps back from me. He spins around and places his hands on the cabinet above his head. I watch his back fall and rise with each breath he takes. I knew I shouldn't have told him.

"J… Josh?" I'm not even sure what I'm asking him. I don't know what I expect or need of him right now.

He turns around and pulls me tight into his arms. My head falls to his chest. "I'm sorry. I'm sorry. I'm sorry," I repeat over and over.

"You have nothing to be sorry for, Emmy. What happened is not your fault. I'm sorry I didn't know. I'm fucking sorry I can't torture the fucking asshole and make him feel even a tenth of the pain you've felt."

We stand there, silently clinging to each other. This is my safe place, in Josh's arms.

---

SITTING UP ON THE ROOFTOP, underneath the stars and twinkling fairy lights, I feel the most relaxed I have in a very long time. When Josh said there was a barbecue up here, it was the understatement of the freaking year. It's not your regular backyard barbecue area. No, it's a gourmet kitchen for the outdoors.

The back wall is lined with a stainless steel benchtop and cabinets. There's a sink and even a four-door, under-bench bar fridge. Blue LED lights frame the outline of the bench, reflecting off the stainless steel.

We're seated on a large outdoor daybed—an outdoor bed that's more comfortable than any indoor bed I've ever owned. There're strings of twinkling fairy lights hanging above that seem so out of place it makes me smile. I remember the night Josh took me back to the cabin after graduation. He had haphazardly hung fairy lights all over the place.

The way the lights are draped out here looks the same, like he has done it himself. I wonder what his fascination with fairy lights is. It's odd, yet I love them.

"Okay, kids, I'm calling it a night. Catch you tomorrow," Sam says, pulling his large frame out of the chair opposite us.

"Thank you for cooking dinner. It was delicious." I smile up at him.

"For you, I'd cook any time, Emily." He winks back at me.

"Huh." This must be what all those heroines in the reverse harem romance books feel like, having multiple men doting on them.

"*Huh,* what?" Josh asks.

"*Huh,* nothing. I just had a random thought pop into my head—nothing important." I can feel my cheeks heating up.

Josh tilts his head and squints his eyes at me, examining my every reaction. I really wish I could go back to high school me, who never let anyone see behind the walls. I need to work harder to build those walls back up.

"It was definitely something. Care to share?"

"Trust me, you really don't want to know."

"I wanna know," Sam pipes in.

"Well, I read a lot of books on my kindle, and I just thought that this must be what the heroines of reverse harem books get. Two men doing nice shit for them." I shrug my shoulders. I feel Josh's body stiffen next to me.

"No! Not a fucking chance in Hell, Emily. You know I'd do anything for you. But sharing you in some fucked-up, reverse harem shit ain't ever going to fucking happen. Fuck. I want to shoot him for just putting that thought into your head." Josh points to Sam, who is standing in front of us with his mouth hanging open.

I burst out laughing. I know that Josh is not the sharing type. Thank God for that, because I certainly do not want to be shared. "Eww, I don't want you to share me with anyone, idiot. It was a fleeting thought about the books."

"You're trying to get me killed, Emily. I knew it! You hate me. It's my cooking, isn't it? Just tell me. Be honest," Sam rambles out.

"Your cooking is fine. I mean, it's not as good as Josh's, but it's good. And I don't hate you. I don't even know you." I take hold of Josh's hand, just in case he does have any ideas of shooting his only friend.

"Well, I'm out. Enjoy your night." I'm not sure I've seen anyone walk out of a room so fast before.

I giggle. "You should really stop threatening to shoot your friends, Josh. You won't have any left."

"I don't need any friends. I already have the best one right here." Josh stands up, pulls out his phone, presses a few buttons and "Behind Blue Eyes" by Limp Bizkit starts playing.

# Chapter 5

## Josh

Pressing play on the music, I hold my hand out to Emily. "Dance with me." Her nose scrunches up at my request.

"You wanna dance? To Limp Bizkit?"

"Babe, I'd dance with you to any music. In fact, there doesn't even need to be music, and I'd still dance with you."

"Okay, I officially know what it means to swoon now." She takes my hand and I pull her up, out of the lounger, and to her feet.

I don't waste time before I have her little body pressed tight against me. The feel of her curves under my palms, her scent surrounding me, hearing her cute little sighs as she relaxes in my hold—this right here is my ecstasy.

I don't know how I survived living all those years without her. Actually, that's a lie. I do know. I wasn't fucking living.

That became evident, really fucking fast, the minute she came crashing back into my life.

I listen to the lyrics to "Behind Blue Eyes" play softly, and the words couldn't be closer to the truth. Because I am a bad man. I don't have a conscience, but I do dream of a future. And every image I can conjure up, they all revolve around this woman.

Back in high school, I hated the feelings she evoked in me. I hated that I didn't understand them. And I fucking hated myself, knowing I couldn't do anything with them. So, I shoved them down. Loved her from the sidelines. Watched her every chance I got.

I'm not sure she even knows the extent at which I used to watch her from the shadows. But how else was I meant to protect her? To shield her from the assholes we went to school with.

Emily tips her head back and looks up at the rafters above us. "This reminds me of graduation night, all the fairy lights. Did you hang them yourself up here?"

"I did."

"Why?" she pushes. I was hoping she'd drop it. If she didn't ask, I didn't have to admit that I've spent countless nights staring up at these lights, recalling graduation night. But she asked, and I won't ever lie to her. Omit the truth? Sometimes. If it's for her own good, sure. But lying is not something I could ever do with her.

"I like fairy lights." I shrug.

"You like fairy lights? Why?" She laughs.

"I like them because the twinkle in them reminds me of your eyes. Every time I used to get a glimpse of your blue eyes back in high school, I swore I could see a light reflecting in them. I've spent many nights up here, replaying every memory I could conjure up of your eyes."

"I don't get it. I know that you love me, Josh. I can feel your love deep down in my soul. I've never doubted it—well, maybe I've doubted it sometimes. But your love, the thought of knowing that there was still one person in the world who loved me like no other. That knowledge got me through a lot of my darkest times. But what I don't understand is why? If you love me as much as you do, then why the hell did you make me leave?"

I can feel her body stiffen the moment she finishes her question. How the hell do I answer that? That's a fucking loaded question. But when I look down into her terrified eyes, I know I have to answer her. She needs to know there isn't a damn thing she should be too afraid to ask me.

I press stop on the music and pull her into my lap as I fall back down on the lounger. My fingers run through her hair. It amazes me how it's always so soft and silky. I love the feel of it in my hands.

"I need you to promise me that whatever I say, you will hear me out until I finish. It's not a pretty story, Em, and I really would urge you to reconsider needing to hear it." I kiss her lips. I need to seal her to me. I need to feel her connection. She already has one foot out the fucking door. After hearing everything, I wouldn't be surprised if it tipped her over the edge and made her sprint for the fucking hills.

"I know that I don't say it much. But I do love you, Joshua McKinley. There is nothing you can possibly tell me that will make me think any differently of you."

Her words somewhat put me at ease. But she doesn't know what she's about to hear. I can barely think about the horrors that the McKinley dynasty was built on. How is someone as fucking perfect as she is ever going to agree to become one of us? Because whether she accepts it or not, she is mine. She is one of us. I've already instructed my team of solicitors to change my will, stating that in the event something were to happen to me, everything I own, my majority shares in McKinley Industries—it will all go to her.

"Okay. I was eighteen, Emmy. My father was still in control of everything. I had no way of protecting you. That's why I had to let you go. Because I knew if I kept you, like every fibre of my fucking being ached to, I would have been signing your death certificate. He would never have let me keep you."

It doesn't escape me that she did, in fact, have a death certificate signed anyway. Thank fuck it was a fucking forgery.

"What do you mean? What did you need to protect me from?"

"My father. The McKinley dynasty. The shady shit my father was involved in."

"What kind of shit?"

I take a deep breath. "Mostly money laundering. However, if it was underhanded, my father probably had his claws in it."

"Money laundering? Why? Your family clearly is not short on funds," she asks.

"It wasn't always about the money. It was about power. My father craved power. He controlled a lot of shady fuckers' money—who, in turn, gave him power."

"Okay, but why would you not be allowed to have a girlfriend?"

"Because love makes you weak, according to him. I had a puppy once. My mother bought it for me when I was six. She read that pets could be a way to make your antisocial child… I don't know… social? Or connect on some emotional level.

Guess it's true, because it worked. I really liked that dog. The moment my father saw how much I cared for it, he made me watch as he slit the dog's throat."

"What? Holy crap, Josh, that's bloody crazy. I'm so sorry, Josh. Wait… you're not… you don't do that illegal stuff now, right?"

"I've mostly cleared the family of all of it. Em, I'm not the monster my father was. There was a time when I thought I was. I know my mother thinks we didn't know what he would do to her behind closed doors, but we could hear everything. Every slap, every kick, every word of abuse he would throw at her."

She tries to climb off me, so I hold her tighter. Her whole body tenses up. I can tell there is a question on the tip of her tongue. She's wanting to ask me something but isn't sure she should.

"Just ask me. What is it?"

"Have you ever…" She swallows, tipping her head down before continuing. "Have you ever wanted to hurt me?"

"Fuck no! All I've ever wanted to do is protect you, Emmy. Love you. Worship you. I would rather chop off my own fucking hands than ever use them to cause you harm."

Her body relaxes slightly. "Okay. So, you work, obviously. What is it exactly that you do?"

"I'm the CEO of McKinley Industries. I'm working on cleaning up shop, as much as I can, babe. I promise nothing I do will ever affect you."

"You can't make those sorts of promises, Josh. What if you end up in jail? *What am I even saying?* I'm the one looking at spending life behind bars. I killed my husband. It doesn't even matter what you do."

Within seconds, I flip her over so she's on her back, and

underneath me. I can't help the growl that leaves my mouth. "Do not say that. He was not your husband, Emily. He was a lowlife piece of shit, not worthy of breathing the same fucking air as you. And I'd put money on it that the marriage documents you signed were fake, just like your fucking death certificate."

"Do you think that's possible?" she asks hopefully.

"Yes. And even if they weren't, he was not your fucking husband."

"Okay," she agrees in a quiet voice.

I can't fucking stand the thought of her calling another man her husband. It should be me. I should be the only one she ever calls her goddamn husband. It should be my fucking last name she takes on.

"Em, when I settle all of this and shit calms down, I guarantee you will be wearing my ring. You will be using my last name. You will take the throne that's always been yours. You will be my queen."

She smiles up at me. "You know proposals are usually formatted as a question, right? Are you really going to order me to marry you? Because I've done that once—it didn't pan out too well."

Shit, Fuck. She's right. "That was not a proposal. When I ask you to marry me, Emmy, there will be no doubt that it's a question, one that I can only pray you say yes to."

I lean down and kiss her. *Claim her.* If I can't put my ring on her yet, I can claim her body as mine. And that's exactly what I need to do right now.

Pulling away from her mouth, I sit up, straddling her thighs. I run my fingertips along the middle of her breast, right down to her midsection. The yellow sundress she has on is already bunched up to the top of her thighs.

Moving backwards slightly, I pull her into a sitting position, my fingers brushing the thin straps of her dress over her shoulders.

"You know, I've always fantasised about having you up here. I've dreamt about making love to you under the stars and twinkling lights more times than I can count. Envisioned spending hours worshiping the perfection you are." I trail my tongue slowly over her collarbone and up the side of her neck.

"Mmm, yes, that. Aghh, I think you should definitely do that." Her throat vibrates as she moans.

My hands find the zipper on the back of her dress, lowering it much slower than I want to. What I want to do is tear the fucking dress in half, bend her over and fuck her until all she knows is the feel of my cock driving in and out of that sweet fucking pussy of hers.

Instead, I take my time. Emily deserves to be worshiped. And it ain't like it's a fucking hardship to worship her. Her body is the definition of a goddess. Her dress falls down past her shoulders. Pulling the straps over her arms, I let the fabric fall to her waist.

Her breasts, full D-sized breasts, call out to me, her pink nipples pebbled and just begging to have my mouth wrapped around them. Cupping my palms over each breast, I feel the weight of them in my hands. I roll my fingers across the globes, without touching her hardened nubs.

The moment her back arches, offering those rosy buds to me on a fucking platter, I don't hold back. Leaning down, I take her right nipple into my mouth, twirling my tongue around it while gently biting down. My fingers pinch and pull on her left nipple, the sounds coming out of her mouth filling the otherwise quiet night air.

"Mmm, I could spend all night just licking and sucking on

these breasts." I bite down a little harder before I move my mouth to the other side. Emmy moans, her thighs tightening underneath mine.

I'm still hovering above her legs, mindful not to make contact with the bruising on her hip. But she can't move them and it's driving her insane. Smiling around her nipple, I can't help but chuckle at how much she's trying to get friction between her thighs.

"Josh, I need…"

Releasing her nipple with an audible pop, I ask her, "What do you need, Emmy?" I want her to ask for it. I want her to fucking beg me for it. My tongue goes back to lapping at her nipple, licking all around the hardened tip.

"Mmm, you know what I need."

"I'm not a mind reader, Em. You're gonna have to say it if you want it."

"Argh, Josh, I need you to touch me." She groans as I bite down slightly on her nipple.

"I am touching you." I massage her breast with both hands.

"Damn it, Josh! I need you to touch my pussy, okay? I need you to make me come!" she screams.

I smile. This is what I wanted. Her so far out of her mind with chasing that pleasure that she's not afraid to say what she wants, to ask for what she needs. "Say *please*." I smirk at her.

Her eyes tighten and her jaw tenses as she spits out, "*Please*."

Laughing, I move my leg, placing it between her thighs to hold them open.

Lowering my hand, I slip my fingers underneath the lace of her panties. Her pussy's already dripping wet, soaking my fingers instantly. My mouth never leaves her nipple, sucking, licking and biting down. Inserting two fingers into her channel, I flatten my palm on her clit and hold still.

I bring my mouth up to her neck, and nibbling on her ear, I whisper, "I want you to ride my hand, Emmy. I want your juices dripping down my wrist. Make yourself come on my fingers, Em. Take what you need from me, before I bury my cock so far into your pussy and take everything from you."

"Mmm, J-Josh." She lets out a mixture of groans and moans as her hips start rotating, her pussy tightening, clenching around my fingers and drawing them in and out. She grinds her clit harder into my palm.

I move my lips back down to her breast, using my free hand to squeeze and pinch one nipple while my mouth devours the other. Her moans get louder, her movements more frenzied. She's close. I bite down harder on one nipple while twisting the other. She detonates, her juices dripping down my fingers. I hold my hand still, until I feel her relax.

Her head's thrown back, her mouth open in that beautiful O-shape. This is a look I want to see on her face every fucking day for the rest of my life. This look right here… she's free. At peace, no demons haunting her, no internal war happening, no struggling with what she wants versus what she thinks she should do.

I watch as her whole body relaxes as I lay her back. Her head rests on a pillow, her blonde hair falling like a golden fucking halo around her. I always knew Emmy was too good for me; she's way too fucking pure to be around someone like me. But I don't give a fuck about any of that. She is mine. And mine, she will be staying.

Pulling my fingers out of her, I bring them to my mouth. The taste of her on my tongue, I've never tasted anything as delicious as Emmy. I can't get enough of her, no matter how much I have.

I loosen the zipper on my jeans and free my raging fucking cock from its confines. I pull on the lace that's covering her pussy, tearing it in half. Lining myself up with her entrance, I look towards her face and wait. She's out of it, that orgasm disorienting her momentarily. There's no fucking way I'm entering her without her knowledge. I really fucking hope it doesn't take too long for her to come back to me, because this is testing my restraint like nothing else ever fucking has.

# Chapter 6

## Emily

I come to with a grin on my face, my body feeling relaxed. The first thing I see when I open my eyes is Josh's smiling, if not strained, face looking down at me.

"Welcome back, Em."

"Ah, thanks?" I have no idea what I'm meant to say. But waking up with Josh hovering above me, this is something I could get used to. Wrapping my arms around his neck, I pull his mouth down to mine. He doesn't exactly put up any resistance. His tongue invades my mouth, and the taste of me on him is overwhelming, arousing. I never thought I'd like my own taste, but tasting it on Josh's tongue is on another level.

"Mmm." The moan slips from me. My hips move underneath him. I can feel his thick head waiting at my entrance. What's he waiting for? Why is he holding back? Tilting my hips, I wrap my legs around his waist, pulling him into me.

His cock stretches the walls of my pussy, the slight sting settling as soon as he's buried all the way in. Josh lifts his head, pulling away from my mouth.

"Fuck, Em, your pussy is the best thing in the fucking world. So warm and wet. The perfect place for my cock to be, really. He should live here forever."

I laugh as Josh leans back in and claims my mouth. No, he doesn't just claim my mouth. He claims all of me. My heart, my soul. He doesn't know that every fibre of my being has always been and always will belong to him and only him. Even when I tried dating other men, it was always him my heart belonged to.

Josh starts to pump in and out of me slowly, ever so slowly. It feels amazing. I can feel his love through his soft, deliberate movements. His frenzied kiss slows, and everything else slows down with it. It's just him and me. Nothing else matters in this moment. It consumes me, this love I have for him, and if I let it, it will take over. I'll go back to being the woman who blindly follows a man. I can't let myself become her again.

Shaking the gloomy thoughts from my mind, I pull myself back into the moment. I let my hands travel up and under Josh's shirt, the feel of his hard abs beneath my palms. Snaking my hands around his back, I hug him closer to me. I want him closer. Always.

I let myself enjoy this moment. My eyes focus on the fairy lights above and I'm taken back to the first time we made love like this. Even if I had known I'd wake up alone, I still would have spent the night with him. If I'm honest with myself, I would have followed him anywhere that night. I still would...

---

LYING HERE in Josh's arms, my head resting on his chest while looking up at the stars, I feel peace like I haven't for a very long time. I also feel dread. This sensation is too good to be true. I know it's going to come crashing down around my feet soon. I just don't know when.

My eyes are getting droopy, but I'm too afraid to let myself fall asleep.

"Josh?"

"Yeah, babe?" He leans down and kisses my forehead. Damn it, why does this little gesture make me want to cry? Happy tears, tears of relief.

"You're going to be here when I wake up, right?" I know I sound like a desperate, whiney, stage-five clinger. But I need to know. I'm going out of my freaking mind.

Josh puts his fingers under my chin, tilting my head up until my watery eyes meet his concerned ones. "There is nowhere else I'm going to be. I promise, Emmy, when you wake up, I'll be right here. Holding you. Probably watching you sleep like the creeper I am." He smirks before leaning down and gently kissing my lips.

"Thank you." I settle my head back on his chest and let my eyes fall closed.

"No need to thank me, babe. It's not exactly a hardship holding you in my arms. I love you, Em."

"I know," I reply.

"I know too," Josh says back. It should be easier for me to tell him I love him. I've said the words before; he must know that I do. Yet, something holds me back from uttering the phrase.

"EMMY, get up. Come on. Put this on." I'm jolted awake to Josh's panicked voice. He's standing above me, holding out my dress he discarded last night.

"What's wrong?" I ask, taking the dress and doing my best not to let panic overtake me. Jesus, if Josh looks this panicked… whatever it is, it must be bad.

"Come on, follow me. Do not let go of my hand, unless I tell you to run. If I tell you to run, you fucking run, Emmy." And I'm officially freaked the hell out. I take his hand, silently following him.

The sun has barely risen, and fog fills the rooftop. Josh swipes up his wallet and both of our phones from the bench. Turning, he tucks my phone down the front of my dress, resting it between my cleavage.

"If anything happens, call Sam or Dean. I've programmed both numbers into your contacts." He turns and starts pulling me towards the opposite side of the rooftop. The door he's leading us to is not the one we came through last night.

"Josh, you're scaring me. What's happening?" My voice trembles. I try my best not to let my fear overtake me. I can't be the helpless, defenceless woman anymore. I won't let myself be her. I need to take control.

He stops, turning and placing his palms against each side of my face. He leans in and kisses my lips. "I'm sorry. I'm not trying to scare you, Em, and I promise I'll tell you everything that's happening… just as soon as I get you out of here. We don't have time to waste, come on."

Okay, here's to that whole blindly following Josh anywhere theory. Because that's exactly what I do. I don't question him any further. I simply grip his hand, like it's the only thing keeping me grounded, and let him lead me to God only knows where.

He cracks open a heavy steel door, peeking inside before pulling me in behind him. Holding his finger up to his lips, he gestures for me to be quiet. We then make our way down flight after flight of stairs. By around the tenth flight, I'm having a hard time keeping up with him. My hip is aching so badly I just want to crumble to the floor.

I can't though. I have to push through the pain, through the exhaustion. Josh notices I'm having difficulties. He turns around and mouths, "Hold on," to me before bending at the waist and throwing me over his shoulder, carrying me down the stairs at a much quicker pace than what we were going.

The speed he is managing to run down these stairs while carrying me is impressive, to say the least. How has he not collapsed yet? Stopped to catch his breath? God, I feel pathetic… I couldn't even keep up with *walking* down all these levels.

We get to the bottom and he settles me on my feet, before opening the door and peeking through it again. Once he deems it okay, he leads me into a garage. A nice bloody garage, with two rows of very expensive sports cars. Josh stops at a sleek, black, Batmobile-looking car. When he presses a button and the doors open upward, I'm almost certain it *is* the damn Batmobile.

He supports me as I lower myself into the car. I can't help but look into every shadow in this place, waiting for something or someone to jump out. When Josh jogs around the front of the car, climbing into the driver's seat, I finally let out the air I was holding in my lungs. It's going to be okay.

I stay silent as Josh starts the ignition, the engine roaring so loudly I can barely hear my own thoughts. *So much for being quiet.* I look over at his profile. His jaw is tense, his eyes scanning every direction as he manoeuvres the car out of the underground garage.

As soon as he hits the street, he floors it. My whole body gets pulled back into the seat, the engine's vibrations coming through the leather interior. He makes a few quick turns before slowing down a little. He's still tense. I don't know what I can do to help. I should be able to help... Whatever it is that's happening, it's because of me.

I reach over and place my hand on top of his. He shifts down gears and brings the car to what would be an acceptable speed. He lifts my hand, raising my fingers to his mouth, and kisses lightly.

"Josh, did you steal the Batmobile? Because I'm pretty sure Batman is not someone *even you* want to mess with," I ask.

Josh's laugh fills the car and his body relaxes more as he settles back into his seat. "No, this car is way better than the Batmobile, babe. This beauty right here is a Lamborghini Aventador, so much better than the Batmobile." He shakes his head, as if the thought of me not knowing what type of car we are in is inconceivable.

"Um, Josh? What happened back there?" I ask tentatively.

"Uh, there were some uninvited guests in the penthouse. I'm sorry I scared you, Em. But you are safe. I promise I will not let anyone hurt you ever again."

"Are you safe though? Is me being here going to end up hurting you? I can't do that to you, Josh. It's not fair."

He turns his head so fast to face me. "The only thing that can ever hurt me, Em, is you leaving. Not being able to wake up next to you every day, that's what will hurt me. No, it won't just hurt me. It will fucking ruin me. Don't do it."

He's pleading for me not to leave. I know that if I did, it would destroy him. But then again, I might just end up destroying him if I stay. "I don't want to leave. I want to wake up next to you every day. I'm going to fight this. I'm going to figure out a way to get myself out of this mess."

"*We*, babe. We are going to figure this out."

"Where are we going now?" I ask. It looks like we're heading into the suburbs, only not the normal, everyday people suburbs. This is the elite, rich people with mansions for guest houses kind of suburbs.

"Somewhere no one will be able to find us. But ah, how good are you at climbing fences? You're good with heights, right?"

"Fences? Heights? Uh, I can climb a fence. You know I was part of the gymnastics club at school. I think I'll survive the heights. Why? Whose fence are we scaling?"

"Emmy, you were in every fucking club at school. We're breaking into the McKinley Residence."

"Ah, Josh, have you forgotten that you are a McKinley? Why do we need to sneak in?"

"So no one knows we're there, of course." He winks at me.

"Don't Dean and Ella live in that house?" I'm sure Ella told me about some museum-type house Dean had her move into.

"Yes, which is why we are sneaking inside. It'll be okay." He pulls the car up to the side of the road. Looking into the rear-view mirror, he says, "Okay, let's do this. Wait until I open your door." With that, he jumps out and runs around the front of the car.

Once I'm out of the car, I notice we are not alone. Sam is leaning against a black SUV, smiling a huge-ass smile.

"Rules: Do not go over fifty kilometres an hour. Stop at every fucking orange light. If you so much as leave a hair in it, you buy it. Got me?" Josh grunts out. Huh, I guess he's protective over his car.

"Sure thing, boss. Although, you and I both know you don't pay me enough to buy one of these beauties. Emily, lovely to see you as always." Sam smirks in my direction.

"Ah, you too?" My response comes out as more of a question than a statement.

"Come on, I'm going to show you how to break and enter into one of the most-guarded, high-tech security homes in this neighbourhood." Josh grabs my hand and leads me up the street.

We stop at a tall green hedge. Josh runs his hands along the hedge until his arm disappears between the manicured leaves. "This way." He tilts his head, pushing his way through the bush. He stands on the other side, holding both arms out to make a walkway for me.

"Wow, Moses parted the seas. Joshua McKinley parted the hedge. I always thought you were god-like." I laugh.

"You know very well I'm not just god-like, Emmy. I am a fucking god." He laughs. Taking hold of my hand, he starts jogging across a large green lawn. And I mean large. It's more like a footy oval than a back yard. I stumble as I try to keep up. Josh slows down.

"Don't even think about it. I can walk," I growl at him just as he was about to pick me up again.

"Yes, boss." He holds his hands up in a surrender motion, before looking at his watch. "We have exactly three minutes until the guards make their way to this side of the yard. Come on."

"Guards?" Shit, that does not sound like a good thing. I follow Josh, jogging across the yard. When we finally stop at the wall of a building, I'm heaving with sweat dripping down my forehead. Did we just run ten kilometres? Shit, I'm out of shape. When I look up at Josh, who hasn't even broken a sweat nor seems remotely winded, I get mad. Like irrationally pissed off.

"I hate you. You know that. Did we really need to run across the yard? Some people are allergic to exercise, just so you know. For future reference, I'm one of those people."

"You're extremely hot when you're angry. I just got a level-ten boner from that little tirade." He smirks, adjusting himself in his pants.

"What the hell is a level-ten? Are there actually different levels? No, wait… don't answer that."

"Okay, when we go through this door, stick as close to the wall as possible. Don't make a sound. The cameras will pick up any sound. The way we are going, they won't be able to see us, but if we talk, you bet they'll record that."

My face must look as terrified as I feel, because Josh leans down and kisses me. The moment his lips meet mine, I can feel my anxiety start to ease, slightly. "It's okay, Em. I own this house, remember? We're not actually breaking in, more like *sneaking in,* so mum and dad won't hear us."

"Okay, but this is Dean and Ella's home, right? It still feels wrong to be sneaking in."

"It's a family property. Dean and Ella just happen to live in this one. Besides, it's not like Ella is going to kick her favourite brother-in-law out on the streets." He smiles, so sure of himself.

# Chapter 7

## Josh

Emmy's grip on my hand is tight. I'm afraid she's going to cut off the circulation in my damn fingers. It's admirable how she feels like she's doing something wrong. Maybe to some people it would seem wrong to sneak into the house your brother lives in. I just don't give a fuck. The way the McKinley trust works is everyone has their shares. I inherited the majority shares, so in actuality, I own the *majority* of this house.

Besides, I'm not afraid of getting caught. I have a secret weapon up my sleeve when it comes to handling my brother now. She comes in the form of a brunette spitfire, who can literally kick my ass. *Ella*. Yep, my brother's new bride happens to be very fond of me. She'd never boot me out of here, or let Dean try to either.

I could have walked through the front door, but what

would be the fun in that? Besides, I want Emmy to myself for a bit. I need time to process what the fuck I'm going to do about this fucking cop who seems to be able to get into my penthouse. A penthouse in a building that is meant to have state-of-the-fucking-art biometric security measures in place. Not to mention, the fucking armed guards who are on my payroll. How the fuck is this fucker getting past all of that?

I squeeze Emily's hand a little, attempting to reassure her that she is okay. That *we* are okay. We will be okay. I will find a way to fix this. Walking down the hallway, I go left, heading to the east wing of the house. A wing that no one ever goes into, apart from me. This has always been my sanctuary when we had to stay in this house, as well as during the countless times I've stumbled in here drunk off my ass, making Dean handle my shit for me when I was too fucking wasted to do anything.

There were a few years after I made Emily leave town where I was wrecked. I drank every night, took whatever drug I could get my hands on, anything that would make me forget. And when you're an eighteen-year-old billionaire, there is no such thing as a drug you can't get your hands on.

For around a year and a half, I drank until I could forget. The only problem? It never fucking worked. No matter how much I drank, what drug I took, every time I closed my eyes, I could see her. She was in every shadow of every corner. Some nights, I'd sneak into the school and sit at the table where we first met. I'd wait like she'd walk through the doors again and we could have a second chance. I could redo everything and just claim her from that first moment.

I probably wouldn't have snapped out of it, had Dean not locked me in a fucking cell for a whole damn month. Yes, literally locked me in the fucking basement to dry me out. He kept me fed, clothed. I had all the luxuries I could want for. Just not the alcohol or drugs I used as a bandage. It worked. By the time he let me out, I had come to terms with my fuck up.

I would live the rest of my life regretting my decision to run her out of town. But I have her back now, and I will slaughter anything I conceive as a fucking threat. Finally getting to the door of my room here, I push it open (expecting the room to be empty), only to find my fucking brother sitting on the edge of the bed, waiting with a fucking grin I'd like to slap off his face.

"You're losing your touch. I knew before you even made it to the building." He laughs.

"Yeah, well, I had to adjust my route and pace. Can we not do this now? I've got shit I need to do." Pulling Emily into the room, I cling to her hand, afraid if I let go, she'll run the other way. I know my brother scares her. I don't fucking understand why, but he does, so I hold her hand tighter.

"I'm sure you do." Dean looks at Emily and then pulls his phone out of his pocket.

"El, can you come up to Josh's room?" We only hear one side of the conversation, but after a few back and forwards, he hangs up—right before the door bursts open.

"Josh, you're here?" Ella comes up and hugs me before slapping me on the chest, to which, I swear I hear Emily growl. I pull her tight against me, wrapping my arm around her shoulder.

"Ella, why don't you take Emily to the kitchen and get her a drink," Dean says.

Ella spins around, hands on her hips. Whatever she was about to say falls dead on her lips as Dean adds a "please" to his demand.

"Well, since you said please and all, but just so you know, I'm not doing this because you told me to. I'd much rather hang out with her than you two anyway." Ella stomps her foot as she spins back around and tugs on Emily's arm. "Come on, let's get some coffee. Have you eaten breakfast yet?"

Emily looks back to me for guidance on what she should do. I hate seeing her so insecure and indecisive. I give her a slight nod. "I'll meet you down in the kitchen in a few. Save me some bacon."

"Okay." Emily gives a small smile back.

"I wasn't offering to cook for you, Josh," Ella adds as they both walk out the door.

I turn back to face Dean. Leaning against the wall, I fold my arms over my chest and wait. I'll stand here and wait him out. Whatever he's got to say, I'm sure it's going to piss me off, which is why he had Ella take Emily out of the room.

Dean attempts to stare me down for a few minutes, silently, before he gives in and shakes his head. "Do you want to explain why I had a cop at the club looking for Emily?" he asks.

My back goes ramrod stiff. Did this fucker tell them she was with me? I'll fucking kill him, brother or not. If he's put Emily at any kind of risk, I'll enjoy choking the life out of his fat neck.

"Relax. Put your fucking murderous thoughts away. I didn't tell them anything. I would like to know why we're apparently hiding out a fugitive though." He raises his eyebrow at me.

"She's not a fucking fugitive. And don't worry about it. I'll fix it. It doesn't concern you."

"It doesn't concern me?" Dean stands and starts pacing the room. "That's where you're wrong. It concerns you, which means it very much concerns me. What exactly are you planning on doing, Josh? I'd like a heads up if my little brother's planning a killing spree, targeting every detective out looking for his girl."

"I'm not going to kill every detective in the country, idiot. I don't have that sort of time. Besides, there's only one looking for her." I shrug. One who I very much intend on feeding to my damn pigs. Would that make my pigs cannibals? Because they'd be eating a pig?

"Why does she have *one* detective looking for her. What'd she do?" he asks.

I consider not telling him. This isn't really my secret to tell after all. But for some reason, I spill the beans. "She killed her husband." I shrug, with a huge grin on my face. I'm fucking damn proud of Emily for doing what she did. That takes guts. It's one thing to have thoughts of killing someone, but to actually go through with it is a whole other level.

"The fact that you're grinning about that is fucking weird, even for you."

"He was an abusive fuck who used her as a punching bag, among other things I don't care to repeat. I won't let her go down for this. I'll do whatever I have to do to get her out of this mess."

"That's what worries me." Dean stops his pacing, standing right in front of me. "I know more than anyone that there is nothing you wouldn't do for that girl. But that knowledge scares the shit out of me. I don't like worrying about you, Josh. Promise me you won't do anything stupid. Well, more stupid than usual."

"You know I can't promise that."

"Well, let me help. Who is this detective after her?" he asks. His eyes scrunch before adding, "Wait… if she killed her husband, why isn't there a nationwide manhunt for her? There wouldn't be just one cop looking for her."

"You don't think I've thought of that? The fucker was a cop, Dean. There's no way her face wouldn't be plastered on every news channel if they were looking for her. No, this detective wants something else. I just need to figure out what."

"Her husband was a cop? Someone's gotta be covering this shit up, but why?"

I shrug. *Fuck if I know*. "Either he's not dead, and she didn't actually kill him, which I hope is the case because I'd love to get my hands on the bastard. Or there's a chance it's got something to do with Emily's trust that disappeared without a goddamn trace three years ago."

"What trust?" Dean knows she didn't come from money.

"The five million dollar trust I set up in her name. Someone withdrew it from her account the day she turned twenty-two. The day after a fake death certificate was lodged."

"So, Emily Livingston is legally dead? Then why the fuck is a cop looking for a dead girl?"

"Because it was that same cop who identified the body for the death certificate. He doesn't want Emily; he wants something from her. And I'm going to figure out what it is, exactly."

"*We* will figure it out. You're not going off alone on this, Joshua. I want to be kept in the loop on all your plans. Come on, let's head downstairs before Ella burns our kitchen down."

"I'll meet you there. I gotta make a call."

"Don't do anything stupid."

"I never do." I smirk.

I wait for Dean to leave the room before I pull my phone out and dial Sam. He picks up on the second ring.

"I'm gonna need a pay raise, boss, or a Christmas bonus in the form of this car," he yells over the sound of the engine.

"I swear to God I will fucking shoot you if you hurt my car, Sam. Now tell me you have something for me," I grunt out.

"I thought you'd never ask. But since you asked so nicely, I'll share what I've found. I'll remind you I missed sleep last night for this."

"Sam, get to it."

"Okay, don't get your knickers in a twist. So, I was able to trace the IP address. The cameras were feeding to a docking warehouse in Botany. The fucker's been getting in and out of the apartment by the fire escape door. He's managed to rewire the passcode. I've since fixed it; he won't be getting back in through that door. CCTV caught a glimpse of him entering the building. It's that lovely detective friend of yours."

"We won't be coming back to the apartment. I won't put Emily at risk like that. Text me the address of the docking warehouse."

"Will do, but it's going to be like finding a needle in a haystack there, mate. It's a shipping container dock. I was able to trace the IP back to that particular dock, but finding where it is within that warehouse is anyone's guess."

"I don't care if I have to burn that whole fucking place down to draw the fucker out. Get me the address."

"Okay, will do."

"And, Sam?" I wait for him to answer.

"Yeah?"

"I mean it about my fucking car, not a fucking scratch." Hanging up the phone, I head for the kitchen to find Emily.

# Chapter 8

## Emily

Ella makes one hell of a cup of coffee, although I'm not sure how much of that is her actual skill set, and how much is that fancy as hell machine she used. Either way, I inhale the warm liquid gold my life depends on.

What Ella doesn't do too well is cook bacon. The whole kitchen is currently filled with smoke as we both frantically wave towels around, trying to… Actually, I don't know what we're trying to do, but it seemed like the right thing to do after I turned off the stove and threw the frying pan into the sink.

We probably look stupid, both of us laughing as we try to ease the smoke. That is, until I notice Dean standing in the entryway watching us. As soon as I see him standing there, the panic sets in. Oh shit, what have I done? Five minutes in his house and the kitchen is nearly burnt down.

I know I wasn't the one cooking, but I still feel responsible.

My legs take steps backwards, as if on their own accord. I just need to put space between us. More space, I need more space. I walk backwards until I hit a counter. My eyes never leave Dean. Although I know it's Dean, the face I'm staring at now is not his.

It's Trent. He's here and I've messed up. I can see his smirk, the twitch in his eye. That same one he gets right before he lashes out at me. I've just given him a reason to get mad. I should know better. I shake my head. I try to open my mouth, try to apologise, but nothing comes out. I can't form the words.

I can see him getting closer. He's closing the distance. He's getting too close. I desperately look around for a way out. A way to get more distance. Maybe if I can find somewhere to hide until he's calmed down… except I'm trapped. I've backed myself up into the corner of the room.

I sink to my knees before he reaches me. I see a hand come out towards my face and I scream. I scream so loud. Hopefully (this time) the neighbours will hear. Someone will hear and help me. Someone has to help me. The hand never makes contact. Something's wrong. Something's different. Why hasn't he hit me yet?

I bring my knees up to my chest and sink my face into my thighs. Closing my eyes, I wait for the abuse to start. It's bound to start soon. I don't understand why he's taunting me.

"What the fuck did you do?" A loud voice roars—a loud voice that shouldn't be here. Josh, he's not supposed to be here.

"Emmy. Emmy, baby, look at me. You are okay. You are safe." Josh's voice is soft. I can feel his hands on me. Maybe I'm dreaming. Maybe Trent knocked me out and I'm dreaming. That's the only explanation I can think of right now.

Except, when those hands gently lift my chin, forcing my face up, my eyes connect with those stormy blue eyes—the eyes that hold the other half of my soul.

"Josh?" How did he find me? I look around. I'm not in my apartment. This kitchen is way too fancy to be anything I've ever lived in. Then it all comes back to me: the coffee, the bacon, the smoke, Dean.

I can see Dean and Ella both staring down at me with expressions that look like pity. I don't want or deserve their pity. I look back into Josh's eyes.

"It's me, babe. You are safe," he says, kissing my forehead.

"Josh, can we go back to your room?" I need to get out of here. I need to get away from everyone else. I know I'm putting a lot on Josh right now. I shouldn't be using him as my crutch, but that's exactly what he's become. My lifeline, my sanity. He seems to be able to break me out of any panic attack I've had. When I wake up in the middle of the night from the nightmares, he's the one there, holding me and letting me cry myself back to sleep in his arms.

"Sure thing. Hold on." I feel his arms scoop me up. I bury my head in his chest. I can't bear to look at Ella or Dean right now.

"I'll bring some food up. Don't worry, I won't cook it," Ella says as we pass them.

"Thanks," Josh replies, walking out of the room with me in his arms, again.

---

IT'S BEEN two weeks since my little breakdown in the kitchen. I haven't stepped foot out of this room. I mean, it's like there's no need to leave this room. It's bigger than the apartment I had back in Adelaide.

There's a large four-poster bed in the middle of the room, and dark wooden beams with white curtains falling down the sides of the bed. Above the bed are fairy lights, strung from beam to beam. It's a lot more feminine than I ever thought Josh would have. But it's like a fairy tale, romantic even. I love it.

The room has its own sitting area with black, plush, leather couches facing a large television that's mounted to the wall. There's even a little kitchenette-bar area off to one corner. It's fully stocked with every beverage you could probably dream of. I haven't touched a drop of alcohol though. I'm not really sure why, but the thought of it makes me want to puke, ever since the last time I tried to drink with Ella and her sisters.

It's late. I'm looking out the window, waiting for Josh to come home. I haven't told him of my growing anxiety every time he leaves. I don't ask him to stay with me, even though I desperately want him to. I know he tells me he's going into the office to do some work, and I do think that at some point during the day he does. But that's not all he's doing.

I know he's out looking for this Detective Jones. I've heard the phone calls he's been having with Sam. I know Josh is frustrated he can't find him. I've been racking my brain for any recollection of someone named Jones. I can't for the life of me make a connection between that detective and Trent.

Josh says it's awfully suspicious that there is no warrant out for my arrest—he had Sam hack into the police database to check. There is nothing on the database to report Trent's death at all. His records show that he is MIA, missing in action. I have this awful fear that I didn't actually kill him and he's out there somewhere, looking for me.

I asked Josh to look into Trent's brother. He was also a cop. According to Sam's research, he's still going about his everyday life. He goes to work and returns home to his family, which, by the way, I had no idea even existed. I met the guy heaps in the first year of dating Trent, and never once did either of them mention any other family members. Sam says that Trent's brother has a wife and two young kids.

Why hasn't he been looking for Trent? Why hasn't he alerted anyone that he's missing or anything? And, my biggest question, where is the fucking body? Josh had a team enter the apartment I shared with Trent. They found nothing; the apartment was completely empty. No furniture, no clothes, nothing. No body rotting on the kitchen floor. Just nothing. The apartment had been cleaned out.

I know he's stressed out. And I know the cause of that stress is me. I've offered to help him. If this detective is after me, why not just call and tell him a place where I'll be. I'll meet with him, see what he wants. Josh, of course, won't even consider using me for bait.

It's 11:00 p.m. now. He's been gone for fourteen hours. Fourteen long hours, in which I have to try to pretend that I'm okay without him. I have taken about six baths today, in an attempt to calm my thoughts. What if something has happened to him? I could text him. Sometimes, when it gets too much, I text him and he calls me straight away, his voice soothing my inner demons.

I don't though. I don't want to be the needy girlfriend. Is that what I am to Josh, his girlfriend? I know he's used the term before, but we've never discussed a label for what we are, other than Josh claiming that I am now and always have been *his*.

I had Ella show me how to use Facebook on this phone

today. I missed out on all the social media blasts from the last few years. She introduced me to TikTok a few days ago. I'm afraid to admit how many hours I've wasted on that app. It just draws you in and keeps you there.

Today I made a fake profile on Facebook. I friended a heap of randoms who live in Adelaide. I also friended Trent's brother (Stephen) and his wife (Veronica). I searched through both profiles. Nothing on their pages mentions Trent. It's like he didn't even exist. I can't find a trace of him online anywhere.

I sent a friend request off to Detective Jones. He hasn't accepted it yet, but I want to try to help figure out what he wants with me. Maybe then Josh can stop looking. He can stop being stressed out.

The rattle of the door handle has my heart beating overtime, until I see Josh walk in and I'm immediately overcome with relief. There's always this niggling feeling that he's just not going to come back one day. I can't seem to shake the thought.

I run up to him and jump into his arms, wrapping my own around his neck and my legs around his waist. I cling to him. Burying my face in the crook of his neck, I inhale his scent. He's freshly showered. He smells like sandalwood, the fancy shower gel he uses all the time. There have been many days he comes home in different clothing than he left in, always freshly showered.

He left wearing a suit. He's returned wearing a pair of black denim jeans and a white t-shirt. Inhaling the intoxicating scent, I ask, "Did you just shower?" before lifting my head to look him eye to eye.

He nods. "I did."

"Why?"

He thinks about it for a moment, then he answers,

"Because I like to wash the filth of my world off before I come home to you."

"What'd you do today?"

"I went to the office, you know, ran a multibillion-dollar corporation. Made the McKinley family more money. The usual." He walks over to the bed, laying me down and falling on top of me.

He starts kissing me up the side of my neck. His attempts at distracting my thoughts always bloody work. As his teeth graze the sensitive skin just under my ear, my whole body shivers with pleasure. My back arches up. Pushing my pelvis into his crotch, I can feel his hardness in his jeans.

The denim rubs against my bare pussy. I purposely didn't wear panties under my dress today. Josh tends to end up tearing them anyway. One of his hands trails up my thigh until it reaches my wet centre.

Josh's body freezes above me. He groans. "Em, please tell me you haven't been walking around the house without panties on all day. Fuck, I'm going to have to shoot anyone who looked at you today," he grunts as his fingers enter me.

"Mm, no one saw me. I didn't leave the room. Well, Ella came in here for a bit. But other than that, no one saw me today. Mm, God, that… Don't stop… that," I moan as he works his fingers in and out of me.

Oh God, I'm going to come embarrassingly soon at this rate. I don't know what it is with Josh, but I can't seem to get enough of him. He's turned me insatiable. It's his own fault, really. If he wasn't so damn good at what he does, then I wouldn't want it as much.

"I'm never going to stop, Emmy. I want you to drip all over my fingers. I want to lick your juices off them. Savour the taste of you in my mouth. In fact…" Josh removes his fingers. I start to protest until I see his head move south.

Yes, *this,* I can get behind. He doesn't waste time before his tongue is circling my clit. He slides two fingers into me while sucking and nibbling on my clit. I'm so close. I'm chasing the edge of the cliff as I shamelessly push my pelvis harder into his face, my centre clenching down on his fingers as I detonate around him.

"Oh my God, Josh, yes, yes, yes!" I scream as my vision blurs. My whole body quakes with my orgasm.

Josh continues to lick until I'm nothing but a spun-out ragdoll, sprawled across the bed. When I open my eyes, Josh is hovering above me, waiting. He always waits. He never enters me until I either take over and make the decision for him, or I nod, giving him the go-ahead. I appreciate him even more for always waiting for me to be well aware of what's happening.

But I don't want him there right now. No, I want him inside my mouth first. I'm starving for a taste of him. I push him onto his back and climb down his body. Holding his shaft in one hand, I slowly stroke him up and down.

My tongue licks the precum spilling off his tip. "Mmm." God, I love the taste of him. I never thought I'd ever like the taste of a man, but Josh is different. I can't get enough of him. Not having the patience to tease him tonight, I open my mouth wide over the thick, hard head of his cock, flattening my tongue as I suck his length in as far as I can take him. I wrap my hand around the base, squeezing and stroking up and down to match the movements of my mouth.

I hollow out my cheeks and moan as his head hits the back of my throat. Attempting to relax my gag reflex to take him even further, I manage to swallow around him.

"Fuck me. Jesus, goddamn, Em," Josh grunts out as his

hands reach down, picking me up from underneath my arms. My mouth leaves his cock. I can't help the pout that I'm now sporting. He smirks at me. "Babe, I was about to come down your throat."

Josh rolls us so I'm beneath him, positioning his cock at my entrance. "I need to be buried deep inside you. Are you ready for me, Emmy?"

"More than ready. Do your best, Josh, please."

# Chapter 9

## Josh

"*Do your best, Josh, please.*" As soon as the words leave her lips, I slam into her. The warm, wet, tight sensations making my balls constrict. I hold steady, buried to the hilt, calming my raging cock down a bit. I refuse to lose control this early. I'm not a fucking rookie teenager.

Once I've got things calmed down a little, I start pumping in and out of her, her juices dripping as the sound of flesh hitting flesh rings out loud in my ears. I needed this tonight more than she will ever know. The knowledge that I could come home and lose myself in this girl is what has kept me going these last couple of weeks.

I clear my thoughts of anything that isn't her, isn't us. This thing between Emily and me is lethal. It has the potential to ruin me. This one woman can bring me to my knees, shatter my already black soul. God help the world if it ever comes to that. Yet the rewards of having her far outweigh the risk.

"Oh God, yes, that. Keep doing that," Emily moans as she pulls on my neck, claiming my mouth. Her kiss is hungry, needy. I push my tongue deep into her mouth, giving her everything. Every piece of me belongs to her.

Our bodies move in sync, her hips arching off the bed. Pulling away from her, I sit up, lifting her legs and holding them in the air, her ankles resting on my shoulders. I hammer into her. I give her what she wanted.

Her head falls back, her eyes close and her mouth opens as I continue to pump in and out. We're both a sweaty mess, both panting for breath, climbing that hill and pursuing that ecstasy we can only get as we crash over the cliff.

Her walls pulsate around me as her body stiffens and she screams my name. There is nothing I love hearing more than the sound of her lost in bliss and calling out my fucking name. I follow her over the cliff, crashing as waves of pleasure run up my spine. My release spills into her, filling her.

I collapse next to her and pull her into my arms, bringing the blanket up to cover us. My fingers trail mindlessly up and down her back. We lie there in silence as we both let our breathing settle, our bodies relaxed. *Sated.*

"Josh, are you okay?" Emily's quiet voice breaks the silence. Am I okay? How the fuck do I answer that without depositing all of my stressors onto her? She doesn't deserve the burden of my worries.

"I will be," is the best answer I can come up with.

"Is there anything I can do to help?"

"You being here, that's helping more than you'll know. Don't worry, Em. All this shit will sort itself out." My lips meet the top of her head.

Her fingertips trace along her name branded on my chest. "I'm sorry," she whispers.

"You have nothing to be sorry for, Emmy. This isn't your fault."

"It is." She picks her head up and connects those blue eyes with mine. "Do you think I'm a horrible person?"

Her question shocks me. It makes me fucking angry to think she would even consider that. "Fuck no, I don't." My words come out harsher than I intended. Emily's eyes widen. She tries to push off me. Holding her tighter, I count to ten in my head. "Emmy, babe, you are literally the best thing since sliced bread. Actually, no, you're better. You are the best fucking thing on this whole planet. Why on earth would you think you're a horrible person?"

She shakes her head no. "I killed someone, Josh. I took a life from someone. And I'm not sorry. I don't feel bad about it. I should feel some sort of guilt. I should feel sorry, but I don't. The only thing I regret is that I didn't do it sooner. And I'm sorry that I've brought this burden to you. But I'm not sorry that I killed someone, and I should be, right? A normal person would feel something."

"Normal is overrated, Emmy. You are not normal. You are exceptional. Never aim to be normal, because normal is average, and trust me, babe, you are anything but average." I lean down, gently kissing her lips. "Also, you shouldn't feel sorry for defending yourself. You should feel fucking proud. I'm proud of you, Em. I'm not sorry that you came to me. I'm fucking ecstatic that you're here. You are not a burden. Don't you ever think that."

"I like having you back too. I wish it were under different circumstances. But I love you, Josh. I don't know what I'd do right now without you."

Maybe she's stopped thinking of her escape route. I feel like the last couple of weeks she's accepted the fact that we are an *us*. That she's not alone, but I still can't shake this sense of dread, this feeling that she wants to leave. Not that she wants to leave me, but the fact that she thinks she needs to protect me.

"I love you too. I don't want you to worry anymore, Em. Go to sleep. I'll be right here when you wake up."

"Okay." She lays her head back down on my chest.

I stare at the ceiling, not willing to close my eyes and let myself drift until after I feel her breathing slow, her body soften under my hands, her light little snores fill the room.

---

"FUCKING. Fuck. Fuck. Goddamn fucking shit piece of thing!" I yell as I throw my monitor across the room. It shatters, glass flying in every direction as it hits the wall.

I've been sitting in this office all fucking morning, going over every scrap of information my team has managed to uncover on Detective Jones. It's not fucking much. So far, we know he's a dirty fucking pig. He's recently been suspended. He's not even a fucking detective anymore. Whatever the fuck he wants with Emily has nothing to do with the law.

It's been three weeks. Three fucking weeks since I had to have Emily hauled up to my brother's house. She won't even leave the bedroom. I need to get this shit sorted, and sooner rather than later. Her words from a week ago replay back to me. "*Do you think I'm a horrible person?*" I've spent the last week trying to prove to her just how fucking perfect she is. The only problem is I've been spending more time here, in this fucking office, and out on the streets of Sydney than I have with her.

I've spent countless hours searching for any scrap of information on this fucker. He's like a goddamn ghost. He hasn't been seen since he questioned Dean at The Merge, the club my brother works security at. That doesn't mean he's disappeared. He's been sending daily emails directly to me. Each day, the threats get more detailed, more graphic. Today's email sent me over the edge, a red haze enveloping me.

*Joshua,*

*You keep ignoring my messages. It would be wise for you to start listening. The longer it takes for me to get what I want, the worse it's going to be when I do get my hands on her. You know, I've heard all about that tight fucking cunt of hers. I've always wanted to see what all the fuss was about. Have you ever fucked a dead girl? You see, there's this moment when the fear overtakes them, and their cunts tighten to a painful point. That's when I'll slit her pretty little throat. I'll enjoy licking the tears from her cheeks, and when I do, you can drown in the knowledge she copped it worse because of you. Hand her over, and I might, just might, go easier on her.*

## *DJ*

IT TOOK Sam and three guys to hold me back when all I could think of was going on a fucking killing spree. He's got family. I've already found them. I have no issues in killing each fucking person off. He wants to threaten the one person I love. Let's see how he fucking likes it when I retaliate by doing the same. But I won't make fucking threats, and he won't see it coming until it's too fucking late.

Even with being held down by four grown fucking men, the only thing that dragged me out of that haze was my phone ringing with Emily's ringtone. She very rarely calls—today she called at the right time.

Now I'm sitting here, like a fucking useless fuck. He wants me to turn Emily over to him. He knows I'm hiding her somewhere. But he will never get to her. I've already got us new identities, passports, bank accounts, and a plane fuelled and ready to go on a moment's notice. I will disappear with her if that's what it takes. There's a little island I purchased under a shell corporation. Nobody knows it exists—well, nobody but me.

I'm hoping it won't come to that. I want to give Emily everything she dreams of, the horses, the grandkids. *Everything.* I want to give her the fucking world. And I can't do that until I find this fucking asshole and deal with him.

Heading to the bar, I pour another glass of whisky, downing the contents as the door to my office gets thrown open. Sam walks in like he fucking owns the place. He helps himself to a glass before sitting on the lounger. He tilts his head at me, looking contemplative, then he speaks.

"Do you really think getting wasted at three in the afternoon is wise?" he asks.

"Got any better ideas?" I shrug as I pour another glass. Getting wasted seems like a really good bloody idea right now.

"Yeah, I do. Give me your keys. I'm driving. You're coming with me."

He stands, waiting for me to respond. "Where're we going?"

"Tony pinged the IP from the last email. It's a warehouse over in Marrickville, near Cooks River."

"Well, why didn't you fucking lead with that? Let's go." I swipe my keys and wallet off my desk and storm out of the office.

"Ah, you're not fucking driving, Josh. Give me the bloody keys." Sam steps in front of me at the lifts, holding his hand out. I only give him the keys because he's right. I can't drive right now. I'd probably end up driving us into the damn river at this point, not from being drunk, because I've only just started to get a light buzz on. No, I'd drive into the river out of pure fucking rage at this point.

I pass the keys over as the doors to the lift open. "Disregard any and all fucking road rules. Just get me to that warehouse."

"Done."

---

"WAIT, HOLD UP. ARE YOU CARRYING?" Sam stops me from jumping out of the car. We've pulled over at a block of abandoned industrial sheds. The place is deserted. For Sydney, that's fucking disturbing as hell. The thirty-minute trip gave me time to sober right up.

"Of course I am. And I'll be more than happy to show you if you do not remove your hand, now!" I grit out. He knows I don't fucking like being touched, unless it's Emily doing the touching, that is. Thinking of Emily, I pull my phone out and send her a quick message.

**Me:** I'm taking you out for dinner. Be ready at seven.

Her response is immediate.

**Emmy:** I can't go to dinner, Josh. Let's just have dinner here.

**Me:** Em, we're going out. Be ready. Love you. xx

**Emmy:** Are you sure that's wise?

**Me:** Yes. Talk tonight. I gotta go.

**Emmy:** Okay.

Sliding my phone back into my pocket, I jump out of the car. Sam's waiting for me with a group of around ten men I'm assuming he's brought along. Walking up to the group, I instruct them, "If anyone sees this fucker, shoot to hurt, not kill. That kill is mine. Let's go."

I get a mixture of grunts and "yes, sirs" in response.

Sam leads the way to the warehouse marked number six. Pushing past him, I kick the door open. I pull the Glock out from my back and storm into the building.

"Jesus Christ, Josh, let the whole fucking neighbourhood know we're here, why don't you."

"Shut up!" I hiss. I stop and listen. I identify and dismiss each distant sound: the wind rattling tin against tin, the dripping pipes, scurrying animals. There's nothing else. This building is fucking empty. Or the fucker's already a rotting corpse, because it sure does fucking stink like decay in here.

It's dark, apart from the light streaming in from the door we just kicked down. There're no windows in here. Looking around, I see a switch on the wall. When I pull the lever down, the warehouse lights up.

As soon as the lights come on, I see the reason why it stinks like rotting corpses. I look back at Sam. His face is pale, a few guys behind him already leaning over and losing the contents of their stomachs.

What the fuck did we just walk into? I can't help but feel like this is a setup, somehow. "Nobody touch a fucking thing," I say as I step further into the room. The sight before me is enough to give the fucking devil nightmares. It's a damn good thing I don't fucking scare easily.

There are three bodies, three female bodies. These women have been brutally tortured; ripped clothing hangs from their rotting flesh. As I inspect closer, my skin crawls. All three women have long blonde hair, their vacant blue eyes open and damning. I feel like they're staring right at me… accusingly. I didn't get here sooner. I haven't caught the bastard before he could do this to these women. The part that disturbs me the most is they all look like Emily.

This could be Emily's lifeless body lying here. Fuck! Turning around, I'm about to walk out when I spot the far wall. Sam's already over there taking photos with his phone of everything on display. As I walk up next to him, my hands are shaking. Spread out all over the wall are images of Emily. Old ones, and more recent ones of her at my apartment and out at the ranch.

How long has this fucker been watching her? There's image after image of her beaten and bruised, a few with casts on her arm. There're images of her spread out on a bed, naked, bruises and cuts all over her body. My gun drops to the ground, the sound echoing in the otherwise silent room.

I start tearing at the images, ripping them from the wall. I don't stop until every single one is in shreds. Once I'm satisfied that every photo is destroyed, I bend down, pick up my gun and walk out.

"Torch the fucking place," I grunt as I walk past the men standing at the entrance watching, waiting and unsure what the fuck to do.

I need to get home to Emily. I need to hold her living, breathing body in my arms. I need to breathe in her fruity scent, feel the pulse in her neck beneath my hand. This fucking prick of an ex-detective is going to have one hell of a fight on his hands if he thinks I'll ever let him get even an inch near her. I should have fucking shot his ass back on the side of the road when the asshole had the audacity to pull up behind me and question me about Emily.

# Chapter 10

## Emily

I'm not sure why I'm so nervous. It's Josh. I'm going out to dinner with Josh. Why the hell am I so nervous? Argh, I wipe my sweaty palms down the fabric of my dress, then recoil at the thought of possibly marking what has to be the softest freaking fabric I've ever worn.

I went in search of Ella's help as soon as Josh texted and asked me to be ready for dinner. Okay, well, he didn't ask so much as tell. But, again, it's Josh. I'm sure if I put my foot down, and really expressed how much I'd rather stay home, he wouldn't push it. He would let me stay here. Argh, why can't I just be normal?

*Because normal is overrated and average.* I hear Josh's voice repeating those words to me, like he has every day this past week. I just need to calm down. Looking at my reflection in the floor-length mirror, I let out the breath I've been holding. I don't know what Ella did, other than wave some bloody magic wand over me, because I don't look like the plain old Emily right now.

I'm wearing a knee-length black cocktail dress. It has a squared neckline, my breasts popping out the top, with probably way too much cleavage on display. The dress is tight, like painted on my body kind of tight. And there is a slit that runs right up the front of my left leg, stopping about two inches from my hip bone.

My hair is loosely curled, falling down my back. My face though… I don't know what she's done, but my eyes look three times bigger than usual, the blue really popping against the gold-toned eyeshadows. And my lips, fire-engine red. This girl looking back at me is not me. She's beautiful. I almost feel like I've got a disguise on. I'm not used to seeing myself look like this. I'm also not used to wearing dresses this nice.

I don't know how I'm meant to walk around without flashing everyone the black lace panties I have on underneath the dress. That's if I don't fall and break an ankle in the black strappy stilettos Ella had me put on. I tried to argue that I wouldn't be able to walk in them. Her response was: *"You'll have Josh to lean on anyway. You know that boy's not gonna let you fall flat on your face."*

The shoes do look really good, and I love how my legs look in them. I am, however, self-conscious of how much skin I have showing right now. What is Josh going to say when he sees me? I don't even know where we are going. What if this dress is too much? I mean, what if he just wanted to take me to McDonald's?

Shaking my hands out in an attempt to ease my nerves, I eye that bar fridge I've not inspected yet. Maybe if I just drink a little something, I can calm down enough to at least pretend to be normal.

I'm bending at the waist to examine the insides of the fridge, because this dress is too tight to bend down any other way. The fridge is filled with tiny bottles, most of which I don't recognise. The two bottles I do recognise are a sweet white wine or champagne. I opt for the bottle of sweet bubbly white.

"You know, I'm tempted to skip dinner and head straight into dessert, with that ass of yours being the only thing on my menu."

I jump out of my skin, straightening up and spinning around, only to slam into Josh's chest. Josh's very naked chest. Very wet, naked chest. Tiny water droplets drip down his torso. The moan involuntarily slips out of my lips.

"Fuck, Emmy, are you trying to give me a heart attack. Because damn, you look incredible." Josh takes the bottle from my hands. Stepping back, he twists the top off before holding the bottle back out to me. His eyes rake up and down my body.

"Thank you." My voice is just as shaky as my hands when I take the drink back and bring the bottle to my mouth. Why the hell am I so twisted about whether or not he likes the dress? I don't care what he thinks about it. I like it and that's all that matters. The lie I'm telling myself isn't working. I do care what he thinks and it's pissing me off, because I know I shouldn't.

Josh stares at my shaky hands. "What's wrong?"

"Nothing," I lie.

"Emmy, I fucking love you. But you're a shit-ass liar. Now, what's wrong?" he says, more persistent.

"I am not a shit-ass liar. When I was fourteen, I had my dad believe I was at a sleepover at my friend Katie's. When really, I went to..." I snap my mouth shut. That is not a story for Josh's ears. That's one of those I'll take it to my grave stories and never tell a soul.

"When you were really what? Go on, finish the sentence. This, I can't wait to hear."

"It doesn't matter. The moral of the story is: if I could get away with lying to my dad, who was a trained special forces soldier, then I think I'm a pretty good liar." I shrug.

"Emmy, I'm aware who your father was and what he did. But I'd love to know what it was you were really doing while you were supposed to be at your friend Katie's? That sounds like a story I should know. Also, we don't keep secrets from each other. Spill the beans, Em." He smirks.

Well, let's see how long he's wearing that cocky grin when I tell him what I was really doing that night I *didn't* stay at Katie's. "Okay, if you're so insistent on knowing, I'll tell you." I crook my finger at him, ushering him closer so I can whisper. Leaning into his ear, I tell him, "I went to the movies with Carter. He was the captain of our school's swim team. Real fast, he was. We sat up in the back of the theatre and..."

My sentence is cut off. Sparks explode throughout my body as Josh's lips smash against mine. His kiss has a way of making me lose all sense of reality. When Josh kisses me, everything in the room fades away, my senses overridden by my body's reaction to his.

"Mmm, I missed you," I mumble as I break away from his lips, fisting his shirt in one hand and trying not to drop my tiny wine bottle that's grasped in my other.

"I missed you more."

"Not a competition. Want the rest of that story now?" I ask sweetly.

"Nope, I'm going to be with your dad on this one and pretend that you really did stay at Katie's house all night."

"Okay." I step back, sipping on the wine. The sweet, fruity taste lingers on my tongue.

"Now, tell me what's wrong?" Josh says. Damn it, I thought he'd forgotten about that.

"It's nothing. Where are we going tonight anyway?"

"Emmy, it's not nothing. I can tell something's on your mind. I can't fix it for you if you don't tell me."

"You know you can't fix everything, right?"

"Try me?"

"Oh my God, you're relentless. Okay, I'm freaking out. Are you happy? I don't know where the bloody hell you're taking me. I don't know what I'm supposed to do. I don't know what I'm supposed to wear. If I look okay or not. If you like my dress, if it's too much… not enough? I don't know what the rules are. How am I supposed to keep to the rules if I don't know them?"

I'm yelling by the time I finish my tirade. I look up to see Josh's blank face. Great, he's got the *I'm not giving you an expression* face on. I hate that face. I can't read that face. I'm trying to replay what I just said to him in my head. Did I say something I shouldn't have?

Instinctively, I take a step to the side, trying to make space between us. The moment I do, that's when I see a tiny flicker of emotion in his eyes. He's annoyed. That's a look I know well. It's just not usually directed at me.

I wait him out. I don't know what to say or do after my little outburst. So, I just stand here and wait, like a deer caught in the headlights. Josh holds up his hand, all five fingers pointed up in the air.

"First, when it comes to you, I will always be relentless." He puts one finger down.

"Second, no, I'm not happy. I'm not happy because I can clearly see that you're not. I can't be happy when you're not okay, Em. I won't be happy until you are." He releases a breath.

"Third, I was planning to take you to a nice restaurant, have dinner, candles and shit. But I've had a change of plans. I'm taking you to The Merge. We are going to let our hair down and let loose." He puts another finger down.

"Fourth, you are fucking stunning in anything you wear. Whatever you choose to wear is the *right* thing. I cannot tell you enough how much I fucking love that dress on you. But if you hate it, then I hate it too. I want you to dress for you, Emmy, not anyone else." Another finger goes down. All I can do is stand here and nod an acknowledgement.

"And Fifth… Rules? There are no rules, Emmy. You are the fucking queen of the McKinley Empire; you make the fucking rules. Do not, and I repeat, do not let any other fuckers try to tell you any differently."

I don't even know what to say. That is a lot to take in, the power he is giving me, the control to make my own choices. As much as I want to be able to do all the things he says I can do, make my own decisions, my own rules, I'm afraid I don't know how to be that girl anymore. There's a constant bit of doubt that lingers in the back of my head, telling me it's just a trick, mind games.

What I can do is pretend. I've been getting better at pretending these last few weeks. I just need to keep doing it. I plaster a smile on my face, straighten my shoulders and fake the confidence that I don't yet have.

"We're going to the club Ella works at?" I ask excitedly. At least the enthusiasm is real. I've heard so much about The Merge. I've been wanting to go and see it for myself. According to Ella, it's the hottest club in Sydney, not that I would know. It's been years since I've been out, anywhere, let alone a nightclub.

Josh smirks and looks me up and down. "We are. But if you'd prefer, we can go to dinner."

"Are you kidding me? I want to see this fancy nightclub I keep hearing about. Are you sure I look okay for that?" I ask, glancing down at my dress again.

"You look perfect. You are perfect. Now, let's go." Josh holds his arm out, indicating for me to go in front of him.

"Fuck, Jesus Christ to all that is holy." He groans. I turn around, confused.

"What's wrong?" I ask.

"Hold on a sec. I just need to grab something real quick." Josh walks into his closet. Moments later, he walks back out, wearing a shoulder holster over his dress shirt. He stops at a chest of drawers and pulls out what looks like a small armoury. He selects two handguns, securing them into the holster.

"Why do you need those?" I ask as he makes his way back over to me while throwing a jacket on. We're only going to a nightclub.

"Babe, have you seen your ass in that dress? Every man in that place is going to have their eyes on you."

My eyebrows rise to my hairline. "You're joking, right? Josh, you can't go around shooting people. Even if they did look at me, which I doubt they will, but if they did, you cannot shoot people in Ella's club. It'll leave a mess."

"I'll pay for the cleaning bill." He laughs as he leads me out of the room with his hand on the small of my back.

# Chapter 11

## Josh

Stopping at the valet out front of The Merge, I turn to look at Emily. "Wait for me to open your door."

I jump out and hand the keys to the guy waiting. "You scratch it, I'll repaint the whole car with your blood." I smile at him. He stands there with his mouth hanging open as I jog around to the other side to let Emily out.

I have to stand directly in front of her while she manoeuvres herself from the car. I wasn't about to let every fucker get a glimpse of those black lace panties I just saw. I have to readjust myself in my pants. I'm a walking fucking hard-on right now—have been ever since I saw her bent over the bar fridge back in our room.

Emmy's grip on my hand tightens as she looks around the crowd currently lined up to get into the club. I pull her into my side, wrapping my arm around her shoulder. Leaning into her neck, I whisper, "The moment you feel like you need to leave, tell me and I'll get you out."

She nods her head, then puts that fake fucking smile back on her face. The same one she's been wearing for a few weeks now. I can always tell the difference (most people can't). But I know the one she's wearing right now is fake as hell. I haven't called her out on it though.

If she needs a mask to hide beneath, then I'll let her. Right now, she's handling whatever inner demons she's carrying around the way she needs to. If she can't handle it anymore, then she'll have me to handle it for her. Until then, I'll be here as her backup.

I walk us straight up to the door, bypassing the waiting patrons attempting to get in. Security pulls the rope aside the moment they spot me.

"Good evening, Mr. McKinley," one greets as he opens the door, at which, Emily giggles next to me. A real giggle, not a fake one.

"Something amusing?" I ask her.

"Just the whole Mr. McKinley thing. It makes you sound old. Wait, oh my gosh, is that a grey hair?" She reaches up, running her fingers through the front of my hair.

"It's blonde, not fucking grey. Also, we're exactly the same age, babe. If I'm old, what does that make you?"

She laughs. "Good point. We can be old together."

I'm leading her straight to the stairs for the VIP area when she just stops. I glance over at her. Her eyes are wide and her head turns, looking in every direction of the club.

I try to see the place the way she might. The walls are lined with red velvet curtains. Three stories high. The top two have balconies, which overlook the huge dance area on the ground floor where we are standing now. There's sectioned-off seating with a variety of bench seats and sofas. There are bar tables and coffee tables—all have a collection of gold sculpted bodies that are merged together in different kinds of erotic positions capped with a glass tabletop.

There's a main bar that runs along one side of the floor; it's already packed with people waiting to order their next rounds. Thank fuck we don't have to line up like that.

"You good?" I lean into Emily so she can hear me over the sound of the music. Her face lights up; a genuine smile greets me.

"This is amazingly beautiful," she yells out.

"I'll be sure to tell the owner," a gravelly voice says from behind us. I turn around, placing myself in front of Emmy and coming face to face with Zac. My brother's best friend. And the owner of this club. There's no love lost between us. We tolerate each other, for Dean's sake. Now, more for Ella's sake, considering this asshole is my new sister-in-law's brother. I don't even know where the hostility between us started. Maybe it's just always been there. I've honestly never cared to try to work it out.

"Zac." I nod my head at him. If he expects anything more, then he can fuck right off.

"Josh. I trust you're not going to go off on a crazy rampage and leave my club looking like a blood bath tonight?" He smirks.

Emily shoves herself in front of me. Where the hell she found the strength to move me, I don't know. It's probably because she caught me off guard. That's what I'll go with. She stands there with her arms crossed over her chest, her breasts popping out of the top of her dress even more. They look fucking delicious.

One thing I'll give Zac, his eyes never waver from her face. His amused smirk though, that pisses me off. I can tell it's having the same effect on Emily. I decide not to step in, and to let her handle this. I'm intrigued as to what she'll do.

"Zac, the only reason you still have your balls attached to your body right now is because I happen to like your wife. *But* I won't warn you again, if you call Josh crazy or make any comment to suggest that he is, I will cut them off. I'll make meatballs out of them and feed them to his pigs. I've heard they particularly like chewing on the balls of assholes."

Fuck me. My boner just got ten times harder. She's fucking hot as hell when she speaks her mind. Zac, however, covers his balls with his hand. He screws his face up in disgust before he starts laughing.

"I'll have to thank my wife for being so damn lovable. Come on, I've got you two lovebirds a table upstairs."

I wrap an arm around Emmy's waist, holding her in place. "We'll be up in a moment." Zac walks away, shaking his head. As soon as he's out of sight, Emmy spins around.

"Oh God, Josh, I'm so sorry. I didn't mean to. I just… I don't know what comes over me. I hate when people try to say you're crazy. It's not okay and I just… God, I'm sorry."

"Don't be sorry. *I'm not.* I'm fucking hard as a damn steel pole right now." I press my cock into her stomach so she can feel exactly what I'm talking about.

"The idea of pigs eating balls turns you on, huh?" She smirks.

I shiver at the image. "Fuck no. *You* turn me on. When you speak your mind, that shit's a fucking turn-on. When you stand up for me, which by the way you really do not need to do, that's a fucking turn-on. A complete other level of turn-on." I look around. There's gotta be a bathroom around here somewhere. A closet? Office? Fuck, I'll take a dark corner at this point.

"Uh, thanks? I think. What are you looking for?"

"Somewhere I can take you and fuck you where no one else will see what's mine. You heard Zac. He doesn't want his club to be a blood bath tonight, which means no fucker can see your face when I make you come. Otherwise, I'll have to shoot them."

"Wow, okay. Um, how about we file that idea for when we get back to your place. Because as appealing as that is, I kind of wanna see what's upstairs. Come on."

Emily grabs my hand and leads the way, following the path she watched Zac take. Pulling her back into me, I wrap an arm around her shoulder. "*Our* place. And I'm not sure I can wait that long. My balls are literally aching right now, Emmy."

"You'll survive. Delayed gratification and all." She laughs.

---

"SAM, YOU'RE HERE." Emily jumps up, throwing her arms around him a few too many drinks later. Sam holds his arms out to his side, staring straight at me and not returning her hug. That is, until he realises she ain't gonna let go unless he does. He lightly pats her back and pulls her arms from around his neck.

"You're seriously trying to get me killed, Emily. You know that, right?" he says to her.

"Stop it. He's not allowed to shoot anyone tonight. Zac said so."

Sam's eyebrows rise as he laughs. "That fucker is too crazy

to listen to reason. If he wanted to shoot me, he would. Fuck, he'd probably even do it in a damn church."

The next thing I see is Sam hunched over, grabbing hold of his balls, right where Emily's knee just slammed into him. I wince for him. Even if he deserved it, that shit fucking hurts like hell.

"You know what? Zac said Josh couldn't shoot anyone. He didn't say *I* couldn't. Josh, hand me a gun." Emily holds her hand out behind her in my direction.

As much as I want to hand her a gun and see what she actually does with it, I also don't want my friend shot tonight.

"Babe, if I can't shoot anyone, then neither can you. Also, you're drunk. You won't even be able to aim properly." I laugh, pulling her down onto my lap.

"I wouldn't miss. I bet I'm the best shot here out of all of you," she says, pointing to each of the men at the table. As soon as Emily and I sat down, it seemed Ella's whole fucking tribe came and crashed our party. Ella, I don't mind so much. She doesn't piss me off every other second. Dean, Bray, Zac and their wives though? Different story. Actually, Alyssa is sweet as hell. Even I can't not like her. Reilly, Bray's wife… that chick is crazier than me. I feel like I always have to be on high alert when she's around.

"Okay, Little Miss Sniper. How much we putting on this? I'm in. There's no way you're a better shot than me," Bray asks Emily.

I've actually never heard if she can shoot or not. But my money will always be on her. I don't even care if I win or lose. Because as long as I have her, I'm already winning.

"One mil?" I offer up a bet, waiting for Bray to either counter or back out.

Emily gasps. She turns and whispers in my ear, "Josh, I don't have one mil. What if I lose?"

"Babe, how confident are you that you can beat him?" I ask her.

She looks over at him, then turns back to me and smiles. "Extremely." She nods.

I don't know if it's the alcohol in her system or not, but I'm not about to let her lose that confidence. "Make it two million," I tell Bray.

He laughs. "Sure, if you wanna throw your fancy McKinley money away, who am I to say no?" he asks.

"Ah, Bray, that's a lot of freaking money. What if you lose?" Reilly asks.

"Rye, relax, there's no way I'm losing. Besides, I married a trust fund brat. I'm good for it." He laughs and dodges her strike.

I've read about Reilly's family. Her dad was a big-time investor before he went to jail; he left her and her twin (Holly) a hefty little nest egg. Not that Bray needs her money, these fuckers have more cash than they know what to do with. Maybe it's not the McKinley kind of money, but they're a long way from begging.

"Josh, this is crazy. You can't waste that much money. What if I lose?" Emily asks again.

"I don't actually care if you win or lose. It'll be fun to watch him sweat a bit. He's far too cocky.

"I'll do my best," she says.

"Babe, relax." Whispering in her ear, I tell her, "We make over a million dollars in one day. We can afford to lose a couple." Her eyes widen.

"*You* make that, Josh. Not me. I'm homeless. I don't even

have a job. I didn't even get to finish university. I'm probably never going to get a job."

"You know you're never going to need a job, Em, but if you want to do something, I'll do whatever I can to make sure you can do it."

"I don't think I can go back to school now. It's been too many years."

"You can do whatever you want."

"We'll see."

"Emmy, people go to Uni at all ages. If you want to go back to med school, I can make sure you get into the best school in Australia."

"How'd you know I was in med school?"

I look over to Sam. "He found your records. Not that I was surprised. You're the smartest person I know."

"No, I'm not. But I do need to pee. I'll be back." She goes to get off my lap.

"I'll come with you."

"You are not coming to the bathroom with me, Joshua. Sit down." She folds her arms over her chest.

"Fine, Ella, go with Emily." Ella doesn't argue; she stands up and links arms with my girl. I nod to the security guy sitting at the bar watching, instructing him to follow.

"You know she's not going to disappear into thin air, right?" Bray laughs.

"Fuck off."

"Just saying. You also don't have x-ray vision, so no matter how much you stare at the wall, you won't be able to see her."

He's fucking right. I can't see her anymore and it makes my skin crawl. I don't like it. I feel like something's wrong. Like I should have gone with her.

I try to shake the feeling and down the glass of whisky Dean puts in front of me.

"Josh, you good?" Sam asks.

"Yeah, fine."

"No, you're not."

"You're right. I'm not." I get up and head in the direction Emily went. Something in my gut is telling me I need to find her. I always fucking trust my gut.

# Chapter 12

## Emily

"Wow!" I don't think I've ever been in a nightclub bathroom this fancy. The floors and walls are covered in white marble tiles. There is a chandelier—a huge, blingy chandelier—in the middle of the room. There's a row of vanity tables with pink fluffy stools. This must be how the other half lives.

"Yeah, I had it redecorated to be more feminine," Ella says as she takes in the bathroom.

"I'm almost too afraid to pee in here. It's too nice." I laugh.

Just then, Ella's phone starts blaring. "Go pee. I'm just gonna step outside and take this."

I nod and head into the stall. I can hear the sound of heels clicking on the tiles as I finish up, straighten my dress and flush the loo. I head out to the basin. Just before I reach the sink,

I'm yanked back by my hair. My whole body freezes. My eyes shut. I can't open them. He's found me. He's not dead; he's here.

My body drops to the floor. "You stupid fucking bitch. You ruined everything." A high-pitched squeal echoes through the room. That's a female's voice; that's not him. It's not him. I'm okay. Well, I will be once I get off this damn floor.

I open my eyes just in time to see the hand flying towards my face and landing with a sharp sting. I smile at her. If that's her worst, she's about to be really bloody sorry for hitting me. I want to know what it is I ruined though. So, before I retaliate, I ask her, "Do I know you?"

I know exactly who she is. She's the stupid bitch who was at Josh's penthouse a few weeks ago. But the look that crosses her face is priceless.

"I'm the future Mrs. Joshua McKinley, bitch. He. Is. Mine. I know he was almost ready to pop the question before you came on the scene."

I think she's delusional. There is no way Josh would consider marrying someone like her. The thought that he even slept with her is disturbing enough. "Look, clearly you've let Josh fuck you. So, I'm sure you know that he has a name inked across his heart. That's my name, idiot. He was never yours." I push her off me and sit up. "He will never be yours."

"That's where you're wrong. I don't care what name he has on his skin. It will be my name on that marriage certificate. *That's* all that matters." She stands up and opens the little clutch she's holding, pulling out a knife.

Well, that puts a damper on my night. How do I get myself out of here? I look to the door and she steps in front of me.

"No one's coming to help you. You won't be walking out of this bathroom." She leans down into my face. Holding the knife at my throat, she says, "I'm going to enjoy fucking you out of his system." Then, as if on cue, the door slams open and Josh storms in.

Without a word, he effortlessly picks Whitney up. "I thought I warned you about going anywhere near Emily."

"Josh, she attacked me. Don't let her do this to us." Josh laughs, before his face becomes passive. Blank.

"You should have stayed away," he says as he grabs the knife out of her hands and slices it right across her throat. She lets out a gurgled sound, and then nothing. The room goes silent.

I can't stop the gasp that comes out. I've never seen anything so graphically violent, aside from my own beatings… and what I did to Trent. But those instances were different… the memories are blurred. Frenzied. I wasn't in the background, witnessing everything like I am now. Josh looks at me. "Fuck." He drops her body, stepping over her. There's blood, so much blood. It's the only thing I can focus on. The blood pooling around her neck…

"Emmy, I'm sorry. I shouldn't have done that in front of you." Josh squats down on the floor next to me.

He shouldn't have done that *at all*. I know that. It's on the tip of my tongue to say. I should say it. But I can't, even though I know what he's done is wrong. I also know what I've done is wrong. I can't look at him and not still be completely and utterly in love with him. Is this what crazy is? I know they say love is blind, but this is beyond that.

"Josh, we need to clean this mess up. Zac said no blood baths, remember? That kinda looks like a blood bath." I nod my head to the body, now limp and framed in red.

"Yeah, babe, don't worry about it. Are you okay? Are you hurt?"

I shake my head no. I'm not hurt. "I'm okay. Are… are you okay?" I ask him.

"I'm fine. Emmy, can I pick you up?"

Why is he asking to pick me up? It dawns on me that he hasn't touched me at all. He's just been sitting in front of me. I nod my head yes. Josh picks me up and settles me on the vanity bench. His hand comes up and brushes my hair away from my face.

"Fuck. Shit. Don't move. Let me clean that." He reaches for a towel from the pile sitting on the bench opposite us. My hands grab his shirt, and I pull him back to me. My lips find his. I lose myself in this kiss, in him. This is what I need. I need him.

He kisses me back tentatively at first, keeping his hands away from me. I need him to touch me. I know it's all kinds of fucked up. I should be disgusted right now. I should be running for the damn hills. But this is the man my soul connects with on such a deep level. Right now, I need to feel our connection more than anything, and he's holding back. I don't know why. He's never held back like this before.

I wrap my legs around his waist and pull him in closer. I can feel the hardness of his cock against my centre. Moaning into his mouth, I rub myself on him. Something snaps in Josh in that exact moment. His hands go straight for my hair, tilting my head back and angling my mouth at a slant that gives him a deeper vantage point. His tongue duels with mine as we both fight for control of the kiss.

Josh trails one hand down my back, pulling me closer to him as he grinds on me. I'm wet, the lace of my panties doing nothing to contain my arousal. I can feel my excitement sticking to my inner thighs.

"Mmm, Josh, I need you," I murmur into his mouth. His response is to growl, biting down on my lower lip.

"What the fuck, Josh!" I hear yelled at us. I'm too drunk on this kiss to even care who it is. I want more. I need more of Josh, and whoever just walked in has interrupted.

Josh breaks away from the kiss, while attempting to pull my dress down my thighs to a respectable level. When he realises it's not going to happen, he gives up and lifts me from the bench, fixing my hem before he turns around.

"Sorry?" he questions both Dean and Sam, who are standing in the bathroom looking down at a lifeless body. Both of whom don't seem too fussed with the scene. More annoyed.

"Sorry… you're sorry? What the fuck happened in here? Emily, are you okay, sweetheart?" Dean asks.

Huh, interesting. I've always had a feeling that he didn't like me very much. Yet he always asks if I'm okay. I nod my head and step in front of Josh. I will not let anyone give him a hard time about helping me. Protecting me.

"I'm sorry. It's my fault. She came at me with a knife and I freaked out. By the time Josh came in here, she was already dead." The lie easily slips from my mouth—a lie I will repeat over and over if it means protecting Josh from any fallout from this.

"Holy shit, Em. I take back what I said about you being a shitty liar, because that was fucking gold." Josh laughs from behind me.

"Josh, not the time for that conversation," I hiss out.

"Jesus, you've got it bad, girl." Sam shakes his head. "Blink once if you need rescuing," he tells me.

I raise my eyebrows at him and tilt my head. "How are your balls feeling, Sam?"

"Yep, that's my cue to arrange a clean-up crew. Be right

back. Don't leave this bathroom, kids. You both look like shit. Well, not you, Emily. You could never look like shit." Sam winks as he exits the room.

"Emily, don't ever lie for Josh again. He's a big boy and can definitely clean up his own mess," Dean says pointedly to me before directing at Josh, "And you, really? Why is it every time you come here, you leave a mess behind?"

"That's an exaggeration, Dean. You would have done the same thing. She had a knife at Emmy's throat when I came in here. Tell me you wouldn't have done the same thing for Ella." Josh takes hold of my hand. I can feel the trembling. I squeeze tight and hold on. This is a sign he's about to lose his shit. I need him to calm down.

"Of course I would have. I would have done the same for Emily too, you know. I'm not saying you did the wrong thing, just really shitty fucking timing."

"Oh my God!" Ella screeches from the doorway before her pale face looks up at us.

"Fucking hell. El, Princess, calm down." Dean wraps his arms around her.

"Calm down, Dean? There's a dead girl in my bathroom and you're telling me to calm down." Her voice rises even louder when two more men come through the door.

"Jesus Christ, Josh, I thought I told you no blood tonight." Zac curses as he looks from the body to me and Josh.

"It wasn't Josh. It was me. It's my fault. I did it," I say, folding my arms over my chest. Zac and Bray both burst out laughing. I square my shoulders.

"What's so funny about that?" I ask.

"She's a keeper, that one, Josh." Bray smirks.

"Ella, you good?" Zac asks, turning to his sister.

"I'd be better with less blood around. Dean, I need a drink, now!" Ella stomps out of the bathroom. I feel bad. She was so proud of how nice this bathroom was, and I've ruined it.

"Emily, are you okay?" Zac asks me. I'm a little shocked. He hasn't really said much all night. He mostly sits there, looking grouchy and staring at wherever Alyssa is.

"Uh, yep. I think so," I answer.

"I'm okay too. Thanks for asking," Josh says. "Sam will have a clean-up crew here in no time. Don't worry, you won't even know they were here."

"Yeah, I think I'll organise my own. Bray, call them in. I want this bathroom remodelled. *Again.* Follow me. There's a bathroom in my office you two can use."

Zac walks out. "Wow, you must have made a good impression, Emily. He won't even let me use his bloody bathroom," Bray says while typing away on his phone.

It dawns on me that no one, not a single one of these men were deterred by the fact that there is a body surrounded by blood on the floor right now.

"Is Zac like a mafia boss or something? Because I get that, you know, it's only family blah blah, but that's probably something someone should have told me before I threatened to feed his balls to the pigs," I question both Josh and Bray.

"Wait, you what? Seriously, what is it with you two and those fucking pigs? It's fucking gross."

"Babe, he is not mafia. You read way too many books." Josh laughs as he pulls me out of the room.

We make it up to Zac's office easily enough. "Bathroom's through there. I'll be downstairs. Try not to kill anyone," Zac grunts as he walks out.

"Sure thing," Josh says, leading me into the bathroom and closing the door behind him. I find myself in yet another over-the-top, luxurious bathroom. Josh is silent as he turns the water on, adjusting the tap until he's satisfied with the temperature.

He's also silent as he removes his jacket, then his holster and shirt. His eyes never leave mine as he toes off his shoes and pulls his pants down. I just stand here. As I wait in the silence, the whole scene of what just happened replays in my head. In graphic detail. The dead look in Josh's eyes as he ran the knife across her throat. My reaction afterwards. All the blood…

I feel nauseous. My body erupts in a cold sweat, causing me to shiver. Oh God, I'm going to be sick. Rushing to the loo, I crouch down over it. Can my life get any more miserable right now? Tears stream down my cheeks as my stomach rejects every bit of liquor I've consumed tonight. My whole body shakes as I sob into the porcelain bowl.

Josh is right behind me, rubbing his hand up and down my back, holding my hair away from my face and whispering how everything is going to be all right. He's wrong. How is it going to be all right? How can we ever be okay? We're both fucked up. Josh and I are two very messed up wrongs. They say two wrongs do not make a right. If that's true, then why does being *his* feel so damn right?

"Emmy, babe, it's going to be okay. We are going to be okay. We have to be."

"Josh, what's wrong with me?" I ask him.

"Em, you're in shock. It's okay. That… I shouldn't have done that in front of you. I will never forgive myself for that. I'm sorry, so fucking sorry."

"That's the thing, Josh. I should care. I should be running right now. Except I don't care. I don't care that I just watched you… you… I don't care about *that.* I should care, but I don't.

That's not normal. Love shouldn't be so blind. We shouldn't be okay with this."

"Emily, look at me." The fact that he called me Emily makes my head snap right up. He rarely calls me Emily. It's always Emmy or Em.

"There is nothing wrong with you. There is nothing wrong with *us*. What we have, it's so much more than love, Emily. What we have, the connection we share, it's unbreakable. It always has been. We have something people spend their whole lives wishing to find. The stuff Hallmark wished they could capture in a card. What we have, whatever it is, it's beautiful. It's extraordinary. Immeasurable. It's unfailing."

Josh kisses the top of my head and lifts me up to my feet. He unzips my dress, slowly pulling it down my body. He bends over and unclips my shoes, removing one at a time before dragging my panties down my legs.

I capture my reflection in the mirror. My hair stained with blood from Josh's hands. My eyes red. My face blotchy. And all I can think is: *I've looked worse.*

# Chapter 13

## Josh

I've been lying here for hours, replaying the events of the night. Emily cried herself to sleep in my arms. Her rest has been unsettled, plagued with constant stirring. My hand mindlessly runs up and down her back in attempts to soothe her, to calm her. For the first time, I'm guilt-ridden after ending another's life.

I'm not sorry for killing Whitney. The bitch deserved it. No, I don't feel guilty over her. I feel like shit because I lost control and let Emily see me do something so horrendous. It's one thing for her to know I'm capable or even willing to do such a thing, but it's completely different for her to witness me in the act.

I'm shocked she's still here. I'm so afraid that she's going to wake up and what I did will suddenly sink in. She's going to see how too-fucking-good for me she is, and she's going to want to disappear again. I've never been afraid of anything like I am of losing Emily, of having her fear me.

I've made so much progress with getting her to trust in me. To trust that I'm not ever going to hurt her like she has been. How can I expect her to trust that fact after what she saw?

It's almost dawn. I'm running on no sleep and I have to go into the fucking office in two hours. I haven't told Emily about the emails or threats.

Until yesterday, I didn't think too much of them. They were disturbing and fucking pissed me off. It wasn't until I saw the evidence left behind of what that sick fuck is capable of that I got scared. That I grasped how real the threat to Emily is. How am I meant to leave her side, knowing that some sick fucker is out to get her? Knowing exactly what he will do if he does get to her?

What I don't understand is the why. Why the fuck is he so hell-bent on getting his hands on Emily? The sooner I pinpoint the connection and determine what he wants, the sooner I can plan how to draw him out and erase the fucking prick.

"Mmm, did you sleep at all?" I look down into the depths of Emily's blue eyes staring up at me.

"A little," I lie.

"I'm sorry. I don't know how to tell you how sorry I am," she says. I wish she would get it through her head that she doesn't need to be fucking sorry for shit.

"Emmy, you have nothing to apologize for." Leaning down, I connect my lips with hers. The moment I do, all my worries get pushed to the back of my mind, my thoughts clear. The only focus is the feel of Emily's soft, plump lips on mine. The sparks that ignite throughout my body. Her scent all around me. I drown in all that is Emily as soon as our lips connect.

Emily pulls away from the kiss. I can't help but pout at her. I want those delicious lips. "I'm sorry for what you had to do to protect me. I'm sorry I've brought so much trouble into your life. It was never my intention."

"Emmy, I fucking love you. So damn much. There is nothing I wouldn't do to protect you. There is no one I wouldn't slay to ensure your safety. Fuck, even God will have a damn fight on his hands when he tries to claim his angel back. Because I guarantee you: I am one devil who won't give up on you."

"Ah, pretty sure my chances of heaven have long since passed. Don't worry, we'll both be going to the same place."

"Babe, you haven't done a damn thing wrong. You are an innocent survivor, who fought her demons and won."

"Then why doesn't it feel like I've won? He's winning even now. His death hasn't stopped my hell. I'm still hiding out. I'm still running. I just want it to be over, Josh. I'm tired of being scared."

"It will be over soon, Emmy. I promise. And then, you and I are getting that white picket fence. We're going to fill stables with horses. We'll have dogs, cats, sheep, chickens… Fuck, I'll get you a damn alpaca if you want one. We are going to have the future you've always dreamt of. The future I've always dreamt of."

"I hope you're right."

"Haven't you heard? I'm always right."

Emily's laughter feeds my soul, illuminating the sombre mood we were both in. Her joy is the best medicine. And it's contagious. I want to hear it all damn day.

"Babe, get up. Put on some swimmers and a sundress. Pack

a hat and sun lotion. We're going out for the day." I roll her off me and jump out of bed with a sudden burst of energy. I've just decided that Emily and I are spending the entire day together. It's my mission to hear that laugh of hers for the duration.

"Where are we going? Don't you have to go to work?" I can feel her eyes on my naked ass as I make my way into the closet. Turning, I catch her checking me out.

"Em, my eyes are up here." I smirk, pointing to my face.

"I know, but that ass, Josh. It deserves attention." She laughs.

"Fair call. We are going everywhere. Ever been a tourist in Sydney? That's what we are today, just regular old tourists, exploring a new city."

"Okay, but is it safe for me to be out like that? What if someone recognises me? What if today's the day they plaster my face all over the news? What if the police are looking for me?"

I walk back over to her, taking both of her hands in mine. "Breathe, Emmy. You are safe. You are okay. We've looked, remember? There is no record of you being wanted by the police. There is no record of a murder, or a body being found. There is only one rogue ex-cop looking for you, Em. We will be fine. I swear I won't let him get anywhere near you."

---

"CAN I DRIVE?" Em asks with a huge-ass smile on her face. My heart literally palpitates. Is she serious? She wants to drive my car? I'm so fucking torn over wanting my car to remain in one piece without a fucking scratch, and giving her what she wants.

I find myself handing her the keys. There's something about the smile on her face. If I have to risk my half a million dollar Lamborghini to keep that smile there, then I will. I might cry if she destroys my car. But I'll get over it. *It's just a car. It's just a car.* I keep repeating the mantra in my head. *She is everything. This is just a car.* My fingers loosen around the keys as I place them in her palms.

"Really, you're letting me drive? Yes! Thank you, thank you, thank you." She throws her arms around my neck as she jumps up and down on the spot, full of excitement.

"Emmy, there is nothing you could ever ask me for that I'd say no to."

She raises her eyebrows at me, mischief written all over her face. "Well, there was this one thing I read about…"

"Almost nothing, babe. There are a few things I'm never saying yes to. So, whatever it is that you've read in one of your romance books, unless it involves only two people—those two people being you and me—don't even ask."

Her lips spread into a smile. "So that's a no to a threesome then?"

"That's a *fuck no*, Emily. There is no fucking chance on earth I'm ever sharing you with anyone."

Emily laughs as she makes her way to the driver's side of the car. "It's a really good thing I don't ever want you to share me then. Come on, get in. I'm about to take you on the ride of your life." She winks as she climbs into the car.

I send a little prayer up to anyone listening. *Please let my car make it out of this in one piece.* Shit, I don't think I've ever even seen Emily drive. Can she fucking drive? Getting into the passenger's side, I buckle in.

"You do have a driver's license, right?" I ask her.

"Ah, not on me. Why? Will it be a problem if we get pulled over?"

"No, but you do know how to drive? I mean, you have passed a driving test before, haven't you?" I can feel the tiny balls of sweat forming on my eyebrows. Fuck, this is making me more nervous than I anticipated.

"Relax. My daddy taught me to drive before I could even walk." She smiles.

I watch as she turns the engine. She runs her hands over the steering wheel, then over the gear stick. "Hold on," she says.

Hold on? For what? I don't get to ask her before the tyres are screeching and she's pulling, *screaming*, up the driveway.

"Fuck, Emily Livingston, slow the fuck down!" I yell as she slams her foot on the breaks, the car coming to a stop just before the huge fucking iron gates at the front of the property—the iron gates that haven't been opened yet.

"No, fuck no. That is not how we drive this car, Emily. You are a Sunday granny driver. We ain't in some Nascar race right now. A leisurely Sunday drive is the vibe we're going for."

Emily stares at me for a minute before she speaks. When she does, her voice is low and quiet. "Josh, I don't have to drive. If you want to swap seats, we can." She actually pouts at me.

Now, I'm fucking confused. Emily has never pouted at me. That low voice she just used was different. What the fuck is wrong with her? I don't know how to handle this. Of course, I want to switch seats with her and take my damn car back. But what I want more is to see that smile back on her face. I want her to be happy and free.

"Emmy, I don't care if you want to drive. I just want you to be safe—that's all." I grab her hand and bring her fingers up to my mouth, placing a kiss on each one.

"Okay, well, as long as you're sure. I've always wanted to drive one of these fancy cars." She beams.

Why the fuck do I feel like I just got played? Did she just emotionally bribe me to get her way? I can't believe I just fell for it that easily. Damn, she's good. The goofy smile I'm now sporting is hard to hide.

"What's wrong?" Emily asks as she ever so slowly pulls out of the driveway.

"Absolutely nothing. Why would something be wrong?"

"Because you're smiling weird. Why?" She stares at my face.

"First, keep your eyes on the road. You're driving around extremely important cargo right now. Second, don't let my girlfriend hear you say I'm weird. She gets a little trigger-happy whenever she hears that." I laugh.

"Your girlfriend sounds like a cool chick. Also, I didn't say *you* were weird. I said your smile was."

"Oh, she's the coolest. Beautiful, smart, loyal, sexy, stunning… Did I mention she's beautiful?" My eyes travel up and down her body. She's wearing a royal blue sundress. It's loose-fitting with thin straps. Her hair is up in a ball of mess on top of her head, her face free of any makeup. Right now, she looks perfect.

"You've mentioned it once or twice." She smiles. "Are you ready?"

"For what?" I ask.

"For the ride of your life, baby." She laughs as she puts her foot down before shifting gears. The car takes off. I'm pulled back into my seat with the force.

Fuck me. I look ahead and see we are merging onto the

freeway. Where the fuck is she even going? Why didn't I know she was such a lead foot?

I look behind us to check that the security detail is keeping up. They're not. "Ah, babe, I need you to slow down a bit. You need to let the security cars tail you. At this speed, they can't keep up."

"Why do we need security cars tailing us? And what kind of security are they if they can't keep up?"

"Because I'm a VIP, baby! And trust me, they're the best. I wouldn't put just any random security on you."

Emily looks in the rear-view mirror. With a huff, she slows down. I can at least breathe a little easier now.

## Chapter 14

### Emily

I pull up in the almost-empty parking lot. The memories of my dad bringing me here, to this beach, hit me hard. This place holds some of my fondest memories of him. I used to hate him. My dad died saving the lives of others, and I hated him for not being able to save himself. Now, I just wish I'd told him how much I loved him.

I remember yelling at him before he left for his last tour. I remember telling him I hated him for leaving us again. That's a regret I will live with for the rest of my life. My dad was one of the best special forces soldiers this country has ever had. I'm proud to be his daughter. Although, I'm not so sure he'd be proud of me. I haven't given him anything to be proud of lately.

"You okay?" Josh asks from the passenger seat.

"Yeah, you ready to hit the beach?"

"Is there a reason you drove us an hour and a half to get to a beach? You know Bondi was only about twenty minutes from the house."

"I like this beach. It's quiet. I like that it's not crowded here. Besides, this is Soldiers Beach, you know. It's just as famous for its surf as Bondi."

I unbuckle and step out of the car. The fresh smell of the ocean assaults me, the sun warming my skin instantly. Josh walks around the car and wraps an arm around me, pulling my back against his chest. He leans his face into the crook of my neck. I tilt my head to the side, giving him better access, his lips leaving a scorching hot trail as they find their way to my ear.

"Have you been here before, Em?" His voice is husky.

"Mmm, uh, yeah. My dad used to bring me here when he was home. Come on, let's go." I remove his arm from my waist and join our fingers together. I never thought I'd like holding hands with someone as much as I like holding Josh's hand.

Walking down the million steps is exhausting, but so worth it to get to the beach below us. Once we make it to the bottom, Josh releases my hand. I look back over my shoulder at him. I can't help but drool a little at the sight before me. Josh pulls his shirt over his head and tucks it into the back of the waistband on his boardshorts.

He's standing here, in nothing but a pair of black boardshorts, all those toned, tanned muscles on display. All those delicious tattoos, for everyone to see, my name sitting proudly in the middle of his chest. I can't help but feel territorial over this man. I mean, my name is literally written on him. That means he's mine, right?

I look around the beach. There're a few people here but not anywhere near as many as what would be at Bondi. I smirk at Josh. I notice a group of young girls who are now openly staring at us, or staring at Josh anyway. I glare at them, not that they notice. Two can play that game. For the first time, in a long time, I feel comfortable in my own skin. I feel like I can be out here and people aren't going to be staring at a battered and bruised woman, my body currently free of any kind of markings. Yes, it's been a very long time since I have looked and felt this healthy.

"Hold these for me." I hand over my bag and hat to Josh.

"Sure. You know I'd carry your shit anywhere for you, babe."

"Well, that would have been useful back in high school when we had to carry around all those damn textbooks. Now, not so useful. But thanks," I say as I drag my dress over my head. I hold my hand out to Josh to return my bag.

He's standing motionless, just staring at me. Shit, I think I might have broken him this time. "Josh." I snap my fingers in front of his face. He shakes his head, coming out of whatever trance he was in.

"Emmy, where the fuck is the rest of your swimsuit?" he growls under his breath while taking my dress from me. I duck as he attempts to put it back over my head.

"This is a perfectly fine swimsuit, Josh. Don't be ridiculous. Now, are we going to stand here all day arguing over my swimmers, or are we going to get in the water?"

"Em, babe, don't get me wrong… you look fucking hot as shit. But seriously, every other guy here is checking you out. I don't know if I have it in me to refrain from cutting all of their eyes out."

I look down at my body. I'm wearing a black string bikini. It's not that skimpy, from the front at least. Josh hasn't seen the back yet.

"Don't worry, I'll keep hold of your hand so you feel less murdery." Taking his hand, I turn and pull him towards the water, dropping my bag and kicking off my slides on the way.

"Fucking hell, I want to kill whoever the fuck designed that thing. Emmy, you know the material that's meant to cover your ass is missing. You should be asking for a refund. Fuck me, everyone's looking at your ass, babe." His hand squeezes mine tighter.

"The only person looking at my ass who even remotely matters is you. Let's not worry about what others are doing, Josh. It's just you and me."

"Okay, you and me. I like that," he says, before picking me up and running towards the water.

Once he gets waist-deep, he lets me go, dumping me into the water. My head goes under as I struggle to get my bearings. Before I can stand upright, Josh's hands drag me towards the surface. I'm coughing and spitting water everywhere. God, could I look any more awkward right now?

My hands go to my eyes, rubbing the salty residue out of them. "Oh my God, I hate you right now!" I yell as I wail in his hold.

Josh laughs and tugs me tighter against his body. Is that? It is! His hard cock is currently pressing into my stomach. How the hell is it hard right now in this cold water?

"No, you don't." He delivers his panty-dropping smirk at me.

"How on earth can you be turned on right now? I literally just spat water all over you."

"Emmy, I just have to look at you to be hard. Seeing you in this pathetic excuse of a swimsuit, all that smooth skin, feeling these curves under my palms… That's making me as hard as a fucking rock."

I wrap my legs around his waist, linking my ankles together to hold them in place. Releasing his neck, I let my body float backwards in the water, stretching my arms above my head. I love floating on the water. I love the feeling of weightlessness.

"Fuck me, Em, you're a goddamn walking pin-up." Josh growls as his hands go around my back, picking me up and pulling my chest closer to meet his.

"Well then, maybe you should pin me," I suggest.

Josh looks around the beach, then the water. "If there weren't so many people here, I would have you pinned to the sand in a heartbeat, Em."

I follow his gaze and look around. There is a good crowd of people spread out along the beach. What catches my attention is the ten men in suits standing in a line, right where I dropped my bag on the sand.

"Don't you think that's a bit of overkill, and why are they wearing suits? We're at the beach. It's odd," I voice to Josh.

"When it comes to protecting you, there is no such thing as overkill. And they're professionals; they're working. They wear suits. Trust me, Em, I'm paying them more than enough to be here." He looks over to where they stand, except one of them is now walking towards the water. Towards us.

Josh's whole body stiffens as he watches the man approach the shoreline. He waits for him to stop at the water's edge before he unclasps my legs and stands me on my feet.

"Wait here. Don't move an inch. I'll be back."

"Okay." I watch as he makes his way out of the water. And so does every other pair of female eyes on the beach. They can look all they like, but that man is mine. I'd die fighting for him if I had to.

Josh's whole body tenses as he glares at something the man shows him. He spins around and runs back towards me, making it to where I'm standing in seconds.

Taking hold of my hand, he pulls me towards the sand. "Sorry, babe, we gotta leave, now!"

"Josh, what's wrong?" I try to tug my hand free of his, which only makes him spin around and pick me up.

"Josh, stop! You're scaring me. Tell me what's going on!" I yell.

"I'll tell you once we're in the car." Josh storms up the beach, pausing at my bag. He puts me down on my feet as his security team forms a circle around us. I'm officially freaked out. Why are they all looking around, one hand each underneath their jackets, like they are waiting for the need to draw out a gun?

I can feel my body start to tremble as the panic sets in. I search Josh's face for answers, but all I can see is his anger, his eyes darkened, his jaw tensed.

"I want two cars in front, two behind. Do not let anyone get between," he directs to the men surrounding us. Picking up our belongings, he throws my bag over his shoulder before looking me up and down. Cursing under his breath, he shakes out his shirt and puts it over my head.

I absently place my arms through the sleeves. Bringing the collar up to my nose, I inhale his scent. It's somewhat soothing to my frayed nerves.

"Em, I need you to not let go of my hand right now. Stay behind me." He holds my hand tight, like I'll float away if he doesn't. I just nod my head and follow his lead.

The crowd has their phones out, filming as we make our

way back to the car park surrounded by the men in suits. I'm sure they think Josh is someone famous or something. Then again, he is famous. His family is one of the wealthiest in the country; they're always in the paper.

I put my face down and let my hair curtain around me. The chances of anyone actually seeing me with all these men surrounding me are slim, but just in case, I don't want to see my face plastered on a tabloid.

---

JOSH WAS super quiet the whole way back into the city. I didn't have the nerve to ask him anything. I still don't know what to say. Whatever happened back on the beach has him on edge. If it scares Josh, then what the hell will it do to me?

I've never known Josh to be scared of anything; he's fearless. He was always the one causing fear in others. To see the worry in his eyes is hard for me to grasp. I want to erase his fears. I want to assure him that it will be okay. I want to slaughter whatever or whoever it was that provoked that reaction from him.

Josh parks the car at the front of the house. His fingers grip the steering wheel, turning his knuckles white. I see his mouth silently reciting each number as he counts to ten with his eyes closed. I don't move. When he opens his eyes and pins that blue gaze on me, I finally let out the breath I didn't know I was holding in.

"Are you ready to have some fun?" he asks me, raising his eyebrows.

Talk about emotional whiplash. How the bloody hell did he just switch his emotions off like that? I'm relieved to see the fear gone—well, mostly gone. I can tell it's still there in the back of his mind, but boy, does he do a good job at faking happiness. To anyone else looking at him, you would think he didn't have a care in the world.

I know though. I can tell. "You don't have to pretend to be okay for me, Josh. Whatever happened back at the beach spooked you. I want to help. Let me help."

"Em, I promise I will tell you all about it. But right now, we have a bet to settle."

"A bet? What bet?"

"You don't remember? Last night, you made a bet with Bray that you were a better shot than him."

"I don't remember doing that. Why would I do that? Hold up… what exactly did I bet?" I ask, panicked. I don't exactly have anything to gamble with.

"Uh, I may have placed a small wager on it." He averts his eyes, looking out the windshield of the car.

"How small, Josh?"

"The details are fuzzy, but from what I recall, it was around two."

"Two thousand dollars? Josh, you cannot bet two thousand dollars on me. That's insane." My voice rises with panic. What if I lose? What if he didn't bet on me to win, and I actually do win?

"Don't be ridiculous, Emmy. I didn't bet two thousand. It was two mil."

My mouth falls open and shut. "Holy bloody shit! Joshua McKinley, no! Just NO! We need a goddamn intervention up in here, because that has to be the stupidest thing I've ever seen you do. And that's saying a lot, because you once hit our math teacher and got yourself a month's worth of after school detention. *On purpose*."

"I got to spend a week in the detention hall staring at you. It was worth it."

"Do you even remember why I was in detention, Josh?"

"No, all I remember is hearing you being given a week of detentions. I knew I was going to be in that hall with you. Do you know the kind of riffraff who frequented the detention hall?"

"You?"

"Well, yeah, but also, all those other jerks. If I hadn't been there, trust me, Em, you would have been in for a week of hell."

I screw my face up. Does he think it wasn't a week of hell having his intense gaze on me? My skin prickling for the whole hour we sat there silently? I'd never been hornier in my life. The things I'd imagine Josh doing to me then… I would snap out of my daydream to see the smirk on his face. He knew what I was thinking about—*the ass*.

"I don't know. I remember spending the week daydreaming and fantasising about a boy. It was hours well spent. I barely even noticed anyone else in the room. But just so we're clear, it was your fault I got detention that day."

"Em, you were daydreaming about *me*. Don't even try to pretend you weren't. And how was it my fault?"

"Maybe I was. Maybe I wasn't. It was your fault because there was a note left at my desk. A note addressed to Emmy. I was so frustrated I didn't know where these notes were bloody coming from that I screamed."

"How is that my fault?"

"Come on, Josh, you are the only person to ever call me Emmy. You and I both know you were writing those notes."

"Maybe I was. Maybe I wasn't. Come on, let's get in and show Bray why you don't fuck with Emmy McKinley."

"Livingston. I'm not a McKinley, Josh."

"If I say it enough, it will eventuate. And trust me, Em, you will be a McKinley."

# Chapter 15

## Josh

Emily stops me before we're about to walk through the front door. "Josh, did you bet on me to lose? Because I can purposely lose if you need me to."

"Fuck no, I didn't bet on you to lose. Em, I bet on you to win. Although, I don't really care if you win or lose. It's just a bit of fun, Emmy. Relax."

"Two million dollars is not a bit of fun, Joshua."

"We make that in a day. It's fine. You *have* shot a gun before, right? Do you need a quick rundown on what to do?" I'm not sure why I expect her to have range experience. She's just always been the girl who can conquer anything she attempts.

She smiles at me. *A mischievous smile.* "I guess we're about to find out."

When we walk down to the basement, where my father

had an indoor gun range built, we find everyone waiting. Bray is jumping up and down like a damn lunatic.

"What the fuck is wrong with you?" I ask.

"Just warming up the muscles. Where the fuck are your clothes?" He bounces around, punching the air.

"Who needs clothes when you look like this?" I ask, waving a hand down my bare chest. I probably should have taken Em to get dressed before we came in here; she doesn't seem to mind though.

"You know you're not getting into the ring, moron. You're shooting a fucking handgun." Looking at Emily, I whisper in her ear, "You are at least a thousand times smarter than him, babe. You've got this."

"This is going to be fun." She laughs.

"Okay, let's get this show on the road. Hope you got your bank on standby, McKinley. Sorry, Emily, nothing personal, but you're about to get beat," Bray says, still jumping around like a fool.

"Well, that's okay. It's about having fun, right? Not winning or losing," Emily replies in a sugary-sweet voice. A tone I haven't heard since high school. I laugh. Whatever she's got up her sleeve, it's going to be good.

"That's what all the losers say." Bray laughs.

I watch as Emily walks off to the side of the room, and to the table that hosts a spread of handguns. She looks at all the choices, biting her lip. Fuck, she seems nervous and unsure. Maybe I overestimated her comfort level...

"Okay, you go first. Show me how it's done, Bray," Emily says quietly.

I pull her into my arms and whisper in her ear, "Em, you know you don't have to do this, right? Just say so, and we'll get out of here."

"I want to do this. Follow my lead, okay?"

"Well, that's easy. I'd follow you anywhere, babe."

Her smile eases my mind. She's okay; she can handle this.

"Bray, calm the hell down before you shoot someone!" Ella shouts.

"Don't worry, El, if he shoots you, I'll make sure he ends up pig food." I wink at her.

"My hero…" Ella pretends to swoon.

"Ella, what the fuck? You are not giving my *favourite brother* title to him." Bray points to me.

"I'm pretty sure you've never actually had that title. Has he, El?" Zac grunts from his perch on the couch.

"You know what? I don't have a favourite brother. I hate you all equally."

"Ouch, what'd I do?" I ask, pretending to be wounded.

"You orchestrated this whole charade. You knew Bray wouldn't turn down a bet. You're a sore loser, Josh. How are you going to cope if he wins and Emily loses?"

"Emily never loses," I say confidently. Emily coughs behind me.

"Ah, Josh, that's not true. Debate team, year eleven. I lost."

"Well, yeah, but you went up against me, babe. Of course, you wouldn't stand a chance against me."

Emily tilts her head. "Okay, well, how about after I beat Bray, you try to beat me at target practice?"

Her tone is way too confident. She must know how to shoot. "What are the stakes?" I ask her.

She leans up and whispers so only I can hear her, "If you win, I'll be your sex slave. I'll let you have any part of me you want."

Her cheeks redden as she looks me in the eye, winking. I swallow, because damn, do I want every inch of her. There's one part I haven't had yet, and I'm itching to claim it as mine. "And if you win?"

"Mmm, if I win, I want the papers to the Lambo." She laughs.

"My car?" I ask, appalled. She did not just ask me to bet my fucking car…

"Are you scared you'll lose, Josh?"

"No, I'm scared you'll win," I reply.

"That's the same as you losing." Ella laughs.

"As long as I've got Emmy, I'm always winning. It's a deal. Now, let's get on with it. I want to claim my prize." I wink at Emily. She swallows, a little unsure.

"Don't worry, babe, I'll make sure I lube up your little puckered hole real good before I make it mine," I whisper in her ear. She lets out a quiet moan before she composes herself, turning away from me with pink cheeks.

"Okay, everyone, muffs on. Bray, I swear to God if you shoot someone, I'll bury you myself," Zac says, handing me two sets of ear protection.

"Where's your wife?" I ask him as I take the equipment.

His body stiffens at my question. "Why?"

"She makes you so much more bearable to be around. You should make sure she's with you everywhere you go. I think you'd find you'd have more friends than just my brother."

"Really? How many friends have you got, Josh? Last I heard, that count was still zero, you know, 'cause everyone's too worried you'll turn them to pig food when you go off on a crazy tangent."

Without thinking, I step in front of Emily and peel her fingers from the firearm she's currently holding. Given the death stare she's delivering Zac right now, I'm not sure she wouldn't actually shoot him.

"I'm just gonna hold this for you, babe," I say, removing the gun from her tense palms.

"Can't I just shoot him once, Josh? I'll make sure it's… like… in a knee or something. Nothing lethal," Emily seethes.

"Trust me, babe, I've had the same thought… *more than once.*" I glance over at Zac's unimpressed face, though he does side-eye Emily as if he's a little worried. He should be.

"Emily, I'm sorry. I'll try to remember to keep my thoughts about your boyfriend to myself a little better."

"You should look in the mirror, Zac. Those who throw stones… You know, glass houses and all."

"Okay, if you all don't shut the fuck up and put those muffs on, I'm starting anyway. I'm sure Richie Rich over there can afford the hearing aids you will all need," Bray calls out as he takes a stance at the firing line, his barrel aimed at the target.

"It's okay. I don't need you to stand up for me, Em. I'm a big boy. I can take whatever any of these pricks have to say," I tell her, securing her ear protection in place.

Bray finishes his turn, dragging the target inwards across the lane. I can see he didn't do too badly, all rounds striking the upper body.

"Your turn, Emily. Good luck beating that." He smiles, proud of himself. I actually don't know if she can beat it. He's a good shot.

Emily looks over the range of handguns. She picks up a few, hefting them in her hands and feeling the weight of each. She doesn't look satisfied with the choices.

"Josh, is this the only arsenal you have?" she asks.

"Are you expecting a whole armoury, Em?"

"Well, yeah, kind of." She shrugs.

I unlock a door that leads to an actual armoury. Our father

liked guns. I've never really been too keen on them, but for some reason, Dean has kept them all here.

"Holy shit!" Emily walks into the room, her eyes wide. She heads straight for the three sniper rifles sitting along the back wall.

Her fingers lightly run over one of the stocks, and a distant look crosses her features.

"Em, you okay?"

"Ah, yeah. I'm good. I don't need these. I'm just going to pick a little handgun." She walks around me and out of the secured space. I follow close behind. Whatever just went through her mind made her sad. I can't fucking stand seeing that despondent look in her eyes. It breaks me every single time.

I watch silently as Emily picks up a handgun. She doesn't even really look at it. Instead, she walks up to the line, aims and shoots. One shot. Turning around, she says to Bray, "Bring it in. I believe you owe Josh a fair sum of cash."

He tugs the line forward. The whole room is speechless as we look at the shot she just made. One clean round, dead centre through the forehead of the printed silhouette.

"What the actual fuck? Of course you'd find yourself a little assassin!" Bray shouts.

"Pay up, Williamson." I smirk at him.

"Fine, but I was duped. You're like the target shooting version of a pool shark. Where the fuck did you learn to shoot like that, anyway?" Bray stares at Emily, waiting for an answer.

"Don't be a sore loser. Sorry, guys, Emily and I have plans." I bend down and throw her over my shoulder.

"Josh, we haven't had our turn. I want to win that bloody car, damn it. Put me down!" she yells as we exit the room.

"You can have the car, Em. I'll buy another one." I take

the stairs two at a time. I need to get back up to my room. We make it to the hallway, but deciding I can't wait another minute, I walk into the first room I see and slam the door shut. We're in the library. This will work.

Laying Emily down on the large mahogany desk, I lift my shirt, which she's been wearing since the beach, over her head and toss it aside. She's left in that tiny fucking bikini. Pulling on all the strings, I remove the scraps of material from her body. She's like an angel laid out before me. A feast fit for a king.

"I'd love to take my time and worship this piece of art you call a body, but I need to be buried inside you now," I growl.

Emily moans and spreads her legs apart. It's like a huge welcome home banner for my cock. I undo my boardshorts and kick them off, stroking my cock a few times as I stare down at Emily's weeping pussy.

"Are you ready for me, Emmy? Are you ready for me to fuck you into oblivion?" I ask as I line myself up with her entrance.

"Yes, Josh, hurry up already."

I slam into her as soon as I hear the word *yes*. That's all I need, her consent for me to let the beast inside me unleash.

I stay still for a few minutes while I'm buried to the hilt in her warm channel. I could die a happy man right now and still feel like my life was complete.

Once I feel her hips start to move, I know she's had time to adjust to my intrusion. I don't start off slow. I don't hold back. I give her everything I've got. I told her I was going to fuck her into oblivion, and that's exactly what I plan to do.

I'm going hard, her screams filling the room along with the sound of our bodies smashing together. I need more. I always need more.

Pulling out, I flip her over so she's lying flat on her stomach, her plump ass on display. My fingers slide down the crack, twirling around the outside edges of her little puckered hole.

"This ass is mine, Emmy." Her body stiffens. She's not ready for that, but she will be.

I slowly guide myself into her wet, warm piece of heaven. Once I'm buried all the way, I tell her, "Hold on, Em, this is going to be fast and rough."

She obeys without question. Her arms go out to the side of the desk as her hands fold over the ledge.

I pump in and out of her. I can feel her walls contracting. I know she's so fucking close, and so am I. Bringing my thumb down to her clit, I circle around while my other thumb goes straight to that forbidden hole. As soon as my digit pushes through the tight ring, Emmy loses it. She screams out my name as well as a bunch of other incoherent words. But it's *my* name that she screams loudest. Anyone walking by would know exactly who's fucking her. Who's made her feel this fucking good. Who's claimed her.

Her walls choke my cock, quivering as I drive into her a few more times before roaring with my own release. I collapse over her, catching my weight with my hands so she isn't forced to bear it.

On shaky legs, I reach for a tissue box and clean her up. Turning her over, I sit her upright and put the shirt back over her head before adjusting my shorts.

"I fucking love you, Emily, so damn much," I whisper into her hairline as I kiss her forehead.

"I know the feeling," she replies.

"Care to tell me where the hell you learnt to shoot with such accuracy?"

"My dad was a special forces sniper, Josh. Who do you think I learnt from?" She raises her eyebrows.

"Your dad taught you how to shoot, Emily? You were fifteen when he died. You shouldn't have even been near guns."

"Calm your farm. I learnt to shoot when I was five. My dad said it was in our blood. I always had good aim," she says proudly.

"Well, you're now two million dollars richer. Thanks to your little sharking ways." I laugh.

"I don't want his money. Tell him to keep it, Josh. I don't need it."

"No, you don't, but it's a lesson for him not to be such a smartass all the damn time. Don't worry, he can afford it, babe. Come on, let's go shower the salt and sand off."

# Chapter 16

## Emily

Josh has cooked breakfast again. I have a full plate of bacon, eggs, hash browns and toast. I'm starting to think he doesn't trust me to cook for him. But damn, this bacon is good. I can't get enough of it right now.

"You do know I can cook, right? Maybe I should cook you breakfast one day," I say around a mouthful of crispy bacon. Josh laughs and places another couple of pieces of bacon on my plate.

"Em, you don't need to cook. I like doing things for you."

"I'm going to get fat if you keep feeding me like this. You won't be so keen on me when I'm the size of this house," I point out.

"You could be the size of an elephant and I'd still fuck you just as much as I do now. I will love you no matter what you look like, babe."

"Charming. But I think I'd like to cook for you. How about dinner? Tonight? What's your favourite meal?" My eyebrows draw down at the realisation I don't know what his favourite meal is. I should know something so simple. He seems to know everything about me… sometimes before I even do.

"Emmy, it's okay. We are going to have the rest of our lives for you to be barefoot and pregnant in our kitchen. But if you insist on cooking me dinner, I like steak." I almost choke on the bacon. I cough it up and it comes spitting out onto the bench.

"You-you want me to be p-pregnant?" I finally manage to get out.

"Well, I'm not opposed to the idea, but if you don't want kids, Emmy, it's okay too. We'll get an alpaca."

"I-I don't know." Shit, is it getting hotter in here? I can't breathe. I pull at the collar of my top, moving it away from my throat. Looking around the room, I eye the door that leads to the outside. I can make it there. If I run really fast, I can make it to that door.

Just as I'm about to get up, Josh's arms hug me tight to his chest. "Emmy, it's okay. You're okay. I'm right here. You are safe. Just breathe, Em." He rocks me as he smooths his hand down my hair and whispers me promises that I know aren't entirely true.

I'm not okay. I'm probably never going to be okay again. This is never going to stop. I thought I was finally starting to be better. This hasn't happened for a while. But now, the mention of being pregnant has pushed me over the edge. The memory of the time I was so happy to find myself pregnant is vividly playing like a movie in my mind.

*I wait the three minutes the box says it takes for the stick to show the results. Nervousness and excitement run through me as I sit here. It's going to be okay. Whatever it says, it will be okay. Trent will be happy with a baby. Who doesn't love babies?*

*Turning the stick over, my heart explodes with an unexpected feeling. I can't pinpoint what it is, but I know it's a good one. Two lines are visible on the display pad. Pregnant, I'm pregnant. I'm going to be someone's mother.*

I shake the thoughts from my mind. I cannot go back there. I won't be that person again. The mother who was too weak to save her own unborn child from the hell her husband inflicted on her. I won't do it.

"Emmy, what the fuck happened? You've been pregnant?" Josh keeps his voice soft, calm, even with his colourful choice of language.

I shake my head. "I-I can't…" I try to lie. I try to tell him no, but the words won't come out.

"It's okay. You don't have to tell me right now."

My whole body relaxes in his arms.

"Em, if you were to get knocked up, you know I'd take care of you, right? I'd make sure you had the best doctors. Your child would want for nothing."

"My child? Josh, if I got knocked up, as you so eloquently call it, it would be your child too. I don't see anyone else painting my walls with their seed around here, do you?" I'm not sure why I'm so riled up all of a sudden. It's not like we haven't had this conversation before…

"No one around here would be stupid enough to even try to get near your walls, Emmy. And yes, it would be my child, but I pray that our children have more of you than me in them. The world could use more angels like you." He kisses my lips gently. I pull him down to deepen the kiss.

"Don't mind me, kids." Sam's voice tears us apart. I glare at him. How dare he interrupt when I finally manage to find my happy place again. I'm aware that this co-dependency Josh and I have going on is anything but healthy. I just don't care enough to do anything about it.

Sam laughs at my icy glare. "Emily, you've been around him too long. That stare is almost a perfect match for his."

"Careful, mate, it's the quiet ones you have to watch out for," Dean says as he digs into the fridge.

"Why are you here, Sam? It's fucking Saturday," Josh grunts, ignoring Dean's comment.

"Ah, I need that fancy signature of yours on some documents for the Casey merger."

I've heard that before. I'd bet there is no bloody Casey merger, and it's some sort of boy's code for: *I've got shit to tell you, but not in front of others.*

"I'll meet you in the library in five," Josh says.

"Hey, Josh, how long exactly does a merger with another company usually take?" I ask.

"It depends on a lot of influencing factors. You want to come be my COO, Em?"

"No, I was just curious. But whatever Sam has to tell you, I want to hear it too."

Josh shakes his head. "You are too damn smart for your own good sometimes. I promise I will tell you whatever you want to know. Are you going to finish your breakfast?"

I nod my head, because, well, bacon. I'm not about to let it go to waste.

"Dean, have breakfast with Emily for me. I won't be long." Josh throws the order out as he exits the room.

Dean's eyebrows go up to his hairline. "Why me?" he asks to the ceiling, before looking directly at me and pointing. "*You*, do not move a muscle, not even a hair. If I return you with so much as a hair out of place, he'll know, and I'll be pig food."

I don't know how to take Dean. Is he joking? He looks serious. I'm not sure why, but I've always gotten this impression that he didn't like me very much. I've never really even had a one-on-one conversation with him. I guess now's my chance to find out why he doesn't like me.

"You don't like me very much, do you?" I blurt out. Dean looks taken aback by my question; he just stares at me contemplatively.

"Why would you think that? I like you just fine," he finally answers.

"No, you don't. Why not?" I can't help the fact that the people pleaser in me wants to come out and fix his impression of me.

"It's not that I don't like you… It's not you at all. It's Josh. You didn't see the mess he was after you left, Emily. For almost two years, I had to pick his drunk ass up off the floor every damn day. He tried just about every drug he could, in order to make not having you more bearable. I'd wake up, night after night, to him screaming out your name in his sleep. So, it's not that I don't like *you*. It's that I don't like the power you hold over my brother. You are the only person on earth who has the power to destroy him. I don't want to see him go down that road of despair ever again."

I'm speechless. How do I even respond to that? I don't even notice that I'm crying until Dean hands me a tissue. "For the love of God, don't tell him I made you cry."

"I won't. But just so you know, I didn't leave him. He told me to leave. He didn't want me here. It wasn't exactly a piece of cake for me either." I get up, suddenly angry that Josh did this to us. Why didn't he come after me? If he was so broken up over not having me, why didn't he just come and find me?

I know he had his reasons for keeping me away, but I'm still filled with irrational anger. I'm angry at him. I'm angry at the situation I've now put us in. And I'm angry at everyone trying to keep us apart. Are we ever going to get our happily ever after? Because I'm more than ready for it. I want it *yesterday*.

I storm towards the library. "Wait! Where are you going?" Dean calls out.

"To slap some sense into your idiot brother," I retort.

"Shit, Emily, wait up. You should just wait for Josh to finish his meeting. Then, I'll hold him down while you slap that sense into him," Dean offers.

I'm not deterred by his attempts to stop me. The force I push the library door open with has it slamming against the wall. When I step into the room, Josh and Sam have guns pointed in my direction. I freeze. I swear they think they're playing an adult-sized game of cops and robbers sometimes.

"Fuck, Emmy," Josh hisses as he lowers his sidearm. "What's wrong?" He looks behind me to Dean, who has just caught up with me.

"Ah, I tried to stop her," Dean says.

Josh pauses in front of me, bringing his palms up to cup my cheeks. I swipe his hands away from my face. He grits his teeth as he puts his arms down. "Em, babe, what's wrong?"

I look behind him to see Sam scrambling to pack up a heap of papers they have spread out on the desk. I look up to Josh briefly. There's confusion and hurt in his eyes. But I need to know what it is they're trying to hide from me.

I walk around Josh and pull the stack of papers out of Sam's hands. He was too stunned by my actions to put up much of a fight. The moment I drop the papers to the desk and fan them out, I wish they had stopped me. This isn't something I can ever unsee.

Spread out in front of me is a heap of photos. Photos of girls' bodies. Photos of me… from when I was with Trent. Photos of my broken and bruised body. "W-w-why do you have these?" I ask directly to Josh. Why would they be looking at these?

I step away from the desk, and Josh's face falls. "Emmy, it's not. It's…" Running his fingers roughly through his hair, he curses. He makes his way towards me, stopping only when he sees me retreat further away from him.

"Emily, this is the work of Detective Jones. He..." Sam's cut off by Josh.

"Get the fuck out of here. Now! Leave!"

I've never heard Josh sound so animalistic. I watch as Sam and Dean both look towards me, unsure whether they should leave me here or not. I nod my head. I'm okay. Josh won't hurt me. I'm not scared *of* him… I'm scared *for* him.

I need to help him. I don't like seeing him so lost. As soon as Dean shuts the door behind him, I walk over to Josh and pull his hands down from where they are currently pulling at his hair.

He looks at me, but his gaze is more vacant than I've ever seen. "Josh?" I don't know what to say to him right now. I should know how to help him.

"Emmy, you shouldn't have seen them. You weren't meant to see them. I should be protecting you from all of this."

I pull him over to the couch and push him down. Climbing on top of him, I hold his face in my hands, so he has to look at me.

"This is not your fault, Josh. You *are* protecting me. Where do you think I would be right now if you never found me?"

"I should have protected you from *that* ever happening. You didn't deserve to endure that… You should never have been there." Josh wraps his arms around my back, pulling my body against his.

"Nobody deserves to live what I went through. But I survived. I'm still here. I know I don't always handle things great… I know I have issues. But I need you to tell me what's going on. I can't be kept in the dark, Josh."

"It's not a burden I want you to carry, Emmy."

"We don't lie to each other, remember? We don't keep secrets. It's you and me, against the world, Josh."

He stares at me without saying a word for what seems like hours, but in actuality, is probably only minutes. Looking over the pile of papers on the desk, he shakes his head no. He doesn't want to tell me.

"The pictures came from a warehouse Sam and I went to the other day. We had a lead on where Jones was hiding out. When we got there, all that we saw were three bodies and a wall of photos. A whole wall… covered in photos of you."

"How would he get those pictures? Some of them are from years ago."

"I don't know. That's not all. Jones has been sending emails. Every day. Graphic messages of what he wants to do to you when he finds you."

"Why didn't you tell me?"

"I don't want you to worry. I'm going to find this arsehole, Em. I will make sure he never gets his hands on you."

"I wish I knew what he wanted with me. I don't recall ever meeting him. I don't remember Trent ever mentioning anyone by that name. Maybe Trent's brother would know something. What if I called him?"

"I don't think he knows anything, Em. I've had guys following him for the past few weeks. He lives a mundane life with his wife and kids. Goes to work, goes home, takes his kids to soccer on weekends."

"I only met him a few times during the first year I dated Trent. After that, I never saw him again. It's worth a try, right? We know there is no real warrant for me. Somebody went to great efforts to cover up Trent's death, to make it look like he left town. I'm not a suspect, right?"

"Em, there's something else Sam just found. That whole marriage paperwork you signed… it was fake. You were never legally married."

"I wasn't…? So, hypothetically, if I wanted to get married today, I could?" I ask him. Visions of running off and marrying Josh play on repeat in my mind. Would he want to marry me? I know he's mentioned it before… but is he serious? Could I just ask him, instead of waiting for him to pop the question?

# Chapter 17

## Josh

My mind is all over the place. The hurt look on Emily's face when she saw the pictures we had of her haunts me. I'm not entirely sure I trust my own brain at the moment, because I swear she asked if she could get married today.

I stare at her face. She looks determined. Fuck, maybe she did just ask to get married.

"Em, is that your way of asking me to marry you? Because if it is, the answer is fuck yes!"

The smile that spreads across her face lightens my heart; it eases the tension in my body. "Josh, will you marry me? Today?" she asks.

"Emily Livingston, you know I'd marry you any day that ends in Y. *But* you deserve a wedding. A proper, fancy-as-shit ceremony. The big white dress, the flowers, all of that shit little girls dream of having. I don't want you to settle for anything less than you deserve."

"I don't need any of that, Josh. All I need is you. All I want is you. *Forever*. But it's okay. I get that someone in your position can't just run off and get married. I can wait." She averts her eyes.

Tilting her chin, so she's looking back up at me, I ask, "What do you mean someone in my position?"

"Well, I don't know if you noticed, but you're a McKinley, Josh. And not just any McKinley. You are the CEO of McKinley Industries. Obviously, you can't marry someone on a whim. You need to take precautions. You need to organise a prenup, which I will happily sign, FYI."

Shifting slightly, I reach for my phone in my pocket and scroll through until I find the number I need. "Hold that thought, Em. And, FYI, we don't need a prenup. Your ass is crazy if you think I'd ever let you divorce me."

I press the number and dial, before placing the call on speaker so Emily can hear. It rings a few times before he picks up.

"McKinley, is there a good reason you're calling me on a Saturday morning?" he groans.

"Judge Thomas, I'm calling in a favour." I smile at Em, who is sitting as still as a damn statue, waiting to see what I'm doing.

"Josh, if you're in the lockup, call your brother to bail you out," the judge replies.

"I don't need bailing out. I need to get married. Today. I need you to do whatever it is you have to do to make it legal. *Today*." Emily's eyes go wide.

"Ah, Josh, are you being blackmailed? Gun to your head?

Or just insane? Don't tell me you knocked up some bird and need to make it official before anyone finds out?"

"No. How long do you need? To have all the paperwork together? To get this done?"

"Ah, I'll have it done by six tonight, my office. If you're late, I won't be waiting around. I'm going to need the details of the poor woman you've convinced to marry you."

"We'll be there. I'll have Sam send you everything you need."

Hanging up the phone, I pull Emily's face into mine, melding my lips with hers. My tongue seeks entrance into her mouth, which she eagerly grants. She grinds down on my cock as she moans against my lips, tugging on my hair. I let her take everything she wants for a few minutes before I lose it and regain control.

Flipping her over and laying her back on the couch, I settle myself between her legs. "Mmm, maybe we should refrain, you know, until after we're married," I mumble into the crook of her neck as my fingers work their way into her panties, circling her little nub.

"You can stop if you want. I'll just go and finish myself off. *Alone*," she growls.

I laugh. "Emmy, this pussy is mine. Your pleasure, it's mine. Mine to give you. Mine to revel in. You are mine." I bite down softly on her shoulder as I insert two fingers inside her.

"Well, your pussy wants to be brought to a quivering mess, Josh. Make it happen."

Holy shit, she's demanding when she's horny. I fucking love how she comes right out of her shell in these moments.

"Say *please* and I just might, Emmy." My fingers pump slowly in and out of her, while I use my weight to hold down her hips, stopping her from being able to chase the tempo she desires.

Emily glares at me, her mouth clamped shut. She doesn't want to say please. Her hips fight my hold, trying to grind into my hand harder. I keep my strokes slow, teasing, my thumb lightly grazing her clit. I know I'm driving her out of her mind. She's so fucking turned on right now her juices are dripping down my hand.

Looking at my left hand, as it pumps in and out of her, I have a vision of this same moment, except with a gold band on my finger. "I can't wait until your sweet juices are running all over my wedding band. Tonight, when you're officially my wife, we're doing this again."

"Josh, you won't live to see tonight if you don't give me what I want, now." Emily's face scrunches.

I chuckle into her shoulder. "But I love having you squirming, wanting, beneath me."

"Please, Josh, I can't take it anymore." She gasps as I increase the thrusts of my fingers, grinding my thumb down hard on her clit as soon as that 'please' left her mouth.

"Oh God, don't stop, yes!" she screams as her core begins to spasm within seconds. Her inner muscles tighten around my fingers, squeezing them almost to the point of pain.

Removing my fingers, I bring them to my mouth and suck them clean, one at a time. Emily's body shivers beneath me while she watches. As soon as I've finished, she pulls my face down to hers. Her tongue swirls around my own. Moaning into my mouth, she groans as I line my cock up with her entrance.

I break our kiss, about to seek her permission, when she tilts her hips up, drawing my cock into her pussy.

"Arghh, fuck, you're so goddamn fucking perfect, Emmy. I never want to go a day without being buried inside you."

"Well, you should probably put a ring on it then." She laughs.

"Six o'clock tonight, babe, my ring will be on this dainty little finger of yours. My name will be yours. Everything I have will be yours," I promise her.

"I just want you. Just give me you," she whispers breathlessly as I start to slowly move.

"You've always had me, Emmy. I'll be yours forever and more."

---

"WHAT DO you mean you're getting married tonight?" Sam asks, downing the shot of whisky, which it's still way too fucking early to be drinking.

"Exactly that. Six tonight. Judge Thomas's office. If you don't want to be there, you don't have to be. I won't lose any sleep if you're not."

"Of course, I'll fucking be there. I'm just having a hard time believing she agreed to marrying you. Should I get her a shrink? I mean, you are both as fucking cr…" Sam cuts himself off and looks around the empty room before continuing in a whisper, "crazy as each other."

The look of utter terror on his face as he whispered the singular word is hilarious. It's hard to think that a six-foot-something man is scared of little ol' Emmy. Don't get me wrong, I won't ever be underestimating her when she's holding a gun ever fucking again. I can't believe I didn't know she was a little sniper.

"It was her idea. She asked me," I say proudly. There was

no begging on my part, although I was fully prepared to beg when I did get around to asking her. I wanted to give her the fairy-tale proposal. What is she going to tell our grandchildren when they ask about the details of her engagement, or what her wedding was like?

Fuck, can I go through with this rushed elopement, knowing I'm ripping her off when it comes to memories? Unless, I give her the memories. I can do that. I already have a ring. I've had it for a few weeks, waiting for the right moment to give it to her. No better time than the present, right?

"I've gotta go do something. Email me the place you found. I'll go check it out later," I tell Sam, before exiting the room.

"Do not go alone, Josh," he yells after me.

I don't bother answering him. He and I both know if I want to go alone, I fucking will. He's pinged Jones's IP address (from today's grotesque email) to a new location. I fully intend to go and check it out. First, though, I need to give Emily the proposal she deserves.

I find Emily in our bedroom. I head straight for the wardrobe, where there is a little safe currently housing her engagement ring. Retrieving the ring, I walk out to her and take her Kindle from her hands; she glares at me while her fingers white-knuckle grip the device.

"Relax, Emmy, I'm just putting it down over here," I say as I tug harder and place the e-reader on the other side of the bed.

"Come dance with me," I say, holding out my hand, waiting for her.

"Dance? You want to dance? In here? There's no music, Josh," she says while taking my hand and standing up, despite her protest.

"Well, I can fix that. Hold on." I pull out my phone and flick through a Spotify playlist I have, which I've filled with songs that remind me of her, finding the perfect song for this moment.

"I Get to Love You" by Ruelle plays softly while I take her in my arms. The words resonate with me. Loving Emily is the best thing I will ever do in my lifetime. It's the only thing I've ever done with my complete heart and soul invested in the outcome.

"Emily, I don't know what I ever did to get you. But whatever mistake God made when he gave me you, it's too late now. I'm keeping you. There're no takebacks happening here." Leaning into her, I inhale her scent, gently kissing her forehead before continuing. I try to swallow the emotions so I can get everything out that I need to tell her.

"I love you more than I've ever loved anything in my entire life. I know that I'm a lot to take at times. I know I'm far from being even remotely deserving of your love. But I promise I will try every day to be a better man, a man worthy of your time. I will do whatever I have to do to ensure that you know just how loved you are. I will cherish you. I will honour you. I will fucking worship you every day for the rest of my life."

Letting go of her, I take the ring out of my pocket and hold it up to her finger. "Emily Livingston, will you do me the honour of becoming my wife, my partner in life, my queen?"

I wait for her response before I slide the ring onto her finger. Her eyes water as she brings her other hand up to her mouth. "Yes, however, I'm pissed you outdid my crappy little attempt at a proposal."

I laugh. "Em, you proposing to me is the best thing that's ever happened to me. I want you to have the kind of stories you can tell our grandchildren about. I don't want to rip away the memories you should have."

"I don't need the memories as long as I have you, Josh."

This girl is fucking everything. I know heads are rolling up in heaven at the fuck up someone made by pairing her with me. I smile because, in this case, the devil really has won.

---

"OKAY, you are going to be at the courthouse, right? You're not going to stand me up, are you?" Emily asks me as I'm about to leave.

"Emmy, I'd never fucking stand you up. I can't wait for you to be Mrs. McKinley. I'll meet you there at 6:00 p.m. *Sharp*. Don't be late," I tell her, kissing her already kiss-swollen lips.

"I don't understand why we can't go together. We've already done every other unspeakable thing together, Josh. It's not exactly going to be bad luck."

"I just have an errand I need to run first. Besides, it's a memory you can share with the grandkids—how you got ready with Ella and met me at the courthouse. You'll tell them how your breath was taken away by how stunning I looked in a tux. That your heart pitter-pattered the moment you got to put that ring on my finger and locked my ass down forever." I give her my best panty-melting smirk, hoping to ease some of her worries just a little.

"I'll tell them all of that and so much more. I love you, Josh. And, in case I forget to tell you later, thank you for choosing me."

"I will always choose you, Emmy."

As I'm walking out of the house, a sense of unease settles in me. It's not prewedding jitters. I have no doubt that Emily is my one. I've never doubted that. But something else is off. I just don't know what it is.

I read the address that Sam sent me earlier. He said he had a couple of guys scoping the place out, but they hadn't found anything yet. If there's even a scrap of information that will lead me to this fucker, then I want it found, which means I'm going to go there and search for myself.

I have three hours before I have to meet Emily. I figure I can check this place out, change in the car and then head to the courthouse.

Pulling up to the deserted house, I'm pretty sure I'm not going to find jack shit here. The place looks like it's been empty for decades. An old fibro cottage, surrounded by overgrown grass and weeds. I double-check that I've got the right address. Looking around the street, I don't see another goddamn car. I thought Sam said he had a few guys staking out the place.

I'll be in and out. I'm going to be fucking pissed if I walk into a goddamn spider web in this mess. Slamming the car door, I stomp towards the front of the house. The door is already slightly ajar. Pushing it open further, I look down the empty entranceway.

The floorboards creak as I walk through the back of the house. Just as I suspected, there is nothing here. Not a sign of life, or of anyone having ever been here. Deciding I'm wasting my time, I turn and head back for the entrance.

I'm halfway down the hall when I hear the footsteps behind me. Turning around, I see him, Jones, right before a sharp pain radiates through my head and my vision blurs. Dizzy and disorientated, I grab onto the wall to hold myself, then there's another sharp jolt to my head and my knees hit the floor.

# Chapter 18

## Emily

"Are you nervous? It's okay if you are. I'd offer to help you escape if you wanted to run now, but I don't have a death wish." Ella laughs.

"Josh would never hurt you. He loves you. I'm not nervous. Should I be nervous? I don't know why, but I'm not. I just feel like I've been waiting a really long time for this moment. I wish I could share it with my mum. I wish my dad were still alive to give me away, but I'm not nervous."

"Do you think your dad would have approved of Josh?" Ella asks, smiling around her champagne glass.

"Ah, no. Definitely not. But he would have come around eventually. He would have seen how much Josh loves me, and that's all that would matter to him. Are you sure this isn't too much? I mean, we're just going to the courthouse."

I stare at my reflection as my hands skim down the floor-length, white silk dress Ella brought up to me. It's beautiful. The dress has a low back, the material dipping almost all the way down to the top of my ass. The halter bodice ties around the back of my neck, leaving two long white ribbons dangling along my spine.

It's low cut at the front, like really freaking low cut. There's a slit right down the middle of the dress, which goes to my belly button. Ella had to put some sort of sticky tape on the dress to keep it in place.

She's been a godsend the last few hours, helping me get ready. She's done my hair in some weird kind of updo with a heap of twists and curls. I couldn't recreate it even if I tried. I instructed her to keep the makeup light, simple and natural. So, with a neutral nude lip colour and a bit of dark mascara, I'm pretty much ready to go.

"I'm under strict orders to make sure you have a dress that you'll be able to tell your grandkids about. And this dress is exactly that. Josh was rambling something about memories. I tuned out after I heard the words *white dress*."

I can't help but smile at Josh's insistence that we create memories together we can tell our grandkids about. I'm still not one hundred percent sold on the idea of kids, but the memories, I'm more than sold on having those to treasure for all time.

"Emily, hurry your ass up. I'm not getting shot because I didn't get you there on time," Sam hollers from behind the closed bedroom door.

Ella walks to the door, opening it to an annoyed-looking Sam. He glances over his shoulder at me, his eyes opening wide before he quickly composes his expression. "Wow, there are no words, Emily. Just… *wow*," he says.

"Ah, thank you?" I reply. "Okay, let's go. I'm so ready for this."

"You know, if you want to run, I can probably hide you really well," Sam offers.

"I'm done running. I've been running from what I want for long enough. It's time to just start taking what I want. The first thing being Josh. So, let's go."

I have no idea why everyone thinks I'd want to run. Have they not met Josh? Any girl would die to be his. And I get to be his. *Forever.* The thought of tying myself down to anyone used to freak me the hell out. But with Josh, I couldn't be more at peace with the idea.

Now that I know I'm not a wanted woman, and the incident I left behind in Adelaide is not going to come and affect Josh in any negative way, I'm not running anymore. Granted, there is still the issue of the crazy detective stalker to deal with, but I have every faith in Josh that he will find him before the man finds me.

I just wish I knew what he wanted with me. Why me? Shaking all the negative thoughts from my head, I focus on more positive ones, like Josh and how he proposed to me, the song lyrics still playing through my mind. This is what I need to be focused on: Josh, and only Josh.

---

OKAY, I wasn't nervous… But sitting in a judge's office for the last forty minutes has me a little shaken. Where is he? Why the bloody hell isn't he here? He said he would be here. He has to just be caught in traffic or something.

"Can you try to call him again?" I ask Sam, who is tapping

away on his phone in the corner. He picks his head up. Whatever he's about to say gets cut off by Dean.

"I'll call him. There has to be a reasonable explanation for why he's late, Emily. He wouldn't miss this for the world. Trust me, there is nothing Josh wants more in this world than to marry you." Dean walks outside as he places his phone to his ear.

"He will be here. We just have to wait a few more minutes," I tell the judge, who gives me a patronising, sympathetic look.

"Miss Livingston, we can always reschedule. I'll give him ten more minutes. If he isn't here by then, we will reschedule for tomorrow or the next day."

"He will be here. He wouldn't stand me up. He wouldn't do this." I know Josh. I know he wouldn't leave me at the altar, so to speak. He wants this just as much as I do. I know he does. However, that doesn't mean I'm not going to wring his bloody neck for making me wait as soon as I see him.

"Fuck!" Sam curses as he storms out of the office. "Dean, get Emily home now." His voice carries through the open door, and I run towards the sound. He knows something and I want to know what it is.

"Hold the fuck up. What's going on, Sam?" Dean asks, blocking Sam's path to the lift.

"Your idiot fucking brother went rogue, when I clearly told him not to do anything alone. That's what. I need to go and find him, and he better not be already fucking dead."

"W-what do you mean?" I ask, coming up behind him. Sam curses under his breath before he turns around to face me.

"Emily, I'm going to find him, okay? I need you to go

home and wait for me there." Sam walks past Dean and stabs at the button for the lift.

"I'm coming with you," Dean says.

"Someone has to get her back to your house, Dean. Get her home. I'll arrange for extra security and I'll text you where I am heading. You can meet me there."

The doors to the lift ping open. Dean looks like he wants to argue more, but he simply nods his head.

"Come on. Ella, call Bray. Tell him he's needed." Dean holds the doors open for us. I look back to the judge, who is now standing in his office doorway. I don't want to leave. Josh said he'd be here.

"Emily, we will come back, okay? As soon as we find him, we will be back here." Dean's voice is soft, although I pick up on his urgency to get me in the lift.

Numb, I'm numb. I want to fight and argue. I want to scream that he will be here, yet I find myself silently walking through the doors and following Dean and Sam's lead.

---

IT'S midnight and there's still no sign of Josh. Sam and Dean still haven't returned, although I've heard Ella on the phone to Dean a few times over the last several hours. All I can do is sit here and wait. Both Ella and Bray keep looking at me like I'm about to break. But they don't know that I'm already broken. I am screaming on the inside.

I can feel something trying to seep out of my pores, something dark. I've never felt like this before. My skin itches and my mind's locked on remembering the pin number Josh entered when he opened his armoury this morning. It's not hard to recall the numbers he used. One, four, one, zero, one, four. It's the date of our first time together.

I'm not sure why my mind is stuck on that room. Something is drawing me towards it though. I think about what Josh would be doing if I were the one out there somewhere. The possibilities of what happened, what could happen, endless... He wouldn't just be sitting here waiting. No, he'd be out there burning down the town until he found me. He wouldn't care how many bodies he left along the way. I just need to know where to start. If I knew where to start, I could come up with a plan. I could go and bring him back myself.

I keep watching the door, waiting for him to walk through. He's going to walk through any minute now and wrap me in his arms. When the doors open, my heart stops as I watch Dean and Sam enter... without Josh. I look behind them but he's not there.

Standing up, I walk over and search down the empty hallway. He's not here. "Where is he?" I ask them, folding my arms around myself.

"Emily, we... ah. We..." Sam attempts. He can't even look at me. I turn to Dean for an answer.

"Emily, we couldn't find him. We found his car parked out front of an abandoned cottage. It's an address Detective Jones was traced to this morning. We searched the house. Josh wasn't there." Dean averts his gaze. Ella slides up to his side and I watch as he wraps an arm around her shoulder.

"You're not telling me something. What aren't you telling me?" I won't be kept in the dark. This isn't something they can protect me from. I need to know. I need to find him.

"There was fresh blood in the entryway of the cottage. We don't know whose it was. All we know is that Josh was there. His car was left there."

"Well, we need to find him. He's out there somewhere and he needs us to find him. We have to find him." I let one tear slip. Swiping at the traitorous thing, I stiffen my spine.

"If you guys can't find him, I will. I'm not going to sit around here and wait. If it were any of you out there, you all know Josh would be the first one on the hunt."

I turn and head towards Josh's room. Now that I know Detective Jones has something to do with it, I know what I need to do. It's not Josh he wants. It's me. My life for Josh's is one I will gladly trade.

"Emily, wait. You have to let us get some more intel. We will find him. I won't give up until we find him. Just give us time." Sam follows me to the bedroom.

"And what if time is something he doesn't have right now? What if he's out there bleeding out somewhere, Sam. I won't lose him. I can't." I slam the door and lock it. I don't want anyone crowding me right now.

Taking out my phone, I open up the Facebook app. Detective Jones still hasn't accepted my friend request. I go through the process of creating a new profile—one using my real name and picture. Once it's set up, I send another friend request to Detective Jones. Clicking on the bubble icon, I type a private message. Please let this work.

**Me: You have something I want back. Let's talk. Emily**

I put the phone down on the bedside table. Walking into Josh's closet, I pull one of his shirts down, changing out of the white dress, the same one that was meant to hold happy memories. I scrunch it up and throw it into the bin in the corner of the room. I will never wear that again; it should be burned.

I crawl under the covers and lay my head down on Josh's

pillow. Inhaling, I can smell him. I know he's still alive. I know he's out there somewhere because if his heart had stopped beating, I would feel that. I would be able to tell. But I can still sense our connection. I've always felt the connection with Josh. Through all those years of torture with Trent, I could still feel Josh's love for me. I cling to my phone, close my eyes and send up a prayer.

In the quiet, dark room, I let myself fall apart. Silent tears stream down my face. In the morning, I will be stronger. In the morning, I will be braver. In the morning, I will find him. And I will bring him home.

# Chapter 19

## Josh

"Fuck me," I groan as consciousness starts to seep in, my eyes slowly blinking open. Why the fuck does my head hurt so damn much? Raising my hand up towards the pounding in my temples, I'm jerked back as my arm is halted.

My eyes then snap open. What the fuck? My arms are tied down to a chair. Attempting to kick out with my feet, I look down. Motherfucker! Realisation sinks in. I'm trapped. Then, I remember how I got here.

I search the darkness of the room I'm in. I'm alone. But I know that fucker is watching from somewhere. "I'm going to fucking enjoy washing my hands in your blood, you fucking asshole!" My scream echoes off the walls.

Fuck! Emmy's face, a vision of pure innocence, comes to mind. She's going to be bloody pissed that I'm late for what is meant to be our marriage ceremony. I'm going to enjoy slaughtering this fucker even more. He's made me late for my wedding day. *For marrying Emily*. The one thing I've wanted to do since I was sixteen.

Wherever the fuck he is, I'm sure he won't be far. If he thinks he's going to break me, he picked the wrong fucking guy. I'm un-fucking-breakable. Let him bring his worst. I've already met the devil. I was bloody well raised by him. I'm the spawn of Satan himself. I laugh into the empty room.

I wonder just how pissed Emily is going to be about me missing our appointment… I focus on wiggling my toes and fingers slightly, to keep the blood flowing. The last thing I need is to get out of these binds and then not be able to fucking move because my limbs give out on me.

There has to be something around here I can use to get myself out of this mess. I can't see shit. There's a slither of light creeping under what must be the door, but other than that, there's nothing. Pure darkness. The room is cold, but I've been colder. It stinks like mildew. Stale, wet air. What I wouldn't do to bury my head in Emily's hair and get a whiff of that fruity, raspberry scent she always seems to smell like. If I close my eyes and imagine it hard enough, I can almost trick myself into believing that's the scent I'm smelling right now.

---

I MUST HAVE DOZED OFF, because I come to with a start when I hear the doorknob wiggling around. It's playtime, motherfucker. This is probably going to hurt a little. Pain can be good though; pain means you're alive.

The light that comes on as soon as the door opens blinds me. I have to squint my eyes to see the shadow of the fucker who thinks he'll survive this. I don't need to see him though. I already know who the fuck this dead man walking is.

"Nice of you to finally wake up. I've been waiting. I don't like to be kept waiting. You see, Joshua, when I get bored, I tend to find young, pretty things to keep me occupied. To alleviate the monotony."

My eyes are trained on his face. It's odd… I've never met anyone who's more psychotic than I am. But this dipshit certainly takes the cake. He's as nutty as they come. He pauses his sentence as he hefts on a rope he's dragging behind him.

"This one here is your fault, Joshua. You shouldn't have kept me waiting," he says, kicking the body of a young woman. She lets out a whimper. She's still alive… If he's expecting me to react, he's underestimated me.

I shrug my shoulders up and down the best I can while my arms are fucking tied to a chair. "It seems more like a *you* problem than a *me* problem."

"Oh, you're funny." He drops the rope and walks closer to me, bending down into my face. I smile. This is exactly where I wanted him.

"You should have given her over when I asked. Now, I'm going to enjoy making you watch as I fuck her battered and bruised body. She was promised to me. She belongs to me. Not you," he spits with visible anger.

My head leans back then forward with as much force as I can gather. I hear the crunch of bone as my forehead smashes into his nose. My vision blurs. Fuck, I probably shouldn't have used my head. But seeing the blood currently running out of his nose makes the pain worth it.

"You will never get your hands on her," I growl out.

His fist comes flying at me, connecting with my jaw. I can't duck or dodge the hit. I just have to sit here and cop it. My head snaps to the side. Spitting on the floor, I straighten my neck and smile at the asshole. I can see I'm already pissing him off. He's only been in the room for two minutes, and I've already managed to fuck with his head.

I look to the girl on the ground. I have no feelings towards her. No empathy. The only thing I can muster is relief. Relief that she's not Emily.

"You know, Emily doesn't even know you exist. Why is it that you think you have a claim to her, exactly?" I've been going out of my mind, trying to figure out what his connection to Emily is.

"I told you. She was promised to me. He was supposed to give her to me. We had a deal. All I want is the girl. So, how about we speed this along, and you tell me where the fuck you have my girl?"

My blood boils at him referring to Emily as his girl. I can't let that shit show. I have to remain calm and unaffected if I want to make it out of here in one piece, and preferably still fucking breathing.

"You might as well go ahead and kill me, because I'll never tell you where she is. You will never get near her." Staring him down, I dare him to make a move closer to me again. He doesn't.

"That's where you're wrong. It's only a matter of time before she's alone again. You left her at the altar, after all. How long do you think she'll wait for you, huh? Either she's going to walk away and forget you existed. Or she'll come looking for you. Don't worry, I'll punish her regardless of the option she chooses."

He bends down to the girl currently on the floor, curled up in a foetal position. She flinches as his hands reach out and run down her arm. "It's a shame really, such a waste of a good girl.

But I was bored, and you were there. You served me well but it's time for you to go." I watch as he pulls out a knife. Bringing it down to where her hands are bound, he slices both of her wrists.

Her screams pierce the air, blood spilling out of her forearms, down over her hands, and pooling on the floor around her. With wide eyes, she looks up at me. I can't help her. There's a slight flicker of helplessness settling within me. Where the fuck that came from, I have no idea.

I clamp that down tight. I don't need now to be the time I start to feel shit I have no business feeling. Instead, I watch, unaffected, as life fades out of her. I don't avoid looking; it's not like I haven't seen a dead body or two before.

The reaction of the detective is disturbing as hell. He's getting off on the fact that he just killed her. I can see it in his heavier breathing, in his dilated pupils. It's fucking sickening.

"You might want to do something about the body. Rigor mortis kicks in after two hours or so, and trust me, disposing of a body after that is not fucking fun."

If I was trying to shock him with my random facts, it worked. His head snaps in my direction, confusion clear on his features.

"Why would I need to get rid of it? She can rot here with you for all I care," he says as he bends down and drags the body over to a corner of the room.

He walks back towards me. I'm preparing myself for the worst. When he stops to retrieve his phone out of his pocket, the sinister smile that spreads across his face does not fucking sit well with me.

"Well, looks like I won't have to get the information out of you after all. My girl has just made contact. She wants to meet me." He turns the phone around and holds it up so I can see the message and profile photo that is unmistakably Emily.

I thought I was prepared for the worst. I wasn't. Why the fuck would she do this? Please, for the love of all that is holy, don't let her be doing this. I start praying right away to a God I don't even believe in.

"Don't worry, I'll be sure to bring her by so you can say one last farewell." He walks out of the room, leaving me alone.

FUCK! I don't scream out loud. I won't give him the pleasure of knowing just how fucking much I'm panicking right now. Emily cannot come here. My mind is whirling with every possible scenario to explain that message.

Maybe it was Sam. He would do something like that to locate the fucker, then find me. That has to be it. It can't be Emily. We do not end like this. I promised her a future. I promised her memories she could tell her grandkids. These are not the sort I want to give her.

---

I'VE BEEN SITTING HERE for what seems like hours. I have no concept of how long it's been. But when the door opens again, my heart stops and all the breath leaves my lungs.

My worst fucking fear—no, my worst fucking nightmare—has just appeared in front of my eyes.

"No! Fuck no! I'm going to fucking kill you, motherfucker. Get your fucking hands off her!" I scream, the rope around my arms and feet burning into my skin as I struggle against it.

"Well, now, that's a reaction I like to see. I believe you've met my girl—Emily," the cocksucker says as he roughly tugs on Emily's hair, pulling her face up high.

She doesn't let out a sound. She has a blank expression as

she stares at me. One side of her face is bruised. This fucker hit her. And I see red.

She mouths the words, "I'm sorry." She's sorry? When I find a way to get us the fuck out of this, you bet your ass she'll be sorry. The lecture I have ready to give her is about keeping what's mine safe and away from psychopaths. Well, psychopaths who aren't me anyway.

Then again, if I can get us out of this mess, I think I'll just hold her tight and never fucking let go. They can pry her body from my cold, dead hands when we're both old and grey and die in our sleep together *Notebook*-style.

"I've waited a long time for you, Emily. You shouldn't have made me wait. Trent promised you'd be mine. Now you are." The detective licks his lips. I want to cut his fucking tongue out of his goddamn head.

"You and I both know Trent was a lying piece of shit," Emily hisses at him. He backhands her across the face, causing her to fall to the ground. She's so close to me. I want to reach out and grab her, to pick her up. Tell her that it's all going to be okay. But it's not. How the fuck am I meant to get us out of this fucking mess when I can't get myself out of this chair?

"I'm going to chop your fingers off one at a time, then I'm going to slice right through your fucking wrist, you sadistic fucking bastard," I seethe at him.

"Words, Joshua, they don't hurt me." He smirks.

"Words might not, but this sure as fuck will." Emily stands up, her own words confident. I'm not the only one who's shocked at what she's doing. The fucking detective's face is priceless. He goes sheet white, staring at her like a stunned mullet.

# Chapter 20

## Emily

I'm watching the darkened screen, waiting for a reply. My phone beeps with the sound of a notification. My heart pounds as I swipe and unlock the illuminated display. Part of me was hoping it would be a message from Josh, telling me he's on his way home to grovel for missing our appointment with the judge.

Hope's a bitch that's best kept buried though. It's not Josh. It's *him*. The detective. I sit up as I read the message.

**Jones: Emily, it's nice to finally hear from you. Meet me at 74 Bourke Street, Newtown. Come alone. Don't lead anyone here. If you do, I'll kill him before you get to say goodbye.**

Shit, okay. *You can do this, Emily*. I'm not the damsel in distress, waiting around to be saved. I'm more than capable of saving Josh.

If it means sacrificing myself to do it, then that's a choice I'm more than willing to make. He's going to be pissed as hell at me for doing this. I can hear his voice in my head now, telling me to stop. To go and get Sam or Dean and let them know of the plan.

I can't risk anything happening to him though. If it were me, he wouldn't hesitate to come to my rescue. I owe him that same kind of devotion. Besides, I need to get him back. It's gone beyond a want. It's definitely a need now. My heart is literally hurting without him. My chest is constricted and aching.

With my mind focused on saving Josh, I head into the wardrobe, since Josh has somehow filled it with clothing for me. I choose black leather pants and a long-sleeve black shirt, matching them with a pair of boots. I then chuck my hair up in a messy ponytail.

Now, I just need to figure out how I can get into the armoury and escape this house without anyone noticing. It's the middle of the night; it shouldn't be that hard. Walking down the hall, I stick close to the walls, trying to stay in the shadows, just like Josh had shown me the first night we snuck in here.

My heart hammers in my chest the whole time. I finally come to the door that leads downstairs to where Josh has his armoury stored. It dawns on me I never did get around to asking him why he has so many damn weapons. Although, right now, I'm not complaining.

The adrenaline that is currently running through me is like nothing I've ever experienced. I briefly wonder if this is how my dad would feel when he was deployed. Did he keep going on deployments just to feel this rush?

I close the door behind me and run down the stairs.

Punching in the code to the armoury, it opens and the light in the little room automatically springs to life.

I really am spoilt for choice here. There are so many weapons. I'm thankful for those hours spent at the range with Dad. I pick up two small knives, securing one in each of my boots. Next, I need to choose a handgun. Something small I can conceal, yet it has to still pack a punch. If I only get one shot at this asshole, I want to make sure it's lethal.

I select a small, .22 calibre, semi-automatic pistol, tucking it into the waistband of my pants. Just as I'm shutting the door, something stops me. I pick up another small .22. Removing the knife in my left boot, I slip the gun in, making sure my pants sit over the top to conceal it.

I then shut the door, locking it behind me. As I'm climbing the stairs, I send up a little prayer that I can get out of this house without anyone seeing. Shit, what the hell do I do once I'm out? How do I even get to Newtown?

Do I try to take a car? Someone's sure to hear and see that. And there's the whole issue of the gates. I don't know what the code is. There are also guards… As soon as they see me trying to leave, they're bound to call Dean.

I remember the black credit card Josh gave me weeks ago. That will work. I can at least get a cab. Sneaking into Josh's room, I close the door behind me. The tiny hairs on the back of my neck rise. I'm not alone in here.

Turning the light on, I gasp when I see the figure sitting on the sofa. I don't know whether I should turn and run, scream, or see what he wants.

"What are you doing in here, Sam?" I ask as calmly as I can. The fact that I have a few weapons on me gives me more courage than I usually would have in this situation. I'm not helpless right now. I can protect myself. I will protect myself.

"Relax, Emily. I came to check on you. Imagine my surprise when you weren't here," he says, not making a move to get up, or get out.

"Well, you've seen I'm still here. In one piece. Now, you can leave," I say as I walk over to the dresser. I'm sure I threw that card in one of these drawers.

"I was surprised that you weren't here, but I was more surprised at what I read on this," Sam says, holding up my phone.

Shit, I left that on the bed. My mind was so set on getting down to the armoury I left it behind. I'm not used to carrying a phone around yet. I mostly leave it in the bedroom all the time. How do I get out of this? I'm racking my brain, trying to come up with a reasonable excuse for those messages. But I've got none.

"Have you completely lost your fucking mind, Emily? Because that's the only reason I can think of that would have you trying to sneak out by yourself to meet a goddamn psychopath." Sam stands up and throws the phone back on the bed.

I'm quick to swipe it up, tucking it into my back pocket. "Maybe I am crazy. But I'm not going to sit around here, twiddling my thumbs, when Josh is out there somewhere. He's out there and he's hurt, Sam. I can't just sit back and wait for a miracle, because in my experience, those don't bloody exist. I'm going to go and get him. Then I'm going to wring his damn neck for making me worry like this. I probably have grey hairs by now."

"Emily, you are not going out there. I'll go. I'll find this asshole at the address and I'll bring Josh back."

"No, you can't. You read the message. He'll kill him, Sam. I can't lose him. I only just got him back. You have to let me do this. Please, I can do this. I can."

"What is your plan, exactly, Emily? Charm him with your sweet personality and get him to let both you and Josh go free? That's not going to happen. You don't know the things this sick fuck wants to do to you, Emily. You don't know the risk you're taking here."

"I know. I've seen the pictures. I know what he wants with me. But the risk is worth it to keep Josh safe."

"Just what do you think will happen to Josh if you ended up in one of those pictures, Emily? What do you think would happen to him if he knew the reason you died was because you were trying to save him?"

"He would be alive," I say. I know he'd be a mess. But he'd be breathing, and his friends and family would help him get past it. I have to believe that he would be okay without me.

"No, he wouldn't. You and I both know he's not going to live without you. Fuck."

I dig through the second drawer in the dresser. Finally finding the card, I tuck it into my pocket and head towards the door. Sam beats me to it, blocking my way.

"I can't let you do this, Emily. Please, just let Dean and me handle this," he pleads.

"I tried that. You came home without him, Sam. I won't stop until I get him back."

"We didn't stop. We came to check on you. We came to make a plan, do due diligence."

"Yeah, well, I have a plan and I'm going, so you need to move out of my way." I fold my arms over my chest.

"That's not going to happen. I'm sorry, Emily. I can't let you leave. Josh would have my balls if I did."

Fuck, I have to get out of here. The longer it takes, the more hurt Josh could be. I pull out the pistol from my waistband and aim it at Sam's leg. I don't want to hurt him, but if I have to, I will.

"I won't ask you to move again, Sam. Get out of my way or I will shoot you."

"You're not going to… AH, FUCK! GODDAMN IT, EMILY!"

Sam falls to the ground, holding onto his thigh. His scream is so loud if the gunshot didn't alert the whole household, his shriek alone would have.

"I'm sorry, but I did try to warn you. Also, toughen the hell up. Stop screaming. It's only a flesh wound. I made sure to avoid any major arteries. You'll survive." I step over him and run down the corridor. I can hear him calling after me. I feel terrible for what I just did. But nothing is going to stop me from getting to Josh.

---

PAYING THE CAB DRIVER, I jump out of the car. With my head held high, I march up to the door and knock loud. My insides churn with nerves, but I'm doing everything I can to not let them show. I will not show weakness. I will be strong. Josh needs me to be strong right now, and I need Josh.

There is no other option. I have to do this. I have to get him back. When the door opens, I realign my shoulders and stare the demon straight in the eyes—eyes, which roam up and down my body slowly, creepiness surrounding his gleam as he takes me in.

*This is for Josh.* I keep replaying the mantra in my head. It seems like we stand here forever, just staring each other down. I will not be the first to break. I won't speak first. He must not like the defiance I'm putting off because he reaches out and lands a left hook directly to my face. I fall to the ground, my fingers itching to pull out a gun and shoot him. I have to wait. I have to know where Josh is first.

"There's going to be one of those for every day you made me wait, Emily. You were meant to be mine. He promised me you would be mine after four years. That was the deal." He reaches down, grabbing me by the arm, and drags me into the house before slamming the door behind him.

I have no idea what deal he's talking about. Who the hell did he make a deal with? "What deal?" I ask.

"The deal Trent and I made when I signed the fake death certificates for you and your mother. He wanted the money. I wanted you."

"Why?" I question.

"Why? Why do I want you? I've been watching you for a long time, Emily. Trent was never meant to have you first. It was supposed to be me."

"No, why did he want the money? What did he do with it?" Maybe I can find out if there is any of it left, then recover it and give it back to Josh. Not that he seems to care about the cash, but I do. That's a lot of money. If I'd have known he made that account for me, I would have sent it all back to him.

"He owed some nasty people some money. He never did learn his lesson. Had a bad gambling habit. Always making the same mistakes. But it doesn't matter now, because you're here. You're mine, Emily, and we can start our future together. However short that may be for you, well, that depends on how good you are."

He runs his fingers down my cheek; it takes everything in me not to recoil. I know if I do, he will just get angry again. I can't very well save Josh if I'm in pieces myself.

"What did you do with his body?" I ask. I need to know that Trent's body is never going to be found.

"Oh, you don't need to worry about that, Emily. I helped you. I got rid of the evidence you left behind. Couldn't exactly have you going to jail for murder, now, could I? I put him through a crematorium, then I sprinkled his ashes over the ocean. He always hated the beach." The detective laughs.

"We had a deal. Let me say goodbye to Josh first," I demand. As much as I try to not let my voice quiver, it does, giving away the emotion I'm feeling right now.

"A deal is a deal. And I would so love for him to see that I have you in my grasp now. Let's go." He picks me up, his grip tight around my upper arm as he pulls me through the house.

The moment he opens the door and shoves me into the room, my eyes go to Josh. The detective grabs me by my ponytail, holding me close to him. I shut all my emotions off. The sight of Josh tied to the chair, the dried blood that's dripped down his face, the bruising I can see… it makes me sick to my stomach.

This is all because of me. He's in this predicament because of me. I mouth the words, "I'm sorry," to him. I need him to know how sorry I am that he's gotten caught up in my mess.

"I've waited a long time for you, Emily. You shouldn't have made me wait. Trent promised you'd be mine. Now you are." Then I see the detective lick his lips as his eyes roam over my chest. It makes me sick.

"You and I both know Trent was a lying piece of shit," I reply to him. It's not until after the words leave my mouth that I realise what I've said. The hand that comes out and slaps me across my face knocks me to the ground.

I can hear Joshua cursing, yelling all sorts of profanity. I need to end this now. With a clear mind and determination, I reach for the pistol in my waistband.

The detective says something about words not hurting him to Josh. He's so focused on Joshua he doesn't notice that I'm now standing and holding a gun aimed at his head.

"Words might not, but this sure as fuck will," I say. I take the slightest bit of pleasure as I watch the shock cross his face.

I don't give him a chance to say anything. I'm not prepared to take the risk of him overpowering me. With my dad's voice in my ear, I focus on the target, breathe, pull my finger back and become one with the pistol.

The sound of the gunshot echoes in the room. The detective's body falls to the ground. I aim the end of the barrel at his fallen form, checking where I actually got him. It's a clean shot, straight in the middle of the forehead. Lowering my weapon, I stare at him, waiting to feel... *something*. Anything. Where's the guilt? The shame? I should feel something other than pure relief right now.

"Emmy, untie me." Josh's hoarse voice breaks me from my inner turmoil.

"I'm sorry... I'm so sorry." Dropping the gun to the ground, I pull out the knife from my boot and cut him loose.

# Chapter 21

## Josh

Emily pulls a knife from her boot and cuts the rope loose, first from around my ankles and then from my hands. I'm in awe as I watch her. Who the hell is this girl? It's like I am staring at an entirely different person from the one who was scared of her shadow a few weeks ago.

When she walked through that door, I felt sick to my stomach. Seeing her get hit was the worst fucking moment of my life. I know I couldn't watch her get tortured, and that's exactly what that sick fuck had in mind. For her. For me.

As soon as my hands are freed, I pull her into my arms. When she winces, I loosen my hold slightly. I'm so relieved in this moment, but also pissed as fucking hell that she put herself in this position.

I hear movement in the hall. Shoving Emily behind me, I bend down and swipe her discarded gun from the floor. Dean bursts through the door, followed closely by Zac. I don't lower the firearm. Dean, however, the trusting fool that he is, lowers his. Zac's smarter than I give him credit for because his gun is still trained straight on me.

"What the fuck took you so long? And why in God's name would you let Emily do something so fucking reckless?" I scream at Dean. There's no fucking way I would ever let Ella put herself in danger like Emily just had. I would have locked her in a damn cage if I needed to.

"First, it took a hot fucking minute to track the payment on the card Emily used for the cab she took to get here. Second, I didn't fucking let her out. She snuck out. Ask Emily just what measures she took to get out of the bloody house." Dean smirks, like he knows a secret I don't.

I look behind me and raise my eyebrows at Emily. She rolls her eyes and huffs. "What'd you do, Em?"

"It was only a flesh wound, Josh. It's not a big deal." She folds her arms over her chest.

"Who'd you shoot?" I ask, confused. I'm trying not to laugh. I shouldn't think it's funny that she shot someone to get to me. But I do.

"Sam, but it was his fault. He wouldn't move out of the doorway. I only shot him in the leg," she defends her actions. She doesn't need to make a case for herself though. Not to me.

"Huh, okay." I turn back to Dean. "Seems like he deserved it."

Dean places himself in front of Zac. "Drop the gun, Josh. You're not going to shoot me."

I tilt my head and stare him down. "Are you sure about that?" I ask him.

"No, but I'd like to think you wouldn't shoot your own brother."

"Okay, well, this little family reunion is great and all, but I'd really like to go home now," Emily says, walking around me. She steps in front of me and takes the gun out of my hand. I'm a little stunned by her boldness so I let her take it.

Cupping her face gently in my palms, I lean in and kiss her forehead. "Let's go home."

"Hey, Zac?" Emily starts in that sugary-sweet voice—a voice I know means that I am going to love whatever it is she is about to say. I've come to know this is the sweet voice she uses when dishing out threats.

"Yeah?" Zac turns around to look at her.

"If you ever point a gun like that at Josh again, I'll shoot your ass before you can even blink. And I don't miss. Just ask the detective back there. Oh, that's right… You can't, because I shot him." Emily smiles. Zac and Dean both stare with slack jaws and wide eyes.

With a shake of his head, Zac says, "I'll take that into consideration, Emily." He turns and continues walking.

"We're going to need a clean-up crew," Dean says before he follows Zac.

"Just torch the place," I suggest as I lead Emily to the Range Rover Zac is currently waiting at.

---

LYING HERE in bed with Emily in my arms, I finally feel peace again. I honestly wasn't sure if I'd get out of that room alive. Emily's been quiet since I had Zac drop us at my penthouse. With the threat now gone, we don't have to hide anymore. I'm at a loss for words. I'm not sure what to say.

I just know I need to get her talking. She didn't say anything in the car, and she didn't say anything as we showered and climbed into bed. She curled up to my side, wrapped herself around me and clung to my chest, her fingers digging into my arms.

"Thank you. I don't think I said thank you," I say as my hands mindlessly twirl the wet strands of her hair.

"What are you thanking me for?"

"You saved me, Emily. You alone. No help. No one else. Just you. As much as I wish you hadn't put yourself at risk like that, I am thankful that you came to my rescue."

"I would never have stopped looking, Josh. I would have done anything to get you back."

"It's over, Emily. The threat is gone. You are free."

"Josh, do you… do you still want to marry me? I understand if you don't." Emily stares down at the ring on her left hand.

"What? Why would I not want to marry you? Emmy, it's not even a question. We *are* getting married. As soon as I can book an appointment with Judge Thomas, we are signing those papers."

"You're not disgusted at what I've done?" she asks. "Josh, I just killed someone… *again*."

"Emmy, look at me." I tilt her face up towards mine. Once I see those blue eyes, I tell her, "There is nothing you could ever do that would make me not love you. You didn't have a choice. What you did was self-defence, Em. You are perfect in every single way. Never doubt that."

"I should feel bad, guilty, or something. But I don't. If I had to do it again, I would. And that scares me. Why don't I feel remorse? It's not normal."

"Normal is overrated, babe," I remind her again. "We are exceptional. Normal is for the masses. You're one of a kind. There's nothing wrong with you." I think about what she says.

I've never felt remorse in my life, other than when I made her leave town all those years ago. "Emmy, do you think less of me? Are you disgusted by me? You've seen me do unspeakable things. You know I don't feel any kind of remorse afterwards. Fuck, Em, I'd slaughter my whole family if it meant saving you. I would sacrifice anyone. If it were a choice between you and them, there is no choice for me. It's always going to be you."

"I don't know how I got so lucky to have you, but I will always choose you too." Her words mean everything to me.

"You should sleep, babe. It's been a really long fucking day."

"Josh, can we go back to the ranch tomorrow? I mean, if you don't need to be in the city, can we go back?"

"We will head back as soon as we wake up. I promise."

"Thank you."

---

THREE WEEKS, it's been three weeks since Emily and I returned to the ranch. She was able to reunite with her mum, and honestly, between her mother and mine, I feel like I've hardly got her to myself. Today's going to be different though. Today is the day I get to make her mine. *Legally*. Today is the day I get to call her my wife.

We decided to rebook and have the judge marry us out on the ranch. We've invited just our family and friends. Emily decided that she's friends with Ella's sisters-in-law, which means I have to endure spending time with Ella's brothers, Zac and Bray. I'm getting used to them being around. Would I call them friends of mine? Absolutely not. But they are friends of my brother's, and now apparently friends of Emily's, which means I can't turn the idiots into pig food.

As much as I'd like to think I can hog all of Emily's attention today, I know I'm going to lose her to the girls. I want her to have that moment, to be surrounded by friends and family when she gets ready for her wedding. Even if we're not having a huge ceremony, no expense has been spared.

I let my mother go wild, with the one condition that only family would be in attendance. No press. No outsiders. She grumbled about how I'm ruining her dreams of a huge wedding, but I reminded her she still gets to do all of that for Dean and Ella, after which she happily arranged everything (happily for the most part anyway).

Wanting to take advantage of the morning, I wake Emily up by burying my head between her legs. This has become my favourite way of waking her. It doesn't take long before she's moaning and squirming underneath me as I slowly swirl my tongue around her clit.

"Shit, Josh, stop. Move." Emily groans as she jumps out of bed and runs to the bathroom.

I follow her, holding her hair back while she prays to the porcelain gods. "Well, that's not the reaction I was hoping for," I say, when she finally stops and leans her back against the wall.

"Oh my God, I'm so sorry. I'm so embarrassed." She covers her mouth with her hands.

Standing up, I fill a glass with water and hand it to her. "Are you okay? Should I call a doctor? Is it nerves?" I really fucking hope she's not getting cold feet.

"I'm fine. I probably just ate something bad. I'm not nervous at all. I get to marry you today. I want to marry you,

Josh. Stop worrying." She sips on the water, then bends straight over the bowl again.

"I'm calling a doctor. Hold on." I run out to the bedroom, grab my phone and find the doctor's number that we use in town and dial. It's seven o'clock on a Saturday morning, but I don't care.

"Mr. McKinley, what can I do for you?" Dr. Kapner answers.

"I need a house call, doc. My fiancée is sick."

"What's the problem? When you say sick, what do you mean?"

"She woke up throwing her guts up. It's our wedding day. We're getting married today. I need you to come and check her over." My voice is panicked. The thought of Emily being sick, of something horrible being wrong with her is too much.

"I'm fine. I'm sure it will pass," Emily groans into the toilet.

"Ah, I can be there in about thirty minutes. In the meantime, make sure to keep her fluids up. Does she have a fever?"

I place my hand on her forehead before she bats it away. "No, she doesn't," I answer.

"Okay, that's a good sign. I'll be there as soon as I can. And congratulations on the wedding." He hangs up.

"Fuck, Emmy, what do I do? How can I help?"

"Josh, stop. You can help by not panicking. It's just an upset stomach. That's all. Also, pass me that dressing gown. I'd prefer not to be throwing up into the bowl while I'm naked."

"Shit, yes. Of course." I stand up, retrieve the dressing gown from the hook on the back of the door and help her into it. "Do you want anything? Tea? Coffee? The doctor said to keep you hydrated. You need to drink something."

"Just water is fine. Josh, I'm okay now. Really. I just want to brush my teeth, then lie down for a bit longer."

I pick up her toothbrush and squirt some paste on it. "Open up," I say, holding the toothbrush up to her mouth. She scrunches her eyebrows at me while grabbing the toothbrush.

"I'm going to pretend you did not just want to brush my teeth for me," she says as she stands over the sink.

"You can pretend all you like, but there is nothing I wouldn't do for you, Emmy."

She mumbles a response with the toothbrush still in her mouth. I don't know what it is she said. I just wait for her to be finished. Picking her up, I carry her to the bed and lay her down, getting in next to her.

I send a text to Dean, telling him to direct the doctor up here when he arrives. Putting my phone down, I settle in next to Emily and pull her into my arms. "I can't believe I just threw up when you were doing that," she groans.

I laugh, then Ella comes storming through the door. "What's wrong? Who's sick? Why do you need a doctor?" she demands.

"What the fuck, Ella?" I groan, then I get a look at what she's wearing, or what she's not wearing, which would be clothing. She's walking around in tiny-ass fucking shorts that look more like panties than shorts and a tank top that's fucking see-through.

Rolling out of bed, I storm into the closet, returning with a hoodie. I dump it over her head. "You do know this house is full of staff and you're walking around butt-ass naked, right?" I say as she fights me off.

"Fuck off, Josh. I'm not naked, idiot. Clearly you're not the one who's sick." She ends up taking the hoodie and putting it on. "I'm only wearing this because it's actually cold in here, not because you told me to." She glares at me.

"Whatever you say, sweetheart." I still win, so I don't fucking care about her reasoning. I'm not about to have my houschold of staff staring at hcr ass and tits.

"Seriously, Emmy, what's wrong? Why are you sick?" Ella asks her, climbing onto my bed. I pick her up and return her to the floor, jumping back in the bed myself.

"Argh, if it wasn't your wedding day and I didn't think Emily would shoot me, I'd have some not very nice words for you right now, Joshua." Ella folds her arms over her chest.

"I wouldn't shoot you, Ella. I like you. And I'm fine. It's just a tummy bug. I'm sure it will pass," Emily assures her.

Ella's face drops. "Oh God, not you too. Don't get me wrong, I love being an aunt. But you and I were the kid-free people of the group. Damn it, Josh, couldn't you keep it in your pants. Seriously, now all my friends are going to be tied down with babies."

What the fuck is she talking about? Pregnant. Emily isn't pregnant. We would know. Fuck, is she? I look over to Emily, who has also just caught on to what Ella's saying.

"Ah, I'm not pregnant," she says.

Although, judging by the look on Emmy's face, she's not one hundred percent certain of that.

"Ella, can you please go wait for the doctor and let him know which room we are in." I stand up and walk her to the door.

"Fine, but I'll be back. Don't worry, Emily, I'll makc you some toast and ginger ale. That always worked for Alyssa and Reilly," she says as I shut and lock the door.

Turning back to the bed, Emily appears terrified. Fuck, I haven't seen this look on her for a few weeks now. She hasn't had any flashbacks; she hasn't been scared of anything. But right now, she looks like she's about to run for her life.

"Emmy, it's okay. It will be okay. When the doctor gets here, we can get him to give us a test. Whatever it says, it will be okay." I'm not sure if I'm trying to reassure her or myself at this point. As much as I want to freak the fuck out right now, I can't. We can't both be freaked out.

"Josh, I'm sorry. I didn't mean to." She has tears running down her face.

# Chapter 22

## Emily

Pregnant, could I actually be pregnant? How the hell did I let this happen? I swore I'd never let myself get pregnant again… after the last time. I couldn't even protect an unborn baby. How am I meant to be a mother?

"Emmy, this isn't anything you've done wrong. This isn't your fault. Please don't cry. I really fucking hate seeing you cry." Josh wipes the tears from my face. Why isn't he mad?

"I… how? Josh, you don't understand. Last time I was pregnant, I couldn't even protect my unborn baby. How am I meant to be a mother? I don't know how." I verbalize my internal fears.

"Em, you are going to be the most fierce, loyal mother this world has ever seen. What happened last time is not a reflection on you. Just a few weeks ago, look how you were so fearless you put yourself in front of a madman to save me. What do you think you'd do for a child who was ours?"

"I'm scared," I admit to him. I'm so fucking terrified of not being a good mother.

"So am I. We can be scared together. We will learn how to do this together. I promise I will be here every step of the way with you." Josh always says the right thing.

Sometimes I have to pinch myself; his love for me is beyond anything I ever could have imagined. His endless support for what I want, it's like nothing I've ever experienced.

"Are you mad? Angry?" I ask him.

"I'm not angry. I'm not mad, Emmy. I'm… I actually don't know how to explain it. It's a different feeling from anything I've ever felt." He looks contemplative, trying to figure out his emotions.

"What do you feel? Maybe I can help figure it out," I offer.

"I feel like I need to protect someone who I've never met, someone who isn't even here. We don't even know if you are pregnant, Em, but I feel this need, this urge, to not let anything happen to that baby you're growing. Don't hate me, but I'm kind of hopeful that you are. The world could use more people like you in it. And I feel this overwhelming love. You know I love you with every fibre of my being, but this is a different kind of love. I don't know how to explain it." Josh looks down at our joined hands as I rub little circles around his palm with my thumb.

"I think what you're describing is exactly what every parent feels. An unconditional love that knows no bounds. Do you really think we can do this? I mean, I might not be pregnant and we may be worrying about nothing. But if I am, we are going to be okay, right?"

"I have a good feeling that you are, and we are always going to be okay, Emmy."

There's a knock at the door. "Come in." Josh unlocks the door and greets the doctor.

"Mr. McKinley, how's the patient?" An older man with greying hair walks in, carrying a medical bag.

"Thanks for coming, doc. This is Emily. She's better, I think," Josh says.

"I'm fine. He really is overreacting. I'm sorry he wasted your time coming here." I hop off the bed, much to Josh's displeasure, and shake the doctor's outstretched hand.

"I'm Dr. Kapner and I don't mind coming out here at all. What seems to be the problem?" the doctor asks.

Shit, how do I tell him I need a pregnancy test? Joshua forced the doctor to do a house call for something we could have gotten from the supermarket.

"We need to start with a pregnancy test, doc," Joshua says proudly.

"Emily, is there a chance you could be pregnant?" the doctor directs to me.

I nod my head. I can't look him in the eye. Why am I suddenly so shy?

"Okay, well, let's start with that, and then we can rule out anything else afterwards if need be."

"Okay."

The doctor rummages through his bag and pulls out a box. "Here you go. Just pee on the stick and wait a few minutes," he says, handing the test to me.

"Thank you." I walk into the bathroom. Just as I'm about to turn around, Josh walks in after me, guiding me backwards and shutting the door.

"What are you doing?" I ask him, mortified. He doesn't think he's actually going to watch me pee, does he?

"We are in this together, Emmy. I want to be there for everything. Including the whole peeing on the stick. So, come on, let's do this." He nods his head to the toilet.

"Ah, no. No way. you are not watching me pee, Joshua McKinley." I place my hands on my hips and stomp my foot to get my point across.

"Em, I've literally seen every inch of you naked, licked every curve and crevice. And you're shy about peeing? Really?"

"Yes, so turn around and switch on the tap."

"Okay, you win." Josh places his hands up and pivots on his heel, before running the water in the basin.

I do what I have to do. As soon as the toilet flushes, Josh spins around. "Did it work? Are we pregnant?" he asks eagerly.

I laugh. "You have to wait a few minutes. Put a timer on for three minutes."

We sit there, holding hands on the floor of the bathroom, and wait what has to be the longest three minutes of my life. As soon as the timer goes off, Josh snatches up the stick and turns it over.

"Yes! I knew my swimmers were fucking good," he shouts. I wouldn't be surprised if the whole damn house heard it.

"Oh my God. Josh, it says pregnant."

"Yeah, I can see that. How do you feel?" he asks.

I can't help the tears forming in my eyes. "Surprisingly okay. It's going to be okay. How do *you* feel?" I ask him, noticing his own eyes are shiny with unshed tears.

"I feel like the luckiest fucking bloke in the world. Thank you for giving me this. For giving us this."

"Pretty sure you had a big part of the whole me being pregnant, Josh."

"Yeah, I did. Fuck, Em, we're going to be a family. You, me and this baby." Josh kisses my lips ever so softly before stopping with an abruptness. "Fuck, Emily, you're pregnant. You should not be sitting on the floor. Wait, do you need something? Food? You should probably eat something. Let me call the kitchen. Come on, I'll help you back to bed." He rambles on as we walk out of the bathroom. It's going to be a long bloody nine months, but I wouldn't have it any other way.

"Are you ready to do this?" Josh asks, standing behind me and looking at our reflection in the mirror.

His hands are rested on my stomach, my very flat stomach. I've tried to tell him there won't be anything there to feel for a few months yet, but he's insistent on having his hands there.

As I look at our reflection, I can't believe this day has finally arrived. I'm getting married today, in a fancy white dress and all. This dress is even more beautiful than the first one I had.

It has a lace bodice with long sleeves made out of the softest material I've ever felt. The skirt is silk with a long slit up the front of my left leg. It's gorgeous. But my reflection has nothing on Josh's. He's wearing a tux, a black and white tux. It should be illegal for that man to wear a suit. Just looking at him now, all I can think of is stripping him down and doing very unspeakable things to the body I know he's hiding underneath.

"More than ready."

"Let's do this then. Shall we?" Josh turns and holds his arm out for me. I hook my hand in the loop of his elbow.

We decided to walk down the aisle together. I didn't want anyone to give me away if I couldn't have my dad. Josh's theory was that I already belonged to him, so no one else had a right to give me away.

I'm glad that we are side by side, that I can lean on him as everyone turns and watches us walk down the red carpet.

My eyes take in the beautiful setup Mrs. McKinley has managed to arrange in such a short timeframe. There are two rows of white wooden chairs seated in front of a gazebo, which is covered in pink and white flowers climbing up the sides and arching over the top.

"This looks like something out of a fairy tale, Josh," I whisper.

"Didn't anyone send you the memo, Emmy? You're my queen. A queen deserves only the best."

"If you make me cry and ruin my makeup, I'm going to stomp this stiletto heel into your foot." I laugh. "Thank you for doing this. I couldn't have pictured anything more perfect."

"Even with mascara running down your face, you'd still outshine any fucker here, Em."

We make it to the front. Josh leads me onto the pergola. Now that I'm standing under it, I feel like I'm on a stage. I look back at all of our family and friends. I'm really glad they're here to share this day with us.

My mother is sitting next to Josh's mum. They're both crying, already dabbing their eyes with tissues. Ella and Dean are sitting next to them with Sam on the end, his crutches leaning against the chair. He smiles a huge smile at me. How the guy can even stand being near me after what I did to him, I have no idea. He says that all is forgiven and water under the bridge. But I still feel a little bad for shooting him. I'd do it again though, if it meant getting to Josh.

On the other side of the aisle are Zac and Alyssa. Ash sits between them, his eyes wide and glued to me. I've grown really fond of that kid over the last few weeks. Reilly and Bray occupy the next seats over. Wait, is he? Oh wow, Bray looks like he's trying to discreetly wipe at his eyes. I catch him though; he knows I've seen him do it and he just smiles at me. The couple has one beautiful red-headed little girl on each of their laps. Those twins are bloody adorable, but I pray to God I do not end up with two babies. They're hard work.

Turning my attention back to Josh, the celebrant begins to talk. I get lost in Josh's gaze and it's not until he squeezes my hand to get my attention that I realise I need to focus.

"Joshua, you have your own vows you want to share with Emily?" the celebrant says.

"Emily, from the moment you sat down at my lunch table, I knew you were different. Then you opened your mouth and started rambling on, and I knew you were going to turn my world upside down in the best ways possible. I didn't know or understand the feelings you provoked in me at first, but now I know that was the day I met my soulmate. You make me a better person, Emmy. For so long, I was lost, until you found and completed me. You are my beginning and end. You're the cream to my cookie, the Tam to my Tim, and the toast to my Vegemite. I promise to love, cherish and worship you every day for the rest of our lives." Josh places a solid gold band on my finger.

"Emily, do you have vows you'd like to share with Joshua?" the celebrant asks.

"Joshua, the moment I first saw you, you took my breath away, and still do every time I look at you. I am the luckiest person on earth because I'm loved by you. I promise that you will always be the cookie to my cream, the Tim to my Tam, and the Vegemite to my toast. You are the best part of me. I promise to love you unconditionally for as long as we both shall live." I manage to get through most of what I wanted to say. With tears in my eyes, I slide the ring on his finger.

"I now pronounce you husband and wife. You may kiss your bride."

Joshua has his lips on mine before the celebrant finishes his declaration. His kiss sends a fiery need throughout my body. This is a kiss that I will be telling our grandchildren about, the kind of kiss that inspires love songs. Everything fades into the background as I lose myself in all that is Joshua.

Josh pulls away first. "Are you ready to begin our happily ever after, Mrs. McKinley?"

"More than anything else in the world," I reply.

# Epilogue

## Josh

2 years later

"MA-MA-MA!" Breanna, my sixteen-month-old daughter, wiggles in my arms, calling out to Emily as we watch her canter on Snow, the new Arabian. She's been out here riding all morning while Breanna and I had a daddy-daughter breakfast date.

I think I wore more of the eggs than Breanna got into her mouth. Then there was the issue of her being covered in syrup. Not that Bree complained about spending half an hour splashing in the bubble bath she then had.

Now, we're sitting on the deck swing. She's trying to jump out of my arms to run towards Emily. I knew from the moment she started moving that Bree was a little daredevil in training. The girl has no bloody fear, no concept of danger. I think I've actually sprouted fucking grey hairs from watching her climb the furniture.

"Isn't Mumma beautiful, Bree-Bree?" I ask, not getting a response other than her chanting, "Ma-Ma."

Turning her in my arms, so she's facing me, I whisper, "I fucking love you, Breanna. Don't ever change for anyone." I know I shouldn't be swearing in front of my toddler, at least that's what her mother and grandmothers keep reminding me. But it's just Bree and me; she's not going to dob me in.

"Dada." Breanna reaches out and pulls on my hair as she lands a very sloppy, open-mouthed kiss to my cheek.

"Did you have a good breakfast?" Emily asks. I was so wrapped up in Breanna I didn't even notice her come up.

"Well, we wore more than we ate, but I think it was good. What do you think, princess? Was breakie good?"

"Ma-Ma." Breanna practically jumps out of my arms as she reaches for Emily.

"Traitor," I tell her when I hand her over.

Emily laughs as she kisses Breanna all over her face. I never knew I was capable of loving something so fiercely, but these two girls are my everything. I can't believe how lucky I am to have them.

Breanna looks just like her mother, absolutely fucking beautiful. I'm sure that shit's going to backfire on me one day, but I'll be ready. I figured I'd buy more pigs when she reaches the age of thirteen. And there's going to be more bodies to fucking bury.

"The Williamsons are coming out this weekend. I've got some workers coming in to set up the yard for the kids."

"What do you mean *set up the yard*, Josh? You've already

built a jungle gym. There's a playhouse bigger than most peoples' actual homes, and a bloody petting zoo. What more could you possibly set up?" Emily asks.

When Breanna was born, I may have gone a little overboard building a play yard fit for the princess she is. I'll never admit that to Emily though.

"Emmy, they're only kids once. I have the means to give them memories they can cherish forever. I've booked some theme park rides for the weekend. Who doesn't love a theme park ride?"

"Josh, they can create memories by playing in the dirt. They don't need their own theme park in the back yard. Come on, baby, let's go tidy up your toy room before the kids get here." Emily walks inside the house with Bree in her arms.

"Ah, Emmy, I might have already picked up for her." Emily has this thing about wanting Bree to pick up her toys and pack away after herself.

"Daddy is going to spoil you rotten, little girl." She tickles Bree's belly. "Josh, how do you think she's ever going to learn to pick up after herself if you keep doing it for her?"

"Em, she won't ever have to. I'll always be here to pick up after her." I smile.

"Ah-huh. I'm going to remind you of that when she's sixteen."

"Argh, why, Emmy? Why do you constantly remind me that she's going to be a teenage girl? Are you trying to give me a stroke?" I complain. The thought of my little princess being a teenager is a fucking nightmare.

"Because it's so fun to see the look on your face. Do you remember when I was sixteen, Josh?"

"Of course I do. How could I forget?"

"Do you remember the thoughts you would have about me?"

"No. Just no. Stop right there. This little angel is going to be a nun. It's already been decided. God wouldn't put such an angelic thing on earth to not have them work for the church." I've already had this discussion with Bray. My girl will be joining his daughters at the convent. We just need to get our wives onboard.

"Yeah, sure. Keep telling yourself that." Emily laughs.

## Emily

Fourteen years later.

"ARGH, I HATE YOU!" Breanna slams the door on Josh's face.

"No, you don't!" he yells back. She opens the door, her arms folded under her chest.

"Every girl my age wears dresses like this. It's not fair that you're making me change."

"Every other girl your age isn't my daughter. I don't care what they wear. What *you* wear, on the other hand, I very much care about that."

I watch the back and forth between the two. It won't be long before Bree wins, and Josh gives in to her. He always does. He can never say no to her.

"I'm not going then. I'll stay home. I'll just stay in this room for the rest of my life, and be the old spinster that still lives with her parents when she's forty."

Josh tilts his head at her and smiles. "Is that meant to be a threat, princess? Because it sounds like a fucking great idea to me."

"Argh, you're impossible. Mum, tell him there's nothing wrong with the dress," Bree pleads. Oh crap, I was really hoping to stay out of this.

Josh turns to me. "Not you too, Emmy. Really?" he says, looking me up and down.

"You're overreacting, Josh. It's just a dress," I try to reason with him.

"Babe, that may be just a dress, but on you, it's a fucking wet dream."

"Ew, gross. I do not want to hear that," our girl interjects.

"Where do you think you came from, Bree? It wasn't the stalk." Josh laughs.

"Lalalala." She covers her ears.

"Come on, we're going to be late. It's not fair to Ash if we're late because you're being the fashion police."

"Fine, but if any fucker looks at either of you the wrong way, the pigs are getting fed."

"Again, gross. Besides, there's only one guy I want looking at me the wrong way. But you don't need to worry, Daddy. He doesn't even know I exist." Bree walks past us both, leaving us speechless.

"Whoever that boy is, he's a fucking idiot, Breanna," Josh calls to her back.

I have a feeling I know just who that boy is, and he's not really much of a boy at all. He's six years older than her. Let's hope, for his sake, he continues to not notice her, because if he does take an interest in my daughter, he won't have to worry about Josh. He'll have me to deal with.

ASH

It's my twenty-second birthday. I tried to tell my mother I didn't need a fucking fancy dinner party or any big deal made. She ignored me and went ahead and arranged one anyway.

I'm now forced to sit at the table all night with my cousins, aunts, uncles, and *her.*

Breanna. She's my cousin's cousin. I know, messy. I've grown up with her. I remember when she was born. I remember when she started talking.

What I don't remember is when she stopped being a little kid who was like a cousin to me, and became the most beautiful girl in the room. And I don't remember when I stopped looking at her like a friend, and started looking at her like she was mine.

She's sitting across from me, wearing a little black dress that leaves nothing to the imagination. I'm not sure how she managed to get out of the house dressed like this. Why the fuck didn't Josh stop her? Doesn't he realise every fucking guy with a cock is staring at her, undressing her with their eyes?

Fuck me, I need to stop. She's sixteen. She's still in bloody high school. I can't think of her like this. Adjusting myself in my seat, I turn and listen to Lily chatting about some party she went to the other night. Or at least I pretend to listen. I have to tune Breanna out, for both of our sakes. At least for a few more years.

BREANNA

I want to strangle the waitress who keeps batting her eyelashes at Ash. I also want to stab him in the face. In that tanned, sculpted, beautiful bloody face. He hasn't acknowledged me all night.

I dressed up in the hopes he would notice me. I thought maybe tonight would be the night he'd stop seeing me as a little kid. *He did notice.* I saw the little tell-tale signs he was checking me out. But just as quickly as he started to drag his eyes down the silhouette of my dress, he stopped and redirected his attention to Lily.

I see my friend Ben from school over at one of the other tables. Excusing myself, I go and sit next to Ben.

"Fancy seeing you here," I say.

"Beebee, what the hell are you wearing?" he asks as he looks me over from head to toe. He's the only one who gets away with giving me a nickname like Beebee. He started it the day I got stung by a bee when we were in the fifth grade and I swelled up like a balloon.

"It's a dress, Ben. People wear them." I slump down in my chair.

He looks over my shoulder to the table I just left. "He hasn't noticed, huh?" Ben observes.

"Not a word. He just pretended like I wasn't at the table." I think I'm over it now. I'm going to just find a nice boy my own age and start dating. I'm not waiting around for someone who doesn't want me.

Ben wraps his arm around my shoulder. Glancing back towards Ash, he whispers in my ear, "Don't be so sure he doesn't notice, Beebee. Right now, he's looking at me like he wants to tear me limb from limb." He kisses the top of my head and I snuggle into his shoulder.

"Thanks, Ben."

"Bree. Ben, it's great to see you again, but Bree is at a family dinner and needs to return to the table." Oh my god, can my dad be any more embarrassing right now?

"No worries, Mr. McKinley. BeeBee, you look amazing. Don't worry about what anyone else says. *Or doesn't say*," Ben offers as I stand up.

Dad puts his arm around my shoulder. "Is Ben the boy who doesn't notice you exist?" he asks.

"Ew, Daddy. God no. Ben's my best friend—that's all."

"That's good. It'd be a shame to have to make him disappear."

As I take my seat back at the table, Ash glares at me. "Problem?" I ask him, folding my arms over my chest. I don't miss his reaction. His eyes travel to my chest and back up. Maybe he's not so immune to me after all.

"Yes, there is. A huge one," he says before looking away again.

# Acknowledgments

I am thankful first to you, the reader, the one for whom this story was written. And I hope that you enjoyed Josh and Emily's story as much as I have.

Josh and Emily have taken me on an emotional rollercoaster. I cried, laughed and cursed them all in the same day. Their story truly touched my heart.

I am thankful for the support of my family. My wonderful husband, whose support and endless encouragement never fails. Nate, I could not have accomplished this without you.

I want to thank my beta readers. Natasha, Amy and Sam, you girls are one of a kind. Thank you for all of the time and effort you put into reading and providing insightful feedback for *Ruining Him*.

I am ever grateful to Danni Giddings, who wrote and composed the theme song for Josh and Emily. "Ruining Me" has been playing on repeat while I wrote and edited *Ruining Him*.

The Kylie Kent Street Team, what can I say? I would literally be nowhere if it weren't for you. I often get asked by other authors how I managed to form my street team. My answer is always the same, one hundred percent pure luck, and I'm not ever giving them back!! I believe I have the BEST street team in the business. Not only do you all ARC read for me, but you all read, promote and share whatever I put in front of you so enthusiastically and with genuine interest and excitement. I freaking love you guys!

Thank you, Kat, my amazing editor, who endures my constant messages and rants about these characters. Without you, this book would not be as great as it is now!

# About Kylie Kent

Kylie made the leap from kindergarten teacher to romance author, living out her dream to deliver sexy, "always and forever" romances. She loves a happily ever after story with tons of built-in steam.

She currently resides in Perth, Australia and when she is not dreaming up the latest romance, she can be found spending time with her three children and her husband of twenty years, her very own real life instant-love.

Kylie loves to hear from her readers; you can reach her at: author.kylie.kent@gmail.com

www.ingramcontent.com/pod-product-compliance
Lightning Source LLC
Chambersburg PA
CBHW070643310726
48982CB00001B/399
*9780645257205*